Dr Simon Curtis has lived in Suffolk, England, all his life. He has been a farrier, shoeing horses and working with iron since 1972. Simon was awarded a doctorate by the University of Central Lancashire, in equine locomotion and physiology in 2017, has lectured in 30 countries on the subject of farriery and published five textbooks. His interest in the Anglo-Saxon period of history has led to *The Swordsmith*, his first work of fiction.

To the historians who shine a torch into the Dark Ages.

Simon Curtis

THE SWORDSMITH

AUSTIN MACAULEY PUBLISHERS

LONDON ∗ CAMBRIDGE ∗ NEW YORK ∗ SHARJAH

A CIP catalogue record for this title is available from the British Library.

ISBN 9781398437050 (Paperback)
ISBN 9781398437067 (ePub e-book)

www.austinmacauley.com

First Published 2022
Austin Macauley Publishers Ltd®
1 Canada Square
Canary Wharf
London
E14 5AA

My wife Beverley gave great encouragement for my original ideas, inspired one of the characters, and supported me during the difficult moments. My four children, who turned any mention of it into a poke fun at dad session, thus persuading me to continue.

Kishli Laister-Scott read the original manuscript many moons ago and advised me on any digression from historical fact. Any mistakes left in are due to my stubbornness.

Sophie and Sergio, who I worked with on the cover concept.

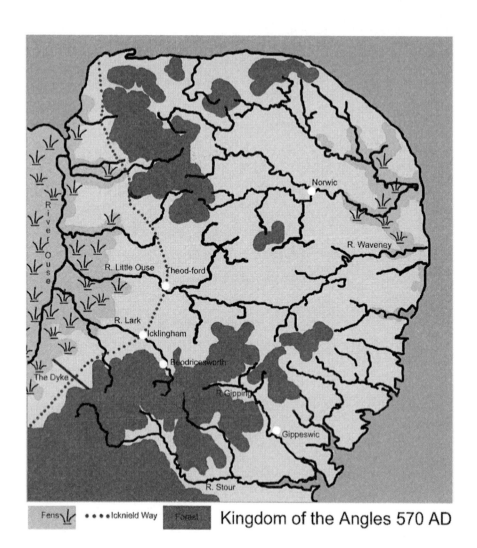

Kingdom of the Angles 570 AD

Place Names	
Bannaventa	Weedon, near Northampton
Beodriceworth (Beo)	Bury St Edmunds, Suffolk
Calchfynedd (Chalk Hills)	Northamptonshire, Huntingdonshire, Cambridgeshire, Bedfordshire, North Buckinghamshire and South Oxfordshire
Cymru	Britain held by the Britons
Erin	Ireland
The Flemish farmstead	Flempton, Suffolk

The Fen Dyke end	Reach, Cambridgeshire
Gewaesc	The Wash, estuary between Norfolk and Lincolnshire
Glastenning	Kingdom of the area now Somerset
The Great Heath	Newmarket Heath, Suffolk and Cambridgeshire
The Great Dyke	Devil's Dyke, Newmarket
Gippeswic	Ipswich, Suffolk
Icklingham	Icklingham, Suffolk
Ivinghoe	Ivinghoe Beacon, Bedfordshire
The Lark ford	Lackford, Suffolk
Lindsey	Lincolnshire
Lloegr	England; literally, the Lost Lands
Lundein	Area around present-day London
Mynydd Baddon or Badon Hill	Unknown battle site where the Britons defeated the Saxons
Norwic	Norwich, Norfolk
Old Country	North Germany and the Jutland Peninsular
Stowe	West Stow, Suffolk
Stubs Worth	Stetchworth, Cambridgeshire
Theod-Ford	Thetford, Norfolk
Valhalla	Great Hall of the brave dead
The Wood Dyke end	Stubs Worth, Stetchworth, Cambridgeshire

Word Meanings (Briton)

Arturius	Arthur of the Britons
Cymru	Britain
Cymry	Britons
Lloegr	England, literally, the Lost Lands
Sais	Any Anglo-Saxon

Chapter 1
560 AD

Osgar shivered, the Grenwald was about to kill Beowulf. He knew the story well but still he feared for his hero. He saw the Grenwald in the leaping shadows in the corners of the hall and listened as the story grew and intensified.

Cynbeald, the storyteller, always told the Beowulf epic. Everyone said that he was the best scop in all East Anglia. He was a tall thin man with grey hair and a neat trimmed beard. He spoke with a deep voice that was clear and unhurried. The tale was told in three parts over the Eostre festival when the Angles celebrated the end of the cold season. They said goodbye to Skadi, the Goddess of Winter and the hunt, and welcomed in Astara, the Goddess of Spring, asking for a warm spring for the planting season.

Upriver, men silently waded across the Lark carrying spears and shields above their heads. They were followed by horsemen who kept their mounts quiet as they crossed in line, their horses, nose to tail.

Osgar and Leofric had crawled into the hall under the wall covering that hid some rotten wooden planking. They sat on the floor in the corner near the headman's chair. Their father's position, at the end of the hall, reflected his status. He sat with his legs between his twin boys, each gripping his calf. By custom, they should not have been there. They were supposed to be twelve years old to enjoy a feast in the hall but such customs were not always adhered to in the hams. They knew that they would not be allowed into the Great Hall at Beodricsworth but here, if they sat quietly, they would not be sent out.

The hall was made of split wood planking around a wooden frame of oak. It was plastered with wattle and clay on the inside to fill all the gaps and keep draughts out. On the floor was a large square fire on a thick bed of sand. An iron chain and hook hung from a beam over the flames. Above the only doorway was a timber carved with a knotted pattern. The walls were covered with hangings showing scenes of hunting and war and the thatched reed roof could be seen from inside. It was not grand like the Great Hall at Beodricesworth where all the timbers were carved and one hundred men could be seated. The hall at Icklingham was modest as befitted a small settlement of eighty Angles without a thegn and few slaves.

As the tale intensified, Osgar moved closer to his twin brother Leofric and gripped his father's knee. Eafwald laid a large hand on each of his boys and thought how good life was. After the twins were born, his wife and he had no more children. He prayed to Nerthus, the goddess of fertility but to no avail. He was content though as they grew enough food. The goatherd was more than twelve in number and he bartered his woodwork for some of the finer things in life. Eafwald downed more ale.

Osgar was in his tenth year and had lived all his life in the ham. His mother and father had crossed the sea from the Old Country and still missed it. They came for the land and said that the weather was kinder in this new country. He had only left Icklingham once and that was to walk for the whole morning with his parents and most of the village to Beodricesworth to see the new king of the Angles. He preferred his ham to Beo. It had too many people and was too noisy and smelly. He thought that seeing the king was something special though and he went into his uncle's smithy. In the dingy workshop, he did not mind the noise and the smoke. When the king passed, his Uncle Anson had kept one foot on the wooden stump that his anvil sat on and had leant forward resting his elbow on his thigh. All the people had bowed but Anson had just nodded his head and given a wry smile. Only Osgar had seen it and the king looked into the forge and gave the same smile and small nod back.

Leofric and Osgar tried to stay awake as the story continued. The Grendel's mother had returned to avenge her son's death. She was even more terrible than her son. Beowulf had traced her to her lair in the lake. He fought her under the water, killed her and there he found the body of the Grendel, decapitated him and returned to Hrothgar with the head. That ended the story telling by Cynbeald and the boys knew that there was one final part to come but it would be told on the last night of Eostre. Osgar and Leofric did not wait for their father to tell them that they must go home to bed. They did not want to upset their mother as she might not let them return for the last instalment of the Beowulf epic.

Suddenly, there were noises outside and one of the village women ran to the door. "Waelisc, Waelisc," she shouted, banging on it.

A man, closest to the door, lifted the latch and swung it open. Osgar recognised the woman just as a spear point was thrust through the back of her shawl emerging through her chest. Most of the men in the hall were slow to react, some already asleep. Three, on the other side to Osgar, who had just begun singing with their arms around each other's shoulders, stopped and looked open-mouthed. The one on the left tried to rise but his cloak was still sat upon by his neighbour. Above, Osgar heard the crackling sound of the thatch catching alight. There were twenty-five men packed into a hall with one doorway, Osgar could no longer see it. His father was stuck at the back of the crowd with him and Leofric. He heard his father shout, "Get your weapons and get out."

Two Angles broke from the hall doorway grabbing seaxs as they rushed out into the dark. The first out was young and brave. He ran with all his force into a shield, knocking its holder over and landing on him as he fell. He tried to stab at the wriggling Briton below him but a spear was thrust into his side and then another and a sword hacked through flesh, sinew and bone into the back of his unprotected neck. The other Angle swung his short sword at three of the attackers as they closed in. He knew he was going to die but would take one with him.

"For Woden and Wehha," he bellowed, as he spun left and right.

He could not reach his attackers with his seax. They banged their shields into him and stabbed at him with sword and spear. Ten or more wounds gushed with his blood. He used his left arm as a shield, it was sliced to the bone and still he fought. He was felled with a sweeping cut to his hamstrings and his head was pulled back by his flowing blonde hair and his throat cut.

The raiders had planned well, attacking late into the night when most villagers were drunk or asleep. They knew where the hall was, set on a hill in the centre of the ham. With only one exit, fifteen Britons easily cut down the men as they stumbled out. Most did not even have time to pick up their weapons in the smoke, fire and mayhem. The Angles tried to fight back, with some of the men grabbing the few seaxs and spears that they owned, but the Waelisc were too many for them and they had horses. Around the ham, they threw burning briars on the thatch and ran down anyone appearing. Men were speared or cut through, the old galloped over, babies killed, the young and the women taken. Everywhere was chaos and confusion, with smoke and flames adding to their terror.

Osgar crawled out of the back of the burning hall. He dragged Leofric with him and slithered along the ground to the pigsty where he hid at the far end among the muck, straw and mud. He had lost contact with his brother and dared not call for him. He saw his father run out of the hall, leap over his fallen brethren and swing a punch at one of the raiders, knocking him to the wet ground, before he was felled. Eafwald raised his arm to protect himself and the enemy sword cut clean through it in a spray of blood. The strength of the blow took away his hand and the blade lodged in his forehead across his right eye. The assailant put a boot on his father's face and wrenched the sword from it. He could see the features of his father's killer as his head spun around towards him, looking for his next victim. Osgar had never glimpsed a Waelisc raider before. He would not forget this one. He lay still and hoped that he could not be seen. The Briton seemed to look into the pigsty for an eternity before finally turning away.

Osgar heard his mother's cries as she was dragged away, and worse, Leofric calling for him. He could not move though he wanted to. He wanted to be Beowulf. He wanted to kill the Waelisc raider to avenge his father. He wanted to cut the horse and rider down and save his mother, but mostly he wanted to show his brother where to hide. He did none of these, he hid, he shook and he wet himself.

Osgar's secure childhood had ended. He lay still and tried to think of anything but the immediate past. He remembered that morning when he had gone with his brother to the river. The women met by the ford to beat their clothes while he and Leo hunted for duck eggs. The sky was alive with birds, the river full of fish and the fens teemed with croaking frogs. Leofric and Osgar swam races in the slow waters. No one lived on the other side of the river and the fen stretched much further. They were told that they must not climb up the far bank as it was not safe but they still swam to that side of the river and found more eggs there, as nobody else bothered to swim it.

The twins then walked over the hillock towards the Lark ford past Stowe. "I want you home well before the sun is below the trees," their mother had called out to them, "the wolves are out there and if they don't get you, the elves will." Leofric and Osgar had shuddered at each other and then run off. They had heard talk of children taken by wolves and they had even heard them howling in the distance but no one had ever really told them of elves taking someone.

Just outside the ham boundary was a group of old buildings. They had been told that these were built by the Romans. They heard tales about these Romans, they were magicians and they were giants. Why else did they live in houses of stone? They both thought that the Romans were stupid for magicians. They had put stones on the roof and now it was fallen in. Their own house had a roof of reeds from the fens and it had not fallen down. They broke some of the flat roof stones, which were not even strong stone like flint. They were red coloured and more like the storage pots at home.

"If an elf fought a wolf," Leofric had asked, "who would win?"

"I don't know, I'll ask old Cynbeald the scop. Even if he doesn't know, he'll tell a good story."

"Don't ask him when it's dark or in the hall," said Leofric, "I nearly pooed myself last time."

They had both burst into a fit of laughter that only stopped when Osgar's digging unearthed a large lump of metal. They knew 'the black', when they found it, because it was heavy and an orangey brown colour.

"Aren't grown-ups daft," Leofric had declared, "they call it black but we find it because it's rusty brown. I think it's a Roman turd."

When they had finally ended their giggling, they carried it back to their father. He had slapped them both on the back and told them what good boys they were. He said that he would take it to Beodricesworth after Eostre and trade it with Anson the Broad, his Jute brother-in-law. Osgar wished his uncle were with him now. He would know what to do.

*****

Aefre struggled to keep up with the horses. She was bound by her wrists to a rope about the length of her body. She feared the snorting animal and tried to keep away from its crushing hooves. She was in pain from a kick to her stomach and punch to her cheek. She tried to jog to keep up but the rhythm of the horse tugged at her aching arms. The full moon allowed her to see for some distance and she perceived that she was being taken southwest.

All of the Britons were on horseback now. When she had first been taken, many of them were on foot and she had been dragged along the ridge above the Lark River towards Stowe. They had passed the old Roman house and met with more Waelisc and then they had continued to the Lark ford. To her left, she saw two Stowe houses burning and could hear the people shouting threats towards them. When she glanced back, she saw the flames turning the smoke above Icklingham red. At the Lark ford, there were more Britons and Aefre could see that they had been guarding the crossing where there were many more horses.

16

She had been tied to a horse and the then the rider had mounted up and moved off.

She knew that Leofric was one of those taken and she thought that there were three more captives. She tried to see who they were. Was Osgar one of them? If he was not with them did that mean that he was dead? She had seen none of her people on the ground when she was pulled from her house. They were near the hall but she had seen a horse and rider run down Mildred the herb woman. Mildred was hit so hard that her head and body snapped back and she landed twisted in the mud. The rider did not even look back.

Aefre did not know how long she had been dragged for. She knew that it was getting light behind her and she saw the shadows in front of her. The trees and grass took on an orange colour. The thicker woods closing into the pathway had now opened out and she knew she was on the Great Heath. She had only travelled across it once when it was still safe to go that far west. There had been Angle settlements on either side of the Great Heath which were now abandoned for the safety of the northeast, behind the Lark River.

The chalk-land heath stretched out in front of them with its low rolling hills, thick grass and sparse trees. The Waelisc riders did not look behind them so often now and jabbered to each other with strange sounds and words. To Aefre, it sounded like nothing she had ever heard and she could understand none of it. She knew that the Waelisc spoke a different tongue but she had never heard it before. Waelisc slaves were banned from speaking a word of their own tongue. She could understand the Saxons and the Jutes easily and the Flemish who lived nearby spoke strangely and with many different words, although she could still talk to them but with these people she may as well have been listening to barking dogs or honking geese.

There was a cry and shouting to Aefre's right and the horde pulled up. She could now see that there were nearly as many riders and horses as there were people in her village. From the front of the group, a Briton wheeled his horse around. He had long black braids of hair down to his shoulders. His eyes were upturned at the corners and he had a slightly hooked nose. He wore a jerkin made of dark leather over a tunic. He carried a shield with a spear behind it on his left arm and by his side was a sword sheathed in a black leather scabbard. All the Waelisc looked towards him and Aefre knew he was their leader. He spoke to his men at the back and one pointed down to an Angle lying on the ground, her arms stretched out by the rope tied to the saddle of the nearest horse. Aefre now

17

recognised the girl and feared for her. It was Nelda, her second cousin, and she was with child.

Cadrod spoke to his men while he looked east, checking that they had not been followed. The raid had gone reasonably well. They had taken five prisoners and killed many of the Sais invaders. The raid on the second village had not been as successful with only two houses burned. That village had heard their first attack and quickly the men were formed up with spear and shield in a line between the houses. The women and children were not to be seen and must have fled. He would remember in future, to either attack villages further apart or at the same instant. Not one man or horse had been lost, although two of his horses seemed lame.

Cadrod knew that they were, by now, well away from danger. The Sais did not use horses and so they were half a day's march from them. He was careful when in Lloegr as too many raiders in the past had been killed or taken by the Sais on raids. It was usually due to carelessness or arrogance, where they had become lost or ridden into an ambush. By god, he hated their thin straw hair and their blue eyes and the girl-like way they wore their clothes. He hated everything about them and this was not their land, it was his people's land. Cadrod slipped gracefully from his horse and handed his shield and spear to one of his warriors. He walked over to the Angle girl and kicked her.

"She is with child," shouted Aefre.

Cadrod turned and said, "Did some Sais bitch just fart? Shut her up."

A fist hit Aefre in the mouth and she was thrown back. She lay on the ground and held her bound hands to her face. Cadrod again looked down at the prone Angle girl and pulled her ragged scyrt up. He looked at her and prodded her stomach with his sword. "The Sais sow is in pig," he said. "That's why she can't keep up." He looked at his men. "Do we need any more Sais pigs?"

With those words, he leant on the pommel of his sword and pushed the tip into the girl's bulging stomach. She cried out and yanked on her binding as the sword broke through the skin and flesh. He pushed until he felt the point touch her spine and then he put his boot on her chest and heaved the sword out.

"We've rested long enough. Let's get on," was all he said as he mounted his dark horse.

Nelda's child had died instantly from the sword thrust. Her mother died more slowly from her wound. In Cadrod's mind, killing Angles was no more than stamping on a mouse in the grain store. He had grown up with tales of how these people had stolen their land and driven his Britons from their homes. He had an all-consuming love for his people, their songs and tales, their language and even the way they dressed. Every Sais invader was an embarrassment to the Britons, showing how soft they had been to allow them to settle in the south and eastern edges of the land. Now more of them came every year and Cadrod knew that they would never be satisfied until his people were gone and they had all the land between the seas.

As the sun continued to rise behind them, they travelled at walking pace across the Great Heath. To their left, the forest edged inwards and to their right they looked out across the fenlands. They could see vast areas of water which glistened in the sun and areas of green reeds. Occasionally, the land broke through the water to form hillocks. On these, it was just possible to make out settlements. The fifty horsemen and four captives followed the path of the old Roman road. Aefre knew that it began near Norwic and went all the way down to Lundein. In places, the road was broken and in other low-lying areas, it was flooded. The bridges across streams were collapsed now as the Angles now had no use for it anyway. They preferred to travel along the ancient trade route on either side. They had used the Icknield Way to travel southwest since the early settlements and were told how this route was there before the Romans. It took them west of Lundein and down to their Saxon cousins in the south. Since the resurgence of the Britons, trade and movement had stopped.

Now that the Waelisc raiders had reached their known territory, the pace was less pressing. The four Angle prisoners were able to keep up without their ropes pulling and tugging. Aefre looked around at the raiders and tried to see the other captives. There was another boy and young woman behind her to her right and to the front, she now saw Leofric. He walked with a limp and his head hung down. He was missing a boot and there was blood around his ankle. His smock was torn and there was mud and chalk up the right side. He was still wearing his woollen breeches but he had no cloak around his shoulders. His beautiful wiry blond hair hung in a tangle. She wanted to call to him to let him know she was there, that his father and the fyrd would now be marching to save them but she knew that it would be dangerous to say anything. Her mouth still hurt and she could taste her own blood. She looked further forward at their leader; the one that they called Cadrod. She saw his leather jerkin and his sword hanging by his side. She could see he was relaxed as he laughed with his riders flanking him. She thought of Nelda and knew he would die. Their King Wehha would kill him if her husband Eafwald did not get to him first. She had been raised to hate the Waelisc but had never thought about them anymore than she did wolves. They were something that attacked others and even when the raids had come nearer to Icklingham, she had felt protected behind the river. How could she have been so foolish as to think that it was safe in this country? She wished she had stayed in the Old Country where her boys would have been secure.

When the sun was at its highest, they stopped by a stream. They were well past the Great Heath. The land had become more hilly and wooded. They could no longer see the fens to their right. The horses were tired and they stopped, drank from the stream and ate the rich grass. Their riders had stripped them of their saddles and tack but they were hobbled with leather straps above their hooves that tied one leg to the other. The prisoners were allowed down to the stream to drink and Aefre watched with distain as the boy and girl nodded thanks to their guards. She recognised them as Milgryd and Athelstan. They had grown up in Icklingham and were cousins of her two boys. Milgryd was about thirteen years of age and Athelstan a year older than his sister; both were known by their shortened names as Milly and Stan. When Aefre tried to get closer to Leofric, she was shoved away.

Cadrod had eaten some dried meat and nuts. He sat on the edge of the wood under an oak and looked at the woman while she washed her face. The blood on her chin was gone and she smoothed back her hair as he watched, she knelt by the stream and scooped water into her mouth. This woman had come to his land and was a breeding vessel for more of these Sais pigs, he thought.

"You two," he said to the men nearest to him, "are you tired?"

"No, *sire*," they both replied in unison.

"Good, then take the bitch in the woods and give her one. I can't be bothered."

Leofric saw the two men grab his mother under each arm and drag her backwards towards the bushes. She saw him and shouted to him to sit down. He moved towards her and was tripped by a spear haft between his legs. A foot stamped on his chest and he felt a pain go through him as two ribs cracked. One of the Waelisc grabbed his hair and pulled his face close. "Did you want to see her shagged?" he said and threw him back to the ground.

Leofric just heard meaningless noises and felt the spittle on his face and the pain in his chest. He did not hear his mother scream because she kept quiet. She had her son to protect until her people came so she made no noise.

*****

It was still dark when Osgar crawled across to his father. There were the bodies of seven other men lying around him, most within ten paces of the hall and two others still in the doorway. The hair on their heads was burnt away and the remains of their clothes smouldered and stuck to their bodies. Osgar could smell cooking pork. The burning flesh reminded him of feast days when a whole pig was roasted on a spit and he vomited between his hands. When he reached his father, he could see that he was still alive. His chest rose and fell and his left eye was partly open. The side of his face away from the burning hall was white and the uncovered part of his right arm and right leg were red and blistered.

Osgar took hold of his father's legs and strained to pull him away. He moved him ten paces from the hall as another beam crashed down and a plume of red sparks rose into the air. He put his father's arms back down by his sides and listened to his father whisper, "Is that you, Osgar?"

"Yes, Father."

"Is your mother and brother here?"

"No, Father, they are not."

"Will you fetch my seax, Osgar?"

"Yes, Father."

Osgar walked towards the burning hall, with tears running down his face. He had listened, from when he could first understand, to tales of heroic men. When he imagined battle, his father was always at the front, his shield smashing the enemy and his seax downing them. If he could just get his father his blade then perhaps, he would recover. He could see where some of the seaxs lay and pulled his smock up to his face to ward off the heat. He recognised his father's seax by the shape of the hand guard and the pommel. The bone pommel was charred although it lay away from the fire. The blade lay toward the hall and the tip was buried in burning ash. He put his hand on the pommel and in a delayed reflex, snatched it away in pain as he burned the tips of his fingers. Now his face was searing from the fire's heat and he wrapped the sleeve of his smock around his right hand and then grabbed and tossed the seax away in one movement. He had thrown it five paces and was glad to retreat away from the fire to where it lay, sizzling in the damp mud. Osgar ran to a nearby house where a wooden pail lay, half full of water. He poured the contents over the seax until no more steam rose from it, picked it up and carried it to his father.

21

He placed the charred handle in the hand of the severed arm beside his father and said, "Your seax is in your right hand, Father."

"I'm going to Valhalla now, my son. You will fetch Aefre and Leo to me."

"I will, Father," said Osgar.

Osgar was ten years old. His father was dead, his mother and brother taken, his village and his life were gone.

*****

As dawn broke, a hand touched Osgar's shoulder. He turned to see Cynbeald standing over him. Cynbeald was covered with scratches, his clothes were torn and filthy, his hair bedraggled.

"I thought everyone was dead," said Osgar standing up beside the body of his father.

He could see more villagers appearing; some women and children but no men and then the Flemish men came. They carried their shields in the fighting position and laid their spears over their shoulders. Some had seaxs in their belts or behind their backs and they moved closely together at the jog. Osgar listened as they spoke in their unusual accent to Cynbeald. Their headman was called Henryk. He had visited Icklingham before to trade their pottery-ware and Osgar had also seen him the one time that they had travelled to Beo. His straight hair was worn longer than the Angles and his beard had a slight ginger colour to it. His woollen smock was high at the collar and more ornate than most with square embroidered patterns around the cuffs. Cynbeald explained all he knew about the attack, which was not much. The Flemish knew more than him. Henryk told him that the raiders had crossed at the Lark ford and followed the river downstream to Icklingham. Some of the Waelisc then attacked Stowe but the villagers had heard them coming and seen the fires at Icklingham so were ready.

"There was no fight," said the Henryk, "the Waelisc could see the line of Stowe men and would not risk a fight against armed men. If they had known how drunken most of them were, the Waelisc may have given battle, ja. I have sent a messenger to Beodricesworth and posted men at the Lark Ford. Once the men at Stowe have sobered up, they will send men to join them."

"Can I come with you?" asked Osgar. "I have my father's seax."

"Come with me where?" said the Flem, looking at the Angle boy holding a charred seax in his right hand.

"To kill the Waelisc, to get my mother and brother back," said Osgar, stepping forward with his chin up looking directly at the Flem.

"They are gone, young man. They have horses and more fighting men than we can gather in a day."

Cynbeald said to Osgar, "Come on, we have work to do."

He turned to the Flem and thanked him. Henryk looked around at the bodies, the burning houses, the dead goats and sheep. He looked at the shocked people of Icklingham. There were no men of more than twelve years of age, all had been killed or captured. Some women carried babies in their arms or led young children by the hand, all of them sobbing. Henryk the tall Flem spoke again to Cynbeald, "Your people were here four generations before mine. You let us settle in peace only a short walk away. You are our cousins and we will help you. Our houses are yours and our food is yours, ja." With that he turned and spoke to his men.

The Flemish carried all the bodies they could find up the small hill in front of what remained of Osgar's house, where the cemetery lay. There they built funeral pyres and burned the bodies. Afterwards, the ashes were placed in large urns that their potters had made in the Flemish settlement. The urns were three hands high and two wide and had simple patterns around the rim and the middle. Osgar dug a hole for his father's urn, long enough to lay Eafwald's seax alongside it. Cynbeald helped him fill in the soil and pray to the gods to accept his father into Valhalla.

"Will they let him enter Valhalla, Cynbeald?" said Osgar, patting the mound of soil with both hands to make it smooth.

"Of course," said Cynbeald, "why do you ask?"

"Because his arm was cut from his body."

"That matters nothing, Osgar. Many men die with more terrible wounds than your father. In Valhalla, they are well and whole. The seax was in his hand when he died. That is all that matters and you put it there."

"I should have saved them," said Osgar, "I should have saved my mother and Leo."

Cynbeald said, "No one could help them. There was just too many Waelisc. But you did save Leofric and me."

"How?" asked Osgar, turning his head up towards the scop in disbelief.

"You pulled Leofric out of the hall under the wall hanging. I saw you and followed. You tried to pull him to the pigsty but he ran to your house. The Waelisc were taking your mother and they saw him and took him too."

"How did you get away then?" asked Osgar.

"I saw you go into the pigsty but I knew that they would see my tunic and cloak because it was my bright one for special occasions. I threw it off and just kept running. I must have been lucky. I ran into the woods by the river and kept running through brambles, nettles and thistles and hid by the river. There were others there also. We waited until dawn before returning."

Chapter 2
Bannaventa

The war-band of riders and horses spent a night under the trees with their four captives. The Britons were relaxed, laughing and fooling with each other, happy that they were in home territory. They had camped within sight of a small settlement. The local Britons walked to the encampment with bread, nuts and meat. They handed Cadrod's men their gifts of food and hugged and kissed them. Some of the locals walked over to the captives who were tied to four trees. They were prodded, kicked and spat on. A Briton woman pulled each head up in turn and opened an eye to look in it. She pulled on the fair hair with a look of disgust. The Briton had never been close enough to touch an Angle. She had seen slaves from Lloegr in the distance but never ones like these, just taken and still wearing their hair in Sais style. All her life, the Briton woman had learned to revile them. They had stolen her people's land and they were all child murderers and rapists.

Milgryd and Athelstan looked at each other, from ten paces apart where they had been tied to trees but did not dare speak. Stan was just glad that his sister Milly was untouched by the Waelisc men. He was still dazed by the events of the last day and wanted to believe that it was a nightmare that would end when he woke up. Milly tried to smile at her younger brother and mouthed 'Stan' to him. She could not sleep and sat hunched up against the tree to which she was tethered. Every noise of the night made her jump and tremble with fear as she awaited the inevitable assault from her captors. She had seen Aefre, from her ham, dragged away and raped by two of the Waelisc and expected to be next. She thought of poor Nelda, her life taken from her in such a gruesome way.

In the morning, the captives were tethered, once more, to the horses and the group of riders and slaves travelled further south and west, over more rolling hills. The Britons' settlements became more frequent and many villagers shouted and waved to the riders. They in turn waved back and sometimes yanked on their prisoners' bindings to jerk their arms. The rider, whose horse Athelstan was tethered to, dug his heels into his mounts' ribs to make him shoot forward. The horse broke into a canter and pulled Stan over to laughter and cackles from the Britons. He was dragged fifty paces, with his arms stretched out ahead of him, along the bumpy turf. Cadrod wheeled his horse around and cantered to the back of his war band to see what was going on.

He looked at the Angle boy, now cut and bruised around the face. Blood was running from his nose into his mouth. "You did that to him, just to give a peasant a laugh?" said Cadrod angrily to his warrior. "And if you had killed him, would you have explained to the King why he only had three more slaves?"

"I thought you wanted them all dead, my lord?" replied the rider, with his head down.

"Of course I want all Sais dead, but these are slaves so they are already dead."

"Bannaventa," announced the front rider, pointing to the town ahead. Aefre did not know what they were saying but she felt that they had reached their destination. It had taken a day and a half, surely that meant that the Angles were only three days march away, she thought.

The houses became more closely grouped together. At first, they were similar to the ham houses that she was used to and then as they entered the town, they became very different. The horde of riders strung out and walked down a stone road between rows of houses and then all the buildings became made of stone. They had thatched roofs but the walls were made of quarried rock. The doors looked solid with iron rivets through oak panels or planks and there were wooden shutters at window openings.

The town's people came out and once more, the Angles were prodded and spat at. The Britons shouted at them in their strange language. The four captives stared ahead and walked. They entered an open area through an archway in the wall. Leofric looked up not trusting it not to fall and there were more shouts so he immediately ducked his head down again. At the far side of the open area was a tower, the like of which none of the Angles had ever seen before. It was the height of a tree and had arched openings in it. Where it joined the wall, there was a larger curved passageway and they could see people standing above the archway. There were colourful wall hangings from halfway up the tower of brighter colours than the four had ever seen. Aefre looked cautiously at these Waelisc people and saw how gaudy the colours of their clothes were. They were not the earth shades of her people's clothes but the bright colours of the sun and sky.

The riders drew their horses into a long line parallel with the tower and wall. The binding ropes were unwrapped from the saddle pommels and the four Angles were led to the front. Three of them stood with their heads bowed. Aefre looked around and kept her chin high. "Mother, put your head down," said Leofric, as quietly as possible, "please mother, put your head down."

"Kneel," ordered Cadrod to the four Angles.

They heard him speak, they even guessed that he was talking to them but it was just a noise that they heard, a nonsense word. Cadrod nodded to his sergeant who walked behind the captives with his spear. He struck Athelstan hard behind the knees with the spear haft. He fell immediately to his knees and Cadrod repeated the order and quickly Milgryd and Leofric dropped to the ground, kneeling in the dirt. Aefre remained standing and was hit from behind. The pain shot through her legs and they collapsed so that she too knelt. She was about to get up but thought better of it. When she looked up, she could see a figure behind the wall in front of the tower. He was old and bald on the top of his head. He had long white hair and a beard and was tall for a Briton. He had bony forearms and long fingers with protruding knuckles. His clothes were brighter than she could ever imagine. He wore a gown of white, trimmed down each side with blue. There was a red vestment below the gown and a gold band on his head. He leant on a white stick that had a gold orb just above his handgrip.

"Welcome to Calchfynedd," he said looking at the four, "I trust that you have enjoyed your journey here and have taken pleasure in my son's famed hospitality."

Cynwyd, the King of Calchfynedd, knew that not a word he was saying was understood by these Sais but he was enjoying himself and he knew how to entertain his people. He had been king for nearly forty years, since the death of his father who had founded the Kingdom. His father had taken the land, left empty after the retreat of the Romans and the destruction of the Saxons at Mynned Baddon. The kingdom of Calchfynedd stretched across much of the southern central lands of Britain, from the old kingdoms of the west to the hated Sais to the north, south and east. Cynwyd's father had taken the land, he had held it and made it rich and now his son Cadrod desired to expand it. There was a time when Cynwyd enjoyed warlike pursuits but no longer, now he felt his age and wanted just to enjoy life's pleasures. Once his son, Cadrod, had reached an age where he could lead men into battle, King Cynwyd stopped riding to attack with his warriors. Occasionally, he felt a twinge of jealousy for his son as he left the fortress of Bannaventa at the head of a line of horsemen. He remembered the feeling of war and battle with its excitement, terror and rewards. He stood on the balcony and looked down at his son who he had indulged with all the horses and men that he had asked for.

"You bring me such gifts," he called down to Cadrod, opening his arms and hands. "You are indeed the most famous warrior in all our lands. These gifts will be put to use to our benefit once we know that they are obedient.

"Come, Cadrod, and share wine with me while these four are shown to their quarters, and do make sure that they are comfortable."

The riders and the crowd laughed at the King's sarcasm. Cadrod handed the reins of his horse to the groom, his shield and spear to a nearby warrior and walked to the tower. He was happy to be home and to see his father in such good spirits and showing such public gratitude to him. He loved his father dearly, revering him and his grandfather as the founder and protector of Calchfynedd. As a boy, he had been trained by his father's best fighters in all the arts of war. He could ride as well as any man in the kingdom and had mastered the spear and sword at an early age. He was not impatient to become king and was happy to wait for his father to die in the fullness of time, when God willed it. He enjoyed the freedom that not being king allowed him in roaming the borders of the kingdom, attacking its enemies. There was only one bone of contention between Cadrod and his father and that was the old king's need for younger females, especially Sais girls. To Cadrod, they were as much the enemy as the men and needed to be wiped from the land with all Sais. While his father lived, he would try to ignore his tendencies and concentrate on pushing the trespassers back along the borders. He climbed the tower steps as his captives were removed from the courtyard.

Aefre, Leofric, Milgryd and Athelstan were pushed roughly through the tower archway to the space beyond. It was another enclosed area with a wall three times the height of a man. There were many secondary thatched buildings within it. Most were propped up against the wall, made of wood and appeared to Aefre to be workshops of the type seen in Beodricesworth. Blacksmiths, tanners, woodworkers, dyers and potters' buildings leant against the far fortification, amongst them were stalls with goods for sale. To the left of the open space was a grid made of beech on a large oak frame. It was about two paces by three wide and as they were dragged closer, they could see that the wooden grid covered a pit. It was drawn back and one by one they had their bindings removed and were pushed into the pit.

"Hey," said a voice from some rags in the corner, "don't go over there. That's where I shit."

Aefre looked at the figure lying curled up in tattered clothes and asked, "What did you say?"

"I said don't go over there, because that's where I shit. I am right to believe that you Suth Folk still shit? But I really don't care so if you want to sit in my shit feel free."

"Are you Waelisc?" asked Milgryd.

"Waelisc, bloody Waelisc, of course I'm not bloody Waelisc. Do you think that the Waelisc live in shit pits? Well, do you? I'm an Angle like you. I am from the North Folk. No taking the piss, you Suth Folk sound funny to us as well."

"What are you doing here?" asked Aefre.

"Do you mean what am I doing in this shit hole or the bigger shit hole that is Calchfynedd?"

"Shall we start with this little hole first," said Aefre, becoming annoyed that they could be in such a situation and this person was trying to be funny.

"I stole an apple," said the bunch of rags as a head appeared.

"You stole an apple?" Aefre repeated.

"Yes. Stole an apple, stole a bloody apple. I wait three years for people to speak to and I get you four. You do still have apples in East Anglia? I'm a slave like you lot, I work on the farm. They don't feed me enough but there is always a chance to take food. I got caught and I'm in here for three days. Is that clear now?"

"So why are we here?" asked Milly.

"To break you in," he replied.

"I don't know what you mean," she said.

"That's what they call taming their horses. They break them in, break their will and then the horses do what they want. They will break your will and then you will do what they want."

"I will not," said Leofric. It was the first time he had spoken in two days.

"You must," said North Folk, "take the easy route, submit, work, keep your head down, survive."

"He's right," said Aefre, "survive until our people come, as they will surely come."

"They didn't come for me," said the rags with the North Folk voice.

*****

Cadrod marched towards the oak door. It was studded with black rivets and hinged to a sturdy frame set in the stonewall. One of the two guards opened the door for him to stride through.

"My son," welcomed Cynwyd, "come in, take a seat." He motioned to one of the two chairs by the fire. "Wine," he said to the servant who immediately carried a silver goblet to Cadrod.

The two chairs angled in towards the fire about three paces from it. The fire had a sturdy stone surround two paces wide and high and was topped by a great Bessemer beam of carved oak. It had a knotted pattern carved across it as did the chairs. The walls were covered with hangings depicting various saints and on the table was a gold cross, three hands high, inlaid with jewels. Cadrod made himself comfortable in his chair and drank from the goblet. He had taken the black leather scabbard off and stood it by the door with the sword hilt up. He wiped the wine from his beard with the back of his left hand and looked at his father.

"So tell me of the raid," said Cynwyd.

"The raid went well father and we lost no men and only two horses are lame. We do not have enough slaves to show for our effort though. The plan to attack during their feast night meant that we caught them off guard but we killed too many young men in their burning hall. By the time we attacked the second village, they were ready and lined up in battle formation."

"We had a fifth captive but she was with child and could not keep up so I rid our land of the vermin. The Sais are retreating though, there is hardly one of the Sais living this side of the river."

"Good," said Cynwyd, King of Calchfynedd, "if we push them back and keep weakening them with raids, some will return to their homeland or elsewhere and they will be left with only the old to support their men and then we will destroy them all."

"What is the state of the slaves? They looked fit and young from the balcony."

"Two women, a young man and a boy who are all healthy," said Cadrod. "They are already learning their place although the older of the two women is still haughty. I had two of my men bring her down a peg or two on the way back."

"Leave them in the pit a couple of days," said Cynwyd, "I will have another look at them. Do you want either of the women?"

"You know that I would rather shag a goat, father."

"I hate them just as much as you Cadrod," said the King, "but a straw haired maiden keeps me young."

Cadrod hid his disgust for his father's lust and said, "I had better go and see that my troops and horses are good. Thank you for the wine, Father." He rose and walked to the doorway and picked up his sword, turned and bowed to his father and left.

*****

In the pit, the five shivered as dawn broke. Two of the guards walked over, undid the front of their trews and urinated through the beech wood grid. When they had walked away the North Folk boy said, "Many thanks, always good to have a light rain in the morn."

Milgryd whimpered in the corner and clung to her brother and Aefre said, "You think it is funny, don't you? Do you have a name or has that been taken from you?"

"My name is Sigbert but you can call me Siggy."

"Sigbert's fine," said Aefre. "How often do they do that?"

"Whenever they need a piss," said Sigbert. "Let's hope the food was well cooked last night."

"Are you saying that they don't just pee on us?"

"That wasn't a pee, dear lady. That was a good old piss. Children do pees. And yes, they shit on you in the pit if that is what you are trying to ask."

Milgryd let out another whimper and Sigbert continued, "Oh don't worry, you can see it coming and get out of the way. They are not as accurate at shitting on you as they are at pissing. Of course, with five of us in here it might not be so easy to dodge them."

Milgryd cried, Leofric and Athelstan just hung their heads and Aefre looked daggers at Sigbert. Aefre had no idea what would happen to them all in the future but her priority was that her son survived. She sat next to him in the pit, both of

31

them leaning their backs against the wall. She spoke softly to Leo, trying to make him understand what he had to do to live. She gleaned as much information as she could from Sigbert who, despite his facetious nature, told them everything he could about Calchfynedd and living as a slave.

The next day, just after dawn, they were pulled from the pit, taken down to the stream and thrown in. They gulped in water and washed themselves and their clothes. Leofric stood motionless in the stream that led into the Nene River, his arms were down at his sides and he stared blankly across towards the east. Once Aefre had finished washing herself and her clothes, she moved to Leofric. She ducked him under the water and rubbed his hair just as she would have at home. It made both of them feel good.

"Just do as they say," she said.

"You don't," Leofric replied.

"Stay safe, stay alive and our people will come," she said.

Wet through, they were taken back to the open space in front of the tower along with Sigbert. They stood in a row and King Cynwyd wandered out. He rested his gold-orbed staff against the balcony wall, placed both hands on the stone, stared down on them and paused to look at the two women with their wet dresses clinging to their bodies. He took his time, looking at Aefre and especially Milly and then nodded to a soldier standing behind them.

"Bow," said the guard.

"Bow," said Sigbert so that they understood and they all stooped except Aefre. She continued to look at the King and he looked amused at her. He nodded to the captain of the guards who struck her with the spear haft. She dropped to a crouch and then rose and looked up at the King. She was struck again and this time the guard held her hair tightly at the back of her head and pushed it down, rubbing her face in the dusty ground.

"Ah, spirit," said Cynwyd the King. "We want it in our horses; we want it in our men, but in our slaves, it is only enjoyable in the breaking. It seems that this Sais whore has more spirit than a whole village of Sais men. What fun to break her!"

Cynwyd looked carefully over them and asked the guard, "What work do we have for the boy and the man?"

"We are short in the stables, my lord, and we can always do with more on the building works."

Cynwyd looked again at the two women. The older one would be trouble but was certainly a fine specimen. The younger girl whimpered and was probably a virgin. He was glad that he was a Christian and the Good Lord sent him such gifts. Again this morning, he thanked God in his prayers for the retreat of the Sais and these gifts before him. Life was so good. He had lived over sixty years and he intended to live many more. Both of these women would be fun in their own way.

"The older one to the kitchen garden and the younger to the scullery," he said.

"Yes, my lord," said the guard and led them away.

Chapter 3
Beodricesworth

Hild had her arm around Anson's waist as they watched Osgar play with the other boys. He had been with them for two years now. They stood by Anson's forge which was in front of their house. It was ten paces away from any other house as a fire precaution. Forges with fires do not mix with tightly packed thatch houses. The forge was no more than four paces by five inside and contained a block of iron with a flat top standing on a knee-high stump of wood. The wooden stump sat squarely on the dirt floor with small wedges under its sides to keep it level and to reduce movement. Behind the anvil was the bellows, made of leather riveted to two V shaped wooden boards. At the thick end, the leather formed pleats and at the narrow end a hollow tube of leather supported along the sides with cane, projected outwards. The base of the bellows was heavy oak wood to keep it to the floor. The top planking was thinner and an ash pole ran along it. Over the end of the pole was a bull's horn curving upwards.

Hanging from the low beams at the side of the forge were various tongs, hammers and other tools. On the ground along the wall were lumps of iron, old tools, broken seaxs, axes and rusty spearheads. Everything was covered in a black dust. The sun streamed through the one small window at the back showing the swirling pattern of dust in the air. Underneath the window was a pile of charcoal which was at waist height and about the same width. Mined coal had been becoming more difficult to obtain. Even Anson's famed bartering skills were to no avail in East Anglia where there was no coal. Trade had been restricted by the Waelisc and the only supplies were from Lindsey in the north or from the Jutes in the southeast. Neither could now come directly and shipping coal around the coast made it more expensive. There was a plentiful supply of charcoal, with some hams devoted almost entirely to its production.

The entrance to the forge was a double wooden door with vertical planking and cross beams. At the top of the left-hand door was a bolt that lodged in the beam and another at the bottom to go deep into the floor. In the middle was a hasp which hinged to the other door. It had a barrel lock through the hasp when shut. Anson had made all the ironwork for his doors, including the barrel lock which he was very proud of. Further along the street, which was full of craftsmen's workshops and stalls selling wares, was an identical door. This was the workshop of his friend Wilfrid the carpenter. Wilfrid had made the doors and other woodwork for Anson and had been repaid with Anson's ironwork. Wilf had been friends with Anson when he had arrived in Beodricesworth a young man. As a Jute, he would have been expected to have settled in the southeast corner of the land where most of his fellow countrymen had colonised. Anson always joked that he had been shipwrecked off the Suth Folk coast and was too afraid of the sea to continue his journey. No one believed him but eventually the questions stopped, he opened his blacksmiths forge and married Hild from Icklingham.

Anson and Hild watched Osgar play the running game. One of Wilfrid's sons, who played on the same team was the same age as Osgar and called Seward. They had become pals since Osgar had come to Beo and always wanted to be on the same side. Osgar had picked up a pass from a Seward and was running with the bundle of rags tightly bound with leather. He clutched it to his chest with his left hand although he was right-handed. A boy, two years older and two hands higher stepped into his way. Osgar hit him at full speed with his outstretched right hand. He struck him full in the chest and just kept running and then another of the opposition had the same treatment. He switched hands for the last, hitting him with his flat left hand. He crossed the line between the silver birch trees and dropped the leather-bound rags. His teammates ran to him to slap him on the back and punch his shoulder. Osgar as always just turned back to the start line with the same look in his eyes. They were a grey blue and hard, not the bright sky blue of many Angles. His mates called the look, his 'Kill the Waelisc' eyes. Osgar never laughed at that as it was too near the truth. He had been told more than once that it was only a game. It was never just a game to Osgar; nothing was without purpose to him. Osgar knew that the running game showed that you could defeat a larger enemy by speed and determination.

He walked back up the hill towards Hild and Anson. He hoped that his aunt Hild would not give him a cuddle and a big kiss on the forehead and say something like, "My big brave soldier." Seward rambled on about the game, as he always did while Osgar walked silently beside him. He had settled well with his new family, never shirking the tasks that a boy of his age was expected to carry out. Hild worried about his long quiet periods when he withdrew into his own world. Like all boys, he had fallouts with others but they had never been told of him starting a fight, only that he never backed down, whoever confronted him.

Anson, Hild and Osgar sat down to eat their evening meal. It was a stew of cabbage and carrot with dried beans thrown in.

"Cabbage and carrot again, Hild," said Anson.

"No, this time it's carrot and cabbage," said Hild.

Osgar smiled, his aunt and uncle were always like this. Their house was always full of friendly bickering, jokes and leg pulling. Hild did not think she was doing her job properly if she was not stuffing them with some food or other.

"I have some good news for you, Osgar," said Anson.

Osgar's heart beat harder as he thought of his mother and brother.

"I have spoken to Tedmund, our Thegn and to the town's Freeman and you are allowed to start an apprenticeship."

Osgar was still distracted by his thoughts about his mother and brother and so just said, "Yes."

"I thought you might just have shown some more enthusiasm," said Anson.

"He was just elsewhere for a while, Anson," said Hild, rolling her eyes at him, "Let him think about it."

Osgar had snapped out of his thoughts. "Thanks, uncle, when do I start?"

"First, we have to get you sworn in at the Great Hall. You have to learn the words so when the Thegn asks you to swear an oath to me and the town and, of course your King, you can say it correctly."

The next week on Thunor's day Osgar stood in front of his Thegn in the Great Hall. He had walked in beside his proud uncle, known to most as Anson the Broad, although others sometimes called him The Jute. Around the hall were the most prominent people in Beodricesworth and some from the surrounding hams. He recognised the headman from Stowe and Henryk, the leader of the Flem settlement, who had come to Icklingham on the day after the raid. Cynbeald, the Storyteller, had patted his shoulder as he passed through the carved doorway and then they waited patiently for the Thegn.

"All stand," said Thegn Tedmund's Reeve.

36

Osgar and Anson were already standing but most of the others had been sitting on the benches around the hall. They rose to their feet and clapped their hands slowly in unison as the Thegn walked in. "All who are not Freemen to leave the hall," announced the Reeve.

Nobody moved as everyone knew that when a ceremony was performed in the hall that no women, children or slaves were allowed to be present. The slaves and women returned after a ceremony to serve food and ale.

"Do you, Anson the Broad of Beodricesworth, take this man, Osgar of Icklingham as your apprentice?"

"I do," said Anson loudly.

"Will you teach him the mysteries of your ancient craft so long as he serves you in a true and diligent manner?"

"I will," said Anson.

Then Tedmund turned to Osgar and said, "Do you Osgar, late of Icklingham, desire to be apprentice to Anson the Broad, where you will smite the black."

"I do, *sire*," said Osgar. His voice wavered and he hoped that it was not obvious. He spoke little anyway, so speaking out loud in public was something he would never choose to do. Cynbeald had tried to give him some training but he did not even like speaking loudly to the scop. He looked straight at Thegn Tedmund as he had been told.

"Then make your declaration to your Thegn and the Freemen of Beodricesworth," said the Reeve.

"I will serve him truly and keep all the mysteries of his said craft secret. I will come to this hall when summoned by my Thegn or my Thegn's Reeve or Thunor will be my judge."

The Reeve spoke, "You will return here after seven summers and with the good grace of the God, you will become a ceorl. Do you understand?"

"I do, sir," said Osgar. He bowed to the Thegn as he had been taught, stepped backwards for three paces, turned and walked from the hall.

"Well spoken," said Cynbeald outside. "We'll make a scop of you yet." And again, he slapped Osgar on the shoulder. "I'm going back in the Great Hall to enjoy the company of Freemen but we will talk later."

Osgar walked back to the forge. Inside the hall ale was passed around, toasts made and songs sung. The Thegn cornered Anson when a chance arose, "Your young apprentice, he's related to you?"

"Yes, *sire*, he is my nephew," Anson replied, showing deference in his voice.

37

"I looked into his eyes when he made his oath. I have had grown men in front of me in this hall almost wet themselves, men that have seen battle shake over just a little oath. Though he did not like speaking out, he had no fear."

"He has his fears, *sire*," replied Anson. "They are not the fears of most twelve-year-olds. He is not afraid of dragons in the night or even you or me. He fears he will not reach his mother and brother before they die."

"And what will you do for him, Anson?"

"I will teach him to smite the black. I will teach him the difference between good iron and bad. I will teach him to make a blade that will cleave armour and the man within it. I cannot teach him to be a soldier but you as Thegn can. When the day comes, as it surely will, I will stand beside him in battle."

"On another matter," said the Thegn, "I need some new shields. I know that you can make the bosses and rivets but who would be my carpenter?"

"*Sire*, you are in luck," said Anson. "Over there is the finest carpenter this side of the Waveney. Hey Wilfrid, come over here," he called.

Wilfrid and Anson walked down the hill from the Great Hall towards the craft street that faced the water meadows. "You told him what?" asked Wilfrid and then answered his own question, "You told him that I was the best shield maker in all Suth Folk?"

"It can't be that hard," said Anson.

"No, and it can't be that hard to be an arse, when you are a Jute, as you have just demonstrated."

Within a week, Wilfrid had walked to Sudbury where there was a shield maker. He did not want to tell Wilfrid anything of the craft of shield making but once Wilfrid had sworn that it was for his own thegn alone and he was staying in Beo and that he had a gift of a good adze, the shield-maker relented. Wilfrid learned how to stress the planks to achieve a curve and to apply bone glue to the joints. Linden or poplar wood was used, sometimes alder or willow. These woods produced light shields that resisted splitting. On returning to Beo, he had walked to the woods to select a good tree and felled it with Seward, splitting it where it lay. They carried it by handcart back to their carpentry shop to cut and glue the curved planks. He then went to the leather worker in the craftsmen's street for the shield covering and instructed him as he had been taught. Five triangles were cut for each shield and a leather rim to go around the outer edge. The leather was attached with more glue. Long sinews from slaughtered cattle were boiled and set around the rim which then shrank to strengthen the shield further.

Anson, the Broad, made the boss for each shield and the rivets to hold it in place. There was either a single or double strap behind each shield, for the arm, and this also was riveted to the thin planking. The boss bulged from the middle of the shield about the size of a hand held over a fist. It was the same angle as the shield where it joined and was riveted. Then it came straight out for three finger widths and finally finished with a pointed dome. If protected the shield holders left hand from spear, axe or sword and was effective when smashed into an enemy's face. The boss did not have any patterning on it as this would have aided any blow by providing grip to a blade or point. Anson forged the metal over a former, the shape of the boss. He turned the glowing metal with large tongs while Osgar struck as directed with the sledgehammer. Anson held the tongs in his left hand and a hand hammer in his right. Osgar first pumped the bellows at the back of the fire by gripping the horn at the end of the pole. He pushed down and the air was forced out by the collapsed leather bellow chamber. The air rushed into the back of the fire making the coals in the centre burn brightly. Anson used a leather beaker to cup water from the hooped pail by the forge. He tipped the water in a circular motion around the fire to dampen the coals and stop the fire spreading too wide, wasting precious fuel and creating a ring of fire that singed the hand.

"Tight and hot," he said to Osgar, "just like a good woman. And don't tell you aunt I said that."

Anson tended the fire and turned the boss to get an even heat while Osgar pumped the bellows. The air was sucked into the bellows through a hole at the top of the bellows' back. This had a leather valve that closed under pressure of the down stroke but immediately fell open on the upstroke. Anson tapped his hammer on the anvil and the ding told Osgar to hurry round and pick up his own sledgehammer that stood against the anvil stump. Osgar's sledgehammer was five pounds in weight. Heavy enough for a twelve-year-old boy, even of his strength. Anson's sledgehammer was eight pounds. For some jobs, Osgar held an object on the anvil with two hands gripping long tongs while Anson struck with his own sledge. Osgar loved forge work and he admired Anson's strength speed and accuracy. When he next struck for Anson, he tried to hit with the same rapidity.

"Slow, slow, slow," said Anson. "Get the timing and the accuracy right. Speed and power will come. Do you smack your hand on a maiden's arse as hard as you can and grab it firmly? No, of course you do not, well striking is like that. And don't tell your aunt I said that."

"He won't have to," said Hild from the doorway. "Is that what you promised to teach him in the Great Hall?"

"Enough for the day," said Anson, pulling a face at Osgar, "Time for ale."

The next day, Osgar lit the fire and checked that the troughs were filled with water and the hooped pails were also full from the well. He dug the clinker out from the centre of the fire and loaded more charcoal on the hearth. Osgar pumped the bellows while Anson turned the metal boss in the fire. When it reached a yellow temperature, he pulled it out of the coals and in one movement had it in position on the anvil. He swung his two-and-a-half-pound hammer exactly where the boss rested on the former. Osgar's following blow landed on the same spot as Anson had hit. Anson moved the boss around by half a finger width and hit it again with his hammer and Osgar followed. This tempo continued until Anson decided that the metal had lost too much heat and he moved it back into the fire. Osgar stacked his sledgehammer down against the anvil stump and walked to the back of the fire and again began to pump the bellows. They repeated this all morning, never rushing, never stopping. The rhythmic ringing of the anvil carried across town and was part of its life.

At about noon, Hild brought two wooden bowls of soup from the house and then fetched them a lump of bread each. They sat outside on a bench facing down the hill to the river, enjoying the afternoon sun. "I was told something last night," said Anson.

Osgar said nothing as it was probably one of Anson's verbal traps. Eventually, the Jute could not help himself and said, "King Wehha is coming to Beo. He will come for a moot in the Great Hall. That's why our thegn wants the new shields. He wants to impress the King."

"Well, you had better get a move on then, hadn't you?" said Wilfrid, who had crept up beside them.

"So how many shields have you made then?" said Anson.

"I can't finish a shield without the bosses and rivets, can I?" said Wilfrid. "I have three ready when you give me the ironwork."

"There's one finished inside the doorway and we will have another done by this evening. The rivets are in a leather cup on the shelf inside the door."

Wilf walked inside the forge, picked up the finished boss, tipped the rivets into it and walked thirty paces to his woodwork shop. That evening, Anson,

Osgar and Hild stood outside Wilfrid's doors and admired the finished shield. It was circular, about a pace wide and had a slight curve to the disk. The boss protruded from the centre and was held firmly in place by the five rivets. The triangles of cattle hide formed a spiral pattern and the rim was covered by leather and sinew that had been shrunk to it. They all patted, stroked and tapped it. It was taut, strong and light.

Each boss was taking some days to make, leaving no time for their normal assorted work. Broken knives, scythes and other objects were starting to collect in the doorway. They ran out of charcoal for two days and had to take a handcart to the nearest ham to buy some more. Finally, a week before the Celebration of Yule and the feast to Skadi, they finished. Their Thegn had supplied the iron but Anson was still looking forward to the agreed payment of cloth, goats, more iron and charcoal plus four ounces of silver and eight ounces of copper. Payment arrived before the Kings visit. The goats were taken down to their enclosure on the water meadows and one was kept at the house to be slaughtered for the festival. The cloth was passed to Hild who hugged it liked a child. She would use it to barter for food and other needs. With the doors closed and the window covered, Anson and Osgar lifted the anvil off the stump and moved it over. Anson dug a small tight hole and put the silver and copper into it. They moved the stump over the hole and lifted the anvil back, covering the cavity.

Taxes were collected from all of the town's people to pay for ale for the Yule festival. By tradition it lasted for three days or until the ale ran out. The town of Beodricesworth prepared for the winter feasting and the visit of their King. Hild had brought out a cheese that she had made especially for Yule with milk from her goats. She had bought plovers from a trade stall as a special treat and honey to make honey and almond cake. The bakers would be producing special breads for the feast which she would buy fresh. Hild loved all festivals because she had the chance to cook and feed Anson and Osgar and share her specialities generously with friends and family.

Wehha, the new king, entered the town from the north. He had visited the North Folk and had journeyed from Theod-Ford where he had stayed the previous night. He had been travelling around his Kingdom of Angels since it had been united. He wanted his people to see him to reassure them that the union that they had recently been entered into was strong. The Wuffingas, his family, had been a force in the eastern area of the Suth Folk for generations. The Angles, like all their cousins in the Anglecynn, chose their Kings by acclamation of freemen and thegns. They usually stayed with the same family but the crown was not always handed down to the first-born male of the next generation. Sometimes the crown passed sideways or even jumped a generation. This way the people of the Kingdom felt that their king was their choice.

The town was decorated as well as possible for the visit. Winter was never an easy time to make a town look joyful but the Great Hall was covered with sprigs of berried holly and some ivy and mistletoe hung inside the hall. Wall hangings had been especially painted of the winter god Skadi and Woden giving gifts to children. Outside the entrance to the Great Hall the Thegn of Beodricesworth's men stood, five either side, all with matching leather covered shields. Anson and Wilfrid smiled as they filed into the hall. It was packed full of the towns people and surrounding hams.

"All stand," announced the Reeve, "let no man stay who is not a Freeman."

There was a passageway between the crowds of about two paces that passed to the left of two burning fires. As Wehha stepped into the Great Hall, the measured rhythmic clapping started and continued until he mounted the low steps at the far end of the hall and turned slowly to face his people. He removed his helmet and with a small nod to all in Great Hall, he sat.

King Wehha's white cloak hung around his shoulders with the fur on the inside, a wolf pelt trimmed the edges. As he sat, he did so with a practiced bob that pulled the cloak up behind him so that it was not tight down his back. He flapped the corners of the cloak from either side of his legs so that it wrapped around and they were almost covered. He wore the traditional wear of any thegn but his clothes were made in the best manner and were spotlessly clean. He wore an embroidered smock made of linen and woollen trousers. These were loose and held up with a leather belt adorned with a silver buckle. They stopped just below the knees beneath which the legs were covered with bound garters. The bindings were of leather in the Angle criss-cross pattern and finished at leather boots. He rested his hand on the golden pommel of his sword showing his ringed fingers. On his left arm above his elbow were gold and silver armbands. His helmet was placed on the small table to his left, facing the crowd with the gold band around it contrasting with the burnished iron of the rest of the helmet. It was also adorned with precious agates along the brow. The helmet had locating holes along the forehead and above the ears. These were to attach the cheek and face plates when used in battle. Wehha looked comfortable and relaxed as he leant back in the dark oak chair.

"Do you accept this man, Wehha, who according to his birth right is the son of Wilhelm, who was the son of Hryp, the son of Hroðmund, son of Trygil, son of Tyttman, son of Caser, son of Woden, now as your king?" called out the Reeve.

"Aye," the room said loudly in unison. If it had been a moot outside on a hill as was sometimes the custom, then they would have thrust their spears towards the sky. Because they were meeting in a hall, all arms were left outside. The cheering died and Wehha, King of the East Angels rose to speak.

Chapter 4
Enslavement

Milgryd climbed the stone steps towards King Cynwyd's rooms in the Tower. The head kitchen maid had told her that she had been summoned by the King. The order was given with a sneer of distain and finished with 'whore-pig'. She had been a slave of the Waelisc for more than two years since when she had been separated from Aefre, Leofric and her brother Stan and taken to the kitchens. The head cook was a plump woman who had five others working below her and she had disliked Milgryd instantly. She had hated her hair and her eyes, her stupid voice and most of all she had hated her whimper when she had smacked her. The cook knew why the Milgryd had been given a job in the kitchen rather than a harsh placement in the fields and she knew how angry the King would be if she was spoiled in any way. The cook was careful not to mark her but had told the other kitchen staff that a punch in the stomach never showed so that was what little Sais bitch was to expect least once a day. She now spoke some of the language, understanding much more and therefore heard every day, the constant stream of insults to her and her people. They were usually just called names; the women of whatever age, whores and the men cowards or pigs. She knew that the punishments and insults would never end. The trips, the casual punches, the insults, would increase as she got older.

"Ah, come in little Milly," said Cynwyd, "you've come to serve my wine. So good of you to come."

Milgryd poured wine from the pitcher that she had carried up the stairs and placed it by the half-filled goblet. She picked the goblet up, carried it to Cynwyd and passed it to him with a little bob.

"Stand by me girl but don't block the fire," he told her.

He looked at the girl; a little plump maybe, he thought, she must be stealing food from the kitchen. He would tell them to thrash her when he was finished. The bruises would be gone by the next time he wanted her.

"You look a little warm here by the fire. Why don't you take off your clothes?"

"Thank you, lord," said Milgryd, with her best attempt at a little coy smile to him.

He held his goblet in his left hand and took a sip while his right hand was placed between her legs. He moved his hand feeling her soft warm skin. She felt his cold bony hand; she felt sick.

*****

Athelstan had worked on the fallen defensive wall to the north of the tower since he had been separated from the others. Its lower level was Roman and the upper had been added to by the Waelisc. Where it was finished, it was the height of five men with crenulations along the top. It was obvious that the lower portion was better built, with the stones larger and more tightly fitted. The kitchen gardens and beyond the river, were to Stan's left, the town was to his right. As always, he had been awoken at dawn to be taken down to the wall from the shack that he slept in. He had some thin soup before he started. He was gaunt, his cheekbones stuck out and the tendons of his arms and legs showed. He walked with a pronounced limp where his foot had been broken. A guard had thought it funny to drop a rock on it and he had been given no treatment and had been kept working, consequently the broken bones had never healed and every step was painful. He moved the stones to rebuild the wall all day long, loading them into a handcart from the barges that stopped by the river and then pulling it up the slope. If there was no barge or no more stones to move to the wall, he carried those at the bottom of the wall up ladders one by one. If he stopped or tried to talk to another slave, he was cursed at and whipped. In the winter, he was fed nuts and grain in the morning, a thin soup at noon and bread in the evening.

He had only spotted Milgryd twice in the time since they had been separated. She smiled and waved to him and he was happy that she was safe. Her clothes were neat and her hair brushed and he could see she was carrying a pitcher of some sort. He saw Aefre in the distance more often because he worked in sight of the kitchen garden. She was at least one hundred paces away, too far to speak too. She seemed to tend the garden there and he thought that she lived in the hovel at the end. He spoke rarely to anyone and had learned little of the language. He understood all the orders that the Waelisc gave, having soon learned from being struck whenever he had hesitated for an instant. He had been beaten more times than he had cared to remember, often it was just casual violence. One of the guards always found it amusing to trip him, another had more than once slammed the haft end of his spear down on his broken foot. He had learned to keep his head down and to keep moving.

*****

Aefre had been taken to the kitchen gardens behind the tower. There was a small courtyard outside the kitchens surrounded by a wall the height of two men, facing the door. Opposite the kitchen door was a gateway with a solid oak arched door set in it, leading through to the gardens. It was part of a small farm which included goats and chickens and at one side there were some pigs under the trees in an enclosed fenced area. A grass pathway led from the gateway straight down to the far end, where there was a hovel. It was poorly thatched, about three paces square and only had a raised area for sleeping in. There was a fire hearth on the ground inside the door with a metal cauldron hanging from the middle beam. This was where Aefre was lived.

The kitchen garden was run by an old Briton and four under gardeners, two women and two men. As the only slave, Aefre was at the bottom of the order and given the very worst jobs. If there were brambles to clear or nettles to weed, she was given the task. She had been allotted the specific job of caring for the herb garden. Aefre had been happy and keen to do this, as she had assisted Mildred the herb woman in her village, but she had made sure that her delight was not seen. She had thought of her friend Mildred, the herb woman from her ham, who had taught her much about herbs for cooking, healing and poisons.

Aefre had risen each morning as the sun came up. She always left her hovel turning right out of the door and stood with her hands on the woven wicker fence, staring into the east as the sun broke above the distant chalk hills. She knew that her people would come from that direction when they marched to rescue her and her son, so each morning she looked east for the fyrd, imagining Eafwald in the front, in a line of shields. She had envisioned her rescue and the destruction of Bannaventa by her people for two years now. It was the only thing that kept her alive; that and the occasional distant glimpse of her son Leofric. Aefre leant on the fence and felt the early rays of the sun, thinking that there would not be many more warm days before Skadi brought winter. She looked to the horizon and to the furthest chalk hill where the sun rose. "Come, come soon," she said and then turned to her own small herb garden. She had been collecting herbs and planting them in the area that she had cleared and dug by her hovel.

Everything that she had learned about plants had been from old Mildred in her ham. Mildred had been the herb woman in Icklingham since before Aefre and Eafwald had arrived from the Old Country. She had immediately bonded with the woman and at nine years old became Mildred's assistant. Her little helper, Mildred had called her. She had learned where to grow the herbs which thrived in light or shade, or needed dung on them and which required more water and after that, she learned how to prepare them so that their properties were best used. Aefre had been taught which ones should be dried or given as herb tea or whether to pound them into a paste.

Aefre picked her usual herbs and made a tea in a small cauldron hanging from a tripod over her fire. She had done this daily from the time that she had found the herbs she was looking for. The herbs stopped her being with child, a precaution she still took although it was a while since she had been called to serve the King. She had been unable to hide her hatred of him and finally she had been whipped in public. The pain of the lash, she could bear but being stripped to the waist in public humiliated her. She had been sent to the King since then and she had hidden her feelings but he knew that she had no respect for him so she was not called very often. As she drank her herb tea, she cursed the goddess Gefjum, the goddess of fertility, just as she had been taught by Mildred.

Aefre had learned some of the Waelisc language but only out of necessity. She hated every word of it and resented using it. She prayed daily to her gods and despised the Waelisc and their Christian god on his idiotic cross. What type of people would worship a man nailed to a cross, she thought, and if he were any god, he would break the nails and climb down. How like the Waelisc it was, for them to think that their one god was a match for all the northern gods.

The bullying, punishment without reason and humiliations continued. Now it was worsened by understanding more of the Britons' language. Aefre was always referred to as the pig-faced whore, despite her obvious good looks, by the head cook. Aefre just looked at her with her icy blue eyes and thought, no thegn in all Anglia would eat the muck that you produce. If she looked at the cook for more than an instant, she was slapped in the face. Aefre did not cry, she just thought, my people will come and when they do, I will kill you. She had only seen her son Leofric in the distance a few times since they had been taken. One day a string of horses were led past the fence at the bottom of the garden towards the river. She noticed the way that one of the grooms was walking and knew in that instant that it was Leo. He was a hand higher now and his hair was in the Waelisc style of braids. She stared through a gap in the wicker fence as she knelt weeding and tried to make it look from behind that she was still working while she watched him.

Was it possible that her son was controlling one of those beasts, she thought, her Leofric? "Keep safe," she said to him, though out of earshot and then said a prayer to Eostre the goddess of good luck and the east. As she was watching, the horse held by her son span around, swinging him in a following circle. The other horses and grooms scattered, two of them almost lost their charges and then Aefre watched in astonishment as her son patted the horse and appeared to talk to it. She was too far away to hear his words but she could see that he was talking to the horse. His right hand still held the rope attached to the halter around the horse's head. He stood on the horse's left side and switched the rope from his right hand to his left and patted the horse's neck very lightly and then he rubbed its shoulder while all the time he talked to it.

Aefre looked at the beast's flared nostrils, the steamy snorts shooting from them in bursts. She could see the horse's eyes bulging in their sockets and thought that this is what a dragon must look like. Leofric was now rubbing the horse's nose and the bursts of steam were slowing while still he talked to it. Had he learned the magic language of horses, she thought? Did horses understand the Waelisc? Is that why they could control and sit on the back of these great beasts? Had her son become Waelisc? She looked again at Leofric wearing the gaudy colours of the Waelisc with his hair worn in their style. No longer was it cut shoulder length, now it had grown and was braided either side. The colour had darkened somewhat, it was still fair but no longer as blond as his early years. Had he given up on his people? Was he now Waelisc? She watched in concern as the only one of the group without a horse walked over to her son, he shouted at Leofric and then kicked him. No, her son was still a slave and strangely, it made her happy, better to be a slave than a Waelisc.

Leofric rubbed the back of his leg as he walked. The kick hurt and the guard that did it was an idiot. They had given him the most difficult and fractious horse to lead and he had just spent time calming him after some geese took off from the riverbank and had frightened him. They were taking the horses to the enclosed area just up from the river. Now that winter was almost come, most of the horses were turned out of the stables. The raids only took place in the warmer months and so they only kept a small number in the stalls, ready to mount. The reduced troop was still able to patrol the eastern border of the Kingdom and mounted a guard if the King or his son Cadrod wished to travel. The horses turned out in the meadows could be returned to service within a day.

When he had been made a slave, Leofric had been taken to the stables where the horses had stood in lines on either side of a passage fifty paces long. The horses faced away from the aisle way towards the wall where they were tied to a fixed ring, attached to a rope halter over their heads. The smell of urine and dung was strong and the horses whinnied and snorted, steam spurted from their flared nostrils. Leofric had run alongside a horse for two days, fearing every moment that the beast would attack him or crush him under its hooves but now he no longer feared them. He had been placed with one of the grooms who showed him how to remove the muck. Every time he was less than perfect, he had been cuffed but when the groom was not looking, he had stolen grain from the manger and stuffed it in his mouth. His first job of the morning had been to fetch water from the stream with a yoke over his shoulders which carried two pails. He had learned to rub down the horses after their exercise every day and to feed and water them. He had slept on straw since that day, in a stall at the end of the passageway, away from the other grooms. From the first, he was awoken at first light and finished at sunset.

Leofric took comfort in being a horse groom and identified with the horses now. They were tied up, made to go and do their masters bidding and were kicked in the ribs if they did not obey in an instant. It was not like that at the start. He was terrified of them at first with everything about them frightening him, especially their size, their teeth and their unpredictability. As he came to know them, he realised that they were not so unpredictable. They needed to see you and just as importantly they needed to hear you coming. Sudden noises or movements frightened them and when strange noises came from somewhere that they could not see, it made them snort and look every way. When he was first put into the stables, he thought the Waelisc talked to the horses. He listened to them making their strange sounds and believed that they spoke a magic language to the horses but when he tried to copy it the other grooms and slaves found him hilarious. Then it came to him that it was not the words that made the horses respond but the way they were voiced. Once he realised that, he began to speak to the horses in his own language. As he groomed them, he told them about his land and his people. He was always given the most difficult horses to work with and the Waelisc grooms tried to get him hurt. One day, one might throw a bucket over his stable partition or a grooming cloth would be flapped outside the stall. His solace was to talk quietly to the horse so that the Waelisc couldn't hear and tell the horse that Waelisc were ugly and needed to be kicked or trod on or bitten.

When Leofric had been in the stables for only one week, he saw something that astounded him. Outside the stables at the far end of the passageway that faced south, was an open area which was partially mud and grass. Fifty paces away was a building that looked similar to this uncle Anson's forge in Beo. He could see through the open door an anvil of similar design to his uncle's and the fire behind it. After that, it was just too dark to see into from the stables. Outside a horse was held by his groom as the smith walked out of the forge building carrying an object with tongs. It was red hot and looked like a ring. He walked to the horse, picked its foot up and placed the object on it. It seemed to set fire to it and smoke shot out from the foot so that for a short while he could see neither smith nor horse. Slowly, they emerged from the cloud of smoke and the smith walked back into the forge.

Sharply, Leofric was cuffed around the head and shouted at so he continued to pick up the urine-soaked reeds from the stable floor and carry them to the pile just outside the stable passageway. Sometime later, he saw the same smith carry out, not a ring as he first thought but an incomplete ring the same shape as the bottom of the horse's hoof. He had realised that it was now cold because the smith took it in his hand this time, and not with tongs. A young boy carried a box beside him and the smith picked the horse's foot up and placed it between his legs while he faced the horse's rear. He could do this because his leather apron had a split up the middle to his groin. The apron was only to the waist, unlike his uncle's, in Beo, which had a bib section protecting his stomach and chest. Leofric had then watched in incredulity as the young helper passed the iron object to the smith and he began to hammer nails through it into the foot. He had not been able to understand how the smith could do this without causing pain to the animal but the horse just stood still. He had thought that he must be too far away to see blood but he still could not think why they were doing this.

During the last two years, he had become experienced with the horses. He had learned to care for their every need so that his charges were always fit and healthy with gleaming coats, he even understood the shoeing of horses with iron. Some of the other grooms now had a grudging respect for him. He had been given the most difficult and dangerous horses to work with and had survived. That did not stop them hitting him or ridiculing him at every opportunity. The incident with the horse earlier was typical of the way he was treated. He rubbed his leg where he had been kicked by the head groom and walked back towards the stables. Before he rounded the corner of the castle wall, he looked towards the tower where he could see a female figure standing on the battlements. The figure had blond hair and he guessed that it was Milgryd.

Aefre had been planting all day and straightened to stretch her back. She had just seen her son with the horses and was thanking the gods that he was safe while she arched her body, she looked west towards the sunset over Bannaventa. She could make out the silhouette of a female figure standing atop the battlements. The figure paused and then turned to face outwards. She had not seen Milgryd in a while but was sure it was her. Aefre prayed to her gods. Beneath the wall in the distant shadow was the usual group of slaves and overseers. She believed that Stan was amongst them but could not make him out. She knew how the slaves suffered by the wall, frequently hearing them cry out.

Athelstan was tired. He had worked the whole day below the castle wall collecting stones and carrying them to the stonemasons. His foot hurt him and he had been beaten twice by the guards. He saw the shadow from the castle battlements near to him and thanked the gods another day was nearly over. He would return to the slave's hovels and his lice infested mat, where he would lay down and dream of home. He noticed all the guards and other slaves looking up at the girl, who was staring down at them. It took a while to realise that it was his sister, perched precariously on the battlements edge.

*****

Wehha, king of all the Angles, stood up in the Great Hall at Beodricesworth to speak. He undid the golden clasp that held his cloak just below his neck, near his left shoulder and handed it to one of his men. The cloak was rolled and placed on the table to alongside his helmet. Wehha enjoyed the adornments of power and showed his wealth publicly at all times. He had been born into a powerful family, the Wuffingas, who had dominated the eastern area of Anglia since the early settlement after the Romans. His family had always had ambitions to rule but none of his ancestors would have dreamt that one day all of East Anglia would be ruled by their house. It was the nature of the Angles, as it was with their neighbours the Saxons and Jutes to continually wage war. Wehha thought that he had waged his war though, first holding the Suth Folk and then vanquishing the North Folk, and wanted no more fighting amongst the Anglecynn in his time. The threat from the west was growing as each year passed. When his family first came to East Anglia, they had chosen their land and moved the Waelisc off it. They had left without a fight. He believed that the Waelisc were a weak people, who under the Romans had forgotten how to wage war, but now they had gained strength from their old kingdoms of the far west.

"My Thegns; good people of Beodricesworth," he said in a voice that carried to the end of the hall, "thank you for greeting me as your king and for your hospitality."

He told them that he was there to listen to them and to answer their worries. He finished by rallying them. "You, the Suth Folk, have known my family for many generations. We came to this land together and settled it together; we built our hams together and we drove the Waelisc away together. Today we are one people, Suth Folk and North Folk. One Kingdom of the East Angles and one king."

King Wehha sat down amid the cheering thegns and freeman. The Reeve banged his staff on the wooden floor and announced, "Let the Moot begin."

There was only one subject that interested the Moot that day. Thegn and freeman told the King of the attacks by the Waelisc upon the people. They described the terror of the raids, the losses and the effect it was having on all of the people of the area. He was told how the boundary of the Angles was receding eastwards and northwards and how his people had abandoned hams only a day's walk from Beo that had been occupied for three generations. How their hams could not cope with the influx of these refugees.

"The Waelisc are cowardly," said one thegn. "They will not stand and fight. We cannot bring them to battle. They run around us on their horses. If they catch a few men away from the line, they cut them down. If they see a shield wall, they scurry off."

"We need to attack them, *sire*," said another. "Raise the fyrd and march to Chalk Hills and slay Cynwyd in his lair."

The King answered, "You are my brave people and you have suffered greatly. I know that you will follow where I lead but I have to secure our Kingdom. We have only just united with the North Folk and I cannot risk that union. We wait while we are growing stronger and then we will destroy this usurper of our lands and his son who does his terrible work. If we have to, we will pull back behind the Lark. We now have all crossing points defended. My people remain safe."

*****

"That was a great speech," said Wilfrid the carpenter over a tankard of ale. Cynbeald the storyteller and Anson the Broad did not nod in agreement.

"I could have made a better speech than that," said Cynbeald, "and I would have had the hall cheering."

"I bet you would have," said Anson, "and your jokes would be better. He told us nothing except he thinks that the union with the North Folk is a good thing. He told us about guarding the Lark crossings. That had been done before he had ordered it."

Osgar and Wilfrid's son Seward and Lynne his daughter arrived. She was wearing a new dress and shawl and sat down opposite Osgar. Seward sat at the bench and shifted along towards Wilfrid. Cynbeald called for some more pottery mugs and a refill of the ale pitcher. He poured barley ale into the two new vessels and topped the others up.

"How did it go, uncle?" said Osgar. "When will the fyrd be raised for war?"

"Not yet, my boy," said Anson.

Osgar looked around the group. As he looked at them, their eyes dropped to the ground. They all knew what he was thinking. "I will go on my own then," said the boy, jutting out his chin.

"You will not, Osgar," said Anson. "You will stay and finish your apprenticeship. You will fulfil your oath to me and your thegn and when you have learned to smite the black you can go and fight your enemies."

"You are all cowards," shouted Osgar.

Anson grabbed Osgar by his smock at his chest and lifted the boy towards him. He spoke almost in a whisper, "No man is a coward here. Each one of us desires nothing more than to march together to the Chalk Hills and help you rescue your mother and brother. You need to remember that they are Hild's sister and nephew as well. We will go when the King calls the thegns and our thegn calls us. Don't ever let me hear you call me or any Angle a coward again." He dropped Osgar who turned and ran back to the forge.

During the three days of Yule, no one saw Osgar. They only heard him because he was using the forge and making the anvil ring. He worked the bellows himself and then hammered the hot iron. He worked with the doors shut and slept in the forge at night. Hild placed a bowl of stew or soup with bread outside the door twice a day and worried about him but Anson reassured her that he was just being a boy. When Yule was over Anson opened the doors of the forge and said, as if nothing had happened, "What have you been making, boy?"

"I have made a scaramaseax, uncle. You said I could have the old iron that has lain against the wall for a year."

"Let's have a look then," said Anson.

"It's not finished yet," said Osgar, "I need you to show me how to harden it by tempering and I don't know where I will get a handle." Osgar passed his metalwork to his uncle and Anson took the long blade in his hand and turned it over. It was about the length of his forearm, from the crook of his elbow to the tips of his fingers.

"Good hammer work," he said running his fingers along the blade, "and a good back."

The scaramaseax only had a blade on one side unlike a double-bladed sword. They came in all sizes, from a short sword down to a kitchen knife size. It was the Angles' utility weapon and tool and was usually just called a seax. After Osgar had forged the blade with its tang for the handle, he had sharpened it. He had spent a whole day honing it with a whetstone until the blade edge was the correct angle along its entire length.

"We will go and get some antler horn later, but first let's harden the edge," said the Jute. "Go and ask your aunt for some pig fat. She will have plenty after the feasting."

Anson looked again at his apprentice's work. He stood by the door in the sunlight and turned the seax over and over and again and ran his fingers along it. *There are men who smite iron all their lives that do not hammer as well as this,* he thought. He had made sure that Osgar gripped his hammer handle the right distance from the head and that he used his wrist first and brought his elbow into use for heavy work. He had shown Osgar how a run of hammer blows, with each overlapping the previous, took out dents and marks but this boy was a natural.

54

When Osgar used the sledgehammer, he would swap his leading hand and was just as comfortable working a left or right lead. Once Anson had asked Osgar why he sometimes worked left-handed and it was clear from his answer that he did not think about when he used a sledge, and was comfortable either way when working two-handed.

Osgar returned with the pig fat which was set in a pottery bowl. Anson warmed it by the fire, for it to melt and poured it into a long trough. Anson heated the seax carefully until it was a good even red along the blade. He dipped the cutting edge of the blade a reed's width into the fat along the whole length of the blade. The fat boiled, sizzled and spat and then he pulled it out and held it in the light. "See the colours, Osgar? Like the rainbow and they seem to move away from the edge. It's the straw colour that we want for this iron."

Osgar watched the rainbow colours move and change and when the very edge of the blade turned yellow Anson plunged the whole blade into the fat and held it there until it was cool.

"Let's try it out," said Anson.

He took it to the anvil and to the boy's dismay, he aimed the blade at the base of the anvil where it fanned out before sitting on the wooden stump. He struck a gentle but firm blow into the iron and then held the blade up for Osgar to inspect. There was no notch in it, to Osgar's relief and Anson leant to look at the anvil base. He pointed with his stubbly finger to a spot and Osgar looked carefully. There was a fresh notch cut into the iron of the anvil as if it were wood. Osgar's eyes widened. "Thank you, uncle," he said, again inspecting the perfect blade.

"Let's go and get that handle made," said the Jute.

They walked alongside the craftsmen's street, past Wilfrid the carpenter who was working with Seward helped by another of his sons. His daughter, Lynne had just delivered some food and ale and they were invited to join them. Lynne eagerly ran to get more when she saw that Osgar was stopping. She handed him cheese and a pottery mug of ale and watched him as Anson showed Wilf the seax. After thanking Wilf for his hospitality, they moved on. The potter was just placing another urn outside in the sun for the clay to dry before firing so Anson and Osgar stopped to pass the time of day with small talk. The potter's son was inside puggling clay with a pole when he came out, he saw it was Osgar and asked, "When are you coming back to play the running game?"

"I'm too busy," replied Osgar. "Anyway, you were not too happy last time when I ran past you."

"You did not run past me," said the potter's son smiling. "You ran over me and I hurt for a week. I want you on our side."

They all laughed, Anson and Osgar moved on passed the dyers until they reached the bone and fur dealers. Outside the skinner's shop were hung furs and hides from many animals including sheep, goats, cattle and in pride of place a wolf's pelt. All pelts and skins were brought out to display each morning and only taken in at sunset or if it rained. There were stacks of cattle horn and antler from red and roe deer, displayed in wicker baskets.

"We need some antler horn for a large seax and an off-cut of sheepskin, enough for the scabbard," said Anson.

"What do you have in return?" asked the trader.

Osgar looked at Anson. "I have nothing," said Osgar with his head down.

"Don't be silly, boy," said Anson. "You have something that you can give in payment any day and still keep to use again."

Osgar looked at his uncle and thought that he was not in the mood for his uncle's riddles so he said, "What's that?"

"Your skill and your craft and your hard work," Anson replied looking pleased with his riddle and then he turned to the trader and said, "he will make you a skinning knife with the best blade you have ever felt. In return, we need enough horn for two large fighting seaxs and for two small hand seaxs. He also needs the sheepskin off-cut for the two long seaxs and leather for the scabbard belts."

The trader looked dubious, a skinning seax needs the sharpest blade of all and he did not want to have to continually sharpen it. Before the skinner could answer, Anson took the scaramaseax from Osgar and placed it in front of him. The skinner turned the weapon in his hand and ran his thumb casually along the blade. Suddenly, he snatched his thumb from the blade and looked at the line of blood on it. Anson laughed and the trader looked at Osgar in approval.

"We have a deal?" said Anson.

The skinner nodded in agreement and replied, "Yes."

Anson walked along the street with his arm on Osgar's shoulder. "Why enough antler for four handles and enough leather and sheepskin for two long seaxs?" asked Osgar.

"You will have to pay the leather worker for making the scabbard for your seax and you need enough antler horn for a small seax to pay him with."

"But why the extra sheepskin for another long seax?" asked Osgar.

"Because you are making me one. Do you think I am going to have an apprentice walking around Beo with a finer seax than mine?" Anson laughed and shoved Osgar.

It had taken all morning to walk up and down the craftsmen's street. They had stopped and passed the time of day with most of the tradesmen and their apprentices. They arrived back at the forge to a big welcome from Hild. Osgar managed a feint to the left to avoid a cuddle and kiss but accepted the bowl of stew. "Cabbage and carrot?" asked Anson.

"Not today," said Hild. "Today it is carrot and cabbage."

Osgar shook his head at them, and started at his stew. He dipped the lump of bread in it and ate quickly. He wanted to get in the forge and start work.

*****

Cynwyd looked at the girl standing on the battlements. He had come out of his rooms to see where his wine was and the girl bringing it. On the wooden floor lay a pitcher on its side, most of the wine was spilt from it, the tray and a silver goblet lay beside it. The girl was crying and looking over the wall and back to Cynwyd and he could hear a voice coming from the ground below the wall calling to her. It was a Sais voice and it made him cringe.

"Milly, Milly, please Milly, go back," called Athelstan.

It was the first time she had heard or seen her brother in more than a year. She knew work had been going on repairing the wall but she had not been able to see it from the kitchen or her hovel where she slept with the rest of the kitchen workers. She felt her stomach; the bulge was obvious. It had been noticeable to the others in the kitchen and the spits, punches and trips had increased. She now understood the insults aimed at her. She was the 'King's tart', the 'Sais pig' or the head cook's favourite the 'King's hole'. She hated them and now she hated herself as much. She did not want a child. She did not want to bring a baby into this Hel and she certainly did not want to carry that old repulsive man's child.

She did not know what to do. She stood on the battlements where she had intended to throw herself off and now, she heard her brother. Just hearing his voice gave her hope and she turned to see Cynwyd. He walked towards her leaning on his staff with his left hand gripping the small gold orb at its top. He picked it up in both hands, pointed the end towards her and pushed her in the stomach with it. She tumbled backwards off the battlements and landed on her back across a rock by her brother.

Aefre had watched the silhouetted figure of Cynwyd push the girl off. It was the first time that she had cried for more than a year. She went into her hovel and crushed more herbs between a smooth pebble in her fist and a slate. She scooped the contents into a small, wooden cup that she had found and added hot water from the cauldron. When the tea had cooled somewhat, she sipped it. She had known Milly since she was born. She had played with her twins, Leo and Osgar, when they were small and now her body lay broken on the ground. Aefre swore to the gods that Cynwyd and every Waelisc would pay for her death.

Cadrod rode around the castle and saw the Sais figure lying dead on the ground and the young man bent over her. He looked up to see his father, the King and said to the guard, "Tell the Sais pig to throw that turd on the fire."

Athelstan tried to pick his sister up with his hands under her armpits but he was too weak. He had been worked every day since he had been enslaved. Only on their festive days did he get a rest because the guards and masons were enjoying a day off. He had been fed the minimum to keep him alive. Two of the guards pushed him out of the way and took hold of Milgryd's limp body by the wrists and ankles. They walked over to the fire of burning waste and threw her on. She landed face down.

Cadrod rode on, followed by his warriors. In the middle of the line were five boys tethered to the saddles of the horses. All of them looked in horror at the scene while Cadrod laughed and chatted with his riders and looked forward to reporting more good news to his father. Once that he had seen that the horses were stabled and his two wounded men were being cared for, he ordered his sergeant to throw the captives into the pit and he strode up the tower to report to his father.

"How did the raid go?" asked Cynwyd.

"It went well," answered Cadrod. "We went south as planned to where the Sais lurk. We killed many and burned their houses and I have also brought five more slaves for you."

"So I saw," said Cynwyd after sipping his wine. "No women though."

"We don't need women father," said Cadrod. "We need young men to work in the fields or on the walls and finish this castle. Their sows are no good to us."

"You speak for yourself," said the King. "A little fair-haired bitch keeps me alive."

Cadrod shuddered. "I do not know how you can touch them, father, but I promise you I will bring back one for you on the next raid and I know just where to go. We can go north and east again over the great heath and cross the river. They will not be expecting us to attack the same place."

"Thank you, my son," said Cynwyd smiling, "for keeping this old man happy. Now tell me more of your venture to the south."

"The Saxons live like all Sais vermin. They settle in small villages with only wooden houses as they are unable to make civilised buildings from stone. Their houses are gathered close together and they farm all around each village. You cannot tell what is farm and what is village."

Cynwyd screwed up his face at that but did not interrupt.

"All their men are farmers or craftsmen and they all fight. Some are well armed with shield and spear and a few have short swords but when they fight, they are cowards. They will not come out and battle like us, man to man. They huddle together behind their shields and stick their spears out and when there are many of them, they form two lines. The line at the back has spears almost the height of two men. It is like trying to get at a hedgehog and no horse will ride through that. However, if we turn them or get behind them or even split them then they are easy. No Sais on open ground can beat one of my warriors."

"Sometimes they fight with an axe. That is how we lost a horse and rider. We caught them at a village as they were forming their line. We went in before they were organised and tried to hit them hard, one of their great oafs swung an axe. It almost cleaved the horse in two. He swung it at an angle hitting the horse on the shoulder and sweeping it down. Man and horse hit the ground. In the confusion, we pulled our man away before they could butcher him. The horse had broken the line but as one, they took two steps back and soon filled the gaps."

"Your grandfather used to tell of how the Sais were destroyed at the Battle of Mynydd Baddon by Arturius," said the King.

"He knew the Sais weaknesses," said Cadrod.

"He knew their strengths as well," said Cynwyd. "That is just as important. If Arturius had lived longer and all our peoples had been behind him we would have driven all the Sais from Lloegr."

"I am the new Arturius, father. I will finish what he started."

"I believe you," said the King to his heir. "You will have to use foot soldiers as well as cavalry and fight them on ground of your choosing. That is what Arturius did. The Sais thought it would be easy but they were trapped and they were all slaughtered, thousands of them. It stopped their advance and threw them back and they have still not recovered. Your grandfather took these chalk hills and made it the Kingdom of Calchfynedd."

When Cadrod left his father, Cynwyd settled back in his chair and sipped his wine by the fire. He called for his servant who stood outside the oak door, "The Sais bitch that lives in the hovel in the herb garden?"

"Yes, my lord," said the servant.

"Have her fetch me wine. I haven't seen her awhile. Oh, and get her washed first."

Chapter 5
Return

Osgar and Anson sat outside the small thatched house in the middle of the craftsmen's street that served as a tavern. They drank ale with Wilfrid and his two apprentice sons and had been joined by Cynbeald the Storyteller. The sun was still over the houses although they had finished work. Spring had arrived and they were soon to celebrate Eostre again. A time in the calendar that no longer interested Osgar. Osgar's frame had thickened even more. From being a strongly built boy, he was now a broad-shouldered young man. He had not reached his full height and still had his boyish looks. He had fluff on his top lip and his aunt Hild had considered telling him that it was time to learn how to shave. His hair was cut in the Angle style; straight across at collar length. It was darker than most Angles but his eyes were grey-blue.

"So Cynbeald," said Anson, "you want us to go back to Icklingham and build a forge?"

"Only temporary," said Cynbeald, "I know you would not want to leave your beloved Beo for too long. The ham is getting back to life. There are more settlers from the Old Country and some of the refugees who have been driven eastwards by the Waelisc incursions. They have cleaned up the destroyed houses and rebuilt but they need ironwork." He looked across at Wilfrid. "And they need a good chippy. They can do the rough-hewn stuff but they are not so good at doors and furniture."

Anson said, "Well we have caught up on our work since we finished the bosses and to be truthful, young Osgar here makes my work so much quicker and lighter. We could do with more. What about you, Wilf?"

"Same with me," said Wilfrid, "I need lots of work to keep the two boys busy."

Anson glanced over at Osgar and could see how uncomfortable he looked. Eostre and Icklingham did not mix well with his apprentice. "We all have to face our demons one day," said Anson to him.

"I know," said Osgar, "but I doubt I will face him in Icklingham."

A week later, they set out. They took turns to pull the handcart along the Lark valley. They passed the settlements of Fornham and at Hengrave and at noon, they reached the Flemish settlement and stopped to eat. They unwrapped the bread and cheese that Hild had prepared for them. She had piled enough food into the handcart to keep for a five-day trip, not the half day that it took. Lynne had accompanied them; she said that she wanted to be with her father and brother. Everyone but Osgar knew otherwise.

The Flemish as always, were very welcoming and Henryk their headman, recognised Anson and Osgar. Wilf, Seward and Lynne, were introduced to the Flems, the men formally shaking hands. They ate and relaxed near the river and caught up on the previous two years. When they explained to Henryk why they were back in the area, he told them that his people would have work for them and he thought the people at Stowe were in need of a blacksmith and a good carpenter also.

They finished their midday meal and moved off towards Icklingham. Osgar was feeling more uncomfortable the closer he came to his birthplace. They passed within four hundred paces of Stowe and waved to the figures in the distance there. It was not just a courtesy but a signal that they were friends in unsafe times. The pathway was clearly visible, though the spring growth meant that pulling the handcart was hard work. Wilfrid and his son swapped turns as did Anson and Osgar. They had the bellows and the anvil firmly lodged over the axel and also an assortment of tools and hammers. Anson had arranged for charcoal to be sent directly from Theod-ford, which was closer.

They came down the slight incline into the village before it rose again to the hillock where Osgar's old house was, near to the cemetery. He looked at where the family house had stood and saw that there was no sign of it, except for some ashes; weeds and brambles which had already taken over. Further along, new houses were in various stages of erection. To the left of the roadway, two new houses were partly thatched. There were men on each roof and one below passing up reed. The carts were piled high with sheaths of reeds and had just arrived from the edges of the Lark, the that chers took the bundles and pinned them to the roofs with twisted split hazel.

Most of the rest of the houses were to the right-hand side of the roadway. This was because the land flattened out to the left and there was more chance of flooding. The houses were always built about fifteen feet above the river. The river could be crossed, at this point by fording, but only when the flow was very light. The ham had once spanned the Lark where it split into three. There was one long timber across the main river which had been banked and then on either side shallow streams were crossed with smaller planks. The planks would take a man who was well balanced but no more. If anyone needed to cross with cattle, sheep or a handcart then the river had to be running low so it could be forded.

Opposite the path leading up from the three bridges, the new hall was being built. The shell had been finished and the split planking fitted to it. Wattle and clay lined the building and the roof was thatched with a design along the ridge. There was no doorway in place yet and no decorations inside. It was built to the same size and on exactly the same spot as the old one. Osgar stared at it and then looked up the incline from the hall to the pigsty. It was still there, pigs were in it and Osgar could see where he hid on the night of the raid. He looked at the spot in front of the doorway to the hall where his father had lain dying. Anson put his hand on his shoulder and said, "Let's get the cart unloaded by the house over there. It's our temporary forge."

They had been given two houses that had not been burned in the attack but were abandoned. They were further up the incline behind the new hall. Osgar could see sheep on the hill behind them and when he looked towards the Lark there were a few cattle grazing in the water meadows. By the time they had unloaded their cart into the first of the houses and Wilfrid and his son had unloaded theirs, the sun was beginning to set. They went to the new hall and sat inside on the benches while talking to the villagers. Osgar spoke to more people than he remembered knowing. His cousins from down the west street were sat near him and there were plenty of new faces who had arrived in the last two years.

The villagers cooked over the fire in the centre of the hall and questioned them about everything that was happening in Beo. Osgar remembered when his mother and father were like this and how he had been in awe of anybody from the town. They listened intently when Anson detailed the visit of King Wehha. He repeated his words as he best remembered them. When he was asked by the women what the ladies accompanying him wore, they were disappointed that he could not remember. They ate, drank ale and slept in the hall.

The open doorway of the hall faced east and the rising sun sent its rays inside. Osgar was already awake and sat against the planked wall with his cloak around him. He had slept in his cloak after undoing the neck clasps as was their custom. It was a good cloak but was now looking somewhat short on him as he was growing so quickly. His seax was on his lap in its scabbard, he pulled it slowly out. The scabbard was made of sheepskin with the wool inwards, the natural lanolin oils in the wool kept the blade from rusting. The antler horn handle fitted his hand's width perfectly with a small, carved pommel at the end. The horn carver had not finished it with the traditional orb or batten end but had given it a small hammerhead. Osgar had not asked for it but he smiled when he looked at it. He was after all a blacksmith apprentice and was therefore looked over by Thunor.

Anson adjusted his cloak and rebound his lower legs with the criss-cross pattern of leather over the woollen socks. These went to his knees where the trousers overlapped them. He pulled on his leather boots and helped himself from the cauldron over the fire, using the unwashed wooden bowl that had lain beside him, to fill with some remaining stew. "We'll have a walk around the ham and see what wants doing," said Anson. "Wilf will be getting started on the door for this hall and we will make hinges and hasps once he has it planked up."

Wilfrid was glad that he had come with Anson. The headman had already explained what he wanted with the door to the hall. He asked for it to be carved across the whole face of the door and also the beam above. The headman was not very clear about what he wanted in the way of a pattern but just told him to make it "like the one in Beo."

Wilfrid did not get many chances to show off his carving skills. He had not slept so well that night. Not so much because of the new environment but more so because he was turning patterns and designs over in his head. He could now see the outline in this mind's eye. It was the traditional knot design on either side of a slain dragon. He had yet to work out the door carving as it was unusual to carve the actual door because of the planking and rivets coming through from the cross beams at the back. No matter, it could be done. That morning he would walk with his son to find a good sturdy Linden tree. They made the best carving wood and he would need one of a girth larger than a man could clasp his hands around. The headman had asked that the door could be made and furnished for the Eostre festival. Wilfrid thought, *Why does everyone want something ready by Eostre or Yule but never think to ask you in time.*

"A girl's got more chance of keeping her virginity in Valhalla," said Wilfrid. The new headman of Icklingham was a pompous man and did not think that funny at all. He was a member of the Icke family, from where Icklingham gained its name, and had travelled over from the Old Country after the raid to claim his family land.

"Look," said Wilfrid, "we will find a tree today and then it will take three days to cut it down and split it into planks. When I have selected the best ones for the job, we will make the door. Anson then will make the hinges and hasp to fit. Once I am happy that the door fits and everything aligns, I am going to take the door off again to carve it. Over the entrance, I am going to chalk out my design and then my son will rough cut it while I work on the door. When he is done, I will fine carve it and then my boy will tidy and polish it. If all goes well, it will be done in two weeks, not two days."

"In my country," said the headman, pushing out his chest, "we are more efficient. You take too long."

Wilfrid stood up and turned his back on the headman. He told his son to pack the handcart and he began to pick up his own tools.

"What are you doing?" asked the headman.

"Going back to Beo, to work for people who know something about good woodwork," said Wilf, continuing to pack his tools.

"Come on," said the headman, with his strong Old Country accent, "you can't take a little joke? You know I want you here. I didn't mean to offend you. Please stay."

By all the gods, thought Wilfrid, *an apology from an* An*gle of the Old Country.*

"If what you said was a joke," said Wilfrid, "it must be a bundle of laughs back home, but I accept your apology. You are going to get the best door on a hall outside of Beo. Just leave us to it."

Wilfrid and his son walked off in search of a linden tree. They each carried an axe and a sharpening stone in a pouch hanging from their belts. Wilfrid also had a seax behind his back that Osgar had made. The scabbard was lengthways along the belt and worn in the traditional Angle style. It had a plain wooden handle that he had made and glued to the tang. He was certainly not going to pay for a fancy antler handle when he could make one himself. The handle had a leather leash with a toggle attached to the pommel. This would allow him to pull it quickly from the scabbard.

Anson looked at Osgar to see that he was ready and they rose together. They walked west along the street that ran parallel with the Lark. The pathway was dry as there had been barely any rain since Yule. That was fine up to this time of year, thought Anson, as it meant that the roadways and fronts of houses were not muddy. Travel was so much easier especially if you needed to cross a stream. All the streams and rivers were low but they still flowed and water was always available. It would need to rain soon though, if the planting season was to be a success because once Eostre was out of the way, seeding would begin. Anson had felt the atmosphere had been getting heavier in the last two days and thought that rain was coming.

Osgar and Anson stopped by a house in the west street. It had survived the raid as the Waelisc had not come this far. In it lived three of Osgar's cousins and his aunt. His uncle had died in the burning hall and it was the first time he had seen them since that time. The two boys had grown so much and were now eight and nine years old and the girl, at twelve was a real beauty. She was just starting to show the signs of becoming a woman. The two boys looked wide-eyed at Osgar as only admiring boys can. They saw their broad cousin who carried a seax in the small of his back. They looked at his adult clothes and his forearms of taut muscles and strong hands. They missed their older brother Athelstan and their sister Milgryd.

Anson spoke to his sister-in-law, who was the middle sister between Hild and Aefre and looked much more like Aefre than Hild. Anson wondered what effect that would have on Osgar but he could see him happily chatting to the boys. The daughter stood close to her mother, holding her hand. Anson asked how she and her family were coping and was pleased to be told that they were looking after the fowl and goats and the boys were working to keep the smallholding going. They had no small luxuries in life but the other families did help them. She confided that there was a wifeless man who had come over from the Old Country who she liked and he was clearly looking for a wife. Anson had grinned and told her that given his time again he would be keen for her to be his wife. She smiled at the compliment and he laughed when she said she would discuss it with her big sister Hild when they next met.

Osgar's cousins wanted to talk to him about the night two years before when their brother and sister were taken. They had not been found by the raiders because they had hidden in the bushes with Cynbeald. Osgar knew that he was supposed to say that they would be all right and would come home but he just became annoyed. "Look," he said, "talking about it will not bring them home. You lost Milly and Stan and I lost my mother and Leo. They are slaves now and until we have enough people to go to the Chalk Hills, they stay slaves."

Anson looked at his sister-in-law's house. It was in good order apart from the bottom of the door which was rotten. "I will get Wilf to mend it when he is done with the hall," he said.

"I can't afford a carpenter," she replied.

"It's on me," said Anson then kissed her on the cheek, squeezed her hand and turned away.

Osgar saw him walk away, said goodbye to his cousins and followed the Jute back towards the Hall. When they reached the pathway leading down to the Lark, they took it. The road inclined towards the first bridge. It was only about one hundred paces from the hall but it dropped by a height of fifteen feet. Either side of the pathway was grass and sedge where it was becoming fen. There were a few cattle turned out to their right. The land was dry due to the lack of rain and the cattle walked on the top and did not sink in. The first bridge was only a thick plank about five paces long. It lay across a small stream running parallel with the main river. The ground had been banked either side to channel the water. On either bank, two posts less than a pace apart were driven into the ground. The plank ran between them and was securely lashed to them. A man could walk across the bridge but there was not room to pass and it was too narrow for a handcart.

They walked further down and in another thirty paces, they faced the ford crossing. The Lark was wider here and the water rushed across the stony bottom at only ankle height. Osgar looked at it in surprise as it was the lowest, he had ever seen it. Across the other side of the Lark, the bank rose more steeply but it was still possible to drive cattle up it or pull a handcart over it. There were wheel ruts and hoof marks in it that were now dried. To the left of the ford was another bridge built in the same style as the first. It spanned the main flow of the Lark and was a good twelve paces across. A whole tree trunk had been split to make it. The trunk had a slight wind-swept curve to it and this had been fixed to arch upwards. It bounced as it was walked across which added to the feeling of insecurity. A rope ran along the left-hand side. It was as tight as possible to the posts at either side of the bridge but still dipped in the middle. The posts and the rope were new and Osgar could not remember it like this.

Another fifty paces after the large bridge was the third one. It was almost the same size as the first and was in the same style. Four men worked on the far end where they were digging the postholes either side of the plank. They had shields and spears stacked together on the village side. Anson looked along the roadway that was raised above the fen, as were the roads connecting the three bridges. In another two hundred paces, it began a shallow climb southwards. He asked the men working why it was being repaired. He recognised none of them, so they were probably newcomers from the Old Country or refugees. They told him that the headman wanted to encourage resettlement to the south and west and as they had to have guards at the crossing point then they may as well be working.

Osgar listened and knew that it was not his place to join in the discussion. He found it difficult to understand why they were improving the access to the ham while they were defending it. Osgar would have smashed the bridges down, never to rebuild them. As it was, the two smaller ones looked silly because hardly any water was passing under them. He knew the rains would return soon and then they would look like bridges. He looked again across the fen to the sandy ground rising out of the valley. *How far away is the kingdom of the Chalk Hills?* He thought. How could the people of Icklingham think that making a crossing over the one defence that they had against the Waelisc, was anything but foolish?

*****

Cadrod was waved off by his father and many of the townspeople of Bannaventa. Cadrod was popular with the Britons as he had made them feel secure in the Kingdom of Calchfynedd. He brought a continual supply of slaves who had made life easier and better for many. They were proud of their warriors who rode out and returned a week later sometimes with gold and silver, always with slaves. They thought of Cadrod as their Arturius and he did nothing to dispel the image. He was cruel, but rarely to his own people, saving that for the Sais vermin. He insisted on discipline and he planned every raid carefully. His warriors never knew if they were going south, east or north until they left the fortress. They always travelled on horseback for speed but usually some of them dismounted and fought on foot when it came to a raid. His father's kingdom could raise an army of thousands if needed but for a raid, fifty was the most he used. He knew the day would come when he would gather an army of all the fighting men of Calchfynedd and that day was not so far off. First though he had to soften up the enemy and make them fear him. It also allowed him to assess the enemy's fighting ability, their strengths and weaknesses. He knew that Arturius had smashed the south Sais at Mynydd Baddon with his clever use of cavalry and foot soldiers but he could not find out how. The bards would spin out the story of Arturius over several nights and the battle at Mynydd Baddon for a whole evening but he learned nothing in detail of his tactics. Cadrod's commander was Waljan, who had been his most reliable warrior since he had taken over from his father in leading the raids. Waljan was fearless as a rider and skilled with spear and sword and was as ruthless as Cadrod in slaughtering the Sais.

"All the men and horses in good order?" Cadrod asked Waljan, pulling his horse up alongside him.

"All fit and well, *sire*," replied his right-hand man.

"And what makes you so happy today?" asked Cadrod smiling at Waljan.

"I like going to the eastern Lloegr, *sire*. It's where my family are from."

"Really?" said Cadrod as they crossed the bridge outside the fortress where it spanned the Nene River and the road headed east. "Tell me about them."

"I only know what my grandmother told me, and she's been dead many years. My family had large land holdings which they had even owned during Roman times. The Romans left and my family continued as before, although trade was never as good again. Then the Sais came. At first, we lived almost alongside them, each to our own village, until their numbers grew so much that they wanted it all. We were pathetic. They kicked us off our own land without a fight. My mother and grandfather moved west and settled in Calchfynedd. They had little but they had a king who would fight for them and not roll over at the first sight of Sais."

"When we toss the Sais into the sea, you will get all your lands back and more, I promise it," said Cadrod.

It had been a few years since he had attacked the area that they were heading for. Cadrod knew from experience that by now the Sais pigs would be complacent. He was meeting some informants on the way and had a bag of silver to reward them if the raid was successful. His spies were from the Gwyre people who lived in the fens. They spoke a version of the Britons language and hated the Sais almost as much as he. Despite their hatred, they traded with the Sais, mainly eels and fish and received cloth, ironwork and barley in return. Cadrod thought that it was always good to have inside knowledge.

The ground was firm but not too hard for the horses, it was good for galloping. He hoped to catch some of the pigs in open ground then they would have some fun. His favourite past time was boar hunting but he mused that Sais sticking would be better. He looked at his troops as they sat high in their saddles, their shields and spears to their left. Most had a scabbard with sword in it by their side. They were happy and he knew what they were thinking. They wanted to kill but they also wanted the pleasure of women. Was he the only one that the thought of having a Sais woman made him sick? He did not care though as he would have them slit their throats afterwards. He told his war-band, "First the work and then the play."

*****

Anson and Osgar headed back across the Lark to the ham. At the top of the incline, where the path from the three bridges joined the street, they could see five girls. They were all of similar age and one was a niece of Anson's and another was Lynne. The girls were sewing, sitting in a circle and chatting. As Anson and Osgar neared, the girls giggled and two of them blushed. Anson thought, that is not for my benefit, and looked over at Osgar. He was totally oblivious and lost in thought. Anson sighed and wished he were Osgar's age again. He looked again at the girls whispering and smiling at each other.

"Do we not produce the prettiest girls in the world," he said to Osgar, "what man would not want one?"

The next day, the whole village busied itself with preparations for the first evening of the Eostre festival. The girls helped their mothers with the cooking. They made fresh bread and biscuits with the last of the previous year's grain. Two goats and a pig were slaughtered to be prepared for roasting and their blood collected and stirred to make black pudding. Carrots and turnips were dug up and cabbage cut and barrels of ale were moved from the brewing house to be stood outside the Hall.

Anson and Osgar had used the day to build the hearth in the house that had been given for their use. They had collected flints, which were in abundance uphill from the Lark. They built it with large flints and used smaller and smaller stones for the base. Finally, they dug the sandy soil and lined the hearth with a layer a hands length deep. The tube projecting from the bellows rested at the right height to give a blast of air into the base of the fire. After it was used, it could be pulled back about a foot so that the leather tube did not burn. They lit the fire and tried it out and once Anson was happy that everything was in order he said, "That's us done, we will be ready to start once the Eostre festival is over."

Osgar looked at him and nodded yes but he felt sick in his stomach. The feeling had been getting worse all day. He did not want to be in Icklingham and he certainly did not want to celebrate Eostre. He had not prayed to the goddess Astara since the day of the attack and even if he lived longer than Cynbeald, he never would. He had been pleased to see his aunt and his cousins but he wanted to be back in Beo. His feeling had worsened when they had looked at the Three Bridges. He could not make out why they had done it. It looked to him like leaving the chicken coop open when you knew there was a fox in the area. When they had walked back to the village and had seen the girls, he could only think of the Waelisc taking them. He could not get the thought out of his mind of his mother being captured with his cousin Milly and Nelda, who was with child. He looked southwest to where he knew his mother and brother were and decided the ham could have their celebration without him.

Chapter 6
Three Bridges

Cadrod and his troop had made good time, the ground was firm and the weather was fair. The few streams that they had to cross, on their way, barely came to fetlock height on the horses. They had crossed most of the great heath and were looking northeast from a high point on one of the last rolling hills before the land dropped down into the Lark Valley. Off to the east, there were thunderclouds and he could see some flashes of lightning. The sky above was clear and there was a full moon. He had been watching the skies all day and any storms were a long way to the east and would not interfere with his attack. The sun was behind him, casting long shadows forwards and it would soon set.

He looked over to his right and saw the two figures that he was expecting, standing in the open. He trotted his horse over to them. They were Gwyre people of the Fens. They were Britons and their tongue, though different in accent, could be understood by his people. They lived near the Angles and traded with them. Cadrod hated them for that but they had their uses as traders always had information. They knew the roads and they knew where people lived.

The Gwyre told him how they often walked to Beodricesworth along the northern bank of the Lark. They described how the Angles now had guards at the two crossings, though they had become slack during the last year. Cadrod was interested to hear that the village that he had attacked a few years ago had recovered and been almost completely rebuilt and repopulated. To his astonishment, he learned how there was a bridge crossing directly in the middle of the settlement and that it had recently been improved. The Gwyre described it in detail saying how he would not be able to take horses across it but the river was easily forded in low water and that the flow had never been shallower. The Gwyre pointed directly at Icklingham and Cadrod ordered them to take his troop there. He patted the leather pouch at his belt when asked about payment and confirmed that they would be paid in silver if their information was correct. It was a feast evening for the Sais pigs and that would make it all the easier. As they moved off, he reminded his men that he wanted death and destruction for their enemies, that they needed young slaves and one young girl. He cared not what they did to the other women but one girl would be taken for their King.

*****

Osgar walked east out of the ham towards Beodricesworth and climbed the slight incline that blocked the view to Stowe. At the top, he stopped and sat on a large tree stump looking back at his old ham and then down to the ruins of the Roman house. This was the stump that his mother and father used to sit on while he and Leofric searched for iron and other articles amongst the ruins. It seemed to Osgar, such a long time ago. To the east, over Beo, the sky was black and he caught glimpses of lightning flashes and heard thunder. He thought that if he stayed there for much longer, he would be soaked by the coming rainstorm but decided that he did not care and sat still on the stump.

In Beodricesworth, it had been raining for most of the afternoon. The storm had rolled in from the east making the air suddenly cooler. Hild had run to the water meadows by the Lark to herd the goats in. Other townspeople were moving their animals to safer ground as torrents of water ran off the dry land, unable to soak it up. Along the craftsmen's street, vendors were bringing in their wears before they were rain-damaged. Water was running down the hill from the Great Hall, through workshops and houses, quickly filling the pits up under floor planking. A stream ran through Anson's forge, past the anvil stump and fire and out under the double doors where its colour had changed to black, stained by the coal dust that it picked up. Nobody could remember such a storm as this and many prayed to Thunor begging forgiveness if they had offended him.

Osgar looked away from the east and down toward the Lark and the Fens beyond where the waters reflected the reddening sky. He knew that by now the drinking and feasting would have begun. He sat alone and wondered what he would say if his father was still there. He would show him his seax and his father would be proud of his work. He then thought of his brother Leo and tried to remember what he looked like and stared towards the setting sun, in the direction that he knew they had been taken. He could see a long way, perhaps all the way to the Great Heath and he looked at the horizon again. What could he see at the limit of his sight? He could see some small dark figures and then there was some movement and then he realised that he was looking at a horse and rider. He strained his eyes and held his hand up to exclude the setting sun. He was sure that he could see a horse and rider. Was there more to the left? It was difficult to see; was he looking at horsemen or trees?

Osgar knew what he had to do and ran back to the ham. He ran straight to the hall and in through the open door. The Headman was toasting Astara and, as always, asking for good planting weather. He looked up at the panting figure of Osgar and was annoyed at the interruption so he carried on with his toast. Osgar looked for Anson and saw him scooping ale from a barrel and refilling his mug.

"I'm glad you've decided to come back and join us," said Anson and then saw the look on Osgar's face.

"There are Waelisc horsemen coming," said Osgar.

A few of the men nearby heard him and stopped and looked at him. Now the Headman was very annoyed, he had wanted these craftsmen to come to his farmstead and add some work of quality to it but now he wished that they would just leave. They had neither the discipline nor manners of the Old Country.

"You are just a boy and you run in here and interrupt a toast to a god."

Before the headman could finish Anson said, "There are Waelisc coming, please listen to the boy."

Osgar tried to explain as quickly as he could what he had seen. The Headman said, "How can we know what he saw? No one can see that far."

Anson raised his voice and spoke directly to the Headman, "You stay here and think about it then. Those that do not wish to be burned in their own hall follow me."

He turned to Wilfrid's son. "Seward, run to Stowe and then to the Flemish ham and tell them the Waelisc are coming. Tell them to come quickly to the Lark crossing here."

To Cynbeald, he said, "Get the women and children up the hill and into the woods."

Anson jogged towards the Three Bridges and on the way, he picked up his sledgehammer from outside their temporary forge. Some of the men, including Wilfrid followed, some had shields and spears and others just ran with any tool that came to hand.

From the distant east, they could hear the rolling thunder and the flashes of lightning. The atmosphere was heavy and they felt the first drops of rain for weeks on their faces. Anson led them across the first and second bridges and then he called across the third and smallest bridge. He could see in the moonlight two men who sat leaning against the posts, not the five men who were supposed to guard it at anytime. He ran across the plank and in bounced with each step, he could see the large jars by them and he knew that they were already drunk.

"Why should we be the only ones not to celebrate Eostre?" said one.

Anson guided them back across the bridge and looked at the men who had followed him. Five of the village had come with him from the hall, Wilf was by his side and he had two drunks and a boy. He swung his sledgehammer in a sideways arc and hit the post on the right.

"Cut the lashings," he said to Osgar. Osgar put his right hand behind his back and found the toggle hanging from his seax pommel. In a swift movement, he had it out of the scabbard and swung it at binding holding the plank to the post. With one swing, his blade severed all the ties and cut into the post and he saw that the first Waelisc attacker was upon the bridge.

*****

Cadrod had been led by the two Gwyre spies towards the Sais ham. As the land became sandier, he remembered it from his last visit. The pathway was straight as it gently dropped into the valley, the fens, with their sedge and reeds, extended either side of the slightly raised pathway. Cadrod had thirty of his men dismount their horses; ten were left guarding the horses with the two Gwyre who had again asked for their payment. "On my return," said Cadrod.

He looked over his men and held his hand up and closed his finger and thumb together. They knew the signal for quiet and looked at their leader intently. He split his horsemen so that they spread out on either side of the pathway and let the foot soldiers walk two abreast towards the bridge. As they closed towards the crossing, he heard some banging. Surely, the Sais pigs were not working on it at this time, he thought. It began to rain; Cadrod had seen the storm nearing them from the east and it did not concern him as the rain and thunder covered the noise of his men and horses. The ground was now wet but they had fought in rain and mud before and were sure footed. His shod horses gained enough grip, with their nailed shoes, on any ground. Then he saw the first of the bridges, just as they had been described to him. At the far end of the bridge, he could see two figures, one swung a hammer and it hit the post and behind them were about five others. He did not know what they were doing. They were all supposed to be in the hall getting drunk. They were not military men, he could see that, so he signalled to his foot soldiers and looked to the Lark ahead for an easy route for his horse to cross.

Osgar pulled his seax out from the lashing and wood as Anson finally knocked over the post, on the other side of the bridge. The plank was now free and Anson bent to pick it up and toss it in the river but the weight of the Waelisc raider now upon it prevented him. The plank over the first stream was now very unstable and the first Waelisc attacked felt unsure of his steps. He could make out two Sais pigs in front of him. They carried no shields or spears and wore no armour so the first blood of the night would be his. He held his shield to the front and left of him and pointed his spear forwards. He aimed it straight at the big man who was bent trying to lift the plank. He ignored the boy as he had been taught a hundred times in military drills. "Pick your target and go straight at him," he could hear the sergeant saying. He aimed low at the crouching figure so that the point of the spear was only two foot off the ground.

Osgar saw that the spear was aimed at Anson and he stepped forward onto the bridge and swung his seax down on it. The spear haft was good quality ash but the seax cut three quarters through it and forced the spear point down into the bridge plank. The Waelisc stumbled forward and as the spear point caught in the wood and it snapped with his weight. The momentum of the attacker took him forward and down, Osgar swung his seax downwards again as he passed and it struck him in the back of the neck. He was wearing a chain mail hauberk, covering his neck, shoulders and chest, but Osgar's seax cut through it and lodged in his spine, as he went down.

Boys dream of the glory of battle, every Angle is brought up on tales of daring, of standing in the shield wall and slaying monsters. It is never like that and in the terror and confusion of a fight all men act differently. During the last three years, Osgar had not daydreamed about the glories of war; he only thought of killing Waelisc and rescuing his mother and father. When his first fight came, he felt calm and was surprised at how slowly everything was appearing to happen. He tugged the seax from the back of the attacker's neck and looked behind him to see the next Waelisc crossing the bridge. This one did not carry a spear but held a broad sword above his head and a shield to his front.

The Waelisc looked at the boy on the end of the bridge ahead of him. He knew that a seax was no match for a shield and sword, let alone one held by a boy. He had seen his cousin slip on the bridge and knew that it was the bad luck of battle that had done for him. He came forward carefully in a slight crouch and raised his sword over his head to swing it down. He thought that he might catch the boy unaware, frozen in the terror of battle. The boy might retreat and then they would have the bridge and pour over it. The boy did neither of these but dropped low and ran towards him. Osgar barrelled into the shield of the Waelisc and knocked him back. The sword swung harmlessly over his shoulder. He swung his seax down as hard as he could and it split a quarter of the way down the shield, deep into the grain and it stuck.

The Waelisc raider had recovered from the shock of the boy's charge and the seax blow to his shield. He was annoyed that he had missed with his first sweep but now he had him. The boy was hanging on to his short sword stuck in his shield and he only had to pull him around and thrust his sword into him. The blade stuck through to his side of the shield by half an arm's length so he could not pull the shield too close to himself for fear of stabbing himself in the face. The narrowness of the bridge meant that he could not stand with feet apart, as he wished to gain full purchase and the rain was making the bridge slippery. He could feel the boy tiring as he tried to pull the shield from side to side, thereby preventing him from getting either a good swing or thrust with his sword.

Osgar felt himself becoming exhausted but concentrated on pulling the shield over to wherever the swing or thrust came from. The one post left standing was in his enemy's way and at least he was on firmer ground. He saw that his seax blade was near the Briton's face so he shoved hard and it came within a whisker of poking him in the eye. However, the Briton was too strong and held back his drive. He was close up to his attacker now and was holding on for his life, he knew that he could not survive much longer. Suddenly, Anson's left arm came over Osgar's shoulder and the right arm followed. He held that sledgehammer in the classic striker's grip. The head of the hammer struck the Waelisc raider above his forehead on his iron helmet. The helmet caved in to the shape of the hammer face and the skull below it was pushed in the width of a man's thumb, at the same time the blow cracked two vertebrae in his neck. Behind the warrior attacking Osgar, his fellow foot soldiers were silenced. Just seconds before they had been cheering and making fun of their colleague for not finishing the boy off quickly. They taunted the few Sais that they could see behind the fight and shouted that they were going to get it next. Now they saw one of their best warriors go down.

When the hammer blow hit him, it looked as if his head had been driven into his body. He went down instantly, sprawling towards the enemy.

Cadrod had kept his mounted troops moving forward and they were dropping down the bank into the stream either side of the small bridge. They had spread out about thirty paces on either side of the planked bridge. He could see his foot soldiers waiting to cross and looked on with dismay at their inability to dislodge a boy with a short sword and a man with only a hammer. He knew, however, that once he had horses up either side of the bank, he would cut their escape route.

Anson looked to his right and left and saw raiders on horseback walking through the sedge and stepping down into the stream on either side. He looked back at the men behind and shouted to his nephew, "Osgar, get back over the large bridge now or we are dead."

Anson again shouted to the men behind to fall back over the bridge. They only needed telling once. Osgar gave one more yank at his seax but it was stuck in the shield and the dead Waelisc arm was still through the leather straps at the back. He picked the fallen Briton's sword off the bridge and ran back with Anson, who picked up a shield and spear that one the two drunken guards had left. They ran past one of the drunks who stood open mouthed at the large bridge. He was the first to be run through with a spear by the raiders but by then they were over the second bridge. As they crossed the second larger bridge, it sprang and bounced to their steps. The hand rope was on their right. It was uncomfortable and unnerving for them to swap their weapons to their left hand to get a secure grip. No man feels comfortable holding a spear or sword in their left hand during battle. Anson saw three more men running towards him, down the pathway from the ham. All three carried spears and shields and one had a seax by his side.

Anson looked at his company; there were now ten of them including a drunk and a twelve-year-old boy. They had seven spears, five shields, a couple of seaxs, one sword, an axe, a scythe and his sledgehammer. *We have not quite raised the fyrd,* thought Anson. The rain increased and as water ran down the path off the hard ground, they were standing in rivulets of muddy water. The moon was now covered and even though their eyes were accustomed to the gloom, it was difficult to see anything. The rain running down their foreheads made them squint to see. They were at least looking towards the reddened sky, which gave a background to silhouette their attackers against. It was raining heavily now, as it had been in Beodricesworth and the lands to the east all day. Further upriver, the level rose rapidly but not high enough in Icklingham to stop the crossing of the Lark.

Cadrod looked at how loathe his men were to move across the second bridge. The hand rope was on the wrong side for them and now the footing was wet and slippery. He looked down the bank of the main river, on the right of the bridge, and thought that there the water was too deep. To the left, the river was wider and there was a ford. The water flowed quite quickly but was only at the height of a man's knee and could be crossed with care. He started his horse down the shallow bank and into the river and his men followed, he urged his men on foot to get across the bridge.

A line of Waelisc raiders were slowly crossing the bridge but they could only attack one at a time. Anson stood two of the spearmen with shields behind the posts on the village side of the bridge. He stood behind them holding an aesc, which was a spear of almost two men's height. In a skirmish like this, it was unwieldy and not much use. In a shield wall, the second row could use these longer spears over the shoulders of their own men and double the number of spear points. The first Waelisc advanced to engage the Angles and crouched and moved behind his shield and held his spear firmly at waist height. He prodded and probed and the two Angles held their place with their shields tight together thrusting their spears at the Waelisc. Anson took hold of his aesc with two hands overhead. He stabbed down at the enemy and the spear point hit his target just below the eye to the side of his nose. There was a crunch of bone and his head went back. A thrust from one of the Angles penetrated his shoulder and he went down, the next raider moved forward and he received similar treatment.

Anson looked to his right. He saw the other seven lined up where the ford gently rose upwards to rejoin the pathway. It was about twenty paces wide where it came out of the river. The drunken bridge guard had now found an axe and was waving it and shouting insults to the Waelisc. The river ford was filling with Britons and some of the foot soldiers had decided that it was easier to wade across than use the bridge. The water was at their thighs in the middle. They held their shields and spears high and waded through. Anson could see that again they were about to be cut off and the seven on the bank would never hold out once the soldiers and riders reached them. He shouted for them to retreat behind the last small bridge. They all obeyed apart from the drunken villager, who raised his axe above his head and waded into the river. Anson tapped the two spearmen on their shoulders and told them to get back across the last bridge.

The intoxicated Angle swung his axe around his head, screamed obscenities and told the Waelisc what their wives were doing while they were away. He called into question their looks, their breeding and their manhood, three swordsmen could not get near him. He swung his axe at each in turn as they pushed forward until finally Cadrod rode his horse at him and thrust his spear into his neck; with that the swordsmen hacked at him and he fell, his body washed downstream. The ale-fuelled heroics of the Angle had allowed the others to retreat over the last bridge. It was, only five paces across and was the same design as the first. Osgar had begun chopping at the post lashings as soon as he was across but the sword was not as sharp as his seax. They pulled one of the posts over and pushed the plank bridge at an angle halfway down the bank, it was no longer any use for crossing the stream. The bank on the side that they stood on was steeper than the others as the pathway began the incline up to the ham immediately. It was more of a ditch than a stream which marked where the fen ended and the water meadows began, here the ground was boggier and there were pools of water scattered about. The heavy rain splashed into these puddles which grew in size and then joined.

Cadrod was furious, he had seen some of his men killed and his attack on the village had been slowed by a ragtag bunch of Sais pigs who seemed to be led by a man with a hammer and a boy. He would take his men through them in quick time now that they had retreated past the last bridge, but his attack, which was supposed to be fast and catch the village unawares, was unlikely to deliver the slaves and deaths that he had planned. He knew that the women and children of the village would have fled by now and a search would only turn up a few. He could see that they had disabled the bridge, not that he would have sent any more to their deaths trying to cross singly. Cadrod marshalled his force for one definitive thrust. The ten opposite were spread only twenty paces wide to the left of the disabled bridge. He told the fifteen men and riders to spread out and they covered a fifty-pace front. They moved forward down into the muddy ground. The men went in up to their knees and the horses well above their fetlocks. It was deep and they struggled and moved slowly but they would meet the enemy in only ten paces.

Osgar looked at the mixture of riders and soldiers in front of him. He held the broadsword above his head but he was not sure if this was how he should and wished to have watched the thegns and their ceorls practice on the water meadows at Beo. It was not like holding a sledgehammer, where his hands would be a foot apart and the weight would all be at the end. He spread his feet as he would in the forge and put a slight bend in his knees.

The first Briton reached them and thrust forward his spear; it came up under Wilfrid's shield and hit him in the thigh. He fell back and his hands gripped the spear haft. Osgar brought the sword down with all his strength, he landed the blow on the attacker's shoulder, he was not wearing a hauberk and the blow cut deep, nearly taking off his arm. For Osgar, again time slowed and he looked for his next target. Wilfrid pulled the spearhead from his thigh; he turned the spear around and first used it to get back on his feet and then slung it at the attackers. It splashed harmlessly in the water and he regretted wasting the weapon. A horse and rider were coming out of the ditch with his spear to the front. The horse was trying to gain purchase in the mud with his hind hooves while his front scrabbled on the slippery bank. Osgar swung the sword in a diagonal arc and the blow glanced down the spear, took some fingers off the Waelisc hand and lodged in his thigh, the horse shied backwards and the rider was dumped into the mud. The raiders were now pressing the defenders who were not wearing any armour and had taken spear thrusts and sword cuts. With more men, the Angles may have held out but now they had three men down and were about to be outflanked on their right side.

Anson was at a loss as what to do next. He had practiced with the fyrd on the water meadows at Beo, as was his duty as a ceorl. It was not his job to give orders there, only thegns gave commands. There they practiced with twenty in a shield wall against twenty attackers. Each man's shield locked to the next. They learned to manoeuvre as one and stay together but this was different. They were fighting a skirmish with not enough men to form a wall and they were losing. It was the first time that Anson had realised that they were all going to die. He was twenty-seven years old and had no children, although he had treated Osgar as a son the last few years. He had wanted to see him become a blacksmith and work alongside him and now they would both die on this spot. Then suddenly from behind him, aetgars flew over his head. Three of the slim throwing spears hit horses, one hit a rider, pinning his thigh to his horse and one-foot soldier was hit in the centre of his chest. Anson glanced behind him and saw the Flems, eight had just hurled their aetgars and seven more drew back their arms and on the order hurled them, again most struck their targets. The Flems drew their seaxs from behind the smalls of their backs, raised their shields and spread out on the ditch side.

Cadrod had seen enough and called his men back. They turned in the mud of the ditch and made their way to the other side. The men crossed the main bridge in single file and the riders looked to go across the ford. Anson shouted to Osgar to help and they lifted the plank back into place. The Flems and the Angles filed across, now heading towards their attackers. Two wounded Waelisc lay between the bridges and were killed on the ground with seax cuts. The band of twenty Angles and Flems reached the main bridge as the last of the enemy crossed to the other side. For the horsemen, the escape was not so easy. The rain that had been falling to the east all day had now flowed far down the Lark, raising its level. The horses were spurred on by their riders down the incline to where the ford had been just a short time before, now the water rushed at chest height. The Flems and Angles picked up any weapons that they could find. A pile of large flints, that had been used to strengthen the sides of the bridge posts, were hurled at the horses and Waelisc and then the villagers from the ham appeared and joined in the bombardment.

Cadrod dug his heels into his horse on the far bank and it lurched up. When he was at the top of the bank, he looked back, some of his riders were urging their horses up the slope but two were being swept downstream. Others had lost their horses completely and were trying to pull themselves through the reeds and up the slippery bank further down. To his left most of his foot soldiers were now heading back to their horses a few hundred paces up the roadway that headed southwest. Of the fifty men and horses that came with him, he had lost twenty warriors and fifteen mounts. When he reached his men where they marshalled the horses, he dismounted and strode over to the two Gwyre, "Hold them," he said.

His men obeyed immediately and he took a knife from his belt. He slit the throats of both Gwyre and they began the long ride back to Calchfynedd.

*****

In the morning, Osgar told Anson that he was returning to Beodricesworth. He was sat by the low mound that marked his father's grave. "I cannot stay here, this is no longer my home," he said. "Only a handful came with us to the bridge. The headman arrived when it was all over, killed a half drowned Waelisc and is now bragging of the Icke family's great victory."

"Come on," said Anson, "let's load up the cart."

Anson and Osgar dismantled their forge equipment. They loaded the anvil and the bellows along with their tools and some iron. Anson placed the Waelisc sword that Osgar had won in battle near the front. Osgar had retrieved his seax and it was back in its scabbard behind his back. Wilf and his son were loading up their cart from the house alongside, when the headman approached. Wilf's thigh was heavily bandaged above his knee with cloth. He had a deep puncture to the muscle which the ham herb-woman had cleaned with ale and pasted it with her concoction. She had told him which gods that he must pray to if he wished it to heal and not fester.

"Where are you going?" asked the headman.

Anson replied, "My apprentice no longer wishes to be here and I agree."

"You listen to a thirteen-year-old boy?" said the headman.

"I do," said Anson, "and had you listened to him last night, we may not have lost so many lives. That thirteen-year-old boy is more of a man than you will ever be. He saved your village by warning us and then holding the far bridge."

The headman turned to Wilfrid the carpenter and said, "And you are going because?"

"Because he is my mate and because my son ran to the Flems' settlement and back here with them before you got to the bridge and you still gave him no thanks."

"I will tell everyone that you do not keep your word," he said to all of them.

"Yes, everyone will think that we let you down," said Anson, with heavy sarcasm.

Cynbeald joined them and said to the headman, "I'm leaving also. Even with my storytelling skills I cannot make your story heroic."

On the way back to Beodricesworth, they stopped near Stowe where the people asked them about the raid. Wilf and Anson briefly described the night's events and asked them why they sent no help. They told them that they had formed a shield wall between their houses as they had done, three years previously, and had waited. They could not see that as they were closer to Icklingham they would have arrived before the Flems and the victory would have been greater. Anson tried to reason with the headman, telling him that if the hams acted alone then they would be picked off, one after another but if they came to each other's aid, they would survive. Anson gave up when he realised that he was banging his head against an anvil.

It was past noon when they reached Beodricesworth but for the last two miles, they had not had to pull the handcarts. A crowd grew around them of well-wishers who took turns to pull the handcarts for them as they were quizzed about the fight at the Three Bridges. Osgar became quieter and sullen as they came to the town centre near the Great Hall. Anson smiled and laughed good naturedly with everyone and chuckled when he was called Anson the Hammer of the Waelisc. He looked at his apprentice with his head down, unsmiling and flinching at each pat on the back.

"What is wrong?" he asked Osgar.

"Nothing, I just want to get back to the forge," he said.

Anson noticed him looking at the broad sword laid in the front of the handcart. "What is wrong with the sword?" said Anson. "You should be waving it about to show the people that you won it in battle."

"It's a Waelisc sword," said Osgar. "It's not my sword; it could be the sword that slew my father. I want my own sword, an Angle sword, we could make one Anson."

"You know that sword making is another skill," replied Anson. "One that I have never mastered and the best iron needed to make one is hard to come by."

"We could make one," said Osgar.

"You could," said Anson, "I'm not looking to learn new tricks. I have a cousin in Gippeswic, maybe you could go down there for a month or so to learn sword making."

Osgar immediately picked up his head and smiled.

"On one condition," said Anson, "that you smile when they call you a hero. You must let them share our victory. Many of them have lost family members to the Waelisc and many are refugees and they need to celebrate."

And celebrate they did. When they reached Beo, they saw that the Great Hall was being decorated with flowers and flags. A great feast was organised for that night, at which Osgar, Anson, Cynbeald, Wilfrid and his son were the guests of honour. Tedmund, their Thegn, had them sat at the end of the hall either side of his raised chair. Before the feast began, Anson rose and with great dignity presented the sword that Osgar had taken to Tedmund. He had wanted Osgar to do this but he had said that he would give it to his thegn in private but could not do it in the hall in front of so many. Anson did not press him as he had been much happier since he had promised that he would learn sword-making soon.

Tedmund stood in front of the packed hall and spoke while holding the sword above his head for all to see. "This was taken by our young apprentice Osgar at the recent battle." Everyone cheered and the Reeve let them enjoy the moment before banging his staff upon the floor as a signal for quiet.

Tedmund continued, "He tells me that it is not the best quality, which is an unusual thing to hear from a gift bearer." Everyone laughed, although Anson said to Osgar that his thegn had not been insulted.

"If the blade is not good enough for an apprentice, who is not even a ceorl, then it will not see battle again. We shall have it displayed on the beam behind me to remind us of our victory."

After the toasts to Woden, Astara and especially Thunor, Cynbeald began the tale of the Battle of the Three Bridges and spoke late into the night. For most of his life, he had been known as a scop. He had spoken in many of the halls in the hams in the area. Now that he was older and experienced, he found it harder to walk from settlement to settlement. He loved his art and knew that he had to set the scene, get the atmosphere right and time the climax. His audience always became drunk as the evening wore on but he used that to his advantage. A drunken man will laugh at something a sober man would not. He knew the great tales by heart, everyone knew Beowulf or the history of Horsa and Hengist but Cynbeald always added his personal touch, exaggerating one part or ignoring the part of a story that he did not like. This was the first time he had the task of relating a battle that he had witnessed.

All day, Cynbeald had considered his task. He had his heroes so that part would be easy. The apprentice boy with the seax and his master with a hammer who were aided in battle by Wilfrid the Carpenter and his son the runner. The enemy was also easy to portray as the murderous Waelisc led by their evil leader. But what was he to say of the headman of the village or the people of Stowe who did not answer a cry for help? The Flems were their cousins but they were not Angles, should he even mention them? His last question was answered when he saw some of the Flems entering the Great Hall. How much easier myths and legends were, he thought.

Tedmund, Thegn of Beodricesworth, toasted his guests once more and then introduced Cynbeald to tell his story. Cynbeald took a sip of his ale and looked around the hall, it was full and it was quiet but he delayed a few moments longer. Most men are nervous when asked to speak in public and many would rather face battle than stand before a crowd and talk. Not Cynbeald, he had loved storytelling for as long as he could remember. He was going to milk this opportunity for all it was worth. He told the tale from the perspective of Thunor. He told of a boy whose family was taken from him but had learned the craft that Thunor held dearest. Who had made his own seax and fought beside his master while Thunor's storm raged overhead. He left out the headman but as the tale reached its climax, he told of Wilf the carpenter and his son from Beo, how the father had fought with spear and shield while his son ran like no other could to the Flems who came to help their cousins. The hall cheered and those nearest clapped the Flems on the back and poured them more ale. In Cynbeald's tale, the drunken Angle who staggered into the Lark, swinging his axe and was cut down, became a hero. Some of his family were there and they cheered and clapped at the mention of his deed, others nodded to them in great respect. Cynbeald told them modestly of his involvement, making sure that they all remembered that he was there.

Chapter 7
Aefre

Aefre stood by her hovel at the end of the kitchen garden and looked east. She could see the line of men on horseback crossing the bridge over the Nene. Their heads were down and there was not the usual banter. She was used to seeing the raiding parties go out and return and she knew that this one was almost half the size that it should be. When they came past her, she ducked low at the wicker fence but none of them was looking around. Some of the men and horses carried injuries. Three of the horses were lame and one rider was slumped so far forward it seemed that any moment he would fall from his mount. He did not hold the reins but instead his horse was led by another rider. She said a short prayer to Thunor and hoped it was her people who had inflicted the wounds to the men and horses.

Once the line had passed, she returned to the fire in the doorway of her hovel and squatted beside it. She had a small pestle and mortar that she had stolen from the kitchen, beside it was a sheath of dried wild carrot. She shook the seeds into the mortar and ground them. She had collected them during the last autumn as she did each year. She always made sure that there was more than enough for the year ahead as they prevented pregnancy. When Aefre had finished grinding the wild carrot seeds, she tipped them into a small leather pouch and hung it near the back of the hovel where no rain dripped through the roof. She then returned to the mortar and cleaned it. Left in a small pile by the door were some whole plants in full bloom which had frond like leaves and rosettes of white flowers, the roots were left on the plants. They lay amongst other weeds pulled from the garden and discarded but they had not come from this garden. The previous evening Aefre had walked down to the riverbank to pull them up. She had been careful to do so when no one was watching and had hidden them under her scyrt.

She had been watching the hemlock grow all spring. It grew where there was poorly drained soil and near rivers. Where the cattle had cleared a forage area, it stood almost hip height. The white flowers told Aefre that it had reached full potency and she knew that all of the plant was poisonous, especially the seeds and the root, just six leaves could kill a man. Aefre selected a good root and cut it from the stem, then she sliced it carefully into small discs and dropped them into the mortar. She ground with the pestle until it was fibrous mush and then scrapped in onto a flat stone and left it in a shaded corner so that it did not dry. She continued with the roots until she had a pile the size of a fist. She put the pulp onto a small piece of clean plain cloth that she had kept rolled up near her bed. She gathered the edges of the cloth up and began to twist the pouch she had made over the mortar. Slowly, a liquid began to trickle through the cloth fibres which was clear and odourless. When she had enough, she tipped it into a small clay baked pot not much taller than a thumb-length, and she pushed a small wooden stopper into its top. She dug a hole near her hovel and placed the pot in the cavity. After covering it up, she left an unusually coloured stone over it to mark where it was hidden.

*****

"It did not go well," Cadrod said to his father. "We were trapped and betrayed. The Gwyre led us to a ford that was low and crossable but the Sais pigs had been alerted. Our advance was slowed at three wooden bridges but we won through and were on the point of complete victory when they sprung the trap. Somehow, they flooded the river and they had men with throwing spears waiting for us when we were in the mud. It was only by bravery that so many of us escaped."

King Cynwyd of Calchfynedd looked at his son. He still stood with his head and shoulders back but his tired eyes looked down. "You have won countless battles and skirmishes and this is the first time that you have not returned to me to tell of victory. You have come back unharmed to me and for that, I will pray to the Good Lord and thank him. You and your men will be better soldiers for this one small reverse. Come let's pray together."

They knelt facing the small table with the gold cross upon it. Cynwyd had a kneeler but Cadrod knelt on the mat covering the floor. Cynwyd prayed aloud, thanking God for his son's safe return and calling for all kind of disasters to beset the Sais. Finally, he said, "Amen," and Cadrod rose and helped his father to his feet.

"On your way out, please tell the guard to send for the Sais bitch in the kitchen," said Cynwyd to his son. "As you know, I had hoped that you would bring me a little straw haired girl. I will have to put up with her for a while. She's a good looker you know, but she is as dry as a witch's tit."

Cadrod was disgusted with his father, finding it difficult to understand how he could even touch the pigs. Why did he not have a little Cymry girl? He walked down the stone steps to where the old Roman wall was being rebuilt. As he stepped through the door, there was a shout and a handcart full of rocks rushed backwards past him, catching his leg before it tipped over scattering the stones. He looked down at the gash in his trousers and back up to see a slave on his hands and knees coughing and gasping for breath. He thought he recognised him as one that he had captured only a few years before. The Sais looked much older than he remembered. He had scrawny arms and his spine could be seen through his tunic where it stretched across his bent back. He had teeth missing, some had been knocked out and some had fallen out through poor feeding. One eye was almost closed through a recent beating. Cadrod strode over to him, took an ash stave from a guard and swung it over his head to smash down on Athelstan. He beat him until the staff snapped and then he stamped down on the back of his head and ground it into the rock chippings lying about. Athelstan was barely still alive, he knew he was dying and he welcomed it. His will to live had finally gone from him with the loss of his beloved sister Milly. He was carried to the river by two guards and tossed in where he drowned.

Aefre watched and wept and then she received a message to take wine to the King from a smirking kitchen maid. When the girl had gone, she went to the spot marked by the coloured stone. She dug the loose earth and retrieved the miniature pot, cleaned it and hid it in the folds of her dress. Aefre washed her hands and combed her hair and then walked to the kitchen door and was met with the usual insults. The tray with pitcher of wine and a goblet was ready for her so she picked it up and walked out of the door on the other side. A kitchen hand held the door open for her and bowed low and said, "Your majesty, Queen of the Sais pigs, enjoy your stuffing."

Aefre walked through the doorway with her head up and her shoulders back. She knew that they would not dare to punch or kick her while she carried wine for the King. She did not want to appear nervous. She told herself to act exactly as she had for the past few years. The clothes she wore were in good order. The other slaves wore rags but because she saw to the old King's needs, she was given new cloth to make her dresses. Aefre was still beautiful and in her twenty-sixth year. Her hair was a fair colour, no longer the stark blond of her youth. Her skin was smooth and unmarked and it was a good colour, she did not burn in the hot sun and redden as most of the Britons did. She wore a claret-coloured dress that reached her calves and it was tied at the waist with a cloth belt. From the belt usually hung pouches, tweezers and other implements but she had left these behind. She had a plaid shawl of greens and yellows which draped around her shoulders covering her upper arms.

Aefre walked diagonally across the first large courtyard to the archway leading to the tower. The guards stood aside to let her through. One made a comment that she did not hear as she concentrated on holding the tray close to her and ensuring that the wine in the pitcher did not slosh over the side. The goblet was laid sideways on the tray so as not to fall off. When she reached the tower, she turned left through its archway, passed more guards and faced the stone stairway. There were never any more guards after this point except the one who stood outside the King's rooms. She sat the tray down on the third stone step and pulled the small pot from the folds of her dress behind her belt. She bit the wooden plug that was pushed into the top and pulled it out. She poured the contents into the pitcher of wine and placed the small pot and wooden bung on the tray. Aefre walked up the steps and where they reached the stone crenulations, she checked that there was no one near the wall and dropped the pot and bung over. She turned the corner and was now facing the guard outside the door to the King's chamber.

"Took your time," said the guard.

"I was not dressed," said Aefre.

"Don't know why you bothered," he replied, leering.

He tapped on the oak door riveted through with iron, and lifted the latch for her. As he did, he squeezed one of her buttocks and smiled. She walked through and set the wine down on the usual table and looked at the King without curtseying. *She is a haughty bitch*, he thought, he may just have her whipped in public again and that would bring her back down. Aefre had seen that on the table were the remains of his evening wine. There was a third of a pitcher left with a tray and goblet. She would be expected to return these to the kitchen for washing. He told her to pour him some wine and to take her clothes off. She did as he said but shook as she placed the goblet in his hand.

"Shaking like a virgin on her wedding night," he said with a smile. "Maybe I should give you some wine. It might loosen you up for once?"

He leant forward to pass the goblet back to her.

*****

Leofric was by the master shoeing smith's side. He carried two toolboxes, one in either hand. Each box contained a blade of two hands length and a wooden mallet to cut the hoof, a pair of pincers to grip the shoe and lever it off the hoof and a knife with a curved blade for the sole of the hoof. The curved knife had the traditional deer antler handle. The toolbox in his left hand was newly made and the tools, which were all in good condition, were his master's. The box in his right hand was his, it was worn and chipped and the joints were loose. The tools in it were old cast offs and were chipped and rusty.

He put the boxes down gently so as not to startle the horse. Horsemanship had come easily to him, moving smoothly and slowly near horses and talking all the time so they knew where he was. He talked in his own language to them which annoyed the Waelisc but had made them believe that he spoke a language that horses understood or possibly put a spell on them. Leofric was a strong boy because he had managed to feed himself extra during the last few years. In stables there is always food available and now that he worked for the shoeing smith, he was given extra rations. His apron was tied around his waist with leather thongs, the split up the middle stopped just below his groin. Either side of the split, the leather was worn where the hooves rubbed the apron on his knees, it had been patched with leather once but now the patches were worn and cracked.

He moved slowly to pick up the front foot on the left side of the horse and as he bent to lift up the left leg, the horse picked it up for him. Horses like this were a pleasure to work on, others were not so cooperative. His left hand slipped the foot behind him and through his legs to emerge between the gap in the apron. He closed his knees, now he held the left foot between them and he released his hands to pick a tool out of the box and cut the clenches. The clenches were where the nails exited the hoof wall and had been turned down to hold the nail tight. Once he had cut them, he picked up the pincers and closed them around the heel of the horseshoe and levered forwards. The shoe loosened and he moved the jaws of the pincers to the other heel. He levered that side and then the shoe was loose on both sides, two more tugs and the shoe was off. He placed it on the top of the box and cleaned out the foot. Now that it was spotless, his master took over and trimmed the foot while Leofric returned to the forge to ready the fire for the shoe.

Leofric's master was hard to please but was not cruel. He disliked Leofric and told him he was a useless Sais everyday but he was a practical man and this boy was good and more importantly he saved his back. Those who shod horses were treated almost with reverence by the Britons. In the time of the Druids, horse shoeing had been controlled and carried out only by them. The mysteries of the ancient craft had been guarded by the Druid priesthood then, but were not so now. The Romans, who learned horse shoeing from the Druids, had come and gone and now it was just another one of the crafts. People still viewed the shoeing smith's job with awe. That they could drive nails into such a large beast without apparently causing pain, still gave the forge and those that worked within it an aura. As a slave, Leofric would never be allowed to be a full shoeing smith, all trades and crafts were closed to him. He was a slave, and a Sais slave at that, and was therefore the lowest of the low. He would be his master's assistant for as long as they needed him. He would deal with the menial chores around the forge and much of the heavy and fire preparation work for his master. Leofric's master knew that he was a good horseman as he had watched him from afar and had listened to reports from people he trusted. He needed someone who could tame these beasts as he was getting older and difficult horses caused his back and knees to hurt.

Leofric often thought of home and his mother. He knew she lived in the hovel at the end of the kitchen garden. He sometimes saw her there when they took the horses down that way. Now he did not leave the south part of the castle and so never saw her. He wondered about his brother Osgar, he wanted to believe that he had survived the raid. What would he be doing now? He prayed daily for the God's to release him from slavery. He kept his head down and did his work and he found solace working with the horses which he now saw for what they were. They were no longer terrifying beasts, they were large frightened animals whose defence was to run and when cornered could only bite and kick. Once he realised that, he had understood them and came to admire their strength, speed and beauty.

*****

"I'm not wasting good wine on you, my Queen of the Sais," said Cynwyd, pulling his hand back while laughing.

He drank his wine and looked at the naked Aefre. When he beckoned, she moved over to his side and his right hand moved towards her. How much was needed, she thought. Would he drink enough to die or would he taste the essence of the hemlock?

Cynwyd felt her while she refilled his goblet and passed it to him. "You know," he said, "you are making me feel good and young again."

He looked at his groin while he continued to caress her body. She did not follow his eyes; she was sick with worry and hated this bony old man touching her.

Cynwyd was enjoying this. He sipped more of his wine and considered what he would have her do next. A feeling of tightness was spreading across his body as he sat in his chair. It was quite a pleasant feeling at first and he did not know if it was the wine or the fact that the proud bitch was yielding to him easily. After a while, the tightness became excessive and as he felt it most in his chest, he was having a problem drawing each breath. He looked up at her and she smiled and then he knew something was wrong. He tried to speak but nothing came out and he could not push himself up from his chair.

Aefre busied herself while he watched her. She took the pitcher and the goblet over to the corner of the room. She lifted the rug and poured the contents of both gently between the floorboards. She knew that though the middle of the room was over the archway under the tower, the corner was over the thick wall and the wine would soak into it. She walked over still naked, smiled again at him and partly refilled the goblet, from the remnants of the previous night and placed it on the table next to him. His eyes were open wide and he was just managing to gasp in barely perceptible breaths.

"I am your death," said Aefre to Cynwyd while he could still hear and understand her, "as you have been death to so many of my people."

She dressed while looking at him and when clothed, she patted him on the hand, tweaked his cheek and walked to the doorway. His glazed eyes could no longer focus but he heard her words as he tried to breathe. She pulled the door open quickly and said to the guard, "Come, I think that the King is ill."

The guard rushed in, took one look at the wide-eyed figure in the chair and called for help. He turned to Aefre and said, "Stand there, bitch," and motioned her to wait outside the door.

*****

Cadrod, King of Calchfynedd, looked at his dead father and then around the room. He had already slammed the back of his hand into Aefre's face and said, "Now tell me one more time, Sais whore, what happened?"

Aefre again recounted how she had poured the wine and how he had drunk two goblets while he had talked to her and felt her. Then she said it was as if the life had left him. His breathing had stopped so she went straight to the guard to tell him. Cadrod lifted the goblet of wine and sniffed it and was about to dip his finger in it to taste it when he looked at Aefre and said, "Drink this all bitch, and if you spill a drop, you die now."

Aefre had never drunk wine before and though she found it strange, the warm feeling in her stomach was pleasant. She knew that whatever Cadrod thought, she was in danger of being killed. She stood quietly outside the doorway, a trickle of blood running from her nostril onto her lip. The fear had left her now and she waited calmly but deliberately kept a worried look on her face. She had witnessed Cadrod's anger and knew that any misjudged look could send him into a violent attack. She did not wish to die because it was still her desire to return to East Anglia with her son. At least for now he seemed to be alive and well.

Cadrod had summoned his sergeant and the priest who gave the last rites while Cadrod discussed the events with his sergeant. After some time he walked outside and looked at Aefre. She was nervous but showed no signs of illness. His father was old and few Britons lived to his age so it was not a surprise that he died suddenly. His mind was already considering the implications of him becoming king. He would have to spend some time reassuring his subjects and reconfirming alliances with bordering kingdoms. He had so much important work to do. He waved her away with a dismissive hand and she returned to her hovel.

Chapter 8
Gippeswic

It had been two years since Osgar had returned to Beodricesworth with his master, Anson the Broad. He had grown in height and breadth. His hair was still trimmed straight across at shoulder level in the Angle style. He had the beginnings of a goatee beard. It was not so thick but he kept the sides trimmed. He had endured hours of ribbing from Anson, especially about not going out in the wind in case it blew off. Business had been good and they had delivered twenty shield bosses for the Ealdorman in the last year, with a dozen spearheads. The forge had also made a dozen aetgars which were the lighter throwing spears. Osgar had a reputation for making seaxs whether full length or down to kitchen knife size. He protected the iron while working it so it did not lose quality and could now harden it by tempering with the same skill as Anson. Working with his hand hammer, on his own and striking for Anson with the sledge had exercised Osgar's body so that he was powerfully built for his age.

At fifteen years, he was expected to practice military drills with the other men of age in Beodricesworth. Then Tedmund demanded those that had shields to learn the rudiments of the defensive line. He worked the men on the water meadows between the town and the river. Tedmund had never seen battle and his men knew it but they obeyed him none-the-less. He was enthusiastic and thought up new ways to exercise his ceorls and older apprentices. Sometimes he would have those with shields defend themselves with short staves against shield-less attackers with long staves and at other times, he held a shoving contest. The shield men were divided in half and were pitted against each other, pushed from behind by the rest of the men. They leant into their shields and shouted encouragement to each other and insults at their opposition. They always wanted Osgar and Anson on their side and Tedmund had to part them to make it fairer. Osgar would make sure that he was in the centre where he knew his uncle would oppose him. Anson would try to rattle Osgar by talking to him, calling him a half-shaven boy and that he had seen better beards on Saxon women. The men around him laughed and some tried to match his wit but Osgar stayed quiet, leant into his shield and pushed.

Osgar had mastered every skill that Anson could show him. His ability to produce a blade was well known throughout Beodricesworth. He could forge fine metalwork to produce bracelet, broaches and clasps. His fire welding was clean without leaving any weak spots. The forge had been so busy that Anson had given work to a boy of ten who worked the bellows and fetched and carried for the two of them. Osgar taught the boy to strike, showing him how to put a slight bend in his knees to lower his body and to strike with precision following the fireman's lead. Anson could cope without Osgar for a couple of months and so he left for Gippeswic to learn sword making.

Osgar set off west to walk to the port of Gippeswic where he would find Anson's cousin Hunfrith. He was a sword-maker of renown and had come to East Anglia with Anson. Osgar had set his scabbard behind his back and thrown a large leather bag over his shoulder. In this, he had his own hammer and some tongs that he had made. He did not carry his five-pound sledgehammer as he had recently moved up to Anson's eight pounder. He had another cloth bag across his other shoulder which had been made for him by Lynne. It contained food prepared by his aunt for his journey. Hild, Anson, Wilf, Seward and Lynne saw him off from the Craftsmen's Street. Hild had a tear in her eye and dabbed her cheeks with the apron around her scyrt.

"He is going to Gippeswic," said Anson. "Not the Old Country."

Osgar met up with other travellers heading west and settled into the pace of the journey. Many of his fellow travellers pulled handcarts. Some held their family possessions and others were traders taking their goods to the main port and biggest town of the Angles. They passed people travelling the opposite way. These were mostly traders bringing goods from the docks at Gippeswic. The people were no longer moving westwards to colonise Britain. The west was not safe and attacks by the Britons were having their effect, the tide of Angles had turned.

In the mid-afternoon Osgar reached Stowmarket. He had been told to spend the night there. He walked down to the river called Gipping and sat on the bank. Here it was little more than a stream but he had been told that he should follow this until it became a great river at Gippeswic. He had heard Cynbeald the

Storyteller recount tales of the Angles in their boats moving up this valley in the early settlement times. He pulled the bread and dry meat from his bag and ate some of it before covering up the remainder and placing it back in his bag. Then he ate some early raspberries that he picked himself. He found a dry spot under some large oak trees and unclasped his cloak to lay it on the ground. He pulled his scabbard over his head and laid it by the bag after removing the seax. He rolled half the cloak over himself and held the seax in his right hand under it. He prayed to Thunor to watch over him and make him strong and to ready him for battle. As he drifted into sleep, he thought of his mother and brother. He tried to think about why he thought that learning to make a sword would help him free them. Until he finished his apprenticeship, he would not become a ceorl and would not be free to go to the kingdom of the Chalk Hills. If he could learn to make a sword then he could make one for himself and with it, draw men to him. Thoughts of destroying those that took his mother and brother were mixed with seeing the features of the man who killed his father. He had seen him again at the second attack on his birthplace, leading men towards him. Gradually, he drifted off to sleep.

Osgar awoke at sunrise and ate the rest of the meat, bread and berries while he sat in the sunshine against the tree and looked about him. Then he walked down to the Gipping carrying just his seax and washed his face in the cool water and scooped it in his cupped hands to drink. Once his thirst was satisfied, he returned to his possessions and packed them into the bags. He pushed the seax back into its sheepskin scabbard and strapped it behind his back on top of his smock. He swung his bags over his shoulders and pulled his cloak around him, fixing it with the clasps that he had made from spare iron, with Thunor's hammer as a design. He found the pathway and walked east.

Osgar and his fellow travellers followed the Gipping along its valley as it curved southeast. The closer to Gippeswic that they walked, the more people they saw, and the more frequent and larger the hams became. Osgar noticed a strange smell in the air and was told that this was the sea. They came over the brow of a hill and Osgar saw Gippeswic before him and the estuary widening towards the sea. He had never seen such a large body of water before. He made his way towards the docks as he had been told, the houses crowded together even more than in Beodricesworth. When he reached the water, he saw that all along the riverfront were wharves jutting out. They had ships and boats of all sizes tied up and a stream of people carrying sacks or large baskets either loading or unloading them. Facing the wharves were buildings as large as the Great Hall in Beodricesworth where goods were ware-housed and outside there were stalls selling all manner of produce. Ironware, pottery, cloaks and sheepskins were piled on tables with people gathering around.

He asked strangers where he could find the forge of Hunfrith and found himself outside a group of buildings just one street up from the wharves. He had heard the forge long before he saw it, the ringing of more than one anvil was new to him. Behind the forge smoke arose from a large furnace where two men stood, one was a giant. The huge man, stripped to the waist, was carefully tipping measured amounts of charcoal and iron ore into the top of the furnace. On the other side of it, another smaller but powerfully built man, was pumping a bellows. The giant noticed Osgar and beckoned him over. "You must be Osgar?" he said. "Fetch that pail over there."

Osgar swung his bag off his shoulder and pulled the seax from behind his back; he dropped them on the dirt floor and did as he was told. After passing the pail to Hunfrith, he removed his cloak, rolled it up and put it away from the fire and coke near his bags and seax. He watched Anson's huge cousin adding more charcoal and iron ore to the furnace and saw him bobbing down to look at the open vent at the bottom. On his word, the bellows man stopped and took hold of the largest tongs that Osgar had ever seen. The jaws were at least a hands length long and when they opened, it was by a hand's width. He used them double handed as he bent and grabbed at the bottom of the furnace, pulling out a glowing yellow mass. It was full of pockmarks and white sparks shot from it, making the gloomy forge bright. Hunfrith took his own tongs of a similar size and helped to lift it into an anvil, double the size of Anson's back in Beo. Another man appeared with two sledgehammers and passed one to Hunfrith's assistant. Hunfrith held the lump of molten iron on the anvil as each sledgehammer in turn struck it. On the upswing of a hammer, the second hammer struck and, on his upswing, the first, it returned to strike. The lump of iron was becoming a more recognisable form as the impurities were driven out and the shape became rectangular. The speed of the forging put energy into the iron slowing its cooling. Osgar thought that it never would cool but once it turned red, Hunfrith put it in the bed of a second hearth similar to Anson's. The iron was left to gain heat while attended by Hunfrith's two assistants.

"So its sword making you want to learn?" the giant man said to Osgar.

His muscles glistened with sweat and he wiped his brow with the back of his hand showing the blackened palm. He was clean shaven with neither beard nor moustache, his hair was tied in a short ponytail behind his head.

"I do sir," he replied.

"Well you may just be in luck," said Hunfrith, "I have an order for a sword from the Kings Thegn; Wuffa the aethling, nephew of our good King Wehha. Do you know him?"

"No sir," said Osgar.

"My name is Hunfrith," he said, "I go by that name or Frith to my friends and family and that includes you. If you persist in calling me sir, you will learn nothing. I don't like formality. You will do as I say as soon as I say it but you don't call me sir. You will find me an easy master if you do what I tell you and you will learn a lot."

"Yes, Frith," said Osgar.

Frith looked over at his men attending the hearth with the iron pushed into the glowing coals. "Now the iron is ready for more hammer work," he said pointing. "Use the sledgehammer over there. You can take my place."

The semi-molten block was again removed from the hearth with two pairs of tongs and laid upon the anvil. Frith's assistant struck first and Osgar followed him as instructed. Soon the pace increased and blow after blow flattened the metal and drove the impurities from it. Frith looked at his hammer man who smiled, he had been told that a boy of only fifteen who could use hammer like a twenty-five-year-old would be staying. Even when Frith told him that, he had barely believed his cousin Anson himself. The iron was reheating under the coals and Frith said to Osgar, "Now we use three hammers."

After Frith had helped to lift the iron onto the anvil, he did not take up a position behind Osgar as he had before. Instead, he picked up his sledgehammer and stood to the right of Osgar. The first man swung his hammer down and struck the yellow glowing bar of iron, flattening it evenly. Osgar, as before, followed as soon as the first hammer recoiled away. Hit landed his blow perfectly and as soon as his hammer lifted, Frith landed a blow in the same spot. The pace increased again and because there were now three, the beat increased. Osgar noticed that if he did not land his hammer perfectly and there was a small mark on the bar then Frith's next blow would take it out. When he noticed that the blow preceding his left a mark, he did the same and erased it.

They worked all afternoon until dusk only pausing the hammering while the iron was reheated. What had started as a large amorphous blob of sparking iron that to Osgar, looked like the moon, was now a long bar of shining gray iron. When they had finished, they sat outside and drank ale. Frith explained to Osgar how the iron they had produced that day would be used for sword making, it was not hard iron but had the same consistency of iron that was used for general-purpose tools. Tomorrow they would produce iron that was much harder and the combining of these two types would produce a blade for a sword.

They walked to Frith's house on the hillside away from the noise and chaos of the wharves. His house was of the usual style of boarded vertical planks over a wood frame and a thatched roof. The floor was wood and covered with rugs. The house was twice the size of Anson's but Frith still had to duck his head under the door to enter. His wife, Rowena, stood inside the door with their seven children. The children were all well dressed and varied in age from two years to a large eleven-year-old. Rowena had her left hand on the head of the youngest who partly hid behind her scyrt. Frith introduced them one by one and told them that Osgar was their cousin from the west. The boys wanted him to tell them about the battle of Three Bridges and were disappointed when he told them the story briefly without mentioning himself. Frith came to his rescue and told his family that a true Angle never bragged and they had already had the battle recounted many times. He then clapped his hands and told them to help their mother with the meal.

Osgar had detected that Rowena was not enthusiastic about his stay. She was not rude to him but asked him no questions, in the way that everybody else did and since he was always reticent, he offered her no conversation. Her hair was not long in the fashion adopted by most Angle women who then plaited it or put it in buns but was short and curly. It had a slight ginger tinge to it and she had a habit of patting the curls into place and asking her eldest daughter if they looked all right. She was a big-built, tall woman but not a giant like her husband. She was always busy and rapidly patted and kissed her children but was just as quick to admonish them when they did not behave.

They ate their stew from wooden bowls which was made with carrot, cabbage, beans and peas with some goat. They sat on benches and ate as Frith told Osgar about Gippeswic. It was the first port of the Angles and easily their biggest town. He told of how the people first settled in the Gipping valley, where now the busy wharves received boats from the Old Country and the land of the

100

Franks. They often sent ships northwards to lands that the Angles had settled and to the south to trade with the Jutes and Saxons. It was a good place to trade and his business had flourished, he both smelted iron and forged it. Frith's forge workshop had grown until he now employed two freemen, two apprentices and owned two slaves. Life was comfortable but he was concerned how the growing attacks by the Waelisc had affected trade. The movement of goods was threatened although his weapon making had increased.

Osgar slept in a lean-to next to the house and was content. On his first day, he had learned so much and he looked forward to the second day. He said his prayers to Thunor and lay under his cloak, keeping his seax within reach. Rowena, Frith's wife had made it clear at the meal that she thought that he was just another mouth to feed and she had enough already. When Frith said that Osgar was the nephew of his cousin she replied that on that basis they could be feeding all the Suth Folk people. From other conversations, Osgar could tell that she looked after the business while Frith was happy to work all day in the forge. He had an easy-going disposition and did not rise to any of the verbal prodding from Rowena. Osgar woke when the sun's rays beamed through the opening by the door. He sat on the raised sleeping area and retied the leather thongs in the crisscross pattern behind his calves. When he had finished dressing, he went next door for some of the remnants of the previous evening's stew, scooped water from a wooden pail with a mug, drank it and then walked with Frith to the forge.

He helped prepare the bloomery furnace by clearing out the bottom which was caked in slag and came out in a few large pieces. Once cleaned, and raked out, the fire of kindling wood was lit and as soon as it was burning well, charcoal and iron of the correct proportions were tipped in. Frith explained that how by altering the proportions of charcoal and iron and the amount of air that blasted into the raging fire, the quality of iron could be changed. The previous day they had made wrought iron with less charcoal and less heat and it would be softer, this would make a sword bend from a blow but not break. Today they were going to produce hard iron which was tougher and more rigid and would take a good edge when sharpened. A blow to a sword made only from this steel may snap. The art of the sword maker, explained Frith, was to combine the qualities of soft and hard iron so that a blade could take a sharp edge but not break in battle. They spent the day producing another bar or iron. This time Osgar knew his place and stood between Frith and the other striker. Sometimes people of other trades stood by the door and watched as they had heard the ring of hammer and anvil for years and could tell that the cadence was different. The ringing tones could be heard across all the wharves and up into the town, they came and looked in the door to see the burning fire, Hunfrith the Smith with his giant tongs turning the lump of glowing metal on the anvil. Through the doorway were the four men lit by the glowing fire, one behind the anvil, the other three working in unison, each hammer blow followed swiftly by another.

The next day, they started on the bars of iron that they had forged in two previous days. Frith took the first iron bar which was two finger widths wide and roughly squared. He selected a pair of tongs that held it securely and placed it in the charcoal fire, while one of the slaves worked the bellows. When it was yellow hot, he pulled it out double handed and laid it on the anvil. The same rhythm began and the bar was narrowed and drawn out until it was about a finger width and a man's pace long. He cut it in two with a chisel when it was red and each half was put in the hot charcoal to bring them up to yellow. He fixed a block of iron with a furrow in it on top of his anvil. When the iron was hot again, he pulled it out, placed the iron closest to the jaws of the tongs in the furrow and hammered down with his hand hammer, it was immediately followed by a blow from the sledgehammer. With each two blows, the iron road was squashed and stretched between the hammer and the furrow. He turned the metal around in the tongs and put the thick end that had been in the tong jaws into the hearth. They forged the bar that had been heating while the first piece reheated. When they had the bars drawn out into rods the thickness of a finger, he changed the top tool with the furrow with another that had a narrower furrow in it so that by the end of the day they had a batch of rods of uniform diameter. They were marked at each end with a small punched notch so that they were not mixed up with the harder iron. As usual when they had finished for the day they washed, put their smocks back on and then went to have some ale outside the forge. Osgar, as always, retied his belt and slotted his seax in the scabbard behind his back.

The wharf opposite was full of handcarts alongside a clinker-built ship of about twenty-five paces. It had no mast but benches along the side for rowers. The sea captain was telling a well-dressed thegn that they were missing the tide and would have to delay a day. The thegn scowled at the sea captain and kicked one of the slaves loading the sacks of barley. He wore a fur-lined cloak over a fine wool smock, embroidered down the front. The clasp holding his cloak at one shoulder was silver and he wore gold armbands which glinted in the sun. He turned to Hunfrith and said, "Hey you, get off your fat arse and help unload the handcarts, and that goes for the rest of you."

Frith ignored him and continued to talk about the difficulty of obtaining quality iron ore. Suddenly, the thegn was at their bench and said to Frith, "I gave you an order, move."

Frith put his ale down and said calmly, "I am a ceorl, a freeman, I work for no one but myself and my King."

"I do not care what you are," said the thegn, "You will do as I say and you will load my grain now." He pulled his sword from its scabbard and brought it towards Frith. He aimed it with the blade flat and the edges sideways so that Frith looked down the length of it.

Nobody had noticed the well-dressed young thegn at the next house. He was a blond man with a neatly trimmed goatee beard and he wore a sword at his side. He had rings on the fingers of his left hand which he rested on the sword pommel. He leant against the corner post of the building with one foot up behind him resting on the wall. He was watching what was happening with a wry smile. He had seen the argument from the start and had recognised Hunfrith the sword-maker and thegn Selwyn of the North Folk. He could hear Selwyn ranting at the seated giant and saw him draw his sword from its scabbard by his side and point it at the throat of the smith. The stranger saw a well-built young man rise from his bench and step forward.

In one movement Osgar reached behind his back with his right hand, pulled the toggle on the handle of his seax up and grabbed it and drew it sideways from the scabbard. His hand found the handle as he swung it in an arc over his shoulder. The blade of his seax hit the middle of the sword prodding at Frith's throat and sent it clattering to the ground. Osgar's eyes were open wide and staring at the thegn, he did not move but held his seax down by his side with the blade aimed forward. Frith motioned to him to back away and Thegn Selwyn looked into Osgar's eyes and shuddered. Frith picked the sword up and handed it, handle first, to the thegn. Frith could see that the blade was bent and there was a crack in one side running to the centre. Frith thought that it was not a sword of great quality, for the thegn though, it was a symbol of his status and his authority and it had been destroyed by a boy with a seax. Selwyn determined that instant to make him pay heavily for his insolence.

That evening a message was sent to Hunfrith that he was summoned to attend the Ealdorman's court the next day with Osgar where they were to be sued for attacking Thegn Selwyn and damaging his sword. The Angles had strict rules of compensation for damage and also laws punishing fighting outside a battle. The punishment and compensation, known as wergild, could mean that Frith lost everything he had and Osgar who had nothing could be made a slave. Rowena would not allow Osgar into their house and try as Frith did to explain what had happen, she would not relent. She reminded her husband that she had never wanted Osgar to work in the forge anyway.

"He came here to steal your skills," she said. "He paid us nothing. He eats our food and sleeps under our roof. Now his stupidity will cost us everything that we have worked for."

Osgar slept in the forge and Hunfrith smuggled some food in for him. In the morning, they walked up from the wharves to the town centre where the Great Hall stood. Osgar could still remember how impressed he had been when he first saw the Great Hall at Beodricesworth but his was even grander. There was not a beam showing that had not been carved and outside the entrance, flat stones had been laid so it was not muddy. The door was thick oak and was heavily studded with iron rivets. Either side of the doorway stood men with shields at their sides and their spears shouldered. They were led in by the Reeve to stand before the Ealdorman, who sat in a raised chair and was flanked by thegns. Frith was terrified and his giant body shook while Osgar looked at the Ealdorman and studied him. The Ealdorman did not like being looked at like this and took as instant dislike to Osgar.

"Whosoever brings charges to this court, step forward and speak," said the Reeve after banging his staff on the floor.

"I do," said the thegn whose sword had been damaged.

"Then state your case," said the Reeve.

They all listened to the Thegn Selwyn. To hear him speak one would imagine that he had asked them politely to help and that because he had missed the tide he would pay more for shipping and the people of the north would starve. His main case was that as a thegn, he could not be attacked by ceorls and his sword would need replacing at great cost. The Ealdorman listened sympathetically and tutted occasionally as the tale was told. He ticked off both Frith and Osgar on two occasions when they protested that the story was not true. The thegn produced two witnesses who confirmed that every detail of his story was correct. The Reeve then asked for the compensation claim. Selwyn stated that the sword had a value of five hydes of land or four slaves.

Frith and Osgar were asked to respond and Frith spoke directly to the Ealdorman. He told the story exactly as it happened and then addressed the issue of compensation. "*Sire*," he said, "I am one who smites the black and I know something of sword-making, you can ask anyone here in Gippeswic that this is so. No good sword would bend and crack with a blow from a seax, however well the seax is made and however well it is wielded. A sword made in this country by the pattern weld method from good iron is worth the amount stated but this thegn's sword is just a cheap import, it is not worth more than a cow."

Osgar stepped forward to speak and told of the events and how he could see that the thegn had lost all reasoning and that he believed that he was about to stab his master in the throat. He had acted to save Hunfrith's life without harming the thegn. This raised a chuckle from many in the hall but not the Ealdorman. He considered for a moment, his chin rested in one hand with an elbow on the armrest. He looked from Frith to Osgar to Thegn Selwyn and finally he spoke, "You have produced no independent witnesses to this crime and I am expected to believe that a thegn of some standing would pick a fight with a ceorl and his apprentice and then that he would lie about the quality of his sword and its value. Without a witness of status, I have no option but to order wergild for the full amount."

A voice from the back of the hall said, "I may be of some help."

"And you are?" the Reeve asked gruffly before the Ealdorman could stop him as he knew perfectly well who it was.

A tall young man of impeccable dress stood in the doorway ignored the Reeve and spoke to the Ealdorman as if he had asked the question, "I am, Wuffa, then to Wehha."

"How can I be of help?" said the Ealdorman, in a deferential tone recognising the King's nephew.

"It is not you who can help me, but thank you anyway," said Wuffa, "I am here to help this court decide on this matter, which I witnessed at the wharf yesterday."

He gave his version of events which coincided with Osgar's and Hunfrith's statements. He even confirmed that Hunfrith was the best sword maker in Gippeswic and if he said the thegn had a cheap sword then it must be so. The Ealdorman looked at Selwyn who gritted his teeth and blushed. Wuffa added that even the hero of the Battle of Three Bridges could not break a good sword with a seax. The Ealdorman looked more closely at the apprentice boy and then turned

105

to the thegn and said, "In light of this evidence from the Thegn Wuffa, it is now clear that you have lied to me. You will pay to the Reeve a wergild of two slaves or the equivalent before the week is out. Next case."

Osgar and Hunfrith walked out of the Great Hall and were joined by Wuffa. He was about two years older than Osgar and stood as tall as Frith which made him very tall, even for an Angle and had a relaxed charm about him that immediately put them at their ease. "I wish to thank you," said Frith formally with a small bow, "for speaking to the Ealdorman."

"Think no more of it," said Wuffa. "How else am I to get my sword made? I had come to the docks to find you and to see that the iron ore had arrived. I ordered enough for two swords as you asked."

"*Sire*," said Frith, "there is less than enough for two. I will have three-quarters enough for a second sword."

"It is good ore though?" asked Wuffa.

"The best," said Frith.

"Then keep it as payment," said the Atheling.

The three of them walked across the market place to the alehouse. It had a wooden carving of a swan over the door which was painted black. Osgar, as the apprentice, fetched three ales and sat next to Frith opposite Wuffa who leaned his elbows on the trestle table while holding his ale in his right hand. Osgar noticed that two of Wuffa's thegns stood casually near the door and watched anyone passing close by. Osgar also looked at the gold rings upon Wuffa's left hand and two gold bangles pushed up his forearm, he also had two bronze and two silver armbands on his left arm. He had never been so close to gold before and looked at it intently. Wuffa noticed Osgar's stare and pulled one of the gold bands down his arm and passed it to Osgar to look at. Osgar held it like it was a delicate duck egg.

"You will not break it." Laughed Wuffa. "Bite it."

Osgar looked at Wuffa, who repeated his instruction to bite the gold band. He did as he was told and clamped his teeth on it and bit. He expected a tooth to chip but instead he felt it sink in slightly.

"Soft you see," said Wuffa, "not like the iron that you smite."

He took a gulp of ale and asked both of them, "Are the Angle people made of iron or gold?"

Never had Osgar been asked such a question, his life was straightforward. You ate or starved, lived or died, people were not iron or gold; they were friends

106

or enemies, Angles or Waelisc. The riddles, that so amused Anson just irritated him. He was only an apprentice so he sat still and waited for Frith to answer. "It is a difficult question, my lord. I believe that the people are made of iron, but the black comes in all qualities. Only by forging with the hammer, in great heat is the slag driven from it and then it hardens."

Osgar followed the analogy and was impressed with Frith. He sipped his ale and relaxed, then Wuffa turned to him and said, "And your thoughts, young Thunor?"

"Raise the fyrd and attack the Waelisc," replied Osgar.

Wuffa laughed at the way Osgar had ignored the question and had gone directly to his own subject. He knew something of his story, how his father was killed and his mother and brother were taken in a raid. He had been in King Wehha's company when the report of the battle of the Three Bridges had cheered them all. "My uncle, the King," began Wuffa, "is a strong and brave ruler. No one else could have united the North Folk and Suth Folk. He knows that East Anglia is one Kingdom and that an attack on one part is an attack on all, however, he also knows that rushing in to attack the Waelisc may bring defeat and then the whole country would be at their mercy. We must build our forces, make alliance with our cousins the South Saxons and then fight them on our terms."

"And all the time, they get stronger and kill and take more of our people," said Osgar.

Frith started to reprimand Osgar for speaking in such a forthright way to an atheling.

"I am happy for him speak," he said to Frith. "He has the right to speak earned in battle. Every day I practice with my sword, we have mock battles with the fyrd, but I have never seen a drop of blood spilled in anger. This boy has more experience of war than most Angles."

He turned to Osgar. "The day will come when I will need you and East Anglia will need you. Look after yourself until then."

Wuffa stood to leave, signalling for them to stay seated. He put his hand on Osgar's shoulder while he looked at Frith and said, "Just a work of warning, Selwyn the thegn will not be amused by today's ruling. It has cost him dear and his pride will have been hurt, stay clear of him, he will look for revenge."

Wuffa left the alehouse and his guards walked a few paces behind him. Frith and Osgar watched as he walked casually down the street talking to various street vendors and shopkeepers. Frith turned to Osgar and said, "You now have friends in high places."

"And enemies," added Osgar.

During the next week, they finished drawing out the rods of iron. Frith showed Osgar how to arrange the rods as hard, soft, hard, soft, hard and then plait them when orange hot. The plaiting had to be as tight as possible so that when it was lifted to the light no gaps could be seen. Once this was done, then they used the bloomery furnace rather than the hearth. Only in the bloomery could they get the rods to a white heat.

Frith took the woven metal rods that were the width of three fingers and the length of a forearm and placed it in the bottom of the bloomery. It had been filled with charcoal and air was blasted in from vents and from the bellows. It gave off such heat that all of them had stripped their smocks off and worked in their trousers and boots. Their legs and chests were protected from flying sparks by the leather aprons tired around their waists and necks. They all had a speckling of burns on their forearms and the backs of their hands, Frith had more than anyone as he was usually holding the work in his tongs. Although tongs were about an arm's length, the sparks flew with each blow of the hammer and some reached him.

The bloomery furnace heated the iron almost to melting point, then the outer surface gleamed and an eye, used to looking at hot metal, could see the surface shimmer and move. They called this a wash and it was the perfect time to hammer as the metal would fill every minute cavity and the blade made of five parts would become one. The different grades of iron could be seen distinctly and if the plaiting was even, the hammering symmetrical and controlled then the swirling pattern was constant and uniform along the blade. This was pleasing to the eye but much more importantly, it meant that the hard and soft iron was equally distributed along the length. The soft allowed flexibility in the blade so it did not crack or shatter, the hard iron gave strength for the blade to cut and to take a blow against the edge.

The next day the blade was held in Frith's tongs and the end that would form the hilt was pushed into the bloomery furnace and only brought out when the glow was bright yellow. The end of what would become the hilt was forged square with a pointed section called the tang, drawn out to a sharp tip, this would become the handle. It needed to be as strong as the sword so that it did not bend or snap with a blow from another sword in battle and it must be absolutely central or the sword would feel unbalanced.

Once Frith was happy with the tang and hilt, he turned it again in his tongs and the blade was once more placed in the bloomery furnace. As the process continued, care was given to maintaining symmetry. Frith used his hand hammer more and one of the strikers was dropped, the heavy hammer work was over and now it was pure precision. Frith picked up a flatter which looked like a hammer and had a square face of three finger widths. Each time he laid it carefully on the blade, the striker hit the top of it and it levelled the ironwork below it. Frith constantly stopped to check that he was producing an even thickness. Next, the blade was fullered, creating a trough that ran the length of the blade. Some said it was to let the blood out or that it made it easier to pull from an enemy's guts. The truth is, as Frith explained to Osgar, that it lightened the blade but made it still stronger. Fullering was achieved with a tool that looked like a miniature axe with a blunt and rounded blade. Frith carefully ran it down the centre of the blade. With each soft blow from the sledgehammer he rocked it and moved the fuller towards himself. Every few blows he checked that the furrow was running directly from tang to sword point. When he was content that the alignment was perfect, he took an orange heat and nodded to Osgar to strike. If he thought the blow had not been sufficient, Frith kept the tool in the same place for another blow, if satisfied he rocked the fuller slightly and moved in towards himself. The overlapping work left the gully down the blade an even depth and widened the broad blade some more.

The blade was drawn down either side to an even straws thickness, along the entire length and prepared for the tempering and hardening. It was heated to an even orange along its length and plunged into the water bosh. It boiled the water and more steam arose when it was lifted from the liquid. Now that it was cool, Hunfrith examined it and saw that there were no flaws.

Osgar helped one of the apprentices to lift a long leather trough of pig's fat, which was placed on the floor near the anvil. Osgar had seen his own seax tempered by Anson his uncle and had since learned to do it with all the blades that he made. He knew that you had to understand the metal, the colour when it was cooling and the timing of the final quench. He could do this with one blade made from the same iron, but this was a sword with two edges and it was made from two grades of iron. Frith and his assistant each held the blade with narrow tongs. The blade was brought the fire where it had been turned and moved lengthways until one side of the fullered channel was orange to yellow and the other side red. The sword was dipped carefully lengthways with the red down into the fat to a finger's depth. The fat boiled and spat, then both men lifted the blade evenly, and quickly it was laid on an anvil in the light. Frith watched the rainbow colour move magically towards the blade's centre and at an exact moment, they both lifted it and dipped in water almost to the centre of the fuller. This fixed the hardness. By now, the other side had cooled to red and without delay they carefully dipped this edge lengthways into the pig fat and repeated the whole process.

Now the blade was cool and Frith peered closely at it, again looking for flaws. His eyes traced the swirling pattern where the rods had been woven and then beaten together; this is where any fault would be found. He rubbed the edge hard with another piece of metal. The iron shined and he could see the fixed colour. He continued down each side to see by the colour that there was an even hardness along the entire length.

The next day the sword was honed on a large grindstone standing in the corner of the forge. It was a circular stone on a wooden frame about a forearm across. It had a wooden shaft with a handle through a square hole in the centre which Osgar and an apprentice took turns to rotate. While Osgar turned it, Frith held the sword against the rotating stone. Once Frith had demonstrated to Osgar he held Osgar's hands by the wrists as he stood behind him and helped him grind the sword while an apprentice turned the handle. When the rough grinding had taken the blade almost to its final surface and edge, the grindstone was used with water tipped continually over it. This gave a finer cut and it began to shine, revealing the swirling pattern in the silvery blade.

Suddenly, there was a noise as a pail of water was kicked across the forge floor tipping its contents as it rolled. In the doorway stood the Thegn Selwyn flanked by two armed men.

Chapter 9
Bishop Cadog Ddoeth

Aefre looked east as the sun rose over the far hills and she said the same prayers she had intoned as a slave for five years. She had lived in the same hovel at the end of the kitchen garden during that time. She prayed to the gods and everyday expected her people to come and rescue her and her son. She saw Leofric sometimes with horses and she knew that he was slave to the shoeing smith on the other side of the castle. When she heard an anvil ring, she imagined him there with the fire behind him hammering a horseshoe.

She thought of her ham and the people in it and wondered if it continued the same as before. How many perished in the raid? She did not know that her husband Eafwald had died or that her son Osgar lived. She knew who had been taken that night, of the five of them captured, only her son and her now survived. She was still occasionally spat on, insulted, tripped or beaten without reason but she was no longer the King's whore and it gave her some satisfaction to think back to the death of the old King. The new King Cadrod was not interested in Angle women and she had not been back to the royal rooms in the tower since that day. She kept to the garden and had her own patch of vegetables and herbs. Occasionally, the Cymry, as they called themselves, would come to her for healing. She obliged because it made her life easier and they would give her cloth or meat. She now spoke and understood their language completely, although the Cymry thought that she had a very strange accent and it was a source for more ridicule.

That day, there would be an important visitor. Of course, she was not told who but she recognised the signs, tidying around the castle, game and goats brought to the kitchen and jars of wine brought up from the cellars. She had been told to pick the best vegetables in the morning and take them to the kitchen; she had heard the squeal of a pig taken to be slaughtered.

*****

Bishop Cadog the Wise walked through the streets of Bannaventa. He made the sign of the cross to the people with his right hand and held his tunic out of the mud with his left. He smiled at those that went on one knee and stopped and put his hand on the crown of their heads while he blessed them. He had dressed plainly, wearing a full-length tunic with a gown over it. His tunic was tied at the waist by a woven woollen belt which he liked to think made him a man of the people. His long straight hair was white matching his long beard and he had a straight fringe. His face had large features and his nose was bent sideways, around his neck hung a large wooden cross. His fingers were adorned with just one plain ring with a garnet set into it. As he walked, he leant on the monk to his left and held his staff in his right hand, it was topped with a small golden crucifix. The Bishop's entourage was strung out behind him. They were all dismounted and leading their horses by their leather reigns. Behind the Bishop were two horses with one man leading both while walking between them. The horse on the right was a dark bay and the horse on the left a grey. The grey nodded in time to every alternate step and was lame and distressed. It was Bishop Cadog's own horse and when he had dismounted to help alleviate its pain so had those accompanying him. They had walked for an hour while he had heard the moaning behind him but cared not, as he was not one to inflict pain on one of God's creatures.

He had come to Bannaventa to preach and to see how the rebuilding of the town was proceeding. The Kingdom of Calchfynedd was at the forefront of driving the pagans from the lands. Calchfynedd was still a young Kingdom which it had only come about because of the great victory at Mynydd Baddon. The first King had been Cynwyd's father and the present King Cadrod's grandfather. All of them knew that it was God's work to kill the pagan's and Bishop had reminded all three kings that they would sit beside God in Heaven for their efforts. Sometimes he had to forgive their methods, just as he was sure that the Good Lord would. Bishop Cadog finally entered the castle through the stables on the south wall. He knew that the main gate would be hung with banners but he liked to show his humility to the people. Once in the stables, he called for the head groom and asked him to remove the horse's tack and wash him down. As soon as he had been fed and watered, he wanted his horse looked at to find his lameness. He told the head groom that wanted a report as soon as possible and the best treatment.

It was not the first time that the Bishop had visited Bannaventa and he knew his way. Before he walked to the tower, he looked right through the archway set in the wall running across the fortress, through the arch was the main courtyard leading to the large gate in the eastern wall. He walked to the archway and stood considering the area, to the left were various craftsmen workshops and stalls but most of the area was bare, it was sometimes used for training both horses and foot soldiers and fairs were held there on some holy feast days. He knew exactly what the empty area needed and thought about it as he climbed the stone stairway to the tower and the royal rooms accompanied by two monks.

Cadrod, King of Calchfynedd dropped to one knee before the Bishop, who placed his open right hand on the top of Cadrod's dark head.

"Bless you, my favourite son," said the Bishop. "Please stand."

Cadrod was glad to welcome the Bishop who had known him since he was a boy. He had been his father's priest and had always combined a great gentleness without losing his authority as a representative of God on Earth.

"I was saddened to hear of the death of your father, such a sudden illness," said the Bishop, "Now he will be sat on God's right hand where he will enjoy eternal life."

"Can you be certain of that?" asked the King.

"Certainly," said the Bishop, "this was once a Christian land; your father stopped the pagan advance and drove them back. For that act, he is enjoying the reward of eternal life. You are continuing your father's work and when you drive the last pagan from these lands, you will join your father in eternity. Shall we pray?"

Bishop Cadog knelt and the two monks immediately dropped to their knees followed by King Cadrod and then the Bishop led the prayers. When he could think of nothing else to say, he prayed silently. Finally, he said amen and the two monks helped him rise. "A little stiffness with age," he said. "Now to church matters."

The Bishop told the King of how impressed he was with the rebuilding of the fortress but of his disappointment that there was no church in which to worship within the walls. Cadrod explained how he would build one but it was important to first secure the castle.

"But there is no danger of you being attacked," the Bishop said. "It is the pagans who are being pushed back. I would wish to see work start of my church, King Cadrod."

Cadrod knew better than to argue with the one man who would dare to disagree with him and a man who had always bettered him since he was a small boy. "I have organised a banquet in your honour," said the King. "We have good food and a very good bard."

Cadrod knew how the Bishop appreciated an evening of eating, drinking and entertainment. He especially enjoyed bards reciting epic verses of wit and humour and said it was his favourite pastime.

*****

The head groom was in a panic, he had found that the shoeing smith was visiting his sick mother a day's walk away. He was accompanied by the Bishop's groom who told him that he wanted the horseshoe removed immediately and the hoof inspected. The head groom finally went to the shack which housed the Sais slave to the shoeing smith.

"Go and fetch your tools boy and follow me," he ordered.

Leofric rushed to the shoeing forge, grabbed his rickety toolbox and joined them in the stall where the Bishop's horse stood. The grey was standing with his left forefoot bent forward with the heel off the ground. When he was brought out of his stall, he walked only on the tip of his toe, trying to lessen the pain in that foot.

"Get the shoe off, boy," said the head groom.

Leofric cut the nail clenches as carefully as possible but each tap made the horse flinch. He spoke gently to the horse in this language to calm him.

"Take care boy or I'll have the skin off your back," the head groom warned him.

Leofric took his pincers and lifted each nail from the shoe separately. As he pulled them out, he held them to the light to examine them.

"What do you think you are doing now?" said the head groom.

"I am looking to see if there is any pus or blood on the nail, sir," said Leofric.

"You were told to remove the shoe, so do just that," he said to the slave.

The Bishop's own groom watched while Leofric removed the shoe carefully and cleaned the foot of all straw, dung and mud. He then gently placed the foot

114

on the ground. While he did so he felt the horse give another flinch as he touched one of the heel bulbs at the back of the foot where the hoof ended and the hair began. He looked at his fingertip and there was a faint grey coloured drop of pus on it. The head groom pushed him out of the way and roughly picked up the foot. The horse jumped and his hoof came down on the head groom's foot. He cried out in anger and rammed his elbow into the horse's ribs.

"Have a care," said the Bishop's groom, "This horse has served the Bishop in his ministry for many years. He loves all animals as God has taught us but this horse, he loves more than any other."

"Well, he can get God to fix it then," said the head groom as he hobbled off.

"May I look?" said Leofric.

The Bishop's groom nodded. Leofric carefully picked up the horse's front foot as he spoke calmly to it. "Come on, old boy, the little twats gone."

The Bishop's groom heard only meaningless babbled. "What devil's words are these?" he said.

"Just some words for the horse," replied Leofric.

He examined the heel bulb and then he could see where the skin joined the hoof there was an opening that showed flesh and glistened with pus. He trimmed the sole of the hoof with his curved knife and carefully pared it near the heel. Any pressure made the horse flinch but he had a sharp knife and he cut without pressing down. Finally, there was a black spot in the clean white horn and one more cut revealed a hole, the pus ran out and he could feel the horse relax.

The Bishop's groom clapped his hands softly, so as not to frighten the horse, and then patted Leofric on the shoulder. He had listened as Leofric explained where the infection had run and how to treat it. He had said that he would make a poultice that would wrap around the whole foot and that each day he would bathe the hoof in a tub of hot water and salts. Leofric told him how after three days they would plug the wound and his shoe could be nailed back on. He reassured the Bishop's groom that provided it was protected and cleaned each day that the horse would be fine to ride and the lameness would not return. The groom was impressed by the confidence and clear instructions and walked to the tower to report to the Bishop.

The Bishop's groom was led into the royal rooms where the Bishop was being helped to his feet. He bowed to the Bishop and bowed to King Cadrod.

"Good news, Father," he said, "they found the disease and removed the evil fluid. Your horse is already more comfortable and will be sound to ride in three days. His skills father, are exceptional."

Cadrod beamed, "It seems, my good Bishop that your trip has already proven worthwhile. You see how good the horsemanship of my men is. With our cavalry, we will drive the pagans into the sea."

He smiled at the Bishop's groom. "Tell me, was it my head groom who cured the Bishop's horse?"

"No, *sire*, it was not."

"Well then, tell me," said Cadrod. "It must have been my master shoeing smith?"

"No, *sire*, it was not."

Cadrod was tiring now and said, "Just tell me who cured the Bishop's horse?"

"Leofric, your majesty."

"Leofric," said Cadrod with contempt, "that is a Sais pig name. Tell me now who cured the Bishop's horse?"

"The boy is a Sais slave," said the Bishop's groom. "He is slave to the shoeing smith who was away."

"Cadrod, Cadrod," said the Bishop, deciding to calm an angry King, "you even have slaves that can cure the wounded beast, like the slave Androcles removing a thorn from the lion's paw. I now have to go and get ready for the wonderful banquet that you have prepared for me."

The Bishop Cadog the Wise left with his entourage to wash and change for the banquet, Cadrod fumed and called for his head groom. The head groom did not know why he was summoned to his King but he did know that it would be an arduous journey. His foot was now swollen and he had difficultly bearing any weight on it. He had a crutch under his left armpit and his foot was wrapped in a large poultice, it had been applied by the Sais herb-women who lived in the kitchen garden. His wife had brought her to him when she saw his injury and the Sais woman had said that he had a broken bone, that it would heal but he must not walk on it for two weeks. She had made a poultice that had already soothed it somewhat, now however, he had to climb stairs and that was proving slow and painful.

The limping head groom was shown into King Cadrod's room by his guard. Cadrod looked at him aghast. "So the Bishop's horse is healed and you are crippled?"

The head groom did not know what he was talking about.

"Your Majesty," he said, "the Bishop's horse jumped on my foot, I know of nothing else."

"You made the Sais pig a slave to the shoeing smith and by doing so you have made fools of us all. You are no longer my head groom, so you will now be lifting horse turds, along with the other grooms from tomorrow. Just get out of my sight."

As the demoted head groom hobbled out of the King's presence, Cadrod spoke to the guard who then left. He marched down the steps and called two other guards to him, they went to Leofric's hovel and dragged him out. They beat him senseless, he only felt the first dozen strikes as they cracked his skull and ran the blows down the ribs of his back, continuing along his legs. He was thrown on the muck heap where he lay face down in the steaming heap. When he woke in the morning, he could not move, from the pain across his whole body for the first time in five years he cried. He had endured slavery for long enough, putting up with the jibes and the beatings, working from dawn to dusk, sleeping in the stalls with the horses, hoping as his mother did that the fyrd would appear. He finally gave up all hope of freedom, no longer wanting to live and slipped into unconsciousness.

*****

Bishop Cadog walked with his two monks down the stone steps from his room to the banqueting hall below and they entered the room through an oak doorway. The hall was about twenty-five paces long by fifteen wide and in the centre was a dark wooden dining table set for twenty guests with silver chalices and a row of silver candle holders along the centre. All around the hall were tallow candles flickering and spitting. At each setting was a wooden platter for the food.

Before sitting, the Bishop was given a pottery vessel of mulled wine that he sipped after handing his staff to one of his monks. He was introduced to each warrior by their sergeant. They were dressed in their finest clothes, each wearing bright plaid trews held up with leather belts fixed by buckles. Some of the buckles were silver and all of them wore silver and bronze armbands, some wore as many as six, a few had gold. The warriors did not wear their leather jerkins nor have their legs hooped for riding but wore their trews full length. All were adorned with armbands and they wore rings on their fingers, again of copper, silver and gold, some had garnets set into them. Their hair has been slicked back with oil, they wore it plain and long and sometimes in the braided style, most had full black beards which were also oiled.

The Bishop spoke to each one in turn as he smiled and asked them about their families and especially their wives. With many of them, he remembered their names and even their children's names. The older warriors had known the Bishop as a simple priest who had ministered to them since they were young men. To all the Briton warriors Cadog Ddoeth was a revered figure and they looked upon him as a saint whose words came directly from God. Each one asked for his blessing and he held his right hand on the crown of their head and spoke gently to them. He reminded them that it was their special god-given duty to drive the pagan from Lloegr.

One of Cadrod's warriors in particular impressed the Bishop, he had the same dark looks as the others and one of his armbands was gold but he had an earnest intelligent look. He asked the Bishop whether God accepted a follower of Christ taking a pagan woman for his wife. It was a question that clearly troubled him and the Bishop took his time before answering. The Bishop looked him in the eyes and said, "For a man and a woman to be married in the eyes of God and his church, they must both be followers of Christ."

Bishop Cadog looked deep into Waljan's eyes and said, "This woman that you ask me about does she wish to marry you?"

"No father," he answered, "she is a slave who knows not of my desire."

"Then keep her as a slave my son. Use her as you wish and marry a good Christian girl from Cymru. Listen to me carefully. No good comes of such a marriage to this type of woman." The Bishop smiled at Waljan, blessed him and patted him on the shoulder.

They all sat at their places and awaited their King. Cadrod strode into the hall and beckoned them to sit as they rose in his honour. He wore fine white linen trews with a blue short tunic held at the waist with a leather belt studded with gold, around his shoulders his cloak was linen dyed red. He wore rings on all the fingers of his left hand and armbands above each elbow of gold and silver. On his head sat a banded crown of two finger widths, it was silver with some gold knotted patterning. Cadrod sat at the head of the table with the Bishop to his left, smiled at him, lifted his golden chalice to his lips and sipped. He looked at the array of his most loyal and senior warriors, the Bishop he had known since his childhood and he leant back in his chair as he relaxed to enjoy the evening.

The suckling pig was carried in by two servants head high with candles burning at each end to clapping from the diners. It was laid on a great dresser to one side of the hall and carved. Wine was poured from pitchers into the silver goblets and biscuit-ware pottery vessels were refilled with mead. The Bishop led them in prayer before the meal, when he thanked God for the bounteous meal that they were about to eat and the fine wine and mead before them. He finished by reminding them that they, as Calchfynedd warriors, had been put on God's earth to defend the faith and drive the pagans out.

During the meal, the entertainment began. The Bishop always enjoyed bards more than music or jugglers, liking the way the words were spoken in verse with wit. Cadrod had promised him a bard and so he was anticipating a good evening but when the bard entered, the Bishop clapped his hands in delight and thanked the King. He recognised him immediately as Taliesan the greatest of all the bards of the Britons. Taliesan was bard to the Count of Urien of Ryeyed whose Kingdom was Cumbria.

The whole gathering quietened as Taliesan introduced himself theatrically and explained to his audience that he would recount the twelve battles of Arturius.

"The first battle was at the mouth of the river called Glein," began the bard. His poem played on the double meaning of Glein as pure. The table cheered as he won his first battle, the Bishop laughed and banged the table in joy and Cadrod listened intently to the story of his hero.

The bard took them through the second, third, fourth and fifth battles against the Scots and the northern Britons by the Dubglas River. Cadrod cheered as Arturius defeated the Scots but was not so sure about his victories over fellow Britons. Cadrod wanted all Britons united against the Sais who had stolen their land, Lloegr was theirs and it would all be Cymru again.

"And Arturius defeated the great northern King Caw by the Bassas," Taliesan, the bard, recounted as if he had stood on the banks of the river and seen the battle. He moved on to the seventh battle of Arturius and now he defeated an alliance of the Sais, Scots and Picts. With the mention of the Sais, there were jeers and whistles and Taliesan delayed his verse to let them calm.

"In his eighth battle, Arturius carried an image of the Virgin Mary upon his shield," intoned the Bard Taliesan. It crossed King Cadrod's mind that maybe he should do something similar. Again, Arturius defeated a Sais King and once more they cheered around the table.

"Arturius had ranged far and wide to defeat his enemies, both Cymry and pagan," recounted the bard, "and now he fought his ninth battle in the west in Caerleon, at the old fort of the Romans."

Bishop Cadog mouthed some of the verses that he knew while he listened intently to the tale. King Cadrod imagined himself on horseback alongside Arturius. Waljan looked and tried to listen but he sipped his wine and thought of the beautiful woman in the kitchen garden.

"Arturius fought his tenth battle beside the river called Tryfrwyd," said Taliesan the bard, "alongside Arturius was Cai Hir his foster brother and was Garwlwyd."

The table was getting restless, they had eaten all they could and they were filled with mead and wine. The poem was leading them towards Arturius' final battle and they wanted the bard to reach it quickly.

"On the hill called Agned, Arturius gave battle his eleventh time," recounted the bard. "It was in the northerly Kingdom of Gododdim."

The bard had spoken for most of the evening and still his audience had sat and listened. They had laughed with him and cheered when they should, he had even noticed one or two of these hard and tough warriors wipe tears from beneath their eyes, thinking that no one would notice. He had spoken at many a feast, in the company of Kings and Bishops and he knew how to work his audience. He enjoyed toying with the story and changing a subtle line or emphasising a part more if he felt it would increase the tension. He was a master of his craft and he knew it. "And now," he said, "we will take a break, nature calls me and I am sure that some of you would welcome the chance to relieve yourselves."

They did want a break but most of them just wanted to hear of Arturius' final battle. Once they had all settled again, the Bard Taliesan began. He reminded them of Arturius' life and his previous fights and then moved to his final and most famous battle where he routed the Sais. He told of how many were slain by Arturius alone, how the traitor was killed by Arturius but in doing so, fatally wounded him. He did not finish with the body of Arturius being carried to the Isle of Avalon, accompanied by the sorceress Morganna. The last part of the tale paid homage to Arturius and drew lessons of how the people of Britain, when united under a great leader, would always defeat the pagan invader and how the victory at Mynydd Baddon had pushed the Sais invaders back and led to a long period of peace.

Cadrod knew now that he was the man to finish the work that Arturius had started. He knew that neither Saxon nor Angle could match his cavalry and he would drive the pagan from the land of the Britons. There would be an even greater ballad told of his, Cadrod's achievements in times to come and when he finally departed his life, he would sit at the right hand of the Almighty.

*****

In the morning, Bishop Cadog was accompanied by his two priests to the stables, there he met his groom by the side of his horse. The grey was standing squarely on all four legs and was eating from a nosebag, his ears were pricked forward and his eyes flickered this way and that with each noise around him. As the Bishop approached talking to his priests, his mount stopped eating and moved his head towards his master as far as the rope tether would allow and neighed in recognition.

"He is a different horse from the one led in here yesterday," said the Bishop patting his horse.

He looked down at the left fore foot which was wrapped in muslin tied at the top with a strip of cloth. The groom removed the poultice, picked the hoof up and showed the wound at the heel to the Bishop. It was a neatly cut hole into the sole of the hoof. The poultice had cleaned the horn and even the exposed flesh was pink and healthy. The Bishop leant forward supported by one of his priests and sniffed the wound. "There is no foul odour," he said and gave his horse another pat. Bishop Cadog looked at his groom and said, "Tell me, where is the boy who treated my horse?"

He noticed his groom's discomfort and delay in replying. "He is not here this morning, father," he replied.

"So the master shoeing smith is away and his slave also, how strange?"

The Bishop called over the new head groom of the stables and said to him, "Tell me, my man, where is the boy who treated my horse? I wish to speak to him."

Again, there was a delay and the head groom looked at the straw on the stable floor as he spoke, "He has been kicked, father."

"Well, you can take me to him at once," said the Bishop.

"I am not sure that I can find him," said the groom.

"And I," said the Bishop, "am not sure that I believe you."

The new head groom led the bishop down the passageway of the stables with the rows of horses either side eating their morning feed. Outside he stopped but clearly did not know where to go. The Bishop followed his eyes and saw them glance across the yard to the pile of muck and then just as quickly gaze in another direction. The Bishop looked carefully across to the muck heap and there he saw two soldiers urinating on a bundle of rags lying among the muck, he saw a foot sticking from the pile of straw. Bishop Cadog made his way over to the muck heap. He was accompanied by his two monks, on either side of him and the head groom close behind. The two soldiers shook themselves and tied the front of their trews, as they turned to pick up their spears, they saw the Bishop and each dropped to one knee.

"What is the meaning of this?" asked the Bishop pointing to the figure lying in the muck heap. He had noticed that the body was barely breathing.

"He's drunk, father," said one of the soldiers.

The Bishop turned to the groom and asked, "Is this the boy who treated my horse?"

"Yes, Father," he said.

"So after being kicked all this way by a horse from the stables, he then stayed here and became drunk?"

The groom hung his head and did not answer. The two soldiers began to quietly move away.

"Did I give you leave to go?" said the Bishop to them and they stood to attention.

The Bishop used his staff to lift Leofric's tunic. There was blue and purple banding down his back where each blow had landed. He had blood caked around his right ear which was partially washed away by the action of the soldiers.

"Have you ever seen a horse kick that has left a bruise like this?" he asked of the groom.

The groom found something important on the ground to look at and stayed quiet.

"You two," he said to the soldiers, "go and fetch a litter to carry him on, and hurry."

The two soldiers trotted away and soon returned with a wide plank. Leofric was lifted on by the two monks and the Bishop walked alongside as he was carried back into the castle and up the stone stairway to the Bishop's rooms. The soldiers were curtly dismissed and the two priests under the gaze of the Bishop began to wash and treat Leofric. He was still barely conscious but he could feel gentle hands washing him. His bruised and battered body was covered with a simple linen tunic and he was given wine diluted with water to drink. The Bishop's groom had been sent to find someone to treat his wounds and bruises. He went to the kitchens to seek help and was directed down the garden to the hovel at the end.

Aefre asked what the injuries were and then gathered fresh Liverwort to heal the wounds and stem any bleeding. She picked handfuls of Melissa balm which grew invasively amongst the other herbs, easily recognised by its square stems and white flowers. She boiled her cauldron and made a tea with the balm and poured it into a pottery jar. She made another infusion from the Liverwort and poured that into another pot. She told the head groom to take it to the victim and use it to wash his bruising with the first pot and his cuts with the second. The Bishop's groom reminded her that she was expected to come herself.

"First I must make some balm ointment," she said, "and then I will come. Make sure that the guards are expecting me."

As the man left, she picked all the Melissa balm that she could find. She tore bunches of the Melissa, shredding the leaves and stems and placed them in her mortar to crush them up into a paste. When she had used all, she could find, she put the contents into another pottery jar, washed her hands and set off to the castle. She was allowed into the Bishop's room by the guard and could see a figure laid on his side on a rug. She saw that one of the priests was washing his bruised legs with the balm infusion and the second was treating a large cut to the side of his head. With his fair hair, she recognised that it was her son and immediately knelt beside the figure.

"My poor Leofric," she said in her own language. "What animals could do this to you?"

The priests asked her what else they should do and she showed them the oily paste that they were to smear on the worst bruising. "Do you know this young man?" asked the Bishop from across the room.

"I do," said Aefre carefully, "I was enslaved with him."

"Will he live?" he asked.

Aefre rolled back Leofric's eyelid and looked at his blue eye. She prodded and felt his stomach and his sides under his ribs. She struggled to control her emotions that were demanding that she cry at the sight of her boy and rant at those who had done this. She prayed to her gods to heal Leo and to give her the opportunity for revenge. She had kept secret that he was her son for fear that it would bring more pain and suffering to both and would not change now.

"I believe he will live," she said. "But he will need rest and good food, I will make some more infusions for him."

It was the first time that Aefre had touched her son in five years and now she knew that she had to leave. She kissed two of her fingers and touched them to his forehead saying, "Become strong and live, they will come for us."

"What were those devil words?" said the Bishop. "Tell me what magic they meant?"

"They were neither words of the devil, as you say," said Aefre. "Nor were they magic. I was saying goodbye and telling him to get better."

Bishop Cadog the Wise believed her and told her to bring more tea the next day. She nodded, picked up her jars and left.

Leofric was dreaming that he was still ten years old and by the Lark with his mother and father, playing with his brother Osgar. As he awoke, he could feel his body ache and feel the pain in his head. He remembered the beating that he had been given and laying in the dunghill, and that he wanted to die and then he finally knew that no one would come for him. The fyrd was not coming and his life would continue to be one of pain and humiliation until they finally killed him as they had Milly and Stan. He knew that if he died now, he would not be taken by the Valkerie to Valhalla. He had been deserted by his people and by his gods. Through the pain and despair, he could hear voices. They were male voices and they were Waelisc but they were not shouting or violent. They were calm and he heard one voice asking that their God make him better and save him. The voice reassured him and he felt his body being covered by a paste that soothed the pain. He tried to open his eyes but only his left would open. Leofric could just make out the Bishop who had come to the castle with the lame horse.

The Bishop asked him, "Do you want to be saved?"

"I do," muttered Leofric.

"Will you renounce your gods and be saved by Jesus?"

Leofric did not know what this man was talking about but he had given up on his gods and so said, "Yes."

During the next three days, Leofric became stronger and he drank that tea that was brought to him twice a day, though he never saw who brought it. The balm ointment was rubbed into his bruised skin and he felt in penetrate through his muscles. He was expected to kneel with his hands together and pray with the two priests and the Bishop; his knees did not hurt so he found this easy. He ate good food, drank dilute wine and believed that the heaven that the Bishop spoke of was here on earth and he was already in it. On the fourth day, the Bishop told Leofric that he was well enough to travel and that they would leave to go west that day. He told him that he had talked to the King and he was now his slave and would be a groom to his horses. Aefre saw him leave with the Bishop's entourage and she was pleased to see him well but did not know where he was going. More than ever, she felt alone.

Chapter 10
Thegn Selwyn

Osgar stood beside the giant master blacksmith Hunfrith. They were behind the first anvil in the forge and one of the apprentice boys was stationed by the bellows two paces to Frith's left. Behind them was another anvil and fire in which the charcoal glowed, all three smiths were quiet and looked at the three men standing in the doorway. In the centre was the Thegn Selwyn and on either side of him stood a ceorl with shield and spear. Selwyn smiled and stepped over the threshold and his two guards followed one by one and again flanked their thegn. Neither of them showed any emotion, they stared at the huge blacksmith and his two apprentices. Frith leant on his hammer handle that was vertical with the hammerhead resting on the anvil.

"Do come into my humble forge," he said to Selwyn and then he turned to the boy behind him and said, "Boy, where are your manners, fetch ale for our visitors."

Osgar stood still and felt his pulse quicken, he was surprised at Frith's cool and polite invitation and did not understand his instruction to the boy to fetch ale. Frith was renowned for his ale drinking but it was a strict rule that there was no ale in the forge.

Selwyn stared into the gloomy workplace, he had stepped in from the bright outside sunlight and his eyes needed time to adjust. He was attired in his fine cloths but was without any weapons, his men were dressed as if called to the fyrd. They wore their trousers to below the knee where they were joined by their woollen socks banded in a crisscross pattern. They both wore leather jerkins, a chain mail hauberk cowl and simple helmets. Their spears almost scrapped on the low beams of the forge and they held their shields on their left arms. Behind them, the door closed and they heard the locking beam drop into place on the outside. The apprentice boy had done his job and now the three men felt uncomfortable. In through the door behind Frith and Osgar came the two blacksmith assistants and then the apprentice who had followed his master's coded instructions. With the shutting of the door the forge had darkened some more. The two armed men felt very different now from when they had marched down the street to the wharves, then people had jumped out of their way. They were from the North Folk and liked to show these Suth Folk their superiority. Their Thegn was known throughout East Anglia for his wealth, he traded along the coast of this land and with the Old Country across the sea.

"What do you want?" said Frith.

"I want what is rightfully mine," said thegn Selwyn. "I demand that I am paid wergild for the loss of my sword. I will take the boy as a slave until it is paid."

"You heard the judgement of the Ealdorman," answered Frith, still with a calm voice.

"He had made a judgement in my favour until that young pup Wuffa interfered. The boy comes with me."

"If you leave now, I will do no more," said Frith, looking directly in his eyes.

"Take the boy," Selwyn ordered his men.

They stepped forward and lowered their spears; one caught on a beam and was pulled back and only then tipped down. Osgar picked up his seax and Frith a shovel while one of his assistants held a hand hammer and the older a sledge. All four, along with the apprentice boy backed off. The guards moved cautiously forward, they had to part to go around the first anvil. As they did Frith swept his shovel into the pile of glowing charcoal and continued the arch scattering burning coals and ashes onto the closest guard. He dropped his spear and tried to shake and brush off the hundreds of sparks that burned his arms and face. Frith let the shovel slip from his hand, stepped forward and hit the man squarely on the jaw. His punch landed with a crack and the soldier's legs gave way under him. Frith picked up his shovel, filled it with more hot coals and said to the remaining ceorl, "You next?" The man retreated stumbling over tools on the floor back to Selwyn.

"Tell him to drop his shield and spear," Frith said looking at the thegn.

Selwyn nodded and his ceorl placed both shield and spear on the dirt floor. Frith turned to one of his men and said, "Put him out," looking at the still writhing guard and pail of water was thrown over him.

Frith stared at Thegn Selwyn and said to him, "I will not tell the Ealdorman that you have tried to break his ruling but I will keep your spears and shields.

You may return in one year to collect them. You should know better than to cause trouble in a forge, you anger Thunor."

The door behind the men opened, as the standing ceorl helped his colleague to his feet. It was pulled back by a smiling apprentice boy who had just had the best fun in his life. Selwyn turned and was followed by his two unarmed men. As they walked out there was a shout from one of the fishing boats tied at the wharf only twenty paces away. "Look, it's Selwyn the Swordless."

"Selwyn the Swordless." Laughed another and slapped his thigh.

The three made their way along the wharf and then up the incline towards the town. Their heads were low, avoiding any eye contact and jeers and jokes followed them all the way. Although it was only mid-afternoon, Frith said that there would be no more work for the day. They sat in the area behind the forge near to Frith's house. His wife, Rowena, brought stew and smoked herring and fresh bread. The two youngest boys went to fetch ale as was always their job.

"Selwyn the Swordless," said one of Frith's assistants for the tenth time and laughed. "He will have that name here in Gippeswic for as long as he lives."

"And what name for his men?" asked Frith's second journeyman blacksmith.

"I think that they are the unarmed fyrd," he said laughing.

Osgar smiled but did not laugh. Frith looked at him and said, "You would have used your seax?"

"I would," he said. "My mother and brother were taken and there will be no more slaves in my family."

"I only met your mother once," said Frith. "She is my second cousin. I think she is the most beautiful women I have ever seen, she looked like a queen. She will be safe and if your brother Leo is anything like you then he also will survive."

Frith changed the subject. "We will finish our work on the sword tomorrow and then it will be passed to the handle maker and jeweller, the pommel alone will be covered in an ounce of gold. Only King Wehha will have a more jewelled sword, but no amount of jewels kills your enemy and I believe that we have made the finest blade in all Anglia."

"You have learned the craft of the sword maker well," Frith continued, "You need to return to Beodricesworth and Anson quickly, it is not safe for you here. Three times, thegn Selwyn has been made to look foolish; he will not forget and will want his revenge. You may take the rest of the sword making iron. It is not enough for a full blade but I am sure that you will put it to good use."

128

"Master," said Osgar, "I can take no payment. I am an apprentice and you have sheltered me, fed me and you have given me skills that few others possess. I cannot take the iron."

"You are not my apprentice, and calling me Master is beginning to irritate me," Frith answered. "You are my cousin Anson's boy and have worked diligently these past six weeks. You use a hammer better than either of my journeymen. The two apprentice boys look up to you; they now know what they can achieve in five years. Take the iron as a gift from one second cousin to another."

Chapter 11
Theod-Ford

The final two years of Osgar's apprenticeship had passed quickly. When he returned from learning sword making in Gippeswic, he was treated as if he was already a journeyman blacksmith. Anson's forge had continued to flourish and there was ironwork waiting for him. The new boy was working the bellows and striking when required. He struck with the sledgehammer for Osgar, making seaxs, shield bosses and the occasional helmet. Anson continued to make hinges, hasps and bolts for the town.

Osgar was fully grown. He was an average height for an Angle but he was wide shouldered and his arms and legs were as solid as the iron he worked. He kept his beard closely cut with shears that he had made himself. His seax was always with him and also had a dagger tucked into his belt, that he had handmade it in the pattern welding method. This was unnecessary for such a small blade but he had wanted to practice the techniques learned in Gippeswic.

The apprentice boy had questioned him constantly, on his return two years previously, about all he had seen. The boy had never seen wharves and ships and had dreamed of going to the town of Gippeswic. Osgar had never been one for small talk and was only willing to tell the boy of Hunfrith's forge and the sword making. He did this because he knew that by describing it from start to finish, he would retain it in his memory. The boy had wanted to use the iron that Osgar had brought back to make a sword. Osgar explained that it was insufficient to create a full-sized sword so the iron bars had lain together in the corner of the forge. Although the bars sat on wood to keep them off the damp floor, they gradually turned brown with a fine layer of rust over their surface.

The day came when Osgar was to be released from his apprenticeship and become a free man. Hild clucked around like an old hen making sure that his hair was brushed and his beard trimmed. She had made him a new tunic and trousers which he changed into. He walked up the hill from the craftsmen's street with Anson and Wilfrid the carpenter. They walked together talking while alongside Osgar was Wilf's eldest boy Seward who was also being made free that day. Seward was nervous and chatted incessantly. He did not believe that Osgar was not worried about standing in the Great Hall in front of Thegn Tedmund and reciting his oath. "I know that I will forget the words and look stupid," he said to Osgar.

"Look," said Osgar, "What is the worst that can happen? You get a couple of words wrong and they correct you. You are not the first to do this, for Woden's sake. Now act like a man."

"Thank you for those few reassuring words," said Seward, "you are a real pal."

"Well, think of the butter-maid who stops to talk to you each day," replied Osgar. "She has been waiting for you to be free for two years."

"And you think of my sister Lynne," retorted Seward, "She won't wait forever, you know."

They reached the Great Hall and Osgar was reminded of how much grander was the one in Gippeswic and how much more difficult it had been to stand before the Ealdorman worrying whether he would be placed into slavery. There was a large crowd of well-wishers outside who included Hild and Lynne. Hild had her hair plaited and tied over her head in a bun. Osgar could see the look on her face that meant she would rush forward at anytime to cuddle him. He looked sternly at her to dissuade her from such an embarrassing course. He could hear her say to Wilfrid's daughter Lynne that he could be such a serious boy at times. Lynne was fifteen years old; she wore a fawn coloured peplo dress pinned with a brooch at each shoulder. The dress reached her calves and she wore leather boots with a pattern of holes cut into the supper surface. Her hair was blond and long with a narrow plait hanging down from each side of her fringe. Her eyes sparkled as she watched Osgar and not her brother.

At the entrance, Osgar could see the giant figure of Hunfrith who was talking to Henryk, the Flemish headman. Henryk nodded seriously to Osgar but Frith put his thumb up and winked. Osgar looked for Cynbeald and finally could see him leaning on his ash staff. He had never looked young to Osgar but now he seemed to be very aged. He had told Osgar of all the halls and hams that had employed him to tell the tale of the battle of the Three Bridges. He said to Osgar that it now took a whole evening to recount the tale, and that according to his version, Osgar had almost wiped out every Briton to set foot in East Anglia.

"Give me a chance," was all that Osgar had said.

"I have dined on that evening by the Lark these past years," said Cynbeald, "and I want to be around to tell of more heroic acts. After the ceremony, we shall sip some ale and you can tell me of your time in Gippeswic."

Seward stood beside Osgar in front of Thegn Tedmund who was standing out of his high seat. The freemen and thegns of Beodricesworth and the surrounding hams were packed into the hall, standing and looking at the young men's backs. Seward shook and his voice was quiet as he said his oath. His father had agreed to release him from his apprenticeship and had told the whole gathering of his devotion to his craft and his honesty in his dealings with all men. They both bowed in unison to the thegn and the craft elders either side of him. Wilfrid put a hand on his son's shoulder to turn him and they returned to their places.

"Will Osgar of the Icke family, late of Icklingham step forward to make his declaration," called the Reeve after banging his staff on the wooden floor. Osgar took five paces forward and stood in front of the Thegn. "Will his master, Anson the Broad of Beodricesworth join him," said the Reeve and Anson stepped forward.

"Do you release him from his apprenticeship?" inquired the Reeve.

"I do," said Anson loudly so that all could hear.

"Has this man been diligent in his work," asked Thegn Tedmund, staring down at Osgar.

"He has."

"Has he been honest and fair in his dealings with you and other tradesmen?"

"He has."

"Step forward Osgar of the Icke family," said the Reeve, "and make your declaration in full."

Osgar had memorised his words and practiced them with Cynbeald. Cynbeald told him to stand with his shoulders back and speak slowly and loudly so that even those by the door could hear. "I Osgar of the Icke family, late of their ham by the Lark, do swear before my fellow craftsmen to be good and true to my King and my thegn. To come whenever summoned unless I have just cause to be absent. I shall do no harm to my fellow craftsmen and shall be honest and true to the people of Beodricesworth."

The thegn spoke directly to Osgar, "You are now a Freeman. You may trade as a blacksmith in all the lands of the Angles. You may carry a sword and you may marry a woman of your choice. When the fyrd is called you must attend your thegn with shield and spear or your will pay wergild the value of your goods or where they are insufficient you will forfeit your freedom."

Anson and Osgar bowed in unison to the thegn and returned to their places as the last two were called forward. Osgar could see at the far end of the hall the door slightly ajar and there at the threshold stood Hild and Lynne. Hild kissed her hand, waved it to Osgar and she said something to Lynne who did the same.

When the last, a leatherworker, was released from his apprenticeship and made a freeman ceorl they all filed out. The benches at the nearby tavern were crowded but they found space for all. Henryk the Flem sat beside Osgar with Cynbeald opposite and Hunfrith on the next bench with Anson, Hild and Lynne. Her brother, Seward sat next to her and her father Wilf, stood. Pitchers of ale were brought, their contents drunk from pottery vessels and bread was broken and passed around.

While the others talked, Osgar thought of his future. He had always only ever thought about rescuing his brother and mother and avenging his father, who he still believed he had let down. He kept looking at Lynne, sitting next to his mate Seward. He now realised just how pretty she was but also how she laughed and joked even when she was telling off her brother or father for a rude story. She gave a wry smile and a feigned frown of displeasure. She never complained about the work around the house, helping Hild, nor caring for the goats, milking and herding them. This was the first time that he had imagined her as his wife. He suddenly realised that she was a total distraction to his purpose in life and chided himself for being disloyal to his family.

Henryk saw Osgar deep in thought and asked him what his plans were now that he was a freeman. He told the Flem that he wished to make war upon the Waelisc by any means and if that meant that he had to leave East Anglia and join the Saxons in the south then so be it.

"You need not look for war," Henryk said to Osgar. "It is coming but you need to be amongst those you can trust. See Wuffa and talk to him, he is an aethling now and is his uncle's right-hand man. In the meantime, come to our settlement. You know the Lark Valley and I have work for you. We do not have a forge in our ham but we need one who can smite the black. I have enough silver for a sword and I want one now. We have eighteen men of fighting age, if I am to lead them, then I should carry a sword."

"Sword iron is hard to come by," said Osgar.

"But you have some," said Henryk, "in your forge."

"That is not enough for a broad sword and it is for me anyway."

"There is a new type of sword," said Henryk. "I saw one when I went to Wensum."

Henryk described the style of sword that he had seen. He told how the Franks across the water were making a different design of sword which was pattern welded as before but drawn to a tapering point. It took even more skill to ensure that the overlapping pattern remained consistent along the length so that there were no flaws to the structure. The sword was lighter and required less iron, by a quarter and the tapering style still allowed for over the shoulder swings but was better for stabbing and thrusting between shields. Because of its finer point, it would more easily penetrate a chain mail hauberk and especially thick leather armour.

"Someone with your strength does not need the weight at the end of a sword to cut through a limb," said the Flem, "I know what you can do with a seax which is still only half the weight of this new sword."

"I will talk to Anson about building a bloomery furnace and you see if you can buy some good iron," said Osgar.

"I will see if I can get some at the Moot," replied Henryk.

Both Anson and Wilf stopped talking and Anson said with surprise, "Has a moot been called?"

"Ja," said the Flem, "thought you knew. It's at Theod-ford. Every thegn has been summoned, with so many attending there will be good trade."

"Why has it been called," asked Wilf.

Osgar immediately said, "To raise the fyrd and attack the Waelisc."

"No," said Anson, "If King Wehha was going to do that, he would not call a moot."

Osgar sat and looked at the ground. After a short while, he placed his unfinished ale on the bench, stood and left. The men raised their eyebrows at each other and Lynne rose and followed Osgar walking quickly to catch up.

"I'll walk with you," said Lynne.

"I'm not going anywhere," he said, "I have work in the forge."

"Today?" said Lynne, "I'll come and help."

Osgar said, "No," and increased his pace. She gave up when he would not answer her and returned to her father and brother drinking with the others. By the time she sat down beside her father Wilf, the ringing of an anvil could be heard in the distance.

"That young girl would make any man go and hammer his anvil," Anson whispered to Henryk so that Wilf did not hear.

"What's that?" said Wilf.

"I was saying that at least he didn't call us all cowards this time."

Wilf laughed and nodded and the party returned to their celebrations and speculating about the moot.

The moot was called for Lughnassadh, the feast of bread, when the harvest was in. Every ham in East Anglia was busy with reaping and gathering in the harvest. When it was safely stored, the thegns and their entourages made their way to the town where the Thet and the Little Ouse rivers were forded. It was in the centre of East Anglia where the lands of the North Folk met those of the Suth Folk. They travelled south from the northern coast and Wensum, westwards from Gippeswic along to Gipping Valley and north from the hams along the Lark. As they came closer to Theod-ford, they gained in number. Thegns walked only carrying their swords and their freemen ceorls carried shield and spear. Many thegns had slaves to attend them and pull their handcarts. Traders loaded their handcarts with goods and food for the three-day feast. Many were accompanied by women and children who would not be allowed to take part in the moot. Goats that had been fattened during Spring and Summer were herded along the pathways. Ducks, fowl and hares hung from the carts or from staves between two people walking.

The traders, thegns and ceorls of the Angles camped within a thousand pace diameter of the old iron-age fort guarding the Thet and the Little Ouse. The mound behind the earthworks had been occupied in advance for Wehha and his closest thegns and family. The next best areas were taken by the Ealdorman of Gippeswic and Thegn Selwyn. Other important thegns, such as Tedmund, were close to the centre their position between the river and the mound surrounded by lesser local thegns and freemen. Osgar and Anson along with Wilf and others from Beodricesworth stayed close to Tedmund, their own thegn. Everyone spent much of the time milling about, meeting old acquaintances, settling debts and making new deals. After the first day of feasting, the Moot was assembled. King

Wehha sat on the highest point of the mound and his closest advisors and family, which included Wuffa, were nearby.

On the morning of the second day, the Moot began. All were asked to welcome the King and show their loyalty. The crowd of men thrust their spears skywards and chanted their Kings name. When the cheering finally died down Wehha spoke. He thanked them for coming, without mentioning the wergild fines if they had not. He told them that that his dream had been the union of the Angle people and how much stronger they were now that the North and Suth Folk were under one rule. He finished his welcoming address and then invited all and any of them to speak. There were some who raised petty boundary issues and squabbles over trade agreements. They were told that the moot was for more serious discussions of interest to all attending. Eventually, the subject moved to the topic which concerned most. The Waelisc attacks had cost almost every family of the Suth Folk; many reported that their trade was down and some said that they were considering taking their family back to the Old Country or for a new start in the land of the Franks.

Wuffa stood and bowed to his uncle the King and then spoke of the suffering of the people in the forward areas. He recounted the cruelty of the Waelisc and pronounced that the only cure for their ills was to take the fight to the enemy. At this, Osgar leapt to his feet and cheered Wuffa and he was not alone. The Angles looked to bravery in their leaders as their leaders in return wanted loyalty. Wehha sat in the high-backed oak chair with his left elbow resting on the arm and his hand on his bearded chin. He looked at Thegn Selwyn who rose and bowed to his King.

"My lord and king," he said without any irony, "you have shown great wisdom in not leading us into a costly and futile war. We are growing richer by trade as each day passes. I am sure that we can resolve our differences with the Waelisc so that we both accept our boundaries and in the fullness of time we will live together and eventually trade in peace."

There was clapping and cheering but equally shouts from the crowd and booing. The Thegn Tedmund looked around and saw that no one was willing to stand and speak so he rose.

"My lord king," he began and then bowed, "it is all very well to talk of trade when you are already the richest trader in East Anglia." He looked at Selwyn. "It is fine to talk of peace when you live behind the rivers Thet and Little Ouse, and no Waelisc war-band ever raided this far north. My King, you must know that the people of the Lark Valley do not think of trade or peace, they pray to the gods to stay alive. Each month brings more death and more of our people taken as slaves. The lands to the south of the Lark are empty of our people. Only a lifetime ago we had hams-a-day's walk from the Lark, Anglia is being beaten back."

One thegn after another stood to support either Selwyn or Tedmund. Wuffa had made it clear to all that he favoured war and the Ealdorman of Gippeswic as usual was uncommitted and tried to please everyone. There was a clear split in the people, between those who would attack and those who would defend what they had. Wehha listened intently to what was said and only intervened in the discussion when personal insults were thrown or a thegn wandered off the subject. Eventually, Wehha said that he had heard enough and, in the morning, he would announce his decision. He invited all attending to drink, eat and enjoy the games.

Wehha, King of the Angles, beckoned Thegns Tedmund and Wuffa closer. "We are one people," he said, "and I expect you both to show that you believe it with every word and every act. I shall be sending both of you, Wuffa and Selwyn, each with ten picked men to assess the raids and report to me on how we stop them."

Selwyn said, "*Sire*, this is a busy time for me. Harvest is only just in and there are the final shipments of goods by sea before winter closes trade down."

Wuffa said immediately, "I will go wherever my King sends me and the closer it takes me to the Waelisc the better."

"Of course my priority is to my King," Selwyn rapidly added, "but why not wait until spring?"

"I would not want the name 'Selwyn the Swordless', to gain ground or even change to something worse," said Wehha. "You will do as I say."

"On the subject of swords," said Selwyn, "justice still has not been done to me. My sword was broken by an apprentice and the Ealdorman of Gippeswic had found in my favour until your nephew Wuffa intervened. I demand that the original wergild is re-imposed."

"The wergild was not imposed because you had misled the ealdorman of the facts and even the value of your sword," said Wuffa. "The apprentice Osgar broke your sword because it was at the throat of his master."

The King held up his hand. "Stop this bickering, I have heard enough. Tomorrow at the Moot I will declare upon it."

They all walked towards the river and dispersed into the crowd. There were games of all types being played. On a flat area of land, one ham played another at the running game. The object was to get the rags, bound in leather, to the other end by any means. There was weightlifting where big strong men lined up to lift increasingly larger rocks. Swimming races were held across the Thet. On a signal from the near bank, men raced down the muddy bank on the other side, waded through the weeds and swam towards the crowd. There were no rules, punches were thrown and the swimmers hauled back just as they reached the near bank, finally one emerged and made it to the red flag tied to a spear. On all events, wagers were made and there was good-natured cheering and booing by the spectators.

Wuffa watched all the sports where his men competed. He cheered them along and slapped them on the backs when they were done. All the while that he watched he was choosing his ten men. He saw the giant Hunfrith throw a man to the ground, put his foot on his chest and raise his arms above his head. He looked on as Anson the Broad lead a team from Beodricesworth in the 'tug-of-war' and he watched Osgar in the running game. Strength was certainly needed in the shield wall and Osgar offered something more. Wuffa watched him stoop and collect the bound rags and run, he did not run with his head down but looked left and right to see where everyone was. He only ducked his head when he ran into a defender. A man older and stronger was hit so hard that there was a thud heard from fifty paces. He was bowled over and Osgar ran through to the line. Speed, power and determination, is just what I need, thought Wuffa. When he came off the pitch, Osgar was congratulated by the aethling. He waited while he washed his face and arms and then belted his scabbard to his back. Lynne passed him his seax which she had been holding for him.

"I have been meaning to give you this," said Wuffa as he removed a copper armband from his right arm and passed it to Osgar.

"Why?" said Osgar, and then added, "I am grateful but how have I earned it?"

"You have fought the Waelisc and won and when you did that you fought for the people, my uncle, the King and me. Take it."

Osgar slipped the armband up his left arm. It was a tight fit across his muscles and stayed there. "I want you to come with me to the frontier areas across the Great Heath," said Wuffa.

Osgar beamed at Wuffa and thanked him. It seemed to him the best thing that had ever happened. He had felt that he had marked time for seven long years waiting for this chance to come. It was an opportunity to go to Waelisc territory and a possibility to take the fight to them.

At the Moot the next day, the King stood and announced to all, "I have thought long and hard about the problems of our people and the attacks by the Waelisc. Before I tell you of my decision, I can tell you of new titles. The Thegn of Beodricesworth, Tedmund, will from this day forth carry the title of Ealdorman of Beodricesworth and the Lark. Thegn Selwyn will become Ealdorman of the North Folk and my nephew Wuffa, from this day, is my Kings Thegn. I call for you all to recognise them and show your approval in the traditional way."

The crowd thrust their spears and swords skywards and cheered. King Wehha waited for the crowd to quieten, before he continued, "I have decided to send both the Ealdorman Selwyn and the Kings Thegn, Wuffa to assess the raids along our frontier. I expect them to report to me by the next moon. They have each selected their men."

He turned to Selwyn and Wuffa and said, "Call your men forward."

Selwyn's ten men climbed the mound and stood behind him. Osgar, Anson and Henryk came forward along with Wilf and Seward to stand behind Wuffa and they were joined by five more from the Gipping Valley.

"I have an objection," said Selwyn for all to hear. He pointed at Osgar and said, "He has damaged my property and paid no wergild. I claim him as a slave as was the first ruling of the Ealdorman."

Osgar's head sunk as he thought of being placed into slavery and never being able to fight the Waelisc and avenge his father, mother and brother. He felt for the small hammer pommel on his seax and prayed to Thunor. He would never be able to fight his way out with such a large crowd but considered it might be better to die than fall into the hands of Selwyn. Anson saw Osgar's hand on his seax and gripped his wrist tightly. Henryk mover closer to them both, knowing that the young blacksmith could easily be driven to hasty action.

Wehha was not happy that Selwyn had deliberately caused division. He spoke firmly, looking directly at Selwyn, "My decision on this is that he is no longer an apprentice but a freeman ceorl and he cannot therefore, by our laws be placed into slavery. However, he should never have broken the sword of a thegn and must pay wergild."

Osgar was relieved that he would not be a slave but he knew that a tough wergild that could not be paid by a poor ceorl, amounted to the same.

"Osgar," said the King, looking at him, "you will be made a ward until such a time as you have paid the wergild to Selwyn, Ealdorman of the North Folk."

Selwyn nodded and smiled and Osgar's head sunk lower.

"You are now a ward," said Wehha, "of Wuffa, Kings Thegn."

Selwyn at first looked bewildered and then annoyed, he began to speak but Wehha held up his hand and said, "The decision is made, let me see your chosen men."

Wehha stepped forward to speak to the two lines of men. "Objection," said Selwyn so that all could hear. King Wehha looked at Selwyn and raised his eyebrows.

"This man," said Selwyn pointing at Osgar, "has no shield and spear. He is not fit by our laws to stand by a thegn in battle."

Tedmund of Beodricesworth stepped forward and said, "I will give him a shield and spear as a brave son of Beo."

"That's no good," said Selwyn, "Our laws clearly say that a ceorl must buy his own arms and therefore he cannot go."

Osgar looked around in despair as Selwyn had again prevented him from doing the one thing, he had desired for seven years. He looked to Anson for help and could see that he had no idea how to get him what he wanted. He looked at Wuffa hoping that he would intervene again but he just stared at Osgar's right arm. He tried to catch his eye but the Kings Thegn continued to look at his upper arm. Suddenly, he realised what Wuffa was looking at. He pulled the copper armband from his left arm and held it out for the King to see. "I can buy my shield and spear with this," he said.

"He won it in battle, at thirteen years of age," said Wuffa. "He has obeyed our laws and will stand beside me by right."

The next day the Moot closed and the twenty men set off down the Icknield Way following the old Roman road. Wehha had again talked to both Wuffa and Selwyn to tell them they had to work together as an example to all the Angles of the North and Suth. To Wuffa, he said privately that he was now acting to preserve the United Anglia.

Chapter 12
The Great Heath

The twenty men walked almost due south until they crossed the Lark at Icklingham. They stopped for a rest and the villagers fed them with stew and summer fruits of berries and fresh bread. None recognised Osgar and he did not make himself known. Osgar walked to the cemetery where once his family house had stood before it had been burned down. The mound that marked his father's grave had sunk somewhat but was still distinctive and was covered by wildflowers and grass kept short by the sheep that grazed there. He sat for some time on his own and talked to his father. He told his father of what had happened during the five years since he had last sat by the grave and spoken to him. Osgar renewed his promise to avenge his father and rescue his mother and brother.

The band of twenty-two forded the Lark at the Three Bridges. None of the bridges now stood, they had all been removed and the only way to cross was by wading through the river. The pathway became less marked than before through lack of use, grass and plants grew on it to waist height. It was dry and sandy as they headed towards a ham known to Osgar in his childhood. There was nothing but burned or collapsed houses with a few wicker fences remaining and there was no sign of life. It had been destroyed long before the Icklingham attack and had never been resettled.

They rejoined the old Roman road as the Great Heath widened, to their left was the forest and to their right the Fens. The route curved to the southwest and by evening they headed into the setting sun. They camped on the fenland side of the Great Heath, where the chalk ridge dropped quickly to the edge of the marshland. They slept the night by another deserted ham, posting two lookouts. The next morning Osgar and Seward rose early and went duck egg collecting. They collected over forty eggs by the time that the others had risen and all breakfasted on them.

Osgar and Seward had told of the people that they could see in the fens. They were paddling round coracles made of flexed willow and animal hide. These were the Gwyre, the Celtic people of the fens, who traded with the Angles but kept to themselves. They traded eels, fish and duck and lived in houses on the few clay mounds that emerged from the waters. They spoke a foreign tongue but some could speak with the Angles.

Wuffa suggested to Selwyn that they try to make contact with them and for once, he agreed. Very cautiously with much shouting and beckoning from the Angles, the Gwyre approached. At first, they stayed in the coracles twenty-five paces away from dry land. There were three coracles each with two men in and they had been collecting from eel traps. One of the six men could speak some English and was reassured of the Angles peaceful intentions. He stepped from the coracle helped by Wuffa. Although difficult to understand, he told them that there were no longer any Angles in this area as they had all been killed or driven away by the Britons. They missed the Angles as they had dealt with them and said how difficult it was to get cloth and pottery. The Gwyre shared some smoked eel with the Angles and finally left to continue their trapping.

Wuffa and Selwyn discussed their next move and they all headed due east across the heath towards the forested ridge in the distance. They were all wary of being caught in the open ground without cover and looked all around as they walked. Each one of them knew that they were on the border of the Kingdom of Calchfynedd and if caught exposed by cavalry they would have little chance. By noon, they were on the edge of the woodland and felt safer, and so they stopped to rest, drink from a stream and eat the remains of the smoked eel.

After their rest, they headed northeast along the forest edge where the wide chalk lands became clay. They ventured into various pathways into the forest. These were often less than two paces wide and the branches of the trees hung down to head height. They found the occasional woodsmen at the end of these pathways with houses hidden deep into the forest. At the end of one pathway, they spoke with the Angle family who told them of how most of the hams had gone but a few people deep in the woods could live by hunting deer and boar and producing charcoal. They told them that they kept an eye out for any Waelisc but their raiding parties kept to the heath as horses could not be ridden through the low overhanging branches. They never ventured onto the heath as it was unsafe. The band camped in the forest for the night and though the woodmen could offer little more than berries, crab apples and mushrooms for food, they had mead made from forest honey that they shared.

"What I would do for some decent meat," said Selwyn. "I have had enough of fish, berries and mushrooms. Surely, there must be venison of some sort that we can hunt?"

The woodman ignored his lack of manners in deriding their humble offerings and told Selwyn that there were plenty of deer and boar in the forest. Wuffa was suddenly attentive to the conversation.

"Boar, you say," said Wuffa. "Have you hunted boar Selwyn? Now that is a sport for Kings."

Selwyn did not seem keen and said, "I have of course been boar hunting. Who hasn't? It's not all that it is made out to be."

He had tried to make out that he was an experienced hunter but disinterested. Wuffa guessed that Selwyn was not keen and had some fun in telling him that he was eager to hunt with someone so experienced. Selwyn finally agreed that they had enough men to hunt boar and they would do so the next day. They spoke to the woodman who advised them where to find the boar runs and where the boars would feed themselves during the day. Osgar would accompany Wuffa and Selwyn would have his right-hand man beside him. They would position themselves at the end of some runs and the others would beat the boars towards them. Selwyn described in great detail how the boars would use their runs to escape and that there would be only one chance to kill one. He reminded them all of the dangers of the beasts and that their tusks alone could open up a man and they would savage anyone in their way. Osgar thought that Selwyn must have hunted boar many times as he spoke with such authority.

The next day Selwyn and Wuffa, with their right-hand, men were positioned only thirty paces apart but they could not see or hear each other. They were both in dense undergrowth that had tunnels made by the boars trampling through it. They crouched down facing up the tunnels towards the beaters. In the distance, the beaters could be heard rattling trees with sticks, shouting and clapping. Both Wuffa and Osgar had their spears but not their shields. It would be Wuffa who would make the kill if a boar ran their way. Osgar's job was to protect his master.

"You ready, Osgar?" Wuffa asked Osgar.

"Yes, *sire*," replied Osgar.

"Shall we drop the formalities, my name's Wuffa."

143

"All right," said Osgar, "I will. I've never been boar hunting before. Killing pigs doesn't seem that exciting."

"You just hold that spear ready, if we get lucky, you'll see the difference between a boar and a pig."

When the boar came, its speed shocked Osgar but Wuffa thrust his spear down and forward. It dug into the boar above his dropped head near the spine at the shoulder. The force of the charge knocked Wuffa back but he held his ground as the boar squealed and pushed toward him and swung his head to each side with his tusks bared. Wuffa was shoved back onto his seat and the boar made a grab for his leg. Osgar thrust his spear deep into the boar's mouth and pushed back with all his might. The spear was forced further down into the boar's throat and still he fought but he could no longer push them back and he gave one last struggle and died. Wuffa and Osgar looked at each other and laughed, their hearts pounding with excitement. Then they heard the squealing as another boar ran down a tunnel. Wuffa pulled his spear free and Osgar pulled his seax from behind his back, they both crouched ready and then realised that it was not in their tunnel but the next one where Selwyn waited. They heard a thud and a terrible screaming and finally Selwyn calling for help.

Although they were close, it took Wuffa and Osgar time to force their way through the undergrowth. When they reached where Selwyn and his right-hand man had been, they saw Selwyn trying to climb a small tree with a boar at his foot and his man sprawled on the ground clutching his entrails that hung from his stomach. The boar turned to face Wuffa and Osgar and this time Wuffa stuck his spear straight into its chest and Osgar severed the spine behind the head with one blow from his seax. As the beast rolled over to die, they both looked up at Selwyn clinging to the ash sapling.

"What in Hel's name happened here?" demanded Wuffa.

Selwyn climbed down the tree and stumbled to the ground in an ungainly fashion. He pointed to his aide and said, "He let me down."

"Well, he's paid the full wergild for that," said Wuffa in utter distain for Selwyn.

Osgar was already kneeling by Selwyn's man but could see that his wounds were fatal. He rolled his cloak up and put it behind his head and went to find the beaters to make a litter to carry him back to the ham. They attended the injured man but it was obvious that he would not last long with his stomach and chest ripped open up by the boar's tusks. The boars were butchered and meat given to the woodmen.

The charcoal makers built a huge roasting pit for the boar that evening, but few had an appetite with Selwyn's man moaning in pain from a house nearby. One of the village women tried to dull the pain with herbs and strong mead and in the morning, he was dead. None who was there asked why Selwyn escaped with only a minor injury or how it was that his assistant took the full attack of the boar. Selwyn thanked neither Osgar nor Wuffa for saving him and separated himself from them. He had some bruising and a cut to one heel where the boar had jumped up and grabbed him and he walked with a limp for a week. Wuffa had offered Selwyn a tusk to prolong his discomfort but he refused it as if he was turning down another cup of mead. Wuffa gave one tusk to Osgar, two to the woodmen and kept one for himself.

Osgar resented that they had turned away from Waelisc territory and said to Wuffa, "What is the point of this? We have walked by the fens when we know the Waelisc cannot move through wetlands and now we have walked in and out of the forest we can see that a man finds it difficult to move very quickly. Someone on horseback cannot go fifty paces into the forest, we know that the Waelisc always raid through the Great Heath and attack settlements along the edges."

"Have patience, young Thunor," said Wuffa knowing that calling Osgar this annoyed him, "I have not travelled these parts and I had to see for myself the lands natural defences."

"Maybe we should flood the heath," said Osgar, "or grow the forest across it."

"I'll put your ideas to my uncle," said Wuffa, "I'm sure that he'll be impressed."

They were nearer to the border of East Anglia but still on the heath. Wuffa talked to Selwyn and he stayed with his nine men while Wuffa took his ten on the steep climb from the heath up to the wood covered clay ridge. He had been told that there was still an Angle settlement there called Stubs Worth. When they reached the farm settlement, they were surprised that it had a number of families living there and they seemed quite relaxed about the band of armed men approaching them. Wuffa spoke to their headman who was delighted to welcome a King's Thegn into his settlement.

"Why did you not run or hide?" said Wuffa.

"We have watched you all morning," said the headman, "and could see that you were Angles. The Waelisc will not penetrate the forest this far in, come with me."

Wuffa followed the headman to the other side of the settlement, there a young man stood on a hillock and looked across towards the heath. Wuffa stood next to him and could see the wide stretch of the heath and the water of the fens beyond. "How far is the fen from here?" he asked.

"Less than half a morning walk," answered the headman.

"From sunrise to noon?" asked Wuffa.

"No. After a good morning meal," said the headman, "a youngster would walk there and back between sunrise and noon even in midwinter, it is not as far as it looks."

"Are you going to stand a shield wall across the gap?" Osgar asked Wuffa. He knew that it was a ridiculous thing to say. If all the fyrd of East Anglia was raised, it would not stretch across the heath.

"Maybe, you just never know," was all that Wuffa would say.

Chapter 13
Erin

Leofric sat upright on his horse, in front of him was a monk talking to Bishop Cadog the Wise. Their gowns trailed back over the horses towards their hindquarters and both had their hoods over their heads to keep the rain off. Leofric had never before experienced such rain as had fallen on him since he had travelled with the Bishop. He had been in Erin for more than a year and had hardly known a dry day.

He hated Ireland and prayed each day to God to take him back to East Anglia. He prayed for the people he knew there, his brother Osgar, his father, all the people of his ham and he saved his most special prayers for his mother Aefre. He had plenty of time to pray for them all. Most days they seemed only to ride, eat and pray. At the end of each day he had to see that the horses were safely tethered or stabled and that they were washed down and well-watered and fed. He picked the hooves out and checked the shoeing by feeling for risen clenches and wrenching at the shoe with his hand to see that it was tight. His duties included arranging for shoeing once every three months. He had some tools and nails for replacing lost horseshoes but did not have any equipment for complete horseshoeing.

Everywhere that they went, the Bishop attracted a large following. Monks, priests, nobility and the people came to listen under thatched roofed churches or in the open. He combined authority with kindness; to him there was no difference between a prince and a pauper. Leofric loved him as his saviour but still desired only to return home with his mother. He still dreamed of his village, its river, the old Roman house and the hall with its feasts. He was now a devout Christian but he missed Cynbeald's tales of the old gods. Now he thought of them as mythical stories, no different from the Beowulf epic.

The Bishop often spoke to Leofric as they rode through the country; he would pull his horse back so that it was alongside Leofric's. The Bishop wanted to know everything that there was to know about East Anglia and the Angles. Leofric sometimes had to remind him that he had now lived for eight years amongst the Britons and that he had only been ten years old when captured. He told the Bishop of a land where there was always food and where it only rained for a few days in the spring, just enough for good farming. Bishop Cadog wanted to hear about paganism and tutted at times as Leofric told him stories of their gods.

"Tell me," the Bishop asked one day. "When you talk to the horses do you use a magic language that they understand?"

"Father," said Leofric, "when I was enslaved and brought to the land of the Waelisc, as we call the Cymry, I could not understand any words, everything was just noises. I watched the grooms with their charges and I thought that they were speaking to the horses. When I learned what these words meant I realised that they were not special words but they were said to calm the horses and it was only the sounds not the words that mattered."

He patted his horse and said, "Good boy," in the Briton tongue and then patted his horse again and said, "good boy," in the Angle's language.

"You see, father, it does not matter which tongue I use. The horse understood both."

"Or neither." Laughed the Bishop, and then he laughed and laughed until his monks ahead turned around on their horses and looked back at him. "How funny," he said, once he had his breath back, "you thought we spoke magic words to the horses and now we think that you do. I will put this in my next sermon to show how the Lord's message comes in many tongues."

Leofric had wanted to catch the Bishop in a good mood and now he took his chance, "Will you let the monks teach me to read, father?"

"You are a slave and an Angle and have no need to read," said the Bishop.

"But I could study the disciples' words better if I read the language of the Romans," said Leofric.

"You have learned some Latin by listening to us and joining in prayers. You have no need to read and that is an end of it," the Bishop kicked his heels into his horse's ribs and rode his horse forward leaving Leofric.

*****

Aefre quietly went about her work in the kitchen garden where she was mainly left to herself. Whenever she had to go into the kitchen, she still faced a barrage of insults. Now that the old King Cynwyd was dead and as she was not called to him, she had been given no new clothes. She was called the Old Kings widow or the Hag Queen along with the usual Sais pig and whore.

They tripped her and spat at her when she was close enough but when they were ill or injured, they sought her help. The horsemen and foot soldiers frequently had cuts and abrasions from jousting and training and sometimes they would return from a raid with a serious wound. She cleaned and stitched gashes and protected them from infection which was feared above all else and all the time she hated every last one of them. She wished them dead and she wished them pain but she knew her life depended on her success as a healer. Each day she looked to the rising sun for her people to come for her and in the evening as she watched the setting sun, she thought of Leofric who had been taken west by the Bishop. She loved her people but now occasionally could not stop her thoughts wandering to considering that they may never come and rescue her. It was then that she felt most alone.

The only Angle that she ever had any contact with was the slave Sigbert who she had met on their first day of captivity. He worked in the pigsties which were near Aefre's hovel and was able to see her sometimes. He had never believed that they would be rescued so did nothing to raise her spirit. He wore his clothes and hair in the style of the Britons, allowing his hair to grow long so he could braid it and never clipping his beard. Sigbert seemed charmed as he avoided most of the punishments inflicted upon the other slaves. In some ways, she admired how he accepted his lot and made the most of it. She could not bring herself to act like this though and so adapted her clothes to look Angle and kept her hair plaited in the same fashion as when she was captured.

One day he brought her some meat as a give. "Thank you," she said, enjoying the thick cuts of pork, "where did you get them from?"

Once he had finished chewing the lump that he had stuffed into his mouth, he wiped his chin and said, "I have to collect the swill for the pigs, sometimes there's some real tasty bits in it."

Aefre looked at the piece she had in her hand, put it down and said with a look of disgust on her face, "Pig swill, you brought me pig swill."

"It's not pigs swill until the bloody pigs eat it, is it? I thought you might be a little bit more grateful than that?" he replied, winking at her.

She realised that he had put himself at risk to bring her food. He could easily have scoffed it all himself when hidden near the pigsties. She had few enough visitors or people that she could talk to and did not want to lose Sigbert's company. He did try to keep her informed of anything happening in Bannaventa and sometimes brought news of East Anglia that was told to him by captured Angles. She was disconcerted by the suggestive wink that he had given her.

"I'm sorry," she said, patting him on the knee. "I didn't mean to sound ungrateful. Please don't stop coming to see me when you can but don't take risks. I don't want to lose you."

"That's all right," Sigbert said, moving closer and putting his hand on her thigh, "You must get lonely here and I'm only trying to help."

Aefre rose and smiled at him. "I'll make some nettle tea for you, Siggy and then you must go."

The warrior Waljan was a frequent visitor with even the most minor cuts and bruises for her to treat. At first, she thought that he was just weak but soon realised that it was her that he was interested in. She dealt with him in the same curt manner that she used with all the Britons who came to her. He would leave her food and sometimes cloth for making clothes. She did not understand him. If he wanted her, he could rape her at will. Occasionally, she thought that he was a handsome man who was polite and well dressed and then she put such thoughts out of her mind.

"Why do you hate me so?" he asked one day, when he had brought her yarn.

"I don't hate you. You are a kind man to me but you and your people enslaved me. You have killed us and destroyed our villages ever since we came to this land."

"And whose land is it," said Waljan, losing control of his temper. "Do you think that it was empty? The Cymry have always been here, even since before the Romans. How many of my people have the Sais killed? How many of us have been taken as slaves? Do you think I want to fight forever?"

Waljan looked at the beautiful woman sitting cross-legged in front of him. He tried to calm himself down and could see that she was now frightened of him. He did not know why he was so fascinated by her and often told himself she was just another Sais slave.

"Look, Aefre," he finally said, "we are never going to agree on this, so let's not talk on it anymore. Tell me about your gods again. You know I like to hear about them."

So Aefre told him about the gods of the northern people. She explained Yggdrasil, the mystical tree where everyone's web of fate is woven by the three wise women called Nornir. She taught Waljan to say the days of the week in her tongue and explained each god in turn. He was amazed by the number of gods, their different functions and how they even fought one another. Finally he had to leave and rose, kissed her on the top of her head and left.

He was not her enemy, she thought, although he had been in the raiding party that had burned her ham and taken her and Leofric captive. Maybe she should accept that she was a slave and would never be rescued by her people. It was not unknown for Angles to be raised out of slavery. Perhaps she should take the easy path for once and succumb to Waljan's obvious advances. Then she thought of Nelda's death and how they were followed by Stan and Milly's murders and she felt guilt for her thoughts.

Chapter 14
The Dyke

King Wehha of all the Angles, walked around the banked earthworks of the iron age fort at the Theod-ford. With him was Selwyn, Ealdorman of the North Folk and Wuffa his nephew, the Kings Thegn. Wuffa had asked them stand at the highest part and pointed to the ditch below that followed the bank around to the river. The ridge where they stood was the height of eight men from bank top to ditch bottom. "The three of us could hold this ridge against twenty men," said Wuffa.

"I agree," said the King, "but the Waelisc are not going to come here to fight us so what is your point?"

"My point is, my lord, that if we can build a defensive earthwork like this from Stubs Worth straight as an aetgar across the heath to the fens, then no Waelisc will ever again invade our land."

"How long would this take?" asked the King.

"If all the thegns sent men, we could do this in one year, two at most," said Wuffa.

Selwyn scoffed, "It was tried, years ago, south of the Lark and the Waelisc simply rode around it and destroyed the hams."

"I know it was," replied Wuffa, "I have been and looked for myself. Only three hams joined together to build it and they called it 'Black Ditches' on account of the fetid water that collected in the dykes either side. It was a poor design, in the wrong place and they had not the people to build it. What I'm proposing is of a totally different scale."

"This is a dream," said Selwyn. "There are not enough men in all East Anglia for such an earthwork. Who will get in the harvest and who will carry on trade? The cost is too great, and when it is finished how can we man it? It would take hundreds of men to ensure that the Waelisc did not just walk over it."

Wehha stood and considered the proposal and thought about Selwyn's comments, finally he said, "This is not about cost or lost trade, it is about whether our Kingdom survives. We draw our line and we make our stand, and those who do not wish to be part of this will not be part of Anglia. They can return to the Old Country or make a life elsewhere."

"Selwyn, Wuffa, raise the fyrd; no man is spared and wergild will be enforced. There will be no exceptions. Wuffa, you will oversee the building from the Stubs Worth end and Selwyn, you will begin where the heath drops into the fens."

The news that the fyrd was raised was spread from town to town and ham to ham. Men took up their spear and shield as they were obliged to. Those that had aetgars or fighting axes took them and the rich thegns brought their swords. Their ceorls and slaves travelled with them, many were accompanied by wives, elder children and especially sons. They drove their sheep and goats with geese and pulled their handcarts with every tool and utensil needed. The North Folk headed south and west to join the Icknield way at Theod-ford. The Suth Folk travelled west along the valleys of the Gipping, Waveney and Lark. They joined the Icknield way after crossing the Lark at Lark ford and Icklingham. The ancient roadway had its grasses and plants flattened by the numbers walking along the route.

*****

The people of Beodricesworth had been busy for three days now. Their Ealdorman Tedmund had promised Wuffa that they would be at the Great Heath within the week. The craftsmen finished any current work that they could and then packed every necessary implement into the handcarts. They made arrangements for those who were not going to care for their property and animals. Anson and Osgar packed the handcart with an anvil and bellows and took their forging tools and iron. Their handcart was more substantial than most. Wilfrid had checked the wheels, axel and frame before it was loaded. The two solid wheels were under the centre of the cart which was about two paces long by over four feet wide. It had two curved handles. Many of the carts had only one handle in the centre and a few of the largest had four solid wheels. The handcarts were usually pushed with the handle at the back but on steep hills, they were dragged with one or two people pushing the flat back. Wilf and his eldest son Seward packed their handcart with their carpentry tools. They needed iron and wood wedges for tree splitting, axes for tree felling and thinning planks and adzes for shaping. They carried no wood as they knew that the forests nearby were full of all the types of timber they would need.

Two of Beodricesworth's many brewers had packed large four wheeled carts with copper cauldrons and sacks of barley, also taking elderberries and honey for flavour. Their brews took only a few days to produce ale and then they sieved it and strained it through cloth which allowed them to collect and reuse the yeast. They also sold excess yeast to the baker for his breadmaking. The ale was drunk within two days, because if left much longer it became stale. They made their way to the valley that ran across the Great Heath. Meandering through the dip in the middle of the valley was a narrow stream. It was the only watercourse of any sort to cross the heath which, being chalk-land, soaked up all rainfall. Although they already numbered hundreds, the Angles camped to the southeast where the tree line met the heath. No one felt safe on the grassland, for generations anyone out in the open there was in danger from the Britons' horsemen.

Beech, oak and ash trees were soon felled in the woods and used to make shelters. Branches were woven to make enclosures for the farm animals. Every man kept his spear and shield within reach at all times and they sent out patrols to the southern and western edges of the heath. Beacons were prepared on high points that would be lit to warn of any approaching attackers. While the new town was built in the valley of the heath, Wuffa and Tedmund were surveying the site of the dyke. They lit beacons at the fen edge and the wood edge which allowed them to align ash staves pushed into the chalky ground of the heath. The line of stakes ran straight across the Great Heath, following the rolling undulations. A row of turfs was removed to chalk depth through the topsoil, in many places it was only a foot deep marking the heath with a great white line across it.

Wuffa was concerned that the North Folk had not yet arrived so he sent a runner. Two days later, he returned to tell Wuffa that Selwyn sent his compliments and said that delays and the distance to travel had held them up. Wuffa was furious, Selwyn's support was half hearted but he knew that the Suth Folk could not build the dyke alone. He did not trust Selwyn and thought that King Wehha had made a mistake in promoting him to Ealdorman of the North Folk. It was not clear if his own status as new Kings Thegn put him above the Ealdorman or not. During the months leading up to Yule, the numbers of North

Folk working on the dyke increased but never reached the figures demanded by Wehha to complete the task in two years.

At Stubbs Worth, the dyke building was moving along at pace although it was the toughest section due to requiring the felling of trees, the heavier soil and steep ground. Even when the trees were cut down their massive root stumps remained. These had to be hacked at with axes and pulled from the heavy clay land. The ditch was cut into the ground in a steep V shape, loading the clay soil into wicker baskets. These were carried out of the ditch and tipped on the north side to create a bank. As the bank grew, the workers had to climb higher before depositing their loads. Wuffa watched his people labouring industriously on the dyke. They looked like ants building a nest to him, a continual movement of people, not moving fast but never stopping. He stood on the crest of the bank and after observing the work for some time, he turned to look down the bank at the encampment behind. It was larger, with far more shelters and permanent buildings than he had intended. Many of the builders had become fed up with the continual walking to and fro from the safety of the valley beyond. They had built so many houses and pens for their animals that the settlement was larger than most hams. Many had even brought their children with them and the old who could not be left behind. Wuffa felt unsure about these peoples' security as he had not envisioned any settlement until the dyke was completed.

Wuffa walked back to the valley in the heath and saw the large encampment of homes and workshops. This was where he had expected all the dyke builders to live. He stopped to speak to Anson and Osgar who were working in their forge. After addressing each other in the correct manner and the usual pleasantries, Anson told him that they needed good supplies of charcoal and were running short.

Wuffa said to Anson, "Why do you not go to the village in the woods past Stubs Worth, you know, where we went boar hunting. They make charcoal there and it would be good to see that all is safe, and to tell them about the dyke that we are digging."

"We shall go in the morning," said Anson.

The next day, they set off with their handcart containing only their shields and spears. Charcoal was light but bulky so they had extra planks to slot into the sides so that they could carry more. They headed south and kept to the treelined fringe and after a while, they crossed the white chalk line, where it cut through the turf. They looked to the wooded hills on their left and could see the giant earthwork protruding from the trees.

"I am still not sure what is going on here," said Anson.

"Wehha is building the longest and tallest shield wall ever seen," said Osgar.

"What?" said Anson.

"Forget it," said Osgar. Then he thought for a while and said, "You saw the old fort at Theod-ford, where the moot was held; well, we are building the same thing only in a long line."

They had moved from a master apprentice relationship to one of being mates. Osgar now knew that Anson was not the best smith in the world. He had seen that Hunfrith had more skills and understanding of the iron. Anson was his uncle and he had taken him in when he lost his family, he had fed, clothed and housed him for seven years. There had hardly been an angry word between them in that time and Osgar now accepted when there had been it was his fault. He had come to love Anson's wife, his aunt Hild and he realised how rotten he had been to her, openly resenting her cuddles and patting and over fussing. He wondered if Hild's sister, his mother Aefre now looked like her.

*****

Cadrod strode back and forth across his chambers. He had now heard three reports of an army massing to the east. One of the Gwyre people, whom he no longer trusted, first told of fires burning and a strange line and row of staves across the heath. Then an escaped slave had told the tale of Sais on the Great Heath, describing a huge white bank in such terms of awe that Cadrod had refused to believe him at all. The Briton had said that he was one of many slaves sent to build it and had taken the opportunity to run toward home one night. Finally, after riding day and night, Waljan had returned to report to him from a spying mission with a small troop of horsemen. Waljan as always was clear and concise and he reported to his King that it did not look like an army massing to attack Calchfynedd. It looked to Waljan as if the whole Sais people had moved a day's walk westwards. He had viewed the ditch digging and bank building, from a distance, at either end and he thought that they were building a defensive line.

"But they have no cover," said Cadrod. "They are in the middle of the heath, we will slaughter them."

"They have too many armed men," said Waljan, "for our usual size war band to beat them."

"Then we attack through the woods and come in behind them," replied Cadrod. He was furious that the hated Sais had dared to try to push their border into his land but was energised at the thought of battle.

"I think that they are building an earthwork fort up in the woods where it nears the heath," said Waljan, "I could not get close enough but there seems to be woodworkers felling trees and diggers putting up a bank."

"Then that is where we attack," said Cadrod, "and when we get behind them, we will slaughter them all. The Sais pigs will be pushed back into the sea."

*****

Anson and Osgar reached Stubs Worth and settled down for their noon break amongst the dyke diggers. Tree fellers had cleared the ground to the west of the hilltop that Stubs Worth sat upon. The wood was being split by thirty men and boys, among them Wilf and Seward. All around lay the fallen beech trees, some as they fell, and others with branches removed and some being split for planking.

Wilfrid and Seward split the giant beech methodically, they used two iron wedges almost the size of a hand and they drove them into the felled trunk about a pace apart. Wilf had spent some time selecting the exact spot and then lined the wedges up edgeways. A few solid blows from the sledgehammer drove the second wedge into the trunk and a fine split join the two wedges. Into it, Wilf inserted two hardened wood wedges and as Seward drove them in the split grew. More hardwood wedges were driven outside the iron ones and the split opened further. They moved the iron wedges along, driving them once more into the wood and soon there was a chasm opening in the trunk. Once the split opened from one end to the other, Wilf again selected exactly where the iron wedges were to be driven. The wood began to split about two finger widths from the first line. Wilf was careful to maintain a good parallel line with first split. Finally, it split the whole length and they tugged at the first plank that they had produced from the tree. The inner ragged edge was trimmed with an adze to an even line. Wilf spotted Anson and Osgar and gave a wave, beckoning to join them. They sat together on the trunk to eat their noon meal of crab apple and hazelnuts. Anson had some salted meat that he shared as he chatted to Wilf while Osgar and Seward sat together and talked.

"My sister asked after you," said Seward.

"She did?" said Osgar.

"She won't wait forever you know," said Seward.

"She will have to wait until my mother and brother return," said Osgar.

"Come on, mate," said Seward, "it has been eight years. No one knows where they are."

Osgar looked directly at Seward, "Once I am able to make a sword, for that arse Selwyn, I will be released from this stupid ward and then I will travel west and find them. Nothing will stop me."

After they had finished their food, they were shown the dyke, it was only four hundred paces long but it already looked impressive. The ditch was a steep 'V' shape dug to a depth of six men and the soil was piled up on the northern side as steeply as possible. Here in the wooded hills near Stubs Worth it was mainly clay and had been patted and smoothed with the flat side of spades. Already the small green shoots of some plants were emerging from its surface. The top of the bank was a sharp ridge with only enough space for a single line of men to stand. Where the ditch inclined down toward the heath there were hundreds of men, women and elder children working. The men were using picks to break the ground and spades to dig and load wicker baskets, which were carried by the women and children out of the steep ditch and tipped to form the bank on the other side. Often there were tree roots and stumps that had to be removed. Men with axes set about them until they could be rolled out of the way. Once a wicker basket was full of soil it was carried up the bank where logs had been set in the slope to act as steps. They were pegged into place and would be moved along as the ditch and bank progressed. Up the left-hand side climbed a stream of women and children slowly carrying their baskets, to dump their contents as directed by a thegn standing at the top and then make their way down the right-hand side of the log stairway.

Anson and Osgar said their goodbyes to Wilf and Seward and continued with their handcart along the fringe of the wood towards the charcoal-maker's village. Once they recognised the entrance to the woods, they cut inwards. They were soon amongst the ham of the charcoal people and swapping tales of the previous boar hunt. Anson and Osgar loaded the handcart fully with charcoal and paid for it with smoked eels and fish that they had earlier bought from the Gwyre.

It was too late in the afternoon to travel so they decided to stay the night. They walked over to where the villagers were working to watch the charcoal making process. Wood was packed tightly together in a dome shape, then this was covered in a layer of damp bracken and finally it was enclosed in turf and clay. A fire was started in the centre where a shaft had been left and this was immediately sealed so that by excluding air, they controlled the burn. Any wisps of smoke escaping the turf and clay layer were sealed with more clay. The stream ran close by and this gave them pails of water to damp down the turf. The burning took a day and a night and the huge clamp was attended all the time. If a wisp of smoke was not sealed, then it would break through and then there would rage a fire that destroyed all the charcoal. The whole process of making a large clamp of charcoal took a week and the work could be lost by one short nap.

Anson and Osgar sat down with the charcoal-makers for their evening meal. They ate venison from a recently killed roe deer which had been hung for a week and was now roasting on a spit above a fire. The settlement had old and young living deep in the forest. One of the young mothers fussed over a small baby and breastfed it until it fell asleep. She wrapped the child carefully in woollen cloth and gently laid it beside her while she ate. Another mother broke bread and cut meat from the roasting deer to hand out. She waited until the meat was cool enough and after one final puff on it, she passed it to her boy. The headman of the village proudly told him that the two children were his grandson and granddaughter. Anson leant against an oak tree surveying the scene and thinking about his busy life in Beo and whether this would be a more relaxed life. He downed another mouthful of mead from a mug and then raised it in appreciation to his nearest host. Perhaps not, he thought, Hild likes the town too much to change to this type of life.

In the morning, Anson and Osgar ate some bread and stew given to them by the charcoal-makers before saying their goodbyes. The ham was busy and they were about to light another clamp while one was still cooling. Even when cooling it needed to be attended as they could burst into life and flame out if not kept sealed. They lifted the motty peg from the centre of the clamp, this was a post around which the wood had been stacked and stuck out through the layer of bracken and the turf and clay layer. Removing it left a tubular cavity to the bottom of the clamp. Burning firewood was dropped into the hole and once it was seen that a small fire burned well within, the hole was sealed. This was the only time that a large plume of smoke arose from the clamp. For the whole of the day until the next morning, any smoke meant hasty repairs and flames only meant failure.

Anson and Osgar headed down the narrow woodland track to the heath. They ducked their heads under branches and made sure that they did not tip the handcart over. It was piled high with charcoal and they did not intend losing any, their shields and spears were laid on the sides of the cart. They did not think that a shield and spear would be effective against the Waelisc if they were caught out in the open but they knew that as the fyrd was raised any thegn or ceorl found without these to hand would pay wergild. Before they exited the tree line they stopped and looked carefully all ways to see that there was no danger. They turned right and headed towards the horizon in the northeast, staying within fifty paces of the tree line.

*****

Cadrod sat high in his saddle and stared into the distance. He was hidden in a tree copse in the middle of the heath, farther back were his dismounted men. He saw a large plume of smoke emerging from the forest, he watched for a while and then asked his war band if anyone could remember a Sais village there and if they had ever attacked that area. They all agreed that they had not penetrated that far into the woods. As they watched the plume of smoke, it dispersed into the air and there was no more. Cadrod made a mental note of exactly where he had seen it, there was a clump of trees in the heath opposite it and the forested hill rose higher than anywhere else close behind it and he could find the spot where there had been smoke. Smoke meant people and he knew there were no Britons there so it must be Sais pigs. They may have been bypassed by previous raids or they had moved forward into this area recently, either way they would pay. As the war-band stood still, hidden in the copse of trees, Waljan pointed to two figures emerging from the forest near where they had seen the smoke. They were pushing a laden handcart before them. Waljan looked to Cadrod as he started to kick his horse forward.

"Wait," said Cadrod, "we will catch those two later, first we find those where we could see the smoke."

*****

Osgar and Anson swapped the handcart pulling duties and enjoyed their walk across the Great Heath. The sun and walking warmed them and they had both stripped their tunics off and laid them on the cart. They walked with their bare chests exposed where their cloaks opened. Both had tan coloured trousers held by belts at the waist. Anson's was leather with an iron buckle that he had made. Osgar's belt had been woven by Lynne and was now fixed with his own handmade buckle. He had also forged the broach pinning his cloak below his neck which had a small hammer in the design.

They could see now where the ditch and bank emerged from the tree line, as here it was dug into the chalk soil. It was fifty paces out of the woods and was stark white against the green grass. As they neared, they could see the system of men with picks breaking into the damp chalk and spade men filling the wicker baskets. Women and children filed around the edge of the ditch and up the log steps. All the men working had their spears and shields to hand and there were thegns keeping watch over the heath. When they came closer, they waved to reassure the group that they were friends. They could see a thegn signalling to some of the working men to take up their arms and stand to. Once they were within calling distance, they shouted their names and the thegns and men of arms relaxed and returned to their duties. They spoke with the thegn once they arrived at the ditch. He asked where they had been and what they had seen. Anson told him of the ham of woodcutters and charcoal makers. He said that they had seen nothing themselves and neither had the villagers.

"Good," said the thegn, "they must have seen by now what we are doing, but how many would they need to attack? Maybe they will come in the spring but not yet."

*****

Cadrod and Waljan found the pathway into the wood that they were looking for and took a group of twenty men, leaving their horses with the rest. The path was made easier to follow by the two cartwheel tracks in the damp woodland floor. They fanned out when they could see that they were near the settlement. The clamps were off to one side of the houses, deeper into the woods towards a stream. When they attacked, they caught the Sais by total surprise, most of the men were working near the charcoal clamps and the women and children were close to the houses. They slaughtered the men and children first. They raped the women and then slit their throats; no one escaped or lived. They searched all properties for anything of value but there was little, a few of the men had copper armbands and some of the women wore bronze broaches but there was no gold or silver. There were some boar's tusks which were always prized and some carved bone handled knives. They did not torch the properties as this would give away their attack. They ate the smoked eels and fish drank mead from some storage jars and complained how it did not compare to their own meads.

Cadrod discussed with Waljan their next move. "We will be quicker if we return to the horses and travel along the margin of the heath," said Waljan.

"They are sure to see us coming," said Cadrod. "If we travel by foot, we can stay in the woods and we will surprise them. We need to get around the earthwork that they are digging and into the camp that they have built the other side. Once there, in the chaos we will kill so many they will return behind their rivers and sulk."

Waljan thought that his King was taking a great risk but he had made his suggestion and he would follow Cadrod's orders. They left ten men to guard the horses and worked their way through the woodland on foot. It took longer than Cadrod anticipated as they had to make diversions around large areas of brambles and there was no pathway to follow. Frequently, they had to stop to assess where they were and to send scouts forward to find a way through. The war-band was twice the size of any that Cadrod had led before and he soon realised the difficulties in controlling and manoeuvring so many in difficult terrain. Behind them, they left a devastated ham; the bodies lay strewn where they had fallen. Men, women and children slaughtered and laying without dignity in the leaf titter of the forest floor. No birds sang and there was no noise but the faint crackle of the charcoal clamps. A small wisp of smoke appeared from one.

*****

Anson and Osgar left the handcart by the ditch at the bottom of the hill; they would collect it in the morning and finish their trip back to their new forge. Both climbed the steep hill alongside the bank on the north side of the ditch, at the top they discovered Wilf and Seward who had found a tree trunk to sit on in the rays of the setting sun. They had plenty of ale and shared it with them. Anson brought out the last of the smoked fish and Wilf uncovered some cheese, wrapped in cloth. As they talked, ate and drank, Osgar noticed a light far in the distance, "Isn't that the charcoal-makers' ham?" he said pointing to where the yellow light brightened.

"Not like them to allow a clamp to burst," said Anson.

They watched it glow brighter and then nearby another light grew alongside the first. "Waelisc," said Osgar suddenly.

"What?" said Wilf looking at Osgar with disbelief. "How can two flames in the distance mean Waelisc?"

"Because they are careful with their charcoal clamps and if two have burst, it can only mean that they are hiding or dead."

Chapter 15
Defeat

Leofric stood on a cliff with the Bishop Cadog Ddoeth the Wise. The Bishop had told him that this was the furthest west that anyone could travel and so it was the end of the world. "When this great island of Erin was converted to follow our Lord Christ by St Padraig the Church in Rome thought that all of the world's people would be saved. Alas, it has not been proven so. Now we are almost cut off from Rome. To travel across the sea, even in summer, avoiding the pagan Sais is a deadly gamble and few do it. Erin is cut off from the Christian world but has become ever more saintly despite that."

Leofric was further from home than ever. He was a Christian and prayed to the one God and he loved the Bishop who had saved him. He was content as a groom, working with the horses gave him a feeling of peace but his heart was still in Anglia and he prayed daily to return. He promised his new God that he would give him anything that he wanted; in return, he wished to be able to take his mother back to their land. He prayed daily for forgiveness, for not rescuing Aefre and for wanting dead every last Waelisc. He hated Erin with its rain and bogs and saintly people.

The Bishop turned his horse towards the west; they would begin the long crossing of Erin. They had been there for more than two years and had visited most of the monasteries and spoken to all the Bishops. His last visit had been to Bishop Brendan of Ardfert who was known as Brendan the Voyager. He was now an old man and all who knew him believed he was destined to be a saint. Cadog the Wise was now refreshed and wished to return to Bannaventa again to see how his church building had progressed. He travelled with two monks and Leofric the groom, they all rode and at the end of each day, it was Leofric's job to feed and water the horses. He rose early and prayed with them and understood some of the Latin that was used but he believed that his only escape was to learn to read. When they came to a river crossing, they would usually dismount unless it was a shallow ford. One of the monks would assist the Bishop while he led two horses. Neither the monks nor the Bishop was comfortable in the streams. The Bishop was frail now and unsure of his footing but Leofric thought that the monks were gutless in the face of a little water.

Leofric stood by the bank of a rapid stream in the pouring rain. He had the hood of his cloak drawn up over his head as the two monks and the Bishop did. He held three of the horses while one of the monks held the fourth on the other bank, only twenty paces away, and watched the monks guide the Bishop through the water. The second monk held the Bishop's left elbow and waded with him across the stream while he held his staff in his right hand. The gold cross on the top of the staff was covered in rain droplets which made it sparkle. Halfway across, the Bishop stumbled and fell into the water. His monk held him tight but the staff was released from his grip. The weight of the gold made cross end sink so that the staff end floated with at least a hands length protruding at an angle from the water. It was swept along by the current, the staff end bobbing and weaving as it headed downstream. The Bishop rose and spluttered for someone to save his staff, "It was given to me by the blessed St Enda of Aran."

Leofric released his horses and pulled his cloak over his head and threw it onto the wet ground. He ran along the bank downstream as far as he could until his way was then blocked by trees, then he jumped into the stream. He had not swum since he was a boy, racing his brother across the Lark. He could see the staff bobbing ahead of him and swam awkwardly towards it. Finally, he caught up with it and took hold, he turned it around so that the cross was held high and made his way to the bank panting and coughing. Near the embankment, the water was shallower and he climbed up the muddy bank and then walked back upstream to meet the Bishop and his two monks. He passed the staff to the Bishop and bowed. He looked tired and bedraggled but nodded his thanks and Leofric crossed the stream again with one of the monks to catch the horses who were unconcerned and grazing.

That evening they found lodgings at a church, and after the horses had been fed and watered by Leofric, he ate his stew in the stalls with them. One of the monks called him in later for prayers, the Bishop prayed loudly for longer than usual and he thanked the Lord for the return of St Enda's cross. He said that it was saved due to the special gifts of swimming that were given to Leofric and how the Lord had sent him to be his servant and groom.

After prayers, the Bishop sat and asked Leofric to stay, "How am I to reward you?" he said to Leofric, "You saved my favourite horse and it was easy to reward you by talking you from Bannaventa and saving your soul. But how do I reward you for saving the cross of the Blessed Enda? Do not ask me for your freedom and do not ask that you return to the pagan Sais. That, I will not do."

"Father," said Leofric, "you know that I do desire to return to my people and to free my mother. However, I also know that you will not do this so I ask only one thing, that I am allowed to learn to read Latin that I may serve the Lord better."

The Bishop knew that he could not refuse and said, "Yes."

*****

Cadrod and Waljan squatted by the edge of the wood, behind a felled beech tree and looked towards the ditch and the bank behind it. Trees had been cleared in front of them for two hundred paces so that they had no cover to get closer. The bank behind the ditch was higher than they imagined, it was at least the height of the stonewalls at Bannaventa but it was only earth and they knew that they could run up it however steep. It disappeared to their right up into the forest and to their left they followed it for four hundred paces as it fell to join the heath. Halfway down, towards the heath, it began to be patterned with chalk and by the time it met the heath, it was pure chalk and became a stark white bank behind the white walled ditch. They could see four people on the ridge of the bank and they carried shields and spears. Cadrod had been told that there was a settlement at the heath behind the ditch and bank. He could just see the start of an enclosure with some sheep and goats in it. He believed that he would surprise the Sais by going straight down into the ditch and up the bank on the other side with half his force and send the other half around the end to attack the settlement. He knew that they would then repeat the day's earlier success tenfold. The rest of the Briton war-band remained hidden deep in the woods waiting for a signal to come forward.

Wuffa stood on the bank ridge looking into the trees. With him were Tedmund the Ealdorman of Beodricesworth, Osgar and Anson. Osgar recounted their day and why he believed that the Waelisc were near. Wuffa could see the smoke rising in two distinct plumes in the distance. He peered across the cleared woods but could see nothing.

166

Wuffa turned to Tedmund and said, "Send the Flemish and ten others to Stubs Worth to guard that end of the bank. Make sure that the beacon can be lit quickly if they see anything. Take Anson to the settlement and make safe the women and children and then send ten men to stand with us on this bank and place the rest at the far end. You must also be ready to signal with your beacon and send a runner north to warm the settlement in the valley."

When Tedmund and Anson had gone, Wuffa said, "It may have been just a scouting party that chanced upon the charcoal makers' ham. If it was, then they will be headed home by now. If it is a large war-band or an army then we will be hard pushed to hold them, if they get past the dyke, they will kill us all."

When Cadrod saw that there was only two left guarding the bank he signalled his men to move forward. Waljan was on the left with a group of nearly fifty and Cadrod was on the right with forty men. When they were fifty paces from the bank, Cadrod signalled them to run and Waljan peeled off to the left with his group to run downhill alongside the ditch. Cadrod's men ran straight down into the ditch heading for the only two figures that they could see. It was steep and about the depth of six men, all of them struggled to keep their footing in the soft clay. Some fell or rolled, others skidded down leaving deep cuts in the soil where each footstep had been. At the bottom of the ditch they gathered themselves together and looked up the bank, Cadrod had already set off up it. The Britons knew that it was a hard climb on difficult ground but they would soon be at the top and on the ridge.

Wuffa and Osgar looked down at the approaching army. There looked like there could be one hundred men attacking. Osgar shouted down the other side of the bank for the men to hurry, he could see about ten Angles making their way up the incline behind them. Wuffa untied the toggle holding his sword tightly in its scabbard and Osgar reached behind his back with his right arm and checked that his seax was easy to release. He was calm and he felt that Wuffa was also ready for battle.

They watched the Britons tumble down the ditch in their hurry to get to them and now they had set off to climb up the bank towards them. They carried their shields in the left hands and their spears in their right. Some of them leant forward and pressed the shield into the soft clay to help push them up. Some dug their spear hafts in with each step to gain purchase, their speed of climb was slowing but three continued to run with short steps digging deep into the soil. Osgar aimed his spear with a right hand thrust at the closest attacker. He caught his enemy near his left collarbone and he tumbled backwards, skidding down the hill into two others coming up. Wuffa used an underhand thrust at the nearest enemy to him and his blow glanced off his targets shield. His spear was grabbed and he thrust it back to make the Waelisc fall but lost his spear in the process. Wuffa drew his sword and saw that an attacker was between him and Osgar. He took two steps forward and swung his sword striking his enemy below his helmet into the back of his neck.

Wuffa and Osgar did not have time to speak, there were now more Waelisc within spear distance. They were tired from the steep muddy climb and off balance and it was difficult for them to stand up straight to use spear and shield. They were being urged on by a leader in their midst, Osgar looked down and knew it was the Waelisc leader who had attacked his ham six years ago. He had never forgotten the upturned eyes and thin smile. Osgar controlled his urge to run down the hill at him. Osgar and Wuffa stood together, keeping their shields low as their enemy thrust at them. Osgar used his spear now for downward overhead thrusts and Wuffa used his sword to chop at any spears driven his way. A spearhead glanced off Wuffa's shin and cut into the side of his calf but he stood and continued to fight. Suddenly, they realised that they had been joined by their own men. There were only ten reinforcements but they soon had a shield wall, with the shields overlapping, left over right and they held their spears high to strike downwards. They kept their shields lower than in normal battle position because the Waelisc were eye level with their knees. Soon their advantage of height and secure footing was paying off. Although they were outnumbered by four to one, many of the Britons had received injuries to face, neck and shoulders and some had fallen back down the hill.

Cadrod could not believe that just two men had stopped his charge. He had experienced himself how difficult the bank was to climb. The first ten paces were easy and like all his men he was fit and could run at full pace with armour, shield and spear but soon each stride became harder and he had to shorten his steps and lean forward to use his shield. He looked to his left and saw that Waljan's men were almost at the end of the earthwork. Once they cleared the corner, they would be amongst the enemy. They would cut their way through them and then he would take his men over the bank trapping all between them. Above him, he could see that his men were now held by some Sais reinforcements and he looked for a way to pass them. He saw the row of logs set in the bank to make steps only thirty paces to the left. Now he knew that he could not be stopped and he shouted for his men to back off and move left. Osgar could see the danger and told Wuffa to move the line of men along the bank ridge to cover the log steps. He shouted to one of the men to run to Stubs Worth to get reinforcements.

Tedmund had called his thegns as he scrambled down the bank with Anson. They did not know that by the time they were at the bottom of the bank the Waelisc had begun their advance. Tedmund told them to form the men up at the far end of the bank and ditch behind the enclosure fence. Women and children were to go out of the back of the settlement and to disperse into the woods. By the time Anson had found Henryk, women and children were running up the incline towards the trees and men were picking up their arms and running down the hill, behind the bank. Anson told Henryk to take his men to Stubs Worth to guard the top of the dyke and he would send men to follow and he reminded Henryk to light the beacon if attacked. Henryk had already set off at the run, his long straight hair flapping backwards and forwards with each step. Tedmund found a runner to go to the valley settlement to warn them of attack and asked to send soldiers if they saw a beacon. He then sent reinforcements to the bank and more to Stubs Worth.

Now Anson heard Osgar calling down the bank for the reinforcements to hurry and he knew that an attack was happening. He picked up an axe and ran down to Tedmund who was organising the line. Anson told him that the bank was under attack, to have the beacon lit and to send reinforcements back to the bank. The beacon was soon ablaze but as soon as Tedmund was about to send more men to the bank there was a roar and the Britons rounded the end of the ditch. Tedmund had never seen armed Waelisc before, he had heard the tales and he had seen the bodies of their victims. He was no coward but he froze when he saw them running straight towards him. They had black trailing hair and long beards, leather jerkins covered their chests and their trews were bright colours of red and green. Many wore iron helmets and chainmail hauberks under their coloured tunics. They ran as a mass towards the Angles shouting loudly and waving spears and swords over their heads.

"Shield wall form," shouted Anson, having waited long enough for Tedmund to give the order.

The twenty men behind the wicker fence enclosure overlapped their shields right over left. They were hurried and knocked shield edges into their fellow Angles' arms and spears before finally making the defensive line solid. They bent their knees and leant forward as trained.

169

"Spears down," ordered Anson and the points were lowered towards the running Waelisc.

The shield wall stood a pace back from the wicker fence that was waist high. Anson held the woodman's axe that he had picked up, over his head; Tedmund had drawn his sword and stood beside him. The pack of Waelisc clattered into the enclosure fence and it gave way in a tangle.

Anson ordered, "Step forward," and the line pressed on step into the mangle of fence and Waelisc.

The shield wall broke near the centre with the weight of Waelisc five deep shoving it. One bearded Angle tripped and was immediately stabbed by a spear from the Waelisc pack in the face. Anson swung his axe at the enemy who were pushing through the gap left by the fallen man. He hit his target on the shoulder, his axe cleaved open the enemy collarbone and lodged deep in his shoulder blade. The Waelisc warrior went down with the blow taking Anson's axe with it. Anson was now unarmed and another Briton held his sword high to kill him. Tedmund swept his sword horizontally and hit him across the side of his thigh, the blade bit deep and he stumbled. Anson had time to pull his boar tusk knife from his belt and ran it into his attacker's neck and then he snatched back his axe. Tedmund swiped his sword from behind his shoulder at the next through the gap and hit the raider across his cheek cutting deep into his face and mouth. He wrenched the sword out as Anson shouted, "Close the gap."

The shields banged together and the wall was whole again. Now that Angle was pressed against Waelisc it was difficult for either to deliver a blow. More Waelisc were joining the press and some Angle stragglers arrived. Anson sent some to the right to widen the shield wall as he was worried, they would be outflanked on that side. He had only three men left and had them form a second line with him and Tedmund. On Anson's orders, they used their spears two handed over the shoulders of their own wall. They prodded and thrust at the enemy heads and made them keep their shields high and heads down.

Anson the Broad, the Jute blacksmith from Beodricesworth, looked behind to see the last women disappearing into the safety of the forest. Now it was just the fyrd's lives to be lost, and losing they were. They had held the Waelisc but the press was pushing them back. Now that the crushed wicker fence had been cleared, the enemy was on firmer ground. They were losing men to spear thrusts and although they had stood their ground, the enemy was still at least twice as many. The Angles were tiring, they had lost men and few of them were uninjured. He wished Wuffa had not sent the men up to Stubs Worth as it was now obvious that the attack was aimed only at this end of the dyke.

Cadrod had manoeuvred his men onto the log steps. The span of the steps allowed three men sure footing and he spread his other men, five either side and the rest on the steps behind the leading three. They pressed upwards towards the Sais at the top with Cadrod in the middle of the first three and all of them had swords drawn. The two rows of three men behind them held spears two handed overhead. Cadrod led his men forward knowing that they would now prevail. He pushed up the steps while his spearmen behind and beside him thrust at the Sais on the ridge of the bank. If they raised their shields, the spear points were aimed at their exposed legs and if they dropped their shields down, they lunged at their necks and faces. One more drive and they would be on top of the bank ridge and these few would be killed.

Two more Sais went down, one to a spear thrust up under his tunic into his groin and another to a chop from Cadrod. He could see that of the five that were left one was wearing fine armour. His helmet had cheek pieces and there was a silver crest running down to the nose guard. He would take the life of this Sais and then he would take the helmet for himself.

Then just as they were about to overwhelm them the soldier to his right collapsed on to him with a javelin in his side. Cadrod looked to see where it came from. On the ridge to his right about fifteen men were moving down towards them, the front four held javelins and threw them at his right flank. Two more of his men fell and as shields were held on the left the body of men had to turn sideways to protect themselves. Straight away the Sais above thrust their spears down at them and Cadrod felt pain in his left shoulder. He saw the spear point that had cut through his dark leather jerkin and penetrated the chainmail into the muscle. Just as quickly, it was pulled back plucking his tunic out through the armour. He used all his willpower to stop himself from dropping his shield and instinctively swung his sword at it and cut into the haft as he backed down the log steps. His men as a group, backed away, turned, ran and rolled down the steep bank. As soon as they reached the bottom of the ditch, they scrambled up the other side.

Cadrod saw two more of his men felled by javelins but they were not followed down the bank and once up the ditch and onto the ground they were at a safe distance. He now knew that it had been a mistake to split his forces. He left the injured and led his men down the hill to where he could hear Waljan's force engaged in battle. When he rounded the ditch and bank at the end, he knew that it was going well for the Britons, they had greater numbers and were pushing back the Sais shield wall. His men joined the throng but were now four and five deep, too far back to get at the enemy. He shouted to them to move left to outflank the enemy.

Wuffa and Osgar were desperately thankful to Henryk and the other dozen or so who had come to their rescue. There were just five left standing and they gasped for breath. Wuffa had a cut to the shin of his left leg, where blood seeped through his woollen socks between the leather bindings and Osgar was cut on his sword arm above his wrist. Henryk pointed to the Britons, now out the other side of the ditch where they had regrouped and were being led down the hill. Three of the men from Stubs Worth began to descend the log steps and Henryk called them back. "You will not get to them that way," he said, "follow me."

The Flem trotted down the other side of the bank, using the logs set into the clay and they all followed, including Osgar and Wuffa. Once into the temporary houses and workshops they could see that there was a battle being fought where the bank and ditch ended. Osgar could make out Anson with an axe and Tedmund with a sword and shield. They were to the right of the main group and trying to stop the Waelisc getting around behind the shield wall. Osgar ran full pelt with his shield across his chest at one of the two Waelisc that Anson was swinging his axe at. He bowled him over and stabbed at him with his seax, the long sharp point cut through the leather jerkin, his tunic and pierced his heart.

Osgar was now in a frenzied state, he had seen the man who had killed his father and was determined that he would kill him. He was aware that Anson and Wuffa were nearby and they had been joined on the right flank by others but he would have fought the same way alone. His seax would be no match for a sword or spear in normal battle but in this cramped fight, it was ideal. He smashed his shield boss against faces and swung his seax overhead or stabbed with it between shields. Years of hatred had prepared him for this and his only thought was to get at his father's killer. If he had to kill each and every one of them to get to him, he would. As before, when he was in battle, time seemed to slow and his enemies' reactions were never as fast as his.

Then the Waelisc line began to give. At first, there was the just the ragged gap in their row caused by Osgar, and then Anson, Wuffa and Henryk pushed in forming a wedge. The Britons had given their all and felt the line collapsing on their left flank. Despite their leaders orders to stand they gave way and soon it

172

was a rout. Some of the Angles and Flemish chased them and cut more down but most were too tired and could now feel their wounds. They looked around at each other barely believing that they were alive.

*****

The next day, King Wehha arrived with his entourage. He wore full armour of a tunic length hauberk with a leather jerkin over it and leather arm and shin. His sword was sheathed in a decorated scabbard on his left side, its guard made of gold as was the pommel on his sword. His helmet was carried by a ceorl. It had iron cheek and neck flanges and a full-face mask hung from the brow. The crest of gold ran down the front of the helmet and joined with a horizontal band of gold running around the brow. Over his jerkin, he wore his cloak which was trimmed with wolf fur. He was met by Wuffa who had his leg bandaged and a large bruise on his forearm. He refused to limp.

It was the first time that Wehha had seen the dyke and he was impressed by its size but, was for the moment, more interested to hear all about the battle. He walked with Wuffa and Tedmund up the log steps to the top of the bank, from there they pointed to where the Waelisc attacked came. Wuffa told him of how few of them held them until they used the steps and how reinforcements arrived and the effect of aetgars thrown down into them.

Tedmund then took over to tell of how he organised the line and sent the women and children away. He told of Anson's role when he had delayed. Wehha looked at him at this point and admired his honesty. His experience was that after a battle those who do little brag and those who fight well are happy to share the glory. Tedmund continued to tell of how the discipline of his men had held but when Waelisc appeared he thought the battle was lost. He turned to Wuffa and said, "Then his young man arrived and we drove them off."

Wehha turned to his nephew and said, "So you drove them off? Is that where you were wounded?"

Wuffa replied, "No, my lord, I received a stab wound to my shin on the bank and as for when this bruise on my arm was given to me, I have no idea. I have learnt, in my first battle, how you are not always aware of your injuries. It was the Flemish Henryk who led us to the right flank where Tedmund's men were under most pressure. It was Osgar, the young blacksmith who broke them, I swear he fought as though Thunor was by his side."

173

The three of them walked around the ham settlement, women and children had returned after a night in the forest. Many of them tended the wounds of their men, some kneeling over the bodies of their husbands and sons. A great pyre was being built by Wehha's men where all the dead would be cremated at once. Twenty had perished in battle and another five had since died of their wounds, and there would be more. Some men had been blinded by spear thrusts and a few had lost the use of arms or hands. Two that had fought on the ridge of the bank had severe injuries to their lower legs.

There was a pile of weapons and armour that had been stripped from the Britons and some spears and shields collected from the ground after the rout. The arm rings that had been pulled from the Britons had all been passed to Wuffa and were shown by him to King Wehha. They were mostly copper but there was one gold and two silver rings. Wehha turned the armband over in his fingers and admired the unusual patterning, then he pushed it up his left arm where it lodged on his biceps. He handed a silver band each to Tedmund and Wuffa who also slid them up their arms. The copper bands he divided and passed to each and said, "Give these to those who fought most bravely."

A messenger arrived from across the Great Heath. He had come from Selwyn and asked if assistance was needed. Wehha said to him, "Please give our compliments to Ealdorman Selwyn and say that I will visit him tomorrow when his assistance will be discussed."

The stripped bodies of the Britons were thrown without ceremony onto a fire. These included some that had been too wounded to get away and had been swiftly killed. Forty bodies had been found in total and Wehha knew that many that had escaped would have serious and maybe mortal wounds. In the afternoon, the bodies of the Angle dead were lifted onto the huge pyre that had been built. It was lit with prayers to Hel, goddess of the underworld and Woden, to ensure that the brave warriors would join him in Valhalla. Ale and mead were brought up from the valley but the mood remained subdued. Osgar sat near the bottom of the bank with Anson, Henryk, Wilf and Seward.

"It was a great victory, ja," said Henryk, examining the sword that one of the Flemish had taken from a body and presented to him.

"If this is what victory feels like then Woden save us from defeat," Wilf said.

The next day King Wehha of East Anglia crossed the Great Heath, he strode along the white line cut into the turf. He was accompanied by many of his thegns and their ceorls. Wuffa and Tedmund were close to their King with Anson, Osgar and Henryk carrying shield and spear close behind. Each of them had two more copper bands on their arms. When they neared the fen edge of the heath, they could see that there was the beginning of a dyke. It was half the height of the section at the wood end and only extended for two hundred paces from the edge of the water. There was digging going on and soil being carried up the bank but work lacked the numbers and energy of the wood end.

Selwyn met Wehha and grasped his forearm in welcome. He led him to his camp and apologised that it lacked any comforts. Wehha ignored him and walked to the ditch which he scrambled down and then paced up the bank to stand on the top. From the vantage point, he looked over the works and counted the people engaged there. He walked down bank in a slow and controlled manner and strode across the heath back to Selwyn.

"Is there a feast today that I don't know about?" he asked Selwyn, "Or maybe you have also been attacked by the Waelisc and your people have gone into hiding?"

"My lord," said Selwyn, "It has not been so easy here. Our people, the North Folk have farther to come and digging is not so easy."

"You," said Wehha quietly and slowly, "are a disgrace to the Angles. While the Suth Folk fell trees and dig in the heavy clay in the hills, you send just one quarter of the people that I asked for. The people at the wood end have fought and won a battle with the Waelisc and you send a message belatedly offering assistance."

Selwyn began to speak but Wehha raised his hand and continued, "You will pay wergild for disobeying your King. You forfeit your ten hides in the Gipping Valley and your five hides near Beodricesworth. The land in the Gipping Valley will be given to Osgar and Anson who are now raised to thegns. The land near Beodricesworth is divided between Henryk the Flem who is also now made a thegn and Ealdorman Tedmund. You will pay to your King fifty pounds of silver and furthermore you will send twenty men for each one that you have here. They will be here in no greater period than one week, if you fail me in this you will forfeit all lands and titles."

As they walked back towards the forest rising into the hills on the horizon, Wehha told them that he expected the Suth Folk to increase their numbers fourfold. He had calculated as he walked that at the present rate it would take ten years to complete the dyke. He still wanted it finished in less than two. Osgar and Anson were excused digging duties not because they were now thegns but

175

because they were blacksmiths and were expected to make armour and arms and to continue repairing spades and picks. They collected their charcoal and walked to the growing camp in the valley, here they expected to live and work for the next two years. For Osgar, it seemed like eternity and he tried to dispel it from his mind.

*****

Cadrod looked at the sword cuts on his right arm and thigh and the spear wound in his left shoulder as he rode home. His wounds were bound and they throbbed. Only half of the horses were ridden, each warrior also led another horse. When Cadrod had taken his men around the earthworks to join Waljan's band he was sure that victory was theirs. He had sent his men to the left where they would outflank their enemy, but then one of the Sais pigs had broken through. He was wielding only a shield and a short sword, he should have been dispatched easily but he fought like the devil and then three more joined him. One was a great strong man with an axe and another was the one that he had seen on the top of the bank. He had a silver crest on his helmet and wielded a fine sword. Cadrod had aimed to have him but in the melee, he was knocked down and only later realised that he had been saved by Waljan who had grabbed him under his arm and pulled him back.

Cadrod was inconsolable. He knew how close victory had been, the Sais line was giving way and his extra men should have finished the battle. They would have wiped them all out and then gone on to slaughter the women and children. The Sais would have been driven back behind their rivers and within a year he could have driven them from his peoples' land, from Lloegr. He would be the new Arturius, greater than Arturius because he would finish the job that the legendary leader had been unable to complete. Cadrod ate nothing during the ride back to Bannaventa and Waljan had had to insist to his King that they stopped and rested the horses by a stream. Cadrod reconsidered every detail of the battle, he counted his mistakes, he had left his horses and lost their speed and power and finally he had split his force. He had fought the pigs on their prepared ground. When they were in a shield wall, they were very hard to shift but with cavalry and open ground he would defeat them. Then he would send every one of them to their deaths.

176

Aefre watched the horses and men return. She saw their heads hanging low and she counted their number. Only half were returning and many of them had injuries. She knew that she would be called to treat them. She found it a pleasure. She would not show her feelings but would gently ask questions of the battle as she washed their cuts with the strongest astringent she could make. She knew that she would not be told to treat King Cadrod as he would not have her or any Anglecynn near him. She saw him ride past, he had put his head up and his shoulders back when he came in sight of the castle. She saw that he was bandaged on his arm, shoulder and thigh and she hoped that his wounds festered and killed him.

She was called as expected and soon used up her herbs and medicines. She told the steward that she had stripped her garden bare and would have to pick wild herbs from the woods and near the river. She was rarely allowed out of the kitchen garden and was accompanied by a guard who called her a witch and the devil's whore. She walked along the riverbank and through the woods occasionally stopping to pick herbs. The guard carried one of her woven bags and she carried two. He was bored and resented having to carry a bag for the Sais whore. She was just as interested in the lay of the land and seeing if there were any alternative river crossings as looking for herbs.

When next Sigbert visited her, she told him of the route that she had seen across the river.

"So why are you telling me?" Sigbert said, "You are the one always going on about getting home to your beloved Suth Folk."

"I'm not going without Leo," was her reply.

"Well, I'll give it a miss then, if that's all right with you," was all he would say.

Chapter 16
Wuffa

"Thegns eh?" said Wilf, "Don't expect you'll drink with us now."

"Don't be daft," said Anson.

"I'm only pulling your leg," said Wilf. "So what land do you have?"

"There are ten hydes near Gippeswic, between us two," said Anson, "Hild is already on her way to see Hunfrith to get control of it."

"And what about yours?" said Wilf to Henryk.

"It's near Beo," said the tall Flem, "So I can run it from my people's farmstead, ja. We needed more land, we can feed another thirty now."

They were sitting at benches in the valley in the Great Heath where the camp was growing fast. Under Wehha's orders, more had come from all over East Anglia and rows of houses had grown up with areas of workshops jumbled in amongst them. The crafts people worked to service the ditch diggers. Wilf and Seward had made hundreds of wooden spades, while Anson and Osgar made picks and iron tips for them. The spades had a lip of iron over the blade and when these wore or broke, they had to be replaced. Women and children had followed their menfolk to the heath. If they did not work on the dyke beside their men, they stayed in the camps by the forest or fen ends or in the growing camps in the heath valley. Women there spent the day caring for sheep and goats that grazed on the grassland or weaving cloth to supply the continual need for clothes. Winter was on its way and still they dug and banked the chalk. Digging kept them warm and the men worked stripped to their trousers while the women just worked in their peplo dresses which they tucked up. They wore no scyrts or shawls. When they stopped and the wind blew across the heath, it was a cold exposed place. There was no shelter from it from the chilling wind and they joked that it blew in all the way from the Old Country across the cold North Sea.

There was a feeling of pride in the dyke they were building. It was impressive to all and from a distance, it looked like a white wall stretching across the undulating grasslands. It was ten spear lengths in height from the bottom of the 'V' shaped ditch to the narrow ridge on the top of the bank. The only days that the digging stopped were feast days. Work closed for three days at Yule time when the women and older children worked to prepare for it all week. Special breads were made enriched with milk and eggs. These were accompanied by cheeses made from the goat and cow milk. Pigs and goats that had been fattening all summer on the rich grasslands were slaughtered. Families hauled great Yule logs from the forest in a ceremony to mark the feasts beginning and the brewers laboured to produce enough ale for all.

The Yule feast included games and sports and these were added to by using the dyke. Wuffa stood and clapped and cheered as men raced down into the steep ditch and then up the bank the other side. He was not so interested in who won but how quickly a group of men could scale it. He gave prizes to groups of five men who could stand on the ridge and hold off twenty. No arms were allowed only wrestling which seemed to include kicking and punching. While he smiled and clapped, Wuffa calculated how many were needed to hold off an army of Britons. Sometimes Wuffa included himself in a team, neither expecting nor receiving special consideration from the opposition. He was as fit and strong as his men and he wanted them to see it. He was already held in high esteem for his leadership and bravery in battle.

On the third day of Yule, Wuffa led a group across the heath from the forest side to the fen side. The gap in between the two earthworks was still more than half the width of the heath. Scouts had been sent south to give a warning if Waelisc were seen and as still no one felt safe in the middle of the heath. Although they were twenty strong and it would have taken a full war band to defeat them, they knew how vulnerable they were to an attack by horsemen. There had been no major assault since the Battle of Stubs Worth ten months before, Waelisc horsemen had been seen since that time but they kept their distance. Wuffa walked with Osgar, Anson and other thegns. They were closely followed by ceorls such as Wilf and Seward. Osgar asked the Kings Thegn when they would march on the Chalk Hills and destroy the Waelisc.

Wuffa smiled and said, "First we secure the Kingdom and then when this Great Dyke is finished, the Waelisc will have to smash themselves upon it. We have been hunted by them for a generation and we have run and hidden, but no more. When the dyke is finished, they will become our prey."

"But when will that be?" asked Osgar.

"When Wehha says so, young Thunor," said Wuffa and then changed the subject, "have you made the sword yet?"

"No, *sire*," said Osgar, "Anson and I cannot keep up with the repair of tools and the need for more spear heads. I do not have enough quality iron for sword making."

Wuffa unknotted the toggle holding the handle of his sword in the scabbard. He pulled the sword up with his index and first finger hooked under the gilded pommel. The sword slipped from the sheepskin lined sheath and he grasped the handle. As they walked, he practiced sword swings and thrusts.

"I have heard of different swords from the Frankish country," said Wuffa, "A sword that tapers from hilt to point. Not broad along its whole length like our traditional blades."

"Henryk the Flemish has told me of this sword blade, *sire*, but why would you want a sword like that?" asked Osgar.

"The only reason to have a sword like this one," said Wuffa, still twirling his sword, "is so that it is heavy when you swing it. When you hit your enemy, it cuts deep like an axe but it is awkward to thrust and stab at a foe. I saw you in battle; you swung your seax and stabbed the enemy. You have the strength not to need the weight in the blade and a sharp point will stab through leather, also the sword weighs less to cart around all day."

"But the sword is not for him," said Anson, looking at Osgar, "He is supposed to make it for Selwyn and he will not accept anything except a traditional broadsword."

"Let me worry about that," said Wuffa, "The King will decide what is good enough for Selwyn. When the dyke is finished, make the sword. Make it in the tapered style; I want to know how good it is. Then you will be released from your ward and we may go to the kingdom of the Chalk Hills."

Osgar was ecstatic and could only think of making the sword and being released from his wergild ward. Wuffa had promised him that he would go to the Chalk Hills and that meant that he would take an army. He had always tried to imagine the enemy kingdom. He knew so little of the place where his mother and brother had been taken and no doubt enslaved. The very few who had escaped and returned to East Anglia told of a rich, powerful and cruel people and their huge fortress of Bannaventa made of stone. It must be like the old Roman house near Icklingham, thought Osgar. He could not imagine what the life of his mother or brother was like but he knew that they were alive and every day he reminded himself of his promise to Eafwald, his father. He would fetch them home once the dyke was finished and he had made the sword.

They came to the beginning of the ditch and bank. Two guards stood atop the ridge keeping lookout. They nodded to the group and waved their spears to guards further along the banks ridge and the message was passed to the camps nestling behind the dyke near the fens, that they were coming. Wuffa climbed the back of the bank and walked along the crest. It afforded him a good view in all directions and as the bank dipped down from the last chalk undulation towards the fen, he looked across the marshlands as far as his eyes could see. The water and reeds were only broken by mounds rising out of the flat scenery. These were mainly wooded but he could see some shacks and animal enclosures.

The camp had grown and spread over the heath behind the dyke. It was like the one at the forest end, with a combination of tents, houses, shacks and animal enclosures stretching north and east onto the heath. Great fire pits now smouldered with logs reduced to small chunks at the edges. The skeletons of goats carcasses remained skewered on spits above the smoking ashes. People were busy clearing the previous night's remains and preparing for the last day of feasting. A guard of honour of about twenty thegns and fifty ceorls were headed by Tedmund as he greeted Wuffa and the others with genuine delight and pride in his camp. Tedmund clasped the forearm of the Kings Thegn and said, "You are welcome, my lord."

"Tedmund, Ealdorman of Beodricesworth, you do us great honour," said Wuffa loudly enough for all to hear.

Tedmund led them to benches set outside but around a blazing fire. They were all passed cups of mead and toasted first the King and then Skadi God of winter, not forgetting Woden who kept them safe. Wuffa's party mixed well with their mainly north folk hosts, Wuffa had briefed them during their walk that he wanted them to find out about the mood of their brothers and fellow Angles. Many previously knew each other or were already related through marriage. There was the usual banter, ribbing and jokes, with many of the North Folk jokes aimed at the fen Gwyre, usually involving either interbreeding or webbed feet. Osgar had been delighted to find that Cynbeald was at the camp. He complained that he was old and that his joints hurt and he should not be camped out on a godless heath. He admitted that he was well looked after and was still dining off his tale of the Battle of the Three Bridges. After a few cups of mead, he admitted that when he told the tale he was now the one that held the bridge and that was against a seven-foot Waelisc giant with an eye in the centre of his forehead. He apologised to Osgar who just laughed and said that was just how he remembered it also.

"Now tell me of the fight at Stubs Worth," said Cynbeald to all of them, "I want to know the heroic parts that you all played? I need the inside story from those who were there."

When they had finished telling Cynbeald of that day's events, he clapped his hands together in delight and shouted for more mead and bread and meat. "This one will see me out," he said, "I'll take this story around East Anglia and they will hear it in all the Great Halls of the Land." I was getting sick of telling the three bridges tale and Beowulf is for kids, "This one will see me out."

Wuffa moved towards a smaller fire and said to Cynbeald, "Bring me some of that good mead and tell me of your adventures around our land. It's a while since we spoke."

Wuffa put his arm around Cynbeald's shoulder and led him away. The others could see that Wuffa only wanted the company of the old scop. The two stood by another fire and Wuffa fed more logs on it until the flames leapt to their head height. As Wuffa tended the fire and Cynbeald spoke, they were out of earshot of the others but all could see that it was mostly Cynbeald who talked. Wuffa looked up from the fire occasionally and stared at Cynbeald.

Osgar and Anson sat with a North Folk ceorl between them. He came from the far north of the country on the edge of the Gewaesc. He was not a tall man but was strong in his arms and shoulders. He had blond curly hair and a neat trimmed goatee, which was the only thing neat about him. His head was dome shaped and seemed too large for his body and his bright blue eyes had a look of continual surprise. The clothes he wore were not well kept, his cloak was cheap and dirty along the bottom fringe and he had a hole in one knee of his trousers. His most memorable characteristic was his moaning. He complained about the weather and he moaned that he should not be on the heath digging the dyke and he whined so much that Osgar and Anson made their excuses and moved to another fire. He rose with them and followed, whinging incessantly.

By the afternoon's end, Anson and Osgar each knew his children's names; that he was on his second wife and that despite being a skilled trader, life had not been fair to him. He spoke much about Selwyn his Ealdorman, sometimes he spoke with great admiration and told of how he, Wilburh, had helped to raise him to his position and sometimes he moaned of how taxed he was by Selwyn. At all times, he gave them the impression that he was a close friend and advisor. At one point, he decided to tell a joke about the Jutes and Anson stared at him in disbelief. The basis of the joke was that Jutes carried their shields on their backs so that they were protected when running from the enemy. Anson told him that if he was stupid enough not to realise that he, Anson was Jute, and did not shut up he would hit him so hard that he, "would be searching in his turds for his teeth."

Osgar saw that Cynbeald and Wuffa had finished talking and jumped up saying to Anson and Wilburh, "Look, I have to speak to Cynbeald, but you two stay here."

Anson glowered at Osgar but Wilburh continued telling how the Waelisc now even interfered with trade across the Gewaesc to the kingdom of Lindsey. "Will you come back to our camp by the forest," said Osgar to Cynbeald, "I miss your stories."

"I would like that," said Cynbeald. "But now I have my new battle story and the one place I cannot tell it is where it happened, too many people who know the truth. I shall go north and tell it to the North Folk, Wuffa wants me to tell them of what a good job their people are doing in building the dyke and how it is protecting them."

As afternoon turned to evening, the temperature dropped and an icy wind blew across the heath. They retired to the tents and temporary housing in the camp. Tedmund took Wuffa from one to another so that he met all the people in the camp. He reassured them that their work was saving their country and how grateful their King was to each and all. Finally, they all rolled themselves in their cloaks and slept.

The low midwinter sun rose as an orange ball over the grey frosty heath. Osgar unrolled himself from his cloak and pinned the broach under his neck. He left the shack that had sheltered him and walked towards the high bank, on its ridge stood Wuffa surveying the scene. The Kings Thegn greeted him as he climbed the frozen chalk bank.

"We shall visit the Gwyre people today," said Wuffa looking out into the fens. "We shall talk of trade with them, I like their fish."

"But, *sire*," said Osgar, "everyone knows that they spy for the Waelisc. They are Waelisc."

"Tell me," said Wuffa, "what do we need to win a battle?"

"Speed, strength and bravery, *sire*," said Osgar.

"A bull has speed and strength," said Wuffa, "and if it bravely charges an oak tree, who wins? You are my bull, young Thunor, and I know you will smash my enemies, but I will not waste you on an Oak. From the Gwyre we shall learn all about our enemies."

Wuffa took Tedmund, Osgar and Henryk along the dyke to where it dipped towards the fen marshes. The ditch here had filled with water for a few hundred paces so that it ran inland like a canal. Several coracles met them at the edge of the fens and they were paddled to a Gwyre settlement on one of the clay hillocks that emerged from the waters and reeds. None of them felt comfortable in the round vessels made of willow and skins, while the Gwyre boatmen paddled them seemingly without effort. Wuffa spoke through a Gwyre interpreter to the headman and thanked him for allowing their visit and the hospitality of their welcome and food. He passed a bag of silver to him and said that was for supplying fish to the people building the dyke and that there would be much more trade for them in the years to come. The headman was clearly happy with this and said that it would be like the old days when they took their eels and fish as far as Beodricesworth and Theod-ford. Wuffa smiled and told him that trade would be even better than the old days once the dyke was finished and that it would not be necessary for his people to cart their goods so far. The Gwyre were told that Tedmund and Henryk would send carts to trade at the fens edge and there would be no need for them to cross the dry land.

"Henryk," said Wuffa, "show them your pottery wear."

Henryk uncovered a drinking cup and passed it to the headman who turned it around in his hand as Henryk's words to him were translated, "This is my gift to you, I can bring a cartload to the water's edge and we can trade with you."

The headman passed the drinking cup around and Wuffa watched them nod in approval. He then said, "You are the people of the water and we of the land, we will not encroach on your territory, we only ask for your friendship and trade."

The headman said, "For this, you will not wish us to trade with the people that you call the Waelisc, our Cymry cousins."

"Not so," said Wuffa, "We would not wish to deny you this trade; in fact we would encourage it."

The headman smiled with relief as Wuffa's words were told to him, "We are so interested in your success in trade with your cousins that we would wish you to tell Tedmund all that you do and see."

*****

The dyke building continued through the cold winter. The Angles were glad to work during daylight hours to stay warm. When the ground froze, they broke it with picks and shovelled the icy humps into the wicker baskets and tipped them onto the bank. They wore the tips off the picks, broke spades and burst the wicker baskets. These were sent back across the heath to be mended or replaced. Anson and Osgar laboured in their forge in the heath valley. There were always piles of tools to repair and when they were not doing that, they were forging spears and shield bosses for Wehha's growing fyrd. They were expected to exercise with all other thegns and ceorls, practicing all the skills of war. Sometimes they fought mock battles using only their shields which Osgar relished and at other times aetgars were thrown at targets. Wuffa drilled his Suth Folk men on the heath until locking shields and moving as one was second nature to them.

Next to Anson and Osgar was another blacksmith forge with three smiths. Anson had a new apprentice boy who fetched and carried, pumped the bellows and struck with the second sledgehammer. Sometimes he struck just for Osgar who heard his own voice repeating the same words that Anson had said to him, "Land it level and follow my lead. Don't try to hit it too hard. Timing and precision, boy, timing and precision. Strike while the iron is hot."

There was a family of bakers between their forge and Wilf and Seward's carpentry shop. The ovens had been made of flat stones and covered with turf. They were filled with wood each day and lit. When the wood had finally burnt down the hot ashes were raked out and the dough placed on the flat stones on the bottom. The dough was expertly dropped into place with a flat shovel-like implement and removed when the baker felt they were ready. Fresh baked bread at their noon break was always a treat. The bread varied according to the grain used, it could be wheat, barley or rye.

The leatherworks were close by, making belts, boots, aprons, and other apparel as well as shield coverings for the richer thegns. There were no potters on the heath as it was easier to make the kilns on the clay woodlands where they were supplied with the two materials they needed. The Flemish carted their wares to the growing market on the heath. They sold cups and storage jars as well as lamps and the occasional burial urn. The lamps were filled with wax and tallow by thegns, who could afford them. Ceorls would rather sit in the dark or by the light of a fire than barter for lamp fuel. Weavers and dyers had also moved to the heath setting up their workshops near one another. Some were the wives and daughters of those engaged in the dyke building or supplying the tradesmen, for others it was their main trade. Thegns always bought the finest cloth that they could afford but on the cold exposed heath, they bought the warmest. Their old clothes were given to ceorls as payment or handed down to slaves. They would only hand down undergarments that were not decorated with fine dying or embroidery. No thegn would allow a slave or a ceorl to be seen in their old outer clothes.

Although it brought back bad memories for Osgar, he was glad to celebrate Eostre, it meant that the hard cold winter was finally over and spring had arrived. It was the first break that they had had since Yule.

"Hello Astara and goodbye Skadi," said Anson raising a cup of ale.

They had gathered by a fire with their usual bunch of friends, craftsmen, traders and guards. Henryk was there as his group of Flemish were off duty from guarding the dyke. "I think that the dyke will finish this year, Ja," he said.

"Then will you come with me to the Chalk Hills?" said Osgar.

"You raising your own fyrd?" said the Flem.

"If I have to, I will," said Osgar.

"I come if Wuffa says so," said Henryk, "and I think my men come too. They want to see you use that seax of yours and see if you are as good as I say, Ja."

"Have you seen anything of the Waelisc?" said Anson to Henryk.

"We see them sometimes," replied Henryk. "But they are few and they don't come close. We sound the horns and light the beacons and the men mount the bank. They are not stupid; they can see we are ready for them."

"I am told that they attack our cousins, the Saxons to their south," said Wilf. "They find it easier to get to their hams. They now suffer as once we did."

"King Cuthwulf of the Saxons has sent a message to our King Wehha," said Henryk, "or so I have been told. That can only mean one thing, ja. He is asking for our help."

"Why should we help them?" said Seward, "When we needed help, who did he send?"

"That's the same as the North Folk say to us," Wilf chided his son, "Together we can destroy them and make this land safe."

"I'll join him," said Osgar, "I'll go with the Saxons to the Chalk Hills."

"And who's going to lead our army then?" said Anson slapping him on the shoulder, "More ale for our leader who is deserting his men before an aetgar has been thrown."

"You have waited too long Osgar, I know," said the Flem, "but your time comes, ja."

They drank ale and shared sweet bread while they watched the stream of people pass them by. Many were carrying goods to trade and some were walking to work on the dyke but many others were visiting the heath just to see the great white bank and ditch. All Anglia knew of it and every ham had supplied workers who had returned home. They told every family of the astonishing work so that even those who had never left their ham in their lives wanted to see it. It became a pilgrimage for many, who walked from every corner of the kingdom to stand in awe at the top of the bank, to look down into the steep white ditch and out across the rolling landscape towards the kingdom of the Chalk Hills.

*****

The emissary from King Cuthwulf of the South Saxons was sat alongside King Wehha in the Great Hall in the Gipping Valley. It was the centre of Wehha's power base, the grandest hall in all of Anglia. All wood panels and beams were carved with geometric designs entwined with dragons, wolves, boars and bears. Wall hangings depicted victorious battles and epic tales while around the tables, women rushed to and fro serving food and ale. Wehha sat with Wuffa to his right and the Saxon thegn to his left. He sat with his hands on the armrests of his high-backed oak chair and ate and drank little but coughed occasionally. His hair was mostly grey and parted in the middle, as was his neatly clipped beard. Behind him, on an oak carved table, was his helmet trimmed with gold. He kept his cloak clipped under the neck with a large gold brooch although the weather was mild. He ordered the Reeve to see that there was more wood put on the fire and listened attentively to the words sent by Cuthwulf, about whom he had heard so much but never met.

187

"My lord, King Cuthwulf," began the emissary, "sends his compliments to you King Wehha of all Angles. He praises you and your fyrd for fighting back the Waelisc and desires to see, one day, the wondrous white wall that you build across the land." The emissary stopped to check that the King was listening to him as his eyes were down. Wehha looked at him and turned his right-hand palm up and flicked his fingers to signal for him to continue. "Now our land is attacked by the Waelisc, they rape and kill our women and our children are stolen into slavery. Our farmsteads are raided and we are being pushed south. My King must attack with all our forces but we may not have enough to defeat them. We ask that you send your Fyrd to attack from the east and north."

"My lord, my King Cuthwulf says this to you. If the Waelisc push us into the sea, where next will they turn? They will turn back to you. Our fight is your fight as yours is ours."

Wehha paused and thought on what he had heard. He sipped the warmed mead from a silver goblet and coughed before answering. "You must tell your King," said Wehha, "that he is my dear cousin and it pains me to hear how he suffers. I am as yet unable to send you my fyrd. The dyke that he talks of is not finished, all either guard or build it and I have no more men in my whole Kingdom. To build this great white dyke we have neglected our fields and our animals so much that we have famine and can barely feed ourselves and our women work like men. We will finish our dyke in the year and then we will speak of taking the fyrd to the Chalk Hills and ridding the world of this demon."

The emissary began to speak but Wehha held up his hand and said, "You stay and enjoy the feast. My nephew, the Kings Thegn Wuffa will speak with you."

King Wehha rose with a helping hand from Wuffa and the whole Great Hall stood. Each thegn bowed as the King passed and stayed erect until he had left the hall. The emissary turned to Wuffa, leant across the empty chair left by the king, and said, "You must change his mind. Surely you see that what my King Cuthwulf says is true."

"I believe it is true," replied Wuffa, "but the King will not change his mind. I have tried many times. When this dyke is finished, then I will convince him that we must join you in a great attack. You must hold them until the feast of Astara comes next year. They will not attack in winter; survive the summer my cousin."

The next day, the emissary left with his entourage of thegns and ceorls. They would march to Gippeswic to begin the long trip around the southeast of the island. Each night the ships would be harboured and would not leave in inclement weather and the journey would take almost a month. There was no choice as the Kingdom of the Chalk Hills blocked the old trade routes which would have been walked in less than a week.

Chapter 17
Waljan

Bishop Cadog Ddoeth the Wise had journeyed across the land of the Irish. For a whole month, he had waited for fair weather and a westerly breeze to take him and his company to Britannia. He gave sermons to the people and was joined in prayer by his monks and the Angle Leofric who travelled with him. The Bishop liked a little mystique to surround him and knew that it made his sermons better attended. Leofric was encouraged to keep his hood down so that the people could see his blonde hair and also to speak to the horses in his strange tongue. He still cared for the horses as the Bishop's head groom but had been given reading lessons as promised. The Bishop was surprised by how quickly he learnt Latin. He supposed that it was because he had already had to master their language or maybe it was a gift from God.

They travelled with traders who were taking their wares to Calchfynedd. Their handcarts contained iron implements and arms while others had fine carved bone and animal skins. They knew that they would get a fine price for their goods as the Kingdom was hemmed in by the Saxons and Angle Sais and could only trade with the Cymry to the west. They received good prices in Calchfynedd as there was always war booty from their raids into Lloegr.

The Bishop, Leofric and the two monks, had travelled to Contac Loch Garman in the far southeast of Erin. There they sheltered for another week while the winds blew towards the south, finally they calmed and swung around to the southwest. Their ship sailed for a day to beach on the most westerly peninsular of the Kingdom of Dyfed, near to the shrine of St David. They paid their respects with a visit before continuing west over the mountains. Leofric was happy, each morning he looked for the rising sun and knew that he was heading towards his homeland. He prayed to the Christian God to preserve him, his mother and his people. He believed in this god who had saved him from a life of pain and humiliation but wanted him to rain death and destruction upon all of the Waelisc. He kept all this to himself, while prayed, worked diligently and learned to read and write Latin.

They arrived in Bannaventa to great acclaim from the crowds. The Bishop dismounted his horse and walked. His horse was not lame this time but he had realised how the people liked him down on their level. He used his gold crossed staff to lean on as he made his way through the muddy street between houses to the Castle. He saw that the walls had been rebuilt but his church had no roof upon it and decided that he would not leave until it was finished. The warrior Waljan greeted him, kissed his proffered hand and led him to his rooms.

Cadrod, as always, had arranged for a feast to celebrate the Bishop's return. He sat the Bishop to his left while they ate, musicians played with flute and drums and sang accompanied by a lyre. The Bishop's monks sat at the far end of the hall. Cadrod had not allowed Leofric in with them.

"Why you have that straw haired devil with you, I do not know," said Cadrod.

"I have been guided by God," answered the Bishop. "He saved my cross, which is blessed by the Saint Enda of Arran. He dived into the raging torrent to rescue it, where no man could live."

"That proves he's a devil," said Cadrod.

"I think I am best placed to decide who is a devil and who a saint. I would wish that he may visit his mother, a garden slave."

"Yes," said Cadrod smiling, "He can say goodbye to her. I am going to sell her west as she is a witch and I will no longer have her here."

Waljan sat on the King's right and looked aghast. Before he could speak, Cadrod said, "You see Bishop, how she has even cast a spell on my best warrior. He is like a puppy dog and seeks any excuse to go to the garden for herb treatments."

"*Sire*," said Waljan, "she heals so many and causes no trouble."

"She is a slave and will be sold tomorrow with other slaves that we have taken from the south."

Waljan's head sunk and he ate no more and when the table laughed and clapped at the bard's tales, he sat silently thinking of Aefre. As each day passed, she seemed more beautiful to him. He knew that she was his to take anytime he wished. Sometimes she even told him this but he desperately wanted her to need him. He had not thought of another woman apart from Aefre since his wife had died giving birth to their son who lived just two more days. She reminded him of his wife with her whole demeanour. Her looks were even similar, although Aefre's skin was darker and her hair lighter, she had the same penetrating eyes, full lips and almond shaped face.

Waljan left at the end of the feast but before he had passed through the stone archway, he felt a hand on his elbow. It was one of the Bishop's monks.

"His Grace asks if you would like to share some wine with him," said the monk.

Waljan was about to make his excuses but thought better of it and said, "A kind invitation. I would be pleased to do so."

"Ah, do come in and take a seat," said the Bishop as he nodded to the monk to pour wine from a silver pitcher. "You did not seem yourself at the feast. The slave woman still troubles you, I know but I was thinking of how little, otherwise, I know of you. I seem to have been aware of you, here in Calchfynedd, since you were a boy. You always attend church and I have seen the sincerity with which you pray."

"Your Grace, as always you see straight through us," replied Waljan, "I think of her all the time and cannot remove her from my thoughts and now my king will sell her west. I can live with her not being my wife but I could not go forever without seeing her again."

"You will find the answer to that problem, I know but what else troubles you?"

"I have always lived by a code passed down to me by my father and his father before him. When my grandfather was driven from the eastern lands of Lloegr, he had nothing but he fought at Mynned Baddon for Arturius. They destroyed the Sais and slaughtered them but there was no child killing and rape. They lived by Arturius' warrior code and that is how I try to live."

"When Arturius died, my grandfather came to Bannaventa with Cynfelyn ap Arthwys, founder of Calchfynedd and father of Cynwyd. He was given land to start a new life with my grandmother and showed his gratitude with loyalty all his life. Likewise, my father served Cynwyd his son and I have served Cadrod. I have risen high by being in the employ of King Cadrod. I have gold, land and influence but not happiness. I find that I can no longer hate the Sais. Father, how can I continue to serve my King?"

Cadog, the Wise, sipped his wine, gazed at Waljan and spoke, "Nowhere did our Good Lord Jesus ask us to hate our enemies, so you can let that trouble you

192

no more. You must find a way to serve your king, here on earth, without breaking your code of Arturius. Just remember though, the Sais are pagans and until they are all Christian, they will be our enemy."

*****

Aefre rose early as always and left her hovel to watch the sun rise. She scanned the horizon but saw no change. She prayed to her gods to keep her family safe, that Osgar was now a fine Ceorl working alongside his father. She prayed that Leofric would return to her and be protected and that he would reject the Waelisc God. She knew that his following the Britons ways had saved him but she still could not bear to think of him as a Waelisc.

Then she saw a group walking down the pathway from the kitchen doorway. It was two hooded monks and her son Leofric. She stared and dare not move in case the vision should disappear. When they reached her, the monks stood back a few paces and Aefre held his outstretched hands in hers and pulled him towards her. She kissed him on both cheeks and gripped him as if she would never let go. She said quietly, "I knew that Woden would return you safely to me."

"I am saved by the one true God," said Leofric.

Aefre stepped back and looked at her son, only his blonde hair made him any different to the Britons. "Are you now a Waelisc?" she asked.

"No mother, with all my heart I am of the people, I am Angle."

"How long will you remain here?" she asked.

"Until the Bishop Cadog says that we go," said Leofric, "that may be some years though because he will not leave until his church is finished."

They sat and talked while drinking tea from unglazed pottery cups. He told all he could of his life during the years that they had been separated and she tried to update him with the few changes in Bannaventa. She had never wished to be parted from her son but she saw before her a healthy young man and enjoyed his description of the mysterious Erin beyond the sea at the edge of the world. After some time the monks signalled that they must leave. Aefre watched them walk back up the pathway and enter the castle through the kitchen door. For the first time in many years, she felt happiness. Leofric was safely returned and although she was still a slave, she would have opportunities to see him in the coming years.

*****

King Cadrod talked with the Bishop while they toured the outer courtyard of Bannaventa. The many workshops against the far wall were busy. There were the usual carpenters and leather workers alongside stalls that sold food, pottery, dyed cloth and metal cauldrons. The blacksmiths shop was noticeable by both the smoke rising from it and the noise of hammer striking hot iron causing the rhythmic ringing sound that could be heard over all other noises. In the middle of the courtyard was the church. The foundations had been finished and the walls rose above the height of two men. The shapes of the twelve windows along either side could be seen. They were arched inward to form the same Roman style of the old castle. The walls were an arm's length in thickness but no mortar held them together as this secret had been lost with the Roman departure. The walls were buttressed between the window gaps to strengthen them where the great oak beams would cross the church to form the base of the roof.

The Bishop was unhappy with the lack of progress and told the King so. He, in turn, explained how in these dangerous times he could not commit more people to the church building. "God punished you and all Calchfynedd for not finishing his church as I had asked," said the Bishop. "He saw that you were defeated by the Sais on the Great Heath."

"Then why does he give me so many victories against the Saxon Sais to the south?" asked Cadrod in annoyance.

"Because he is merciful," replied the Bishop, "and because he wants you to drive the pagans from our lost lands. Build my church, destroy the pagans in the south and the Lord God will show you how to defeat the Angle Sais and their white wall."

As they left the church, a group of Saxon captives were being pulled from the pit. They were naked and huddled as one trying to protect themselves from the blows. Guards prodded and smacked them with staves and they were driven down to the river bound together. They clearly believed that they were going to be drowned but instead they were dunked in the river where the horses were washed and made to clean themselves. They were again herded by the guards to the main courtyard where they were tied to posts. Cadrod looked at them with distain.

"We have more slaves than we need," he said to the Bishop. "Our raids to the south have proven so fruitful and I can sell them to our western Cymry where I hope they will be worked to death."

Through the archway was dragged an Angle woman dressed in decent clothes. The Bishop recognised her as the mother of Leofric. She was taken to a post, stripped and tied to it. She tried to cover herself with her hands. The Bishop was taken by her beauty and how even degraded and humiliated like this there was an aura about her.

"Why is she here?" asked the Bishop.

"Because I want rid of her," said Cadrod, "You want to buy her?"

The Bishop pouted his lips and swung his head from side to side, "A pagan woman is no use to me."

Some of the traders came to inspect the slaves. They looked at them no differently than if they were buying a goat or a sword. Their mouths were opened and if they did not immediately cooperate, they were punched by a trader or prodded by a guard. Arms and legs were felt for strength and genitals squeezed. Aefre went into her own world where she could feel nothing. Her body was someone else's and she thought of East Anglia and prayed to her gods to send these Waelisc to Hel. She did not cry even when she thought of her son Leofric. She knew that he lived and was safe even if he now prayed a Waelisc God. She hated this place but did not want to go farther west, where her people would never find her.

Finally, the auctioning began and the group of traders and some richer Cymry from Calchfynedd moved from slave to slave. The first was a boy of about ten years old who trembled and cried with his head down. There were bids of silver and copper and also goods. Cadrod's slave master laughed at some of the offers and reminded the traders of how big and strong Angles grew.

"This boy is for the future. Work the little bastard in your house and in a few years work him in the fields. Look," he said pointing to the boy's genitals with his silver topped staff and at the weeping blood running down the inside of each leg, "I gelded him myself this morning. He will only think about working and eating now, no other distractions."

They laughed and the offers rose, finally the slave master accepted a small weight of silver for him. Then the group of bidders and auctioneer slave-master moved down the row with the same game played out, of low offers being laughed away by the slave-master who then drew their attention to the attributes of the slave for sale. With each completed deal, they neared Aefre, she did not know whether to remain calm and cooperative and hope for a good owner or fight and spit like a demon so that no one wanted her. By the time they reached her, she had decided just to pray to Woden that she was bought by someone who would work her to death quickly.

The other slaves had understood nothing of what was going on. They had been captives for only one week and could not comprehend a word of the strange language of the Britons. When the group of traders reached her, she stood passively with her chin up and her hands by her side. They could see that she was not a young girl but a grown woman in her early thirties. The slave master extolled her virtues telling them that she already spoke their language so did not need teaching it. She was a herbalist of repute in Bannaventa, her wound cures were legendary and women sought her for fertility and pregnancy treatment.

"Look at her demeanour," said the slave master "We believe that she was a Sais Queen when taken by our great King Cadrod. Think of the fun that you can have with her serving your every need." He licked his lips and looked at each trader. "Do I have my first bid?"

The bids were good, far better than the slave master had expected. He had done a good job he thought to himself and wondered why he had not given her a try out himself. The bids were down now to just two of the traders, the others had dropped out. Three copper armbands and two iron cauldrons against two copper bands and some fine bone handled knives.

"Just look at her," said the slave master. "This very evening on your way west, you will have her warming your bed. Just a little more will secure her for you."

Aefre looked at the fat trader who examined her up and down, sweated and smiled. His counter bidder had a thin face and a hooked nose. Some of his teeth were missing and he scratched his groin as he leered at her. A silver armband was dropped over the staff of the auctioning slave master and rested where it met his hand. All looked round to see Waljan by the shoulder of the slaver master.

"I think that makes her mine?" he said. "Take her back to her hovel, unless anyone cares to pay more silver."

Chapter 18
The Tapered Sword

During spring, the dyke building had slowed as half of the men and women were allowed to return to their homes to plant the fields. They were given one month and then expected to return under threat of wergild. King Wehha and his close councillors knew that without a good harvest that year the people would starve. Disease would then fall upon them and they would be weakened so much that the Great Dyke would be in vain. Wehha had heard also of the dissent that was brewing amongst the North Folk. Selwyn was always first to pull people away from the heath, slowest in allowing them to return. The taxes and deprivations that he placed on them were blamed upon Wehha and his Wuffingas family. The North Folk resented that they were ruled by a dynasty whose powerbase was in the Gipping Valley.

When the planting season was over, all the dyke builders drifted back. The traders and craftsmen returned also and the two ends of the dyke moved inexorably together. Both building sites were on the almost flat heath and were now digging into pure chalk where there were few stones, just occasional flints. The chalk was solid and had to be broken with picks and then shovelled up or lifted into the wicker baskets. The two ends advanced towards each other and the gap closed by almost twenty paces each day. They worked through the hot summer with water carted to them during the day. Lookouts kept watch for any sign of raiding Britons who were sometimes seen in the distance. When this happened, horns were sounded, the beacons lit and the men snatched up their shields and spears and formed up on the bank and at each end into defensive lines. Women and the younger Angles scampered back along the back of the bank to the safety of the defended hams where the dyke joined the woods and the fens.

There were always men at arms ready who exercised on the heath under the direction of their thegns. They practiced the shield wall and all the manoeuvres needed to keep it intact in battle. They held mock fights where some would guard the ridge while others took on the role of attackers. Many of the men had invested in more armour as they had seen the injuries from the battle at Stubs Worth. The men who defended the bank had received wounds to their legs because they stood high and could not lower their shields. Those that fought in the shield wall suffered injuries to their arms, necks and faces. The tanners and leatherworkers were kept busy making cheek pieces and neck protectors to attach to their helmets. They made arm guards and leg guards that could be strapped on. Thegns with more wealth invested in hauberks to protect their necks and upper chests. Chainmail was rare and had to be imported from the Old Country or the land of the Franks. A few had a hauberk that covered the head, cheeks and back of the neck and some of these thegns had thin iron cheek plates and neck protectors that hung from the thicker iron helmets. Wuffa had Anson and Osgar make him a faceplate like Wehha's. It was suspended from the brow of his helmet and had two large eyes cut in it. The plate was thickened in front of his nose and the plate was moulded to the contours of his face. It gave him a strange unearthly appearance when worn but he usually had a ceorl carry his helmet alongside him. The only time he wore it was when the horn sounded or in mock battles.

Anson said to Osgar when he saw Wuffa wearing it, "It scares the shit out of me. What will it do to the enemy?"

"It will bring them to him," said Osgar, "and we shall be alongside him."

"I hadn't thought of that," said Anson. "Do you care?"

"No," said Osgar.

*****

The end of summer came and the time for harvest was upon them. Once more half the people were allowed to go home to gather it in. Work on the dyke slowed for a month while crops were reaped and the grain stored safely away. When they returned the people drove young sheep and goats to fatten on the grasslands. They knew that they were going to have to work one last winter in the middle of the cold heath and then the dyke would be finished. They worked in all weathers without pause. When it rained, the thegns had many of them smoothing the chalk ditch and bank. The wet chalk was beaten into smaller pieces and smudged together with the backs of spades. When it was hot and dry, the chalk was too hard to be smoothed, so they concentrated upon digging and piling the chalk onto the bank. They worked in the bright reflection of the white bank. Their skin was tanned brown and their hair was sun bleached blonde. All of them were stronger and fitter than they had ever been. They carried no spare fat and their muscles were defined on their arms and legs.

When the dyke reached the fens, the ditch filled with water until the bank began to rise up the chalk heath. Where the bottom of the 'V' shaped ditch was dry, Thunorny brambles were encouraged to grow to create another barrier. The only gap built into the dyke was where the old Roman road, following the Icknield Way as it travelled across the heath met the dyke. There was left a gap of five paces wide to allow handcarts through. There had been much debate between Wuffa and Tedmund as to whether even this small gap was a defensive weakness. They decided that there needed to be a place where the few traders ventured through and this was so narrow that twenty men would hold it against an attack. The banks either side were given a palisade and pickets were drawn across the gap each evening. Wuffa believed that the Waelisc might be drawn to attack the only passage through the dyke and therefore drilled the men in its defence.

When Yule came, the distance between the two banks was only four hundred paces. The autumn had been mild with only light rains and digging had continued without delay since harvest time. Because they were so close, the Suth Folk and North Folk met and mixed more. It was a short walk between the two gangs that could be crossed during a break. There was little moaning now from the North Folk as most of the biggest whiners had found reason to be replaced and gone back to their hams north of the Little Ouse and the Waveney. During the two years of digging, many of the young women had found partners and Wuffa encouraged this, especially when it involved a marriage uniting the North and Suth Folks. Wuffa made great play of marriage and encouraged the people to produce children. He married a girl from rich North Folk family himself and soon she was with child.

Anson had mentioned to Osgar a number of times that he should marry Lynne and if he did not, he would lose her. He had been prompted by Wilf who told him his daughter would not wait forever. Osgar only ever said that he would marry Lynne when his mother had seen and approved her as was the custom. It was the only subject that Osgar and Anson ever fell out over.

"You are not the only boy to have lost his parents in a raid," were words that only led to Osgar sulking or beating iron into the late evening. The next day it was always forgotten but Anson knew that only one thing drove Osgar on.

When Yule was over Anson said to Osgar, "It's time we made that sword of yours. A thegn without a sword is like a boar without tusks."

"But it's not my sword," said Osgar, "I will have to give it to Selwyn or I will not be released from my ward."

"I do not think that Wuffa is in any hurry to release you from your ward or to do Selwyn the honour of having you present him with a sword," said Anson. "Let's just make the sword and see. If we have to make another, then so be it."

Osgar bucked up and said to the apprentice, "Come on boy, we have a bloomery to build and then we do some real smiting. No more pick sharpening or spade tips."

Osgar sifted through the tangle of broken implements and pieces of pig iron until he found the rods of iron that he had been given to him by Hunfrith in Gippeswic. Although they had always been laid on wood to keep them off the damp floor, they had a coat of rust on them from condensation in the forge. He looked at all of them laid across the anvil and said to Anson, "Not enough, how can I make the sword without enough good iron?"

Anson looked at the iron bars and said, "We can make the tapered sword that Henryk spoke of. The tang handle does not need to be the best iron. I can find some good iron for you to weld into the blade. You will have enough. In return, you are going to help me make a war axe. I feel more comfortable fighting with one, you can kill a horse with a well-aimed blow. Try doing that with a sword."

During the next two days, Osgar and the boy built the bloomery furnace using the only stone available, which was flint. It was not ideal but it built strong walls and then they lined it inside and out with clay that they fetched from the woodland slopes. They made three trips with two handcarts to collect charcoal. At least the carts were empty going uphill and most of the route back to the valley was downhill. By the time that they were ready, Anson had handed Osgar a final pound of good iron.

"Don't even ask how I got it," he said. "It will be worth it just to see if you have not forgotten how to sword-make or if it was a total waste of time sending you to Hunfrith."

Osgar lit the bloomery furnace with wood and then fed the charcoal into the top of it. He adjusted the air vents until the draught was just right. The apprentice worked the bellows when he was told. Osgar placed one bar of iron in the fire and when it was almost yellow heat, he put the next bar in. The sides of the tongs that he used had rounded jaws to grip the rods firmly. He drew the bar out and tapped it on the anvil to rid it of some scaly slag that had oxidised onto it and then he struck it with his three-pound hammer. The apprentice struck it on the exact spot that he had hit it and he drew the tongs towards him in his left hand as his right hand brought his hammer down again. This time the blow overlapped the first and as he raised his arm with the recoil, the sledgehammer again hit the same spot. He worked his hammer quicker this time and again drew the bar towards himself. The blows speeded up and all could hear the increase in rhythm. Osgar knew just how fast he could push the apprentice before he would tire and mishit the iron. They worked their way down the rod and it stretched and tapered towards the end. It was still orange heat and Osgar turned it sideways. They ran a series of blows down it and then while red, Osgar worked it himself checking that it was an even square taper along its length. He placed the rod next to the fire where he could use it to ensure all five rods tapered the same. By the time he had placed it down, the apprentice was around the side of the furnace pumping the bellows. Osgar pulled the second rod from the fire. It was a yellow heat and they repeated the process for a second time.

Once all five rods were the same length and taper, he heated them again. This time he worked without the sledge. He turned the angle on its edge and run his hammer down the top angle. He turned the rod a quarter turn and did the same. The rod was now octagonal and he then kept resting it on the angle and hammering along the top edge. In one heat, the square taper was now a round taper. He put this rod to one side to use as a template for the other four. Osgar removed his tunic and the sweating apprentice boy did the same and both retied the thick apron thongs behind their necks.

He took the iron that Anson had given him and used it to fire weld all five rods together. Once they were all securely welded at their thick ends, he began the process of twisting and weaving the rods. He could only twist the rods over a couple of times before they had cooled to orange and he could not weave them like rope. The weaving took two days before Osgar was happy enough with the result to move on to the next stage.

The tang at the hilt end had been drawn down to almost its final dimensions. It was still square and not pointed yet so that it could be held securely with the tongs. Osgar checked all the tools, the fire and there was enough charcoal before saying that they were ready to start. Anson was on hand to help and as he watched the process intently. The rods were in the bottom of the furnace and Osgar wiped the anvil face with his apron and blew the flakes of oxidised iron off. He did this between each heat, which was as much from nerves as a necessary part of the process. He pulled the iron from the bloomery furnace and laid it on the anvil. The woven bars and tang were heavy now and in total the metal weighted two and a half pounds.

Osgar could see the shimmering wash of the molten iron moving on the surface and hammered the woven rods. The apprentice struck on the same spot and following his master's rhythm and power of strike. If Osgar hit harder then so did the boy and with each heat, the blade lengthened. Before placing it back in the furnace, Osgar checked that the pattern was symmetrical and that the blade was drawing down evenly. Once he was satisfied that the blade was made and that it was long enough and an even thickness with the correct taper, he cooled the blade. He wrapped the flap of his apron around the blade and placed the tang end into the hot charcoals. Once it was hot enough, he forged it to a tapering point perfectly central to the blade.

The next day, Anson arrived with enough pig fat for them to fill a trough for the tempering process. He carefully watched his nephew and ex apprentice evenly heat the blade and temper it. When the hardening was completed, the sharpening began on the grindstone wheel. The apprentice boy turned the stone wheel, sparks flew and the noise put their teeth on edge. The hilt was made of bronze; it curved away from the handle towards the blade tips. It was a hands width across the blade which was three finger widths at its widest. They forged the bronze carefully as it did not change colour to indicate heat in the same way that iron did. There was always a danger that it would be overheated and would crumble and be ruined. The handle was of polished bone slipped over the tang and the pommel at the end of the tang was bronze and had three lobes. The middle lobe had Thunor's hammer etched into it.

Wilf and his son Seward came to admire the sword, so did Henryk and the Flemish and all the trades people in the valley below the dyke. Wilf made the wooden scabbard to hold it and the leather workers bound the sheath in leather. Anson made the horseshoe shaped chape to stop the sword tip from cutting through the bottom of the scabbard which was riveted with bronze. They all asked to try the sword belt on and pull it out and in turn, they swung it and stabbed at imaginary Britons. They all revered Osgar, the boy who lost his parents and became a thegn. He was one of them.

Wuffa came to see Osgar the next day and wanted to look at the sword. He swished it through the fair and thrust it in front of him. He questioned Osgar about its strength and the difficulty in making it. He wanted a mock duel between them to test the blade. Osgar was loath to do this knowing that Wuffa was a finer swordsman then him. He had practiced a few times with a sword and knew that he had no finesse. He was also worried that his thinner blade would chip or even snap in a blade-on-blade fight.

"It is no good waiting until battle to find out how reliable a sword is," said Wuffa.

"Bit like marriage," said Anson and then gave one of his innocent looks with his palms held upwards as if he did not know his words had a double meaning.

Wuffa ignored him and said to Osgar, "I want to know how good it is and you need training if you are to be my right-hand man in the shield wall. We all know how brave and strong you are but can you wield a sword. Let's go to the heath where we have room."

They made their way to the heath where a crowd soon gathered to watch. Each had a shield and their sword and they wore leather to protect their forearms and thick leather jerkins. Wuffa only wore his helmet without the face, cheek and neck protection as Osgar had none and they were supposed to avoid head blows. Wuffa and Osgar circled each other and then the Aethling attacked, he swung his sword backhand overhead to catch Osgar off guard but he moved his sword quickly to deflect the blow and rammed his shield boss into Wuffa's. The jolt knocked Wuffa back and he laughed but he had felt Osgar's strength. His swordplay caught Osgar unawares and a savage downward blow hit the flat blade of Osgar's new sword with a ring. It was a blow that would have broken a poor quality sword but both Osgar and Wuffa felt the springy recoil of the blade.

"Very impressive but does it hold its edge," said Wuffa and rained blows at Osgar so that he had to use his sword to fend them off and each blow was blade edge on blade edge.

The crashing noise made by each sword strike rang across the heath and they clattered together a number of times, Osgar's strength always ensuring that Wuffa was pushed back. Wuffa's lighter footwork and greater sword play always took him out of trouble but slowly he began to tire and looked for a way to penetrate Osgar's defence. Eventually, Wuffa said, "Enough. You must be the most stubborn man in the whole of the fyrd."

They dropped their swords and shields and gripped forearms to signal to all that their practice duel was over. Wuffa asked permission of Osgar to look at his sword and he nodded. Wuffa inspected it, he looked for the spot that he landed the blow against the flat of the blade and could find no mark. He then examined each side of the blade. He ran his thumb down it and could feel its sharp edge but he could find no notches along it.

"That's a fine strong blade," he said in admiration, "It should be marked."

He passed the sword to Osgar who inspected it himself. Wuffa then lifted his own sword and inspected the blade closely. One third of the length from the point was half a dozen small 'v' shapes cutting into the blade which would not sharpen out easily. He cursed himself for being so stupid as to cause such damage to his own sword.

"May I see yours again?" he asked Osgar.

"Of course, *sire*," said Osgar, turning his sword around and carefully passing it handle first.

Wuffa felt its balance. Because of its tapering style the centre of weight was moved towards the hilt. This made it more comfortable to swing. Most broadswords were too heavy ended for long sword fights and Wuffa could see the advantage of the taper. This sword leant itself to more types of thrusts and swings and Wuffa knew that it was often the variety of strokes that would win a swordfight.

"I think that my next sword will be of such a design," said Wuffa, passing the sword handle first to Osgar, "and I know just the swordsmith to make it. Come, let's drink some ale."

They drank ale and ate salted meat and fresh bread. It was a cold winter's afternoon but there was no wind and they sat near a fire.

"The dyke will be finished in a week," said Wuffa, "What shall we all do then?"

"We could join our Saxon cousins and attack the Waelisc," said Henryk.

"You could lead our fyrd against the Chalk Hills," said Osgar.

"We could build another dyke," said Anson in a serious voice and then adding quickly. "Only kidding."

Before they could decide what they would do next, a messenger ran to Wuffa and spoke to him quickly. The tall Angle listened and frowned, then told one of his ceorls to go to Tedmund immediately and have him come. He walked out on the heath alone and no one followed him, they could see he was deep in thought. They looked at each other but could not make out what the messenger had said. Soon Tedmund arrived and spoke with Wuffa for some time. The winter sun fell and it became dark while still they talked until eventually, they walked to one of the fires in the camps and were left alone. Finally, they approached the group and Wuffa spoke while Tedmund stood silently beside him.

"King Wehha of East Anglia died yesterday," said Wuffa solemnly and formally, "When the sun rises, I leave. I want my fifty best men with me and meanwhile Tedmund will stay here and secure our border. My uncle's funeral will be held this week and I must see that it befits him."

Chapter 19
Reunion

They gathered in the morning before the sun rose. Wuffa insisted that Osgar, Anson, Henryk and his men along with Wilf and Seward accompany him. He took all the men who were without injury and had fought alongside him at the Stubs Worth battle. There were thegns from the Gipping Valley and some from the Lark Valley but he took none who was of the North Folk. They travelled light, without handcarts but carried their shields, and spears and food bags across their shoulders. Now that Osgar had a sword, he realised what an impediment it was to walking. He strapped his across his chest as many did and presented his seax to Seward. Anson carried his new war axe, it was strapped to his back so that carrying shield and spear was easier.

They covered the ground quickly and passed Beodricesworth before their noon break. They marched quicker than everyone else on the route. Those who watched them pass remarked upon their lean strong appearance. Soon after their stop, they came to the source of the Gipping and stayed on its north bank marching southeast towards Gippeswic. They were joined by others who had heard of their King's death, mainly thegns and their ceorls and slaves from the western parts of the Suth Folk but also some thegns from the North Folk.

Osgar was miserable. He had believed that when the dyke was finished and his sword made, he would be released from his obligation to Selwyn and would be free. He would either go west with Wuffa to attack the Chalk Hills or he would seek out the Saxons and fight alongside them. Either way, he would avenge his father and return his mother and brother to their people. Each step took him away from that goal. "I don't know why you are so keen to go to Wehha's funeral?" said Osgar to Anson. "You always reminded us that he was not your King as you are a Jute."

"He's your King though," said Anson, "and he is my wife Hild's King. We need to stick with Wuffa; he has seen us all right. He saw that we were made thegns and granted land and Wuffa has been our ring giver."

Henryk said, "We all got something from Wehha, ja. And what one King gives another can take. The King's younger brother will want the Kingdom or maybe one of his sons. You think we just come to pull the funeral ship? The Wuffingas are not called the family of wolves without reason. They are like all wolves, they protect their family and they devour their enemies, ja. We are the young Wolf's pack and we stay with him, ja."

They slept the night under pine trees to keep the cold off and at dawn headed north of Gippeswic to the Deben. They followed the river south until they arrived mid-morning, at the seat of the Wuffingas power. Wuffa was greeted by many of the people, including thegns and ceorls. Osgar could see how much richer the thegns were than the people of Beodricesworth or even Gippeswic. Sword handles were silver or even gold and some were inlaid with garnets. Their cloak broaches were large and many made with precious metals. Each ham had a hall almost as large as the one at Beodricesworth.

Wuffa spoke to a local thegn and his fifty men were fed and billeted into the hall, houses or hovels. Wherever he went Wuffa was clasped by his forearm by thegns. All the ceorls bowed to him and many knelt. He told them to stand immediately and laughed and put his arm around their shoulders.

The next day all Wuffa's men and many others were ordered down to the Deben estuary. There in the muddy flats was a great ship. It had no mast but had a steer board at the stern, twice the height of a man and the vents for oars numbered fifteen along each side. It was beached on the mud flats and thick heavy ropes fanned out from its bow. They waded into the mud and took up the ropes where one thegn with a booming voice, ordered them to pull on his command. There were eight hundred hands gripping the rope and four hundred bodies leaning back taking the strain. "Pull," shouted the thegn and the ship moved. "Pull," he shouted again and the ships helm rode onto the first of the log rollers. "Pull," he called a third time and they settled into a rhythm that kept the ship moving. It encountered the edge of the estuary where it rose slowly. Now they were raising the ship up an incline but it was on firm ground and the log rollers worked better than in the mud. A team of ceorls ran from the back of the ship with the logs and laid them carefully at the front. Once the ship had been pulled to a flat and firm area of ground, they had a break. Many hung their heads and put their hands on their thighs and panted.

Anson looked around at the men gasping and moaning and said loudly, "Most of these have never done a day's work in their lives."

He looked at his companions from the dyke who all stood tall and awaited the next instructions. Building the ditch and bank for two years and continually exercising on the great heath had made them all harder than they had realised. The shiplay, with the helm aimed towards a low hill five hundred paces away which was to be its final resting place. The area was already surrounded with flags and banners and the trees garlanded with holly. It took two days to pull the great ship up the hill and into position so that it was level and pointed northeast.

The next day the ceremony began and the body of Wehha was carried in an oak coffin that was placed in the centre of the ship. Around him was laid all that he would need in Valhalla. Inside his coffin by his right hand was his jewelled sword. He had not died in battle which was the only guarantee of entry to the Great Hall of Valhalla but none doubted that his wealth and power would not go unnoticed by the gods. On his left side was a leather money pouch containing thirty pieces of silver to pay the oarsmen as well as a small gold box for the steersman. The Valkerie would guide him to Valhalla but his own ship would carry him there. Close to him was placed his round shield with its iron boss and leather surface. He had four spears laid lengthways beside his coffin; two of them were aetgars, one spear and one aesc spear of ten-foot length. His favourite foods were placed in copper cauldrons and pottery contained ale and mead. There was even a bone comb and shears left beside him so that he could maintain his beard during the journey. Finally, a bull was slaughtered in the front of the ship and laid out to accompany him on his voyage.

All those at the funeral were expected to help to cover the ship. There were hundreds of shovels to hand and soil was carted close to the ship by slaves and ceorls and then the thegns and Ealdormen shovelled it onto the ship. The ceremony lasted all day with priests saying incantations and scops recounting Wehha's life and his brave deeds. Osgar had seen Wuffa circulating and talking to many and was surprised when he saw him in the distance speaking to Cynbeald. He had not seen the old scop before at the funeral and now he watched as they conversed for a long period. He could see that it was Cynbeald who spoke mostly while Wuffa looked at the ship or out to sea. He nodded sometimes and occasionally turned to the storyteller to say something. As the sun went down the ceremony continued with fires and torches lighting the work as the ship slowly disappeared. A mound of earth covered the main body of the hill and only the lap strokes running up to the prow and stern could be seen. These finally vanished and the covering ended when a perfect mound was formed.

A moot had been called for the next day to decide on the new King. Osgar and the others mixed with people from all over East Anglia. Many had views on who should be King but also a lot had no idea and would go to the Moot to see what happened. Most came from the east Suth Folk area and believed that it had to be a Wuffing for King. Some went for Wehha's younger brother or one of his sons, usually the elder but all were described as Aetheling. They were glad that many mentioned Wuffa, who had quite a following because of his exploits at Stubs Worth, where his actions were not quite as Osgar remembered them. He had been brave and decisive, that day but to hear some 'you would think he was the next best thing to Beowulf', as Anson remarked.

"Well someone had to tell them," came a familiar voice from behind them. They turned and saw Cynbeald leaning on his staff.

"How else would the East Angles have heard of your heroic actions?" asked Cynbeald rhetorically, "Did they not deserve to hear of the fat old Jute who smites Waelisc as hard as he forges iron and the young Thunor beside him who saved his ham with no more than a seax? What of the lanky Flemish, should they have been denied his story, ja? But most of all would all the Anglecynn not wish to hear of the young wolf who has already won battles and is equipped to be King?"

"So that is why we see you with Wuffa so much," said Anson, "You are working for him."

"Great Woden, no," said Cynbeald, "I am a simple scop who tells his tales all over East Anglia. I am always looking and listening for new tales. A scop is the only one not drunk at a feast. No one wants the storyteller to forget his lines, so I stay sober. You would be surprised what I am told by drunken ealdormen, thegns and ceorls alike."

"Now listen carefully to me. Tomorrow at the moot you do not all stand together but you spread out through the crowd. There will be five hundred there. Wuffa has at least another fifty supporters, some from around here and even some amongst the North Folk. Not many have come as Selwyn has not allowed his thegns here. You watch me and you follow me."

The storyteller turned and walked away into the darkness. They all looked at each other and raised their eyebrows. "Well I never," said Anson, "The old scop is a spy for Wuffa."

"I think we keep the voice down ja," said Henryk. "We talk to our men and do as Cynbeald says."

Osgar desperately needed Wuffa to be King. He knew that he was the only one who would lead the Angles against the Waelisc Kingdom of Chalk Hills. He was sick of having his destiny held by others. If it were iron, he could forge it, a shield and he could smash it but his life always seemed to be in other more powerful hands.

In the morning, the moot assembled. They had all slept in the shelters provided and had been given food. There was still much left over from the funeral ceremony and the Wuffingas has been generous in ensuring that all who attended were fed. Wuffa's men did as they had been told, spreading themselves amongst the crowd. They spoke to those close to them and talked of the weather and women and finally they spoke of their choice of King. They told all around them of Wuffa's kindness and especially his generosity as a ring giver, his bravery in battle and how he already had victories to his name, having defeated the Waelisc.

Finally, the moot was settled and the first speaker was Wehha's younger brother. He was a stout figure who had already taken the mantle of wearing a wolf lined cloak. His broach of gold and his silver sword pommel told of his wealth. He spoke to the Moot of his closeness to his brother and how he would continue to secure the Kingdom. He offered his wisdom and his experience and he stressed many times that it was no time to have youth leading the country. He finished by, in a pointed gibe at Wuffa, asking the crowd, "Does a pup lead the wolf pack?"

There was some cheering but it was mainly in one group of his family and close supporters. The Moot looked to Wuffa or one of Wehha's sons to speak. Wuffa let the young man beside him speak as he was the eldest son. He told of his loyalty to his father and how his father would have wanted him to rule. This brought a low murmur from the crowd as they knew the Wehha had never proposed anyone to be King, it was not the Angle way. He gave the crowd only one reason for them to acclaim him King, apart from that it was his birth right. He told them that his uncle was too old to be King and if he was selected, they may have to do the same again in only a few years' time. This brought cheers of support from some and boos from others. Wuffa's expression did not alter, as he looked attentively at the speaker.

When the Wehha's oldest son, had finished, Wuffa stepped forwards. He had taken off his cloak and passed it to one of his ceorls. He stood in his plain trousers and boots with a tunic of cream woven wool. The sleeves were rolled up to show his strong forearms and his left hand rested on the pommel of his sword.

He looked around the moot, into the eyes of all there and then he spoke, "I am not going to beg you to be your King. I will tell you what this wolf cub has already done and what he will do when King, if you so choose him. I have finished the Great White Dyke which was built by us in just two years and now we have a barrier against our enemies and already we have spread west and the old hams that had been deserted are now peopled by us again. I have fought the Waelisc and I have won."

All around his supporters cheered and most of the rest of the moot joined in. Wuffa held up his hands for quiet and then continued, "But we do not just have enemies to the west, we also have them to the north."

Wuffa paused to let his words sink in. The crowd was muttering that he must mean the North Folk.

"I am not casting a slur on all our Anglecynn brothers in the North Folk. Many are here showing that they know that we only remain strong when we are one people."

Then Wuffa threw his bolt of lightning. "Selwyn, who Wehha made Ealdorman now claims he is King of the North Folk and that it is his Kingdom."

No one had heard of this news and there was a murmur all around. Wehha's brother and sons spoke to each other and it was clear to all that they were as surprised as the rest. Wuffa again held his hands up for the Moot to listen and they were immediately silent.

"Acclaim me as your King now and I march this very day with an army to defeat Selwyn," said Wuffa, "If we ignore this threat, we will have enemies to our north and west."

Wehha's brother was about to say something but Cynbeald stepped forward and in his booming voice shouted, "Wuffa is our King," while thrusting his staff into the air. He started the chant which soon grew and included almost all the Moot. They stabbed their spears and swords at the sky and repeated, "Wuffa, Wuffa, Wuffa," until finally even Wehha's brother, sons and supporters raised their weapons skyward and chanted his name in a show of unity.

So Wuffa became the second King of the Angles. His people would want from him only bravery in battle and a share of any spoils. He would only demand from them loyalty. All knelt before him.

Henryk, Osgar and Anson hugged each other. Their man was King and they knew that this secured the lands that had been given to them. They would be close to the King and that meant power and wealth. Osgar was pleased with the result but despaired that he still would not march with Wuffa upon the Chalk Hills to defeat the Britons and rescue his mother and brother. However, he knew that the bond of his giving Selwyn the sword would be set aside and he would be a free man again. If Wuffa would not attack the Britons and their King Cadrod, then he would travel south and find King Cuthwulf's Saxon army and offer his service.

Wuffa formed an army of three hundred to march on Norwic where he believed Selwyn was. It was there that the rivers Yare and Wensum joined and was also Selwyn's main trading centre. He ordered the men who had come with him from the dyke to secure Theod-ford. It was an important town in the centre of East Anglia and controlled the crossing of the Thet and Little Ouse by the Icknield Way and the old Roman road. Wuffa marched north with his army of three hundred, comprising of thegns and ceorls. They were keen to go and they relished a fight because it would mean booty and they knew that Selwyn was rich and would have a great deal of treasure. Wuffa was known for his generosity, he was a ring giver and it was one reason that Moot had swung behind him. He would keep half of any takings and share the rest with his thegns and they in turn would share with the ceorls.

Henryk led his men west towards Beodricesworth and then directly north to Theod-ford. He only had seventy men but along the way, he picked up another twenty who plucked up their shields and spears without stopping. They wanted to share in the excitement and they hoped that there might be some booty to be had. Wuffa had said to all, that he wished to retake North Folk and reunite the Kingdom without bloodshed if possible. He repeated to them all that the real enemy lay to the west and he needed as many fit men as possible to fight them. The Suth Folk listened to their King and they knew that he spoke the truth. Many of them had family ties with their brothers in the north but the Anglecynn was forged through war and their instinct was battle. Five generations had grown and settled since the Romans had gone, during that time war had become normal and had been only punctuated by short periods of peace.

Wuffa marched directly north to the settlement of Eye. It was a large ham on raised land almost entirely surrounded by water from the Dore which was a tributary of the Waveney, there they stayed the night. They were still among the Suth Folk and more men came to them during the evening from the surrounding hams. They were now well over three hundred and none had seen such an army. They crossed the Waveney into the North Folk country at Scale which was an old Roman town built on strategic crossroads, the east-west road joining Theodford to the coast. They followed the south-north route. The town was deserted as the Angles never lived in the old Roman settlements. They had taken over the farmland but would rather build a wattle and daub house with a thatched roof next to a Roman villa than live within stonewalls and a tiled roof.

By noon, Wuffa's army was at the collection of settlements around the Yare. They first came to Cones ford and met no resistance, then they continued with some caution to cross the Yare between the joined settlements of Norwic and Coolayne. To the west were wharves but little activity and all the North Folk fell to their knees at the sight of Wuffa heading his army. They acclaimed their new King and Wuffa was pleased that he had seized such an important group of towns. Norwic and Coolayne were significant trading centres as the shallow bottomed clinker build ships could sail into the heart of East Anglia along the Yare and Wensum. Here Selwyn traded across the North Sea to the Old Country and that this was where Wuffa was convinced that Selwyn would be found. His thegns questioned the local people who had remained and then reported their findings to Wuffa.

All the evidence told Wuffa that he had made a terrible mistake. Selwyn had decided that it was not possible to defend Norwic or the surrounding area. He had moved his force west to the ford over the rivers Thet and Little Ouse and it was there that he was rebuilding the ancient earthworks and had stationed his army. Henryk, Osgar, Anson and his secondary force were marching straight in the jaws of Selwyn's main army.

*****

Osgar and Anson marched together. They both had their spears over their right shoulder and their shields in their left. They carried an extra aetgar in the same hand as their shield. Osgar had his tapered sword slung across his chest where he could pull it from the scabbard and he also had a woven bag that Lynne had made for him, with some bread and salted meat inside. Anson had a seax in a sheath lying horizontally in the small of his back. He could choose to pull his war-axe over his shoulder or his seax from behind him in an instant. Since the day that Osgar had used his seax with such success eight years before, Anson could sell as many as they could make. He still had the one made for him by Osgar with the handle made of decorated antler and a bronze pommel. Seward was so very proud to now own Osgar's old seax, especially as it had seen battle and killed the enemy. He had gained the habit of taking it out and sharpening it with a whet stone whenever they rested until Anson finally said, "If you continue to sharpen that seax, you will whittle it down to the size of a Saxons dick!"

They marched fast as they had been ordered to do by Wuffa. He told them that word would soon get out about his acclamation as King and he wanted the North Folk to be unprepared. They would think that the funeral and Moot might take another week. He knew that the majority of the North Folk did not care to separate the Kingdom and like all Angles wanted only a strong and decisive King. The fast march was easy for them as they were all fit and used to walking quickly for long distances. When they had patrolled the dyke, they would cover the length from one side to another and back in a morning.

The group wore varying amounts of armour. All had the thick leather jerkins protecting their bodies which they wore over their plain smocks. Their trousers were woven wool and their calves were bound with leather bands. These had become closer together and made from thicker leather since the experience of guarding the ridge of the chalk bank against the spears of the Britons. Only a few thegns had chainmail hauberks and these just covered the neck and shoulders. Many also had helmets with cheek and neck flanges which mostly were leather but Anson, Osgar and Henryk sported them made with thin iron plate.

They had marched west towards Beodricesworth but at Elmswell, they turned north towards the Theod-ford. As they marched across the rolling landscape, the land changed from heavy clay to lighter soil and finally to almost pure sand. The woodlands had been of oak, ash, hornbeam and silver birch but it was mainly a sandy landscape of gorse and heather. In the distance, they sometimes glimpsed deer that sped from view at the sight of the approaching force. They met some people travelling south who at first feared them but then told them what was ahead. The travellers knew that Selwyn had declared himself King and they had decided to return to their families amongst the Suth Folk. Soon they met another group who were Suth Folk refugees and were fleeing the

Theod-ford settlement. Once Henryk, Osgar and Anson had gathered around them they told their story of how Selwyn had declared himself King and was setting up at Theod-ford. They had left because they were expected to swear an oath of loyalty to the ealdorman. At first, they thought that the travellers were saying that he had reinforced the crossing but it soon was obvious that he had his main force there. The travellers could give no idea of the number of men that Selwyn had with him. Henryk thought that it must be two to three hundred. The atmosphere changed and Henryk looked around at the concerned faces. Finally, he said, "If they have reinforced the earthworks, it will be difficult to beat them."

"It would be difficult if there were no earthworks," said Anson.

"But they don't know that we are coming," said Osgar, "We can attack them tomorrow as the sun rises."

"I will not have you all killed," said Henryk. "First we look, ja."

They waited until nightfall and moved their whole force up past the Little Ouse and around to the west of the iron-age fort. Osgar and Henryk crossed the Thet well away from any houses, holding their swords aloft. They crept carefully through marshy areas until they came to the rising ground. Here they were out in the open and waited until the moon went behind a cloud before scurrying to the edge of the bank surrounding the fort.

The fort had been dug by the people before the Romans and was built as two banks with a ditch in front of the second bank. The banks and ditch followed a semicircle in a bend in the Little Ouse River where it was joined by the Thet. The North Folk, under Selwyn, had been busy in digging the ditch so that it was once more a steep V shape. The banks were again smooth and difficult to climb and now the second inner bank was topped with a palisade of new poles rising about ten feet from the ground. There were gaps between each pole of about one hands width and the bottom four feet of the palisade was woven with willow to reinforce it.

Osgar and Henryk crept up the first bank. They could hear a voice talking which boomed out across the ditch from behind the palisade. It was soon obvious that this was someone on watch, talking to another man. He was moaning about being on guard duty after he had spent the day digging. He was naming the people who he had not seen digging and who should have been given his watch rather than him. As he went on and on, Osgar began to realise where he had heard the voice before.

"It's Wilburh," he whispered to Henryk, "You know the fellow at the fen ditch end."

Henryk nodded, remembering the man that he had punched, and pointed down into the ditch. He slowly eased himself down on his back. At the bottom, he began the ascent up the bank. They moved along to ensure that they were not going to climb back directly to where Wilburh was standing. Still his loud talking could be heard and he was saying how his experience at digging a ditch was ignored and that nobody knew how to build a dyke like Tedmund of Beodricesworth did. Henryk and Osgar had to suppress laughter when they heard this. Only Wilburh, who had moaned nonstop on the Great Heath, telling everyone of the superiority of Selwyn could now moan about him and praise Tedmund.

They pulled themselves up the last few feet to the palisade and lay looking through the wicker fencing. There were some fires still burning within the large open area below. These fires and the moon lit the ground and the large hall in the middle. There was little sign of life and they guessed that the main force must be in the settlement with some in the hall. Past the hall were a number of lean-to workshops and then there was a roadway which led to the ford crossing the Thet and after that, the Little Ouse. This route was part of the Icknield Way which joined the old Roman road in the settlement.

Henryk felt the wicker fence and looked at the palisade while he still lay prone. He pulled carefully on the wicker. It was mainly willow and felt strongly woven. He was interested in the poles and he felt around the ground to see how firmly they had been set in it. He carefully pulled his sword out and slid it down by the side of one of the poles. He pushed the sword down and moved it around to feel how firm it was. Then they heard the Wilburh coming, his high volume became even louder as he approached. Osgar and Henryk pushed themselves backwards down the ditch so that they were below the sight line from behind the palisade. They listened as Wilburh moaned that he just wanted to be back with his family. He had already given more than enough to Selwyn who was comfortable in the town. Why they should be guarding the fort was daft, according to him.

"Everyone knows they are still at Wehha's funeral," he said. "Then they will have a Moot and it could be weeks until they decide what to do."

Wilburh and his silent companion walked on around the bank palisade. Once they were more than fifty paces away Osgar and Henryk continued their descent into the ditch and then up the second bank. They made their way back across the open land to the narrow Thet and waded back through the reeds and across the river. Henryk gathered the men together and told them of what they had seen.

"I think that most of their men are in the town," Henryk said. "We cannot tell how many are in the fort but they are not ready for a fight. We take the fort quick and hold it, and then we wait for Wuffa, ja."

During the night, the whole force picked their way silently through the marshes alongside the Thet. Osgar carried a large coil of hemp rope over his shoulder, hanging to his waist, which they had stolen from the boat yard by the wharves. They carried all their arms and their bags of food and once they were on dry ground, they waited in the alder trees that lined the river. When Henryk was ready, he signalled for them to move up to the first bank where Osgar was already at the top listening. He lay against the apex of the first bank and tried to see through the palisade opposite. He had the coil of rope around him and lay with his shield to his left with his sword still behind his back. He could hear Wilburh in the distance, who seemed to be about fifty paces away. He beckoned the group up the bank and set off down into the ditch himself. Osgar was about to climbed the last bank to reach the palisade, it was steep and about the height of ten men from the bottom of the ditch.

Osgar heard a shout from behind the palisade and knew that the men reaching the ridge of the first bank had been spotted. He heard Henryk tell them to move quickly. Osgar picked up his shield in his left hand and clutched the coil across his stomach with his right. He ran up the bank, without using his hands or shield for purchase. He was fit and strong from years of heavy forge work and the last twenty-four months scaling the dyke, practicing manoeuvres, and exercising on the heath. It meant that he had no respect for the steep incline and just ran up it. He heard Henryk and the others scrambling down the bank behind him and soon they too would run up this second bank. As he reached the top of the embankment, he could see two figures silhouetted through the gaps between the palisade posts. He had switched his spear to his right hand and thrust it through a gap and firmly into the body of the nearest man. The man cried out and Osgar yanked his spear back. He would have thrust again but the second man, who he could now see was Wilburh, moved along the palisade with his mouth wide open. Finally, he shouted, "Attack, attack."

He stayed out of Osgar's reach and continued to bellow out the warming. Osgar uncoiled the rope and found the large loop at the end. He jumped up and dropped it over one of the pointed poles. He was joined by some of the men who were now running, as he had, up the bank. The rope loop held near the top of the pole. Osgar tossed the free end of the rope back down the bank and twenty men picked it up. He shouted, "Pull," and they all leant back. They had dropped their shields and spears and looked like they were almost hanging horizontally. The post bent near the wicker fence and snapped. The whole group tumbled backwards down the bank into the ditch. By the time they were standing up and starting to climb the bank, Osgar had removed the loop and hung it over the next post and another twenty grabbed the rope. They had all been told their place before the attack so there were no delays as each man knew what he had to do.

Osgar could hear and see armed men running across the ground inside the fort. There were ten to twenty of them. Enough to stop their attack if they reached the palisade before it was broken. The next post bent back towards the ditch as the twenty Angles pulled together. It splintered with a crack and again those pulling the rope fell backwards. The second post had also snapped near to the wicker fence line. There was now a gap in the palisade but it was less than a pace wide and it was at chest height. Osgar signalled to Wilf and Seward, the two men either side of the gap to use a shield. They each held the rim of Wilf's shield backside upwards and Osgar stepped onto it and immediately jumped through the gap. He was careful not to tumble down the bank. Anson, Henryk and the others followed them through. Wilf and Seward handed over duties to two Flems, who held one of their shields and made a step for them.

Once there were ten of them through the gap in the palisade, they made their way down the final bank into the open area of the fort. Osgar was first to the bottom and had to deflect a spear thrust. He had no spear to fight back with and hacked at his enemies spear with his sword. Henryk slithered down the bank beside him, followed by Anson and soon the ten stood together. Their shields tapped against each other as they fitted them left over right, locking them into a shield wall. They faced thirty men who were now being organised by a thegn.

The North Folk thegn ordered his men into a shield wall and the shields clunked and banged as they locked. They had not manoeuvred as quickly as Henryk's men but expected to drive them back against the bank. They were being joined by others running across the space from the hall in the middle. Their thegn was forming a second line. They should have attacked but still they were sorting the correct shield overlap and those in the second line were not sure where to put their spears. Meanwhile more men were clambering through the gap in the palisade and making their way down the slope to join the Suth Folk attackers. Osgar stood in the centre of the shield wall, without a spear, he was vulnerable and he knew that they must close the gap fast.

"Move us forward now," he called to Henryk.

"Forward," shouted Henryk.

They moved quickly to close the space between them and their enemy and the North Folk men were surprised as they had they had twice the number of men. They barely had time to lower their spears when their attackers hit them hard with their spear points and their shields followed an instant later. The Suth Folk men crashed their shields into their opposition and their second line, who had stayed close behind, thrust down with overhead spears. Osgar felt a cut to his sword arm and a glancing blow from a spear cut across his cheek. He instinctively thrust his sword between the dip, which was where his shield joined Anson's and stabbed the man opposite in his shoulder. "Push," shouted Henryk and they leant into their shields. Their left legs were bent and their right pushed behind them and as one, they shoved. The line moved forward and ten men pushed thirty back.

"Push," shouted Henryk, a second time, and they moved forward again and felt their enemy give. Their spears and swords could no longer be thrust at the Suth Folk as they struggled to keep their footing. The North Folk could not believe the strength and violence shown by their attackers. They had practiced the shield wall and knew all the tactics but those facing them were stronger, quicker and much more aggressive. The Suth Folk shield wall facing them was solid and they could barely see their enemy from behind the first line. Long aescs were thrust into them piercing their arms, shoulders and faces. Their line broke and most turned and ran; those who did not were quickly cut down.

Dawn had come and they had taken the fort. They had some injured men but no deaths. They had not killed any of the injured North Folk, as would be expected but treated them with their own. Henryk left ten men to guard the palisade, now at their back and moved his fifty fit men across the ground to guard the ford which was its only entrance. The ford crossed the Thet, where either side the river had been banked. Henryk could see though, that an attack across a broad front would be almost impossible to fend off, because now they faced an army of five times their number, led by Selwyn.

Selwyn surveyed the scene and saw what he thought was a ragtag group in front of him. There seemed to only be about fifty men, most were covered with mud and some had wounds, many were splattered with blood as were their spear tips. He thought that there might be another twenty guarding the bank and palisade in the distance. He had already dismissed the thegns that he had left in charge of the fort. Whether dead or alive he had proclaimed loudly that their land was forfeit and was now his. Selwyn stepped forwards to the edge of the ford and called for the surrender of those who had taken the fort. He told them that they would be free to go south providing they swore on oath that they recognised him as the rightful King of the North Folk. The men from the south laughed and shouted obscenities.

Henryk said to Osgar, "Step out of the shield wall with me and do as I say. You are going to offer Selwyn his sword."

"You can go to Hel," said Osgar.

"You listen to me, ja. Your King told you to obey me. Now we show them what Selwyn is made of, so you do as I say and put your sheath down by your side and your sword back in it."

Osgar nodded to Henryk and they unlocked their shields and stepped forward. They stood together five paces in front of their men and Henryk looked straight at Selwyn and shouted, "We are all Anglecynn here. We come here on the orders of King Wuffa of all Anglia and we do not wish to fight with our brothers."

Behind him, his men murmured. They were prepared to fight their brothers. Their blood was pumping adrenalin through them and they knew that they were stronger, more disciplined and more battle hardened than those who they faced. Selwyn smiled smugly and his army behind him relaxed and some jeered. Henryk held up his hand and continued, "This young man has brought Selwyn a gift. It is a sword made by his own hand. You may have heard the story of how he broke Selwyn's sword with one blow from his seax. He was ordered by our late King Wehha to replace it."

Then he said quietly to Osgar, "Do not move."

Henryk looked along the line of the North Folk army and spoke so that they could all hear, "Selwyn, you have been swordless for too long, come and get your sword."

Henryk stepped backwards and the shield wall opened, he raised his shield so that it aligned with the others and it became solid again. Osgar stood still, as he had been ordered by Henryk. Blood still ran from the cut on his right forearm and dripped onto the sandy ground through his fingers. He had a graze across his face which ran under his cheek-piece and was caked with blood. Selwyn stared ahead and did not move and his soldiers muttered. They had heard the tales of Selwyn the Swordless and though they were never told publicly, they had laughed about the rich pompous thegn who had become an ealdorman and then claimed the Kingdom. Cynbeald, the most famous scop of East Anglia had travelled to all the great halls. He had enchanted them with battle tales where a young blacksmith held a bridge. Now they realised that it was this very man before them and looked with awe at him as he stood motionless, facing them.

Selwyn spoke to the two thegns nearest to Osgar and ordered, "Go and fetch my sword."

They hesitated and someone called out to Selwyn, "Shame."

Wilburh's voice boomed out, "Selwyn, Selwyn," in a chant but no one joined in. They had heard the tales of Selwyn's lack of bravery and most had believed that they were just founded in jealously but now there was a chance for Selwyn to disprove them. All eyes switched between Osgar and Selwyn. Osgar drew the tapered sword from the scabbard beside him and Selwyn visibly flinched. The Angles were loyal to their thegns and their thegns to their Kings and in return, they demanded only bravery. Three hundred North Folk men, who had earlier been prepared to die for their new king, now looked at him with contempt.

Anson the Broad, the old Jute, thrust his spear high into the sky and chanted, "Wuffa, Wuffa." He was joined immediately by all in his shield wall and soon those that stood opposite chanted Wuffa's name. Selwyn turned and ranted at his own men and without irony accused them of cowardice and Henryk had to move quickly to save his life. The men from both sides mingled without rancour and East Anglia had reunited.

*****

Wuffa arrived the day after the battle for the old fort. He could see that the North Folk army was subdued and quickly had all their thegns swear an oath to him as their King. He released all of them back to return to their hams, once they had agreed to pay a price to him depending upon their status and wealth. From most it was a copper arm ring, from the more powerful it was silver. Wuffa shared half of this with Henryk's men, those who had attacked the fort over the Thet were rewarded the most.

"So, young Thunor," said Wuffa, "you disobeyed me when I told you to give the sword to Selwyn."

"I tried, *sire*," said Osgar, getting his joke, "But he did not seem to want it."

"Then I can only assume that he wanted you to keep it, so you are now released from my ward," announced his new King.

They sat in the afternoon sun, spring had almost arrived and the air was warm. The funeral pyres, shared by the dead of North and Suth Folk had burned down leaving only glowing embers. Prayers had been said to Woden so that all the dead of the previous day would drink ale in Valhalla.

"What will happen to Selwyn," asked Anson.

"That's simple," said Wuffa, "He forfeits all titles and is reduced to the level of ceorl. He is exiled from East Anglia and I don't really care if he goes south to the East Saxons or North to Lindsey. The wergild he pays for his treason is all his land and wealth and if he is seen in East Anglia in one week's time he will die."

Chapter 20
The Church

Aefre often thought of her husband Eafwald and her son Osgar. She wondered if he had been an apprentice carpenter under his father. He would be liable to call-up by the fyrd now and she imagined him with a shield and spear. She no longer blamed her people for not rescuing her, so many others had died or been enslaved and still the Angles had not come. Her life had not changed so much in the last two years. She was no longer a slave to the kitchen garden but she still lived in the hovel towards the river. She was owned by the King's senior commander, Waljan and was tasked with growing herbs and special vegetables for him but she continued as a healer and was sought by all in Bannaventa who were ill or injured.

Waljan was frequently out on campaigns and gone for days. She knew that the raids against her cousins, the Saxons to the south, had increased. After questioning Waljan about East Anglia and why they rarely attacked it, he finally told her of the long ditch and bank of chalk. She spent hours imagining the great white bank, her people building it and her husband and son standing at its top looking towards her. She was proud that her people had made their country safe but wondered if it meant that they would never come. She tried to banish the thought and prayed to the gods.

When Waljan had first bought her from Cadrod and stopped the slaves taking her west, she had taunted him. She invited him to beat her or take her as he wanted, though he never did. He would sit with her for hours, speaking to her of everything. She was sullen and tried not to talk but eventually, she realised that he would not leave her alone and she thought that she might as well gain as much information about her son and what was happening around her. He begged her to convert to Christianity and marry him so that she would no longer be a slave and she would have a better life. She told him she was married to Eafwald and he would come for her and she told him that he was stupid to worship a man nailed to a cross.

Waljan was sitting outside her hovel drinking herb tea, while looking at the beautiful women sat in front of him, when a messenger arrived from Cadrod summoning him. He left the gift of cloth and food that he had brought for her and went and as she watched him walk up the path, she knew that she was softening. Eleven years had passed while she had waited for her people to come and during that time, she had known nothing but insults, pain and poverty. Waljan was the only one who even treated her as a person. From now on, she decided that she would try to be more accommodating towards him.

"I expect you have been giving your Angle bitch one?" said King Cadrod.

After two years, it still annoyed him that Waljan had bought her as a slave. He was, however, his best warrior and had always been unwavering in his loyalty and bravery. Cadrod's hatred of the Sais had increased to an even higher pitch during the last few years. He could not bear even to see them and killed captives without reason and with a cruelty that shocked even his own people. He was angered by the dyke across the heath which had stopped his planned advance. He had intensified the attacks on the Sais to the south, they had no such dyke and he was able to use his cavalry to great effect.

Waljan had entered the King's room and had taken his place among Cadrod's other senior warriors. The King told them that he was pleased with their efforts against the Sais dogs and that they had been pushed back and hurt so much that soon it would have the effect he so desired. He believed more than ever that he was the heir to Arturius. He knew that he would repeat Arturius' great victory at Mynydd Baddon with the same tactics. During the time of his grandfather, the Sais had advanced rapidly into their territory and had been surrounded on a hill. The cavalry had caught them in open ground and had cut through their defences. Now he had information that they planned once more to advance into a Cymry Kingdom, his own Calchfynedd.

Cadrod's success against the Saxons in the south had brought him allies amongst other kingdoms of the Britons. Support had been sent from Caer Glori, Caer Baddan and Caer Ceri, so now he could field an army of more than two thousand men. He needed the Sais to advance deep into his territory so that their supply lines were over extended and he could cut off their retreat. He had hurt them during the last two years and had probed far into the lands held by them. The Saxons had lost hundreds of young women and boys as slaves. The old and the young were slaughtered without mercy and Cadrod knew that they would have to attack or he would push them south into the sea. He wanted them to attack and then he would defeat their army and those that were left would be at his mercy. Once he had annihilated them, he would turn on the Angles in the east. His victory would mean that more Britons would rally to him and his army would double again and then no dyke would prevent him from defeating them.

*****

Leofric visited his mother, as usual going to her hovel once a week. His status as an aide of the Bishop Cadrod Ddoeth allowed him access to her and Waljan wanted her Christian son to talk her into converting. What had begun as a joyful experience for them both was now a chore. They had barely spoken in the first eight years of their enslavement and for three years Leofric was travelling in Erin with the Bishop. Aefre was delighted that her son was safe and well fed but she was unimpressed that he could read and write and was disgusted that he had spurned their gods for the Christian God. Leofric made things worse by trying to convert Aefre to Christianity. He told her that she owed her life to Christ as he did and that they would only be saved when she worshipped the one true God. She retorted that they would be saved when the Anglecynn killed every Briton in the world.

"Take me back to Anglia," she would beg him.

"I cannot," was always his reply, "I don't know the way and we would be caught before nightfall."

"You have spurned your people and their gods," she would say.

"I have not spurned my people," he told her with anger, "I want to go home to East Anglia as you do. We will go home one day."

"And what will you do with your stupid wooden cross and your God nailed to it?" she would say. "Will they come with us?"

"I will preach the word of the Lord to our people," he said. "And they shall be saved."

It always ended like this. He stood and kissed her on the head and left. Aefre had heard that her son had talked to many of the slaves and had converted them to the Christian God. Leofric had them kneel and pray and told them that they would go to God's place when they died and would live for eternity there. Most of the slaves now were from the Saxon lands to the south. The supply of Angle

225

slaves had dried up with the building of the dyke across the heath. Sigbert had told her that he had become a Christian because he was treated better by the Britons, one time when he visited her.

"Do you believe in their god?" she asked him.

"I believe in food and clothes and not being beaten," he replied, smiling and winking at her.

"Don't wink at me," she had told him but wondered if she was making a rod for her own back by denying their god. She only had to pretend, she thought, and life would be easier. She could marry Waljan and if the insults did not stop, they would not be said to her face and never again would she be tripped or punched. She had chided herself for even considering such things and had told Sigbert that it was time for him to go.

*****

Bishop Cadog the Wise began his service in the new church on a very proud day for him. It had taken years to build and had high walls with Roman arched windows. The crossbeams of oak were carved and above them, the roof was thatched. The nave held over a hundred standing and sanctuary ended behind the altar in the new style of apse. The Bishop prayed aloud in Latin and only his monks and Leofric understood. The monks had led him with smoking incense swinging in burners as they had processed to the half-hidden sanctuary. A carved screen allowed the congregation to see them partly but it added to the mystery. All in the church could feel that their Bishop was in direct communication with God and while he prayed in a language that they did not understand, they prayed silently themselves. Some asked that sick relatives were made well and some prayed that their lot was improved. Most asked for the death of all invaders in their land.

The Bishop dedicated the new church to the Saints Peter and Paul. No one had seen such a building before. Almost two hundred crammed into the nave as the Bishop held the chalice high, blessed it and the congregation knew that it had turned into the blood of Christ. It was passed from monk to monk but it was not passed to Leofric. He was not expecting to partake of the ceremony although he had done so in private many times. The Bishop had explained to him that it upset people to see someone, who they believed was a pagan forever, drinking the blood of Christ. The Bishop passed the chalice to King Cadrod. He closed his eyes and sipped. He felt the blood of Christ pass into him and with it he felt renewal. He believed that his prayers would now be answered as the Bishop had promised him that with the building of the church would come victory over the pagans. While the chalice containing Christ's blood was passed to Waljan Cadrod thought of the coming campaign.

The Sais pigs to the east were penned into their little flat land and would be there when he was ready to destroy them. The Sais to the south were almost beaten as his continual raids had weakened and demoralised them. Like a baited bear, they had been goaded until they were now going to attack and he would turn his dogs on them. God had answered his request for more men and the Kingdoms of Glastening and Caer Glori had sent him hundreds of men, all with shield, spear and helmets. Many came with horses and he would command a cavalry of two hundred. They would terrorise the Sais as no man could outrun a horse and his warriors would split his enemy and hunt them down in their hundreds. For them, there would be no quarter, no slavery, only death.

Chapter 21
To Calchfynedd

Wuffa met with the remaining thegns in the old fort where he had already ordered the palisade pulled down. Some of the wood had been used for the pyres built for the battle dead. He was surrounded mainly by men from Suth Folk, with only the North Folk who had remained loyal to him and the unity of East Anglia. All of them wore their new arm rings. Wuffa explained how he would now need to go north to the furthest reaches of his Kingdom. He would show himself to all his subjects so that everyone was assured of his authority. He expected that this would take him all summer and during that time and afterwards, all thegns would spend one month of the year on duty at the Great Dyke. He did not need to say that any absence would be met with a demand for wergild. In good time, he told them, there would be a new Ealdorman of the North Folk but meanwhile, he appointed two of his senior thegns to adjudicate on any arguments or crimes.

When Wuffa had finished speaking, he invited them all to ask questions of him. They asked about the land that they had been given, why Selwyn's treasure had not been found and shared and also many trivial issues. The young King of East Anglia answered all of them patiently and politely and then he looked at Osgar, who never liked to speak in a crowd but knew he had to ask Wuffa one question.

"My lord," he said and took a deep breath, "When do we attack the Kingdom of the Chalk Hills?"

"Osgar," said Wuffa, never calling him 'young Thunor' in a public meeting, "my surprise is not that you ask me this, but only that you have waited two days. We know of your desire to avenge your father's death and you still believe that your mother and brother are alive and enslaved by the Waelisc. Many of our people have suffered as you and have been patiently waiting to take war to the Waelisc. Your waiting is over. Today I have sent a messenger to King Cuthwulf of the West Saxons that I will send an army to support his. Henryk, you will once more command on my behalf and Osgar is your right-hand man. You leave in two days."

Osgar could barely believe it and turned around and found Anson. He hugged him and they both punched the air. Anson had never seen his nephew happier and said a silent prayer that his belief that his family still lived would prove true.

It was a hectic two days for the three hundred chosen to march to the Calchfynedd. There was food to gather and pack for the march. Many of them spent their copper rings buying better armour and weapons and they made sure that their leather boots were in good order for the march. All of them had helmets, many with cheek and neckpieces and they were all expected to carry a spear and two aetgars. Some carried the long aescs, which were so deadly when wielded from the second row of a shield wall. They were difficult to march with, being such an awkward length, that Henryk had to encourage men to carry them. However, their bearers would be stationed in the second row, so as to plunge them over their front line's heads into the enemy and would therefore be safer if the shield wall held. Thegns had swords at their side, some slung them over their backs in Osgar's manner, while others had seaxs in the small of their back and a few, like Anson favoured the war-axe. There was great excitement amongst the people, girls wanted to see the fine men of the fyrd and boys asked to hold spears and would clean swords and seaxs for their owners. The army only had a short time to exercise together and get to know one another but many had fought in the battle of Stubs Worth and also at the old fort. Some had been adversaries but were now allies and the North Folk men were keen to learn how an outnumbered force had shoved them back. Henryk demanded obedience from the start and demonstrated to all that it was the instant following of orders with absolute force that allowed them to overwhelm superior numbers.

They left on a warm spring morning and marched southwest down the Icknield Way. It had been a trade route for two thousand years, following the chalk ridge once the heath was passed. Before that, they marched over the breckland sandy soil between clumps of gorse and broom in yellow flower. There were vast areas of open land with few trees. Larger and greener clumps of trees signified a source of water near the ground surface. They crossed the Lark at noon and stopped on the far bank for a break where many people of the surrounding hams had gathered to see them off. Some people had walked from

Beodricesworth to look at the largest number of armed men that they had ever seen.

Anson's wife was waiting for him by the crossing at Icklingham and gave him a big cuddle and kiss before turning to Osgar and grabbing him before he could get away. She gave him a kiss on each cheek and squeezed his face saying that he was her brave boy, spotted his bandaged arm and then the healing wound on his cheek.

"Let me see to it that your arm is properly bandaged," she said, "I can't have you marching off like that."

"It is fine," said, Osgar pulling his arm away. He realised how curt he had sounded and thanked her and gave her a big hug.

"Here have some ale then," she said filling cups for them, "and I have some dried meat and nuts for you to take."

"Sup your ale, boy," said Anson to Osgar, "that'll heal anything."

Wilfrid and Seward were surrounded by their family including Lynne. Osgar spotted her and could not take his eyes away as she looked more beautiful than ever and now saw him looking at her. She walked over to him and said, "Weren't you going to speak?"

"Of course I was," replied Osgar.

They looked at each other until Osgar finally said, "When I come back, will you be my wife?"

"I will," said Lynne as she clutched him and kissed him on the lips.

Henryk was with a crowd from the Flemish settlement. He was formally shaking hands with all the men who were staying. It was the planting season so many had to remain because if they missed the planting there would be no harvest and they would starve when winter came. Ten Flems were coming with Henryk, now famous throughout Anglia for their accuracy in throwing aetgars and by the example that they had shown of how discipline in battle was critical to survival and victory.

The fyrd crossed the Lark and as the land inclined out of the valley, the soil changed from sand to chalk. They passed the edge of the Black Ditches on its left and now realised how insignificant it was compared to the Great Dyke on the heath. As they marched, the grass became thicker and greener and the trees were noticeably stronger. The leaves were out on all except the ash and oak and they would be fully open in a few days, if the warm weather continued. By late afternoon, they crossed the small water course in the valley of the Great Heath.

Here only a month before had been a large encampment of traders, craftsmen, bakers and brewers. Now only one tenth were still there as all the diggers had returned home and those guarding the dyke were serviced from Stubs Worth and a new settlement at the fen end.

They stayed the night in the valley while Henryk and Osgar went with some men to find the Gwyre people. Henryk passed their leader a pouch of silver from Wuffa. The Gwyre were interested in the army and where they were going but Henryk only said that they wished to travel the Icknield Way to meet their cousins in the south. They needed two guides who could also translate for them and the Gwyre leader haggled over the cost. He explained how few people knew the land and could speak the language of the Cymry and Sais. Finally, Henryk said that he would return to Wuffa with the news that they were unwilling to help and from nowhere two Gwyre appeared able to fulfil the role.

They walked back to the main camp carrying salted and smoked fish that they had also purchased. Two of the Swarbians, who had come with them, talked of settling on the edge of the fens when they returned. All of them knew that war brought death and destruction but it also brought many opportunities. There would be plunder and rewards from their King and there was the chance of new land for the growing population.

In the morning, they filled their stomachs with as much food as they could before marching out. They were accompanied by a crowd of people, men, now too old to fight, wished them well and patted their backs while women wept and kissed their loved ones. Girls blushed at some of the comments that the marching men made, and boys too young to fight marched alongside them, staves held over their shoulders as if they carried spears. They soon passed through the narrow gap in the dyke. All the guards lined the ridge above the ditch, on either side, holding their spears aloft and then banging them against their shields in salute. None of them looked back and soon they had marched out of earshot of the cheering people and the mood of reverie soon changed as they had entered enemy territory. They hugged the chalk ridge close to the tree line and in the distance, they sometimes spotted people who disappeared by the time that they marched by. The fens which they had seen sparkling in the distance to their right were now gone and only rolling chalk-land hills filled their views.

In the evening, they stopped by a stream and camped under the trees. Henryk sent out hunting parties, who went in groups of ten for safety who found two settlements which were deserted on their approach. The men returned with some sheep and pigs which were slaughtered and roasted over fires. Under Henryk's orders, they had not burnt the settlement down as they did not wish to draw the Britons to them yet.

In the morning, they continued the march southwest along the Icknield Way. Here the broad pathway could be more clearly seen as it had continued to be used by traders without break for thousands of years. The grassland ridge undulated and gradually climbed and they had a wide view across the whole country. By noon, they could see their goal in front of them as the land rose sharply toward a mound like hill, at the end of a ridge that towered over the landscape. Before the Britons had cut their trade route, this was a well-known landmark that they had known as Ivinghoe hill.

The three hundred men climbed Ivinghoe hill. It was noon, the sun and the climb made them sweat. At the top was a panoramic view where they could see for a day's march in all directions. Settlements could be spotted by the ploughed land and wisps of smoke seen emerging from trees. They could not see Anglia but they looked northeast. All around were their enemies so they stayed in armour and waited. Here was where they would meet Cuthwulf and his army of Saxons. If he did not come, they all knew they would be in grave danger. Henryk was aware that their small army was not enough to survive so deep into enemy territory. They had no more than three days food and there was no water on the chalk hill that they occupied. Search parties were again sent out and returned before nightfall with water but little food. The two pigs, that they had found and killed, would not stretch to feeding three hundred men. Water was carried up the hill from a stream some distance away. As night fell, it became cold and exposed on the hill without tree cover and rain began to fall. They rolled themselves into their cloaks and tried to sleep.

The next day they awoke wet and cold and looked out across the Kingdom of Calchfynedd and saw nothing. They peered along the chalk ridge route to the southwest but could see no approaching army of Saxons. As the day wore on, Henryk again sent out small raiding parties to look for food. He could hear some of the men moaning and losing heart. "How do we know Cuthwulf is coming?" said Wilburh. "Has anyone met him?"

"He'll come," said one of the few Saxons with them.

"Maybe we are in the wrong place?" whined Wilburh, sharpening his poorly made seax.

"Oh yeah, we're in the wrong place," said Anson. "We're on the highest hill around here, where we're supposed to be. Do you see a higher one, you North Folk twat?"

The day wore on and they were baked in the full sun; there was no shade and they covered their heads with their cloaks. Most sat sharpening swords or spears and a few played with dice made from bone. They scratched out a nine-man-morris in the chalk and used small silver coins as markers. Some of the Angles sung and some told stories while Osgar sat on his own on the edge of the hill and looked southwest. He needed Cuthwulf to come to help him fulfil his ambition. By night-time, he was beginning to wonder if the Saxons would ever appear. Henryk had confided in Anson that he could only allow two more days and then they would have to try to make their way home. They had seen the scouting horsemen more frequently during the day and Henryk said that soon the enemy would come with an army to fight them. Ivinghoe was a great defensive position but without water and food, it was the wrong place for them to be caught.

Seward walked to where Osgar sat and looked out across the vista of rolling chalk hills, woods and tracts of farmland.

Osgar looked up and said, "Sit down, mate."

"Why are we here?" asked Seward, lowering himself onto a tuft of grass next to Osgar and stretching his legs out.

"I'm here because I want to rescue my mother and Leo," he replied.

"And kill the Waelisc?" asked Seward.

"Only the one that killed my father."

"You used to say that you would kill them all if you had to," Seward reminded him.

"Did I?" said Osgar surprised.

Seward pulled his knees up and looked out in the same direction as his pal, "You used to frighten us when we were kids, you know. All you went on about was killing the Waelisc and at thirteen you fought in a battle and killed a man and captured his sword. The rest of us in Beo were still playing soldiers with sticks."

"I've thought about it a lot," said Osgar, "I know they are still alive and I made a promise to my father to fetch them home. I also made a pledge to myself to avenge my father and I will see his killer die but I've just made another promise to Lynn. I've loved her for years and should have been married to her when I finished my apprenticeship. Every time I wanted to say something to her, I thought that I was betraying my family."

"So what changed?" asked Seward.

"Well, your nonstop prodding, for a start," he said laughing and then he was more serious again. "When this is all over, I just want to be a blacksmith and farm a little, maybe even a sword-maker. Wuffa says that if the Saxons are defeated then the Waelisc will again turn on us. I want to have children with Lynn and for them to grow up in a ham like I did, only one that is never raided."

The next day, they again woke with no sign that the Saxons were near but the night patrols reported to Henryk that they had heard an increase of movement at the base of the hill that they thought was the enemy. He sent out more scavenging parties and decided that if the Saxons of King Cuthwulf did not come that day then they would move out in the early hours that night and try to gain some distance from their foe.

In late afternoon, Anson heard one of the hunting parties returning and among their loud chattering he recognised Wilfrid's voice. Anson stood beside Osgar and called down the hill, "Do you have any food. I'm starving?"

"You big fat Jute," Wilf shouted back. "What food do you want?"

"I'm fed up with pig and salted fish," he called back. "Do you have sheep?"

"No," Wilf called in return.

"Well what do you have?" shouted Anson, his hunger making him short tempered.

"We have an army of Saxons," came the reply.

*****

Waljan jumped from his horse and ran from the stables across the courtyard. He took the stone stairway two steps at a time and went straight into the King's room.

"You have news for me?" said King Cadrod.

"I do, *sire*," said Waljan. "The Sais come from the south as we expected but they are joined by the eastern Sais."

"How many?" said Cadrod, looking concerned.

"Twelve hundred or more from the south and two hundred to three hundred from the east," replied Waljan.

"Good," said Cadrod relaxing, "We outnumber them and they are on our land and they have no cavalry. I do not want one left alive. When we defeat them, all of Cymru will join us and we will clean our land of this filth. Now we have much to do. We gather our forces and march in two days. I want to catch them in the open where our cavalry can be used to best effect."

Cadrod poured Waljan wine from a silver pitcher, they tapped their goblets together and drank. Cadrod had never been happier as considered his plan was working to perfection. He was the heir to Arturius and soon, with the defeat of the Sais, all would recognise him as such. The Bishop has been right about building the church, God was on his side and he would in return reward the church with such treasures as had never been seen.

Chapter 22
Cuthwulf

Wilfrid and Seward led the Anglian army down the steep hill towards the woodland. They walked past Saxons posted as lookouts and finally came to a large hidden glade in which camped Cuthwulf's army. The grassy area had been crushed down by the weight of feet. At the margins of the wood some bluebells were in flower, carpeting the wood floor in a blue haze. Fires were being built and the preparation of evening food begun. At the far end of the glade, an awning was covering four poles set into the ground. Under the cover sat the King of the West Saxons who stood to greet the East Angles. He was a man of over forty years with bright eyes that had crinkles at their sides. He had a long moustache that drooped on either side of his mouth and a V shaped beard. It was obvious that he was glad to see them.

Henryk stepped forward with Anson and Osgar and they bowed in unison to Cuthwulf.

"Welcome, welcome," said Cuthwulf, spreading his arms wide and smiling, "to my great hall in the forest."

"My King sends his compliments," said Henryk. "He wishes that he could be with you on this great endeavour but regrets that as a new King he must ensure the security of his region."

"Of course, of course," said Cuthwulf pulling on his pointed grey beard, "How many of you are there?"

"We are three hundred, *sire* and most have seen battle," replied Henryk as the King grasped his forearm.

"That I can see," said the King looking at Osgar's bandaged arm. "I had hoped that Wuffa would send me a thousand or at least five hundred, but you are here and I welcome you."

"Will the fires not tell our enemy where we are?" said Henryk.

"Hope so," said Cuthwulf, "yes, I hope so. Tomorrow, we lead him on a little dance. Your men can march fast?"

"Ja," said Henryk, "they march fast."

"Do we march on Bannaventa?" said Osgar.

"Oh great Woden no," said the King. "No, no, too obvious. We would need three times this number. No young man that is where he wants us. Open ground, defended town, no. We'll find a good spot. We chose our ground not his."

King Cuthwulf introduced them to his son Ceol, the Aetheling, who looked every inch a Saxon prince. His hair and trimmed beard were immaculate and he had wavy fair hair which was held in place by a headband. His tunic was cream with ornate embroidery around the collar and cuffs. The sleeves were full length and the cuffs held together with silver clasps. His ceorl held his helmet with its iron face piece. It had gold on the helmet brows and a gold moustache under the nose of the face piece. The cheek pieces and neck pieces were also iron and notched and patterned.

Ceol eyed Osgar up and down, they were about the same age but there the similarity ended. Osgar was tanned and tightly muscled. His hair and beard were trimmed in the Angle fashion but he had three days of stubble and his clothes were plain and worn. They were dusty from the last weeks marching, the days sat on the hill and his shield showed the marks of battle. The cut on his cheek had scabbed over but he still had a bandaged arm.

"Did you get your wounds in battle practice?" asked Cuthwulf's Aetheling, looking disdainfully at Osgar.

"No," said Osgar, without a 'sire' or 'my lord'.

"Do I need to guess?" said Ceol, annoyed by Osgar's perceived bad manners and lack of answer, "Or will you tell me?"

"They were a leaving present from our brothers the North Folk," retorted Anson on Osgar's behalf, still answering obliquely.

"Father," said Ceol to the King, "if these Angles are fighting amongst themselves, what good are they to us?"

"I tell you what good we are," said Henryk, "Osgar here is worth ten men. He fought a battle while you were still sucking your mother's tit, ja. There's no man in this land I rather have next to me in the shield wall. You going to frighten the Waelisc with your silver, maybe you blow them a kiss."

Ceol reached for the pommel of his sword and Henryk did the same. Osgar watched but did not move. He knew he could cut Ceol's hand off before his sword came near to the Flem. Cuthwulf put his left hand over his son's right which gripped the hilt of his sword. He held his right hand up and said calmly, "Good, good, we are all ready for battle now. All we have to remember is who the enemy is. Now let us eat and drink. We have a little mead left, so let's enjoy it. Tomorrow, we leave our handcarts and only travel with what we can carry."

Henryk pushed his sword back into its sheath and eventually, the Aetheling did the same. Osgar did not take his eyes off Ceol and the Aetheling stared back for a while and then dipped his eyes and turned to go with his father. Cuthwulf said, "Remember that we are cousins. We are Anglecynn. We have only one enemy and if we do not put all our energy in to defeating them then none of us will leave here alive."

It was light early and the joint army unrolled themselves from their cloaks and rose. They ate the remaining food from the previous night, drank water from the stream and left. Behind them, the Saxon handcarts had been piled high and set alight.

Cuthwulf had Henryk walk with him so that he could talk to him about his army and how they would fight together as one. He was careful to keep his son Ceol away and had given him the duty of keeping stragglers up. They were moving fast and it was important that they were not strung out as they marched directly north. Cuthwulf knew that Bannaventa was to their northwest and he was risking being caught on the march by the Britons. His plan meant that speed and surprise was needed. He was heading to the eastern borders of the Calchfynedd where the fens again began. There he would seek his battleground.

That evening they were by the Great Ouse, the wide looping river could not be crossed. They could go no further north and an escape route east was also cut off by the Ivel River and then the fens. They could turn around and head south which would inevitably take them into their enemies hands or they could go west towards Bannaventa and further into the lands of the Britons. Cuthwulf was relaxed and had chatted amiably to those around him as they had marched. He had sent out scouts to survey the area for him. He ate raw duck eggs that had been found in the marshes by the Great Ouse. "Tomorrow, they will find us trapped by this great river. We need to be ready."

*****

Cadrod was furious. He had marched his large army southeast only to be told quite clearly that the two Sais armies had joined and camped at the Great Hill and now before they had even reached it his scouts had told him that they were wrong.

"Well they can't have disappeared into thin air," said Cadrod, "and even the Sais cowards cannot run home that quickly."

"They have gone north, *sire*," said the mounted scout. "It is easy to follow them. They leave such a downtrodden track."

"They have either skirted around us to attack Bannaventa," said Waljan. "Or they may be trying to get to the eastern lands behind the defensive dyke."

"If they go too far north then we have them," said Cadrod. "They will be trapped by the rivers with no way out. Turn the army around Waljan, let's catch them."

*****

Cuthwulf's scouts returned; they had found what he wanted. He moved his army east along the bank of the Great Ouse to where it was joined by it tributary the Ivel. Most of the river fork was a marshy area apart from a shallow hillock forcing the river into a looping bend. The hillock was steeper to the west and dropped down to the east. The land was first flat and dry and then in another few hundred paces west it became marshy. Cuthwulf formed his army on the raised ground, with Henryk and his men formed the right flank on the steepest part of the ridge. Cuthwulf commanded the centre and the Aetheling Ceol, commanded three hundred on the left flank. Their line was less than three hundred paces across and it was only another five hundred paces to the Ivel. The hillock dropped down behind them to the Great Ouse only one hundred paces behind them.

All the men looked around to survey their position themselves. They felt trapped. There was water on three sides and they knew that the Britons would come from the south. They were brave men and they believed in their King but they feared that if the battle did not go well that there would be no escape. Most could swim but not with armour and heavy clothes on and the other side of the river was still enemy territory where they would emerge from the river without arms.

Everyone was set to work, cutting the riverside trees to make stakes. Anson and others with axes, felled suitable ash and elder while the rest with seaxs cut

239

the ends into sharp points and planted them as directed by Cuthwulf. They dug holes and pushed the stakes in, pointing them towards the open ground. The flatter the ground became the damper it was and easier to dig. Cuthwulf hoped that the stakes would deter the Britons from sending their cavalry against his left flank which was almost on level ground.

Osgar carried the cut posts to where Cuthwulf had ordered them to be set. He helped Seward sharpen them with his old seax and dug holes to plant them in.

"You when we were on Ivinghoe Hill and you asked me why we were here?" asked Osgar.

"Yes," said Seward.

"Well I told you why I was here but you never told me why you came."

"I could tell you that I came because I hoped to win rings of copper and silver but that's not why. I want to be like you, we all did in Beo. You've already got wealth, land and a position. The scops use your name in epic tales. What have I got? Who's ever heard of me? I'm a carpenter's son who will soon be looking for work when his younger brothers start at the shop."

"Oh Thunor," said Osgar, realising what his boyhood friend was saying, "Don't say that, don't even think it, mate. You are going to be the uncle of my children. I want to take my son into your woodwork shop for you to make him a toy sword. I want to drink ale with you after work like my uncle and your dad do. Stay away from me in the shield wall. I seem only bring death. Better than that, stay in the back line, you're good with an aetgar."

"Don't be an arse, Osgar, I've never thrown an aetgar in my life and you're not my mother."

"Look," said Osgar, dropping the post that he had been sharpening, "I know I'm not saying this very well but it's stupid you trying to be like me when all I want is for my life to be like yours."

Cuthwulf's army settled down for the night as the enemy had not reached them yet although they had seen horsemen in the distance. Cuthwulf had no doubt, that these were the scouts of his enemy. He thought of the position that he had brought his army to. The battle would be decisive either way, if he lost, his army would be slaughtered and all the Saxons of the south would be unprotected. They had been weakened enough these past few years and if defeated, they would collapse and be pushed back to the sea. However, if they won and could unite the Angles in the north and east with the Saxons in the south then the Anglecynn would not just be an idea and a word. There would be a union stretching across the island.

Cuthwulf pondered his forces. He could see that the Angles, though few in number, were battle hardened. They had marched fast all day and yet the Angles had laughed, sang and made fun of the Saxons. His emissaries had been impressed with Wuffa before he became King. This disciplined young King had an army made in his own image. What of his son Ceol, pondered Cuthwulf, would he hold the left flank? He had made sure that his Aetheling had trained with the best Saxon warriors. He was a master with sword and spear but he had not seen battle. How would he react? Cuthwulf did not doubt his son's bravery but would his arrogance cause problems? He would speak to him in the morning and remind him of the need for his army to act as one. Cuthwulf slept on the ground beside his men. He was rolled up in his ornate fur lined cloak and his jewelled helmet sat on the ground beside him. His sword laid by his right hand, the toggle tying the pommel into the scabbard was undone and the hilt pulled out showing two finger widths of blade.

On the right flank squatted Osgar with Anson, Henryk, Wilf and his son Seward. Anson and Wilf had been playing dice and arguing over how much was owed by each to the other. In the distance, they could hear the booming voice of Wilburh.

"Why have we come here?" said Wilburh to anyone who would listen, "Wuffa would not have taken us here. It's not right, some of us can't swim."

"I wish someone would shut him up," said Anson, "Why in Hel's name did he come with us?"

"Because he has nothing," said Wilf. "No lands, even his wife ran away. Look at his arms; he doesn't own even a copper band. He hopes that for once he is on the winning side and can take a share of booty home."

"I go and tell him to be quiet," said the Flem.

They listened to Henryk trying to reason with Wilburh. "Oh so now I can't talk, can I?" Wilburh said, "I'm a free man. It's not right to tell me what I can say."

Finally they heard the Flem tell him in a firm voice, "I don't give a damn what you say, ja, but you are stopping people sleeping. You must be heard back in East Anglia, now you shut up."

Henryk swung his arm and his fist hit Wilburh in the mouth splitting his lip and loosening a tooth. He walked back to the group in silence clutching his sore fist in his hand. Henryk sat down in a silence only broken by croaking frogs. He wrapped his cloak over his legs and said, "Now we sleep, ja."

In the morning, there was a low mist. In places, it was less than a man's height. Above it, there was a blue sky. The early morning sun would soon start to burn it away and by noon, all the mist would be gone. Cuthwulf's army stood on the low hillock. They formed a wide crescent curling along the ridge edge in a bend in the river. The right flank occupied by the Angles, overlooked the steepest part of the hillock. As the defensive position swung around, it also tipped down to the level ground. The left flank curled around backwards to meet the marshy ground before the river. They could hear the Britons coming before they saw them as they had horns blowing and drums sounding. The army of Britons rounded the bend in the river and were soon lined out across the fork as if their first job was to stop any escape. It looked to Osgar as if they had twice the number of Cuthwulf's army. They were organised into blocks of about two hundred men and behind them were the cavalry. Osgar had never expected to see so many horses and knew the effect that they would have upon foot soldiers caught in the open.

Cuthwulf strode along the back of their line, starting at the right flank and spoke loudly to the Angles, "If you stand and hold this ground, then no cavalry can beat you. Listen to your thegn commanders. Remember, you must not break from the shield wall even if you think that the enemy is defeated. You will only advance on my order or the order of your immediate commander. Henryk gives you your orders and if he falls then it will be Anson."

"This day is our day," he told them and though he was not their King they felt he was speaking for all the Anglecynn. He moved along the line to speak to the soldiers that he was commanding in the centre. On the right flank, they could still hear his voice repeating the same words. As he moved on, Anson stepped forward from the shield wall and faced the Angles. He took his axe from behind his shoulders and held it as he would a sledgehammer, with his right hand closer to the head.

"You have heard Cuthwulf," shouted Anson. "He is not our king but he is our cousin. His people have endured like us. We fight today to avenge our people who have suffered from the Waelisc since we came to these lands. Our people have been butchered, our women raped and our children stolen. When the Waelisc come close look at them and you will see the demons who did all this and if we fail this day, will again turn on East Anglia. Stay together, stay in the shield wall and this day will be our day."

The Angles cheered and banged their spears against their shields. Cuthwulf had moved on past his central force and was now talking to the left flank commanded by his Aetheling, Ceol. Soon all the Saxons were cheering and banging their spears in time with the Angles. Henryk moved behind the Angles on the right flank. He checked that they had their aetgars to hand and reminded them that they were only to throw on his command and he wanted them aimed at the horses if they were near enough. He had arranged those who had carried the ten-foot aescs and some with battle axes, so that they were behind the front row. They were to aim their thrusts over their own men's shoulders down the slope.

*****

Cadrod looked northwards towards his enemy who were clustered atop a small hillock that dropped away to the right. To their left was the broad river which disappeared behind the knoll and reappeared to their right. There the ground became marshy as the river formed a fork with the Ivel. He did not want to take his men and especially his horses into the boggy ground so decided upon a frontal attack. He had enough men to force them off the top of the hill. The ridge was steep but not high and his horses would gallop up it. He would send half his army straight at the Sais and follow behind with the cavalry. Once the Sais line was broken, his cavalry would push through and then he would have some fun and then the bards would be speaking of him and this day in a thousand years.

He ordered his men forward. They marched over good ground with their shields to their front and their spears up. The ground was good and they marched quickly, expecting victory and with it some rich pickings and when they were fifty paces from the Cuthwulf's army the order was given to lower their spears. They pointed them at the heads appearing over the shields above them. The Britons shouted at the Anglo-Saxons, telling them that they were dead and that they would lose the land that they had stolen. Some shouted insults about their parents or their looks or what their wives were up to while they were away. The Cuthwulf's army just heard a meaningless noise and they, in turn, shouted insults and threats back. Osgar just stood silently and looked at his enemy, appraising their weapons, their shields and their armour. He saw that very few had helmets, although some had chainmail hauberks. He looked closely at their shields which did not seem as well made as his own. The Angles had either leather covered shields or flat wooden shields that were painted thickly with bright designs. The heavy paint was important as it hid the grain of the wood and although the Waelisc shields were of a similar style and shape, he could clearly see the grain.

The Britons had moved up from fifty paces away to twenty-five from the Cuthwulf's line. Henryk ordered the men at the back to take an aetgar and to be ready and then they heard shouts from the Britons who lowered their spears. With a great roar, they charged and at that moment Henryk cried, "Throw," and one hundred aetgars rained upon the enemy. Most in the front were missed but the second and third rows were hit, then shield and spear clashed. Spears stuck in shields or were deflected upwards but some found their mark and then the two armies were shield to shield. Henryk ordered the men who had thrown their aetgars to thrust down with the aescs.

Osgar stood in the centre of the right flank and held his shield high on his left arm were it firmly overlapped with Anson's. He picked his targets deliberately and each thrust of his spear from over his right shoulder was with his full strength. He caught attackers in their faces, shoulders and necks. He picked out a target in front and his strength forced his spear point through chainmail and deep into his enemy's flesh. The body fell sideways and before Osgar could yank it clear, the spear was jammed in the melee and snapped. Osgar let go of his spear and pulled his sword from the scabbard. He had not used it in battle before, having only practiced with it on the heath. Wuffa had encouraged him to not just use the traditional over arm swings but to point and lunge. Osgar used these sword strokes now. He was able to swing his sword down on spears cutting through their hafts and to drive the tip of his sword over and between shields.

Osgar could feel Anson next to him, the broad Jute's shoulder banging against his. Anson shouted nonstop, swearing at the enemy, encouraging those around him and even joking. Osgar said nothing as he concentrated on the enemy immediately in front of him. He had seen the man who had killed his father, on horseback in the distance, just before the battle started. He believed that each man in front of him was on that raid that had taken his mother and brother. He fought with a controlled fury, using his strength and speed to kill and injure any Britons unfortunate enough to face him. Finally, the pressure on the line eased and the Britons fell back. They were losing too many men; the Angles and Saxons further down the line had lost men but not in the same numbers as the Cadrod's army. As they felt them fall back, the Anglo-Saxon army jeered at their enemy and a group of Cuthwulf's Saxons took off after them, following them down the hill, hacking at their backs and shoving their spears into them. Some on the Angles flank where it joined Cuthwulf's main force ran with them too. The excitement of victory had grabbed all of them. Osgar tried to step forward but Anson's arm was upon his shoulder. "This is not over, wait for the command to move," Anson shouted.

He then bellowed at the top of his voice to all of them, "Hold, do not move, stand."

Henryk was also stopping men from joining the chase but many had already gone with Wilf and Seward included. At least one hundred Angles and Saxons pursued the Waelisc down the ridge. Those that watched envied them and resented their commanders for halting them.

Waljan had seen the Britons army battering the shield wall with little success. He had been unable to use his troops on horseback to aid them. Although they could ride up the steep ridge, at the point of attack the mass of foot soldiers blocked them from getting near the Sais. Now he could see the attack crumble and run so he pulled his horsemen round and back down the hill. He cantered his horse down to the level ground and over his shoulder, he saw that it was not a general advance by the Sais but a group of about one hundred chasing the retreating Cymry. He swung his horse around and called to his troop of fifty men to do the same. They turned and chased through their own retreating men. Some were knocked flying but Waljan drove his horsemen on. Cadrod sat on his horse and watched.

Seward had the seax out that Osgar had given him. He hacked at a Briton who had been wounded in the shield wall. He had no sword or spear and tried to parry the blows with his shield. Eventually, a low swing caught him on the leg below the side of the knee and the seax cut through sinew and into bone. The leg caved inwards and he went down. Seward hacked at him until he was dead. Wilf had jammed his spear two handed into the back of another Briton and jogged down the hill looking for his next target. Then he saw the horsemen.

On the brow of the hill, Cuthwulf watched more than one hundred good men slaughtered. They had been surprised and cut off by the horsemen. Cadrod seeing Waljan turn his troop and send it into attack had sent in a reserve of his soldiers and the rout was stopped and turned. None survived and those who were not killed immediately were shown to the Cuthwulf's army and butchered so that they could see them die. Anson watched his best mate Wilfrid run through with a spear while trying to protect his son Seward. Osgar saw his boyhood friend Seward, cut down with a sword stroke and then dragged towards them to have his head pulled back by his hair and his throat cut. Anson's hand gripped Osgar's shoulder. Osgar's anger rose beyond his control. His only thought was to attack everyone of the enemy in front of him and gain revenge for his family and now, for one of his few close friends. He could barely hear Anson shouting in his ear and for one terrible moment was about to turn his sword on his uncle to free himself. Anson had dropped his spear and axe and held both his arms around his nephew.

"I killed him," said Osgar to Anson.

"Of course you didn't. Why do you say that?"

"Because he told me he wanted to be a hero in battle like me and I told him not to stand by me in the wall. I should have kept him close."

"Osgar," shouted Anson, though he still gripped him tight, "you've got to stop thinking that you are responsible for every death around you. You are no more to blame for his death than I am Wilf's and throwing your life away will not help Leo and your mother." Anson lowered his voice and said, "Let's both stay alive. We know how to do this."

Osgar wiped his sword-arm across his mouth and nose and nodded, "Yes."

Cuthwulf had seen nearly one tenth of his army destroyed in a wild undisciplined charge. The shield wall had held well and though they had taken losses, the Britons were falling at three times their rate. He had picked a good site to fight and now his enemy knew it. He spoke to his men and told them that they must now believe that they had to stay in formation or die. His commanders repeated his words up and down the line. Cuthwulf's army was now muted. They had seen that war was not glorious as described by the scops. It was ugly and full of horror and death.

Another attack by the Britons was underway across the whole front of Cuthwulf's army. This time there were gaps in the attacking foot soldiers where the horsemen could gallop through. The charge was supposed to intimidate and break the defensive line but Cuthwulf's army stood its ground. No horse will charge through a shield wall with spears pointing out of it. The stakes in front of the middle and left flank deterred the riders also and the result was the same as the first attack. The Anglecynn army held, they took injuries and losses but they held a tighter shield wall than their enemy. They held a better position and they were slaying their enemy by at least three to one. If a man was killed in the shield wall the tight pack would hold him up until he could be pulled back out of the way. Most of them now carried injuries, from glancing blows and chops that had cut them. Their leather jerkins may save their life, by reducing the depth of a cut but they were still wounded.

In the lull after the first attack, they had collected weapons from within thirty paces of their line, leaving the relative safety of the shield wall. While they kept a wary eye out for their enemy, they had retrieved aetgars which were taken back behind the line and shared out. Dropped shields and a few swords were picked from bodies and brought back and even broken spears were fetched as these could still be tossed randomly from the back of the line of defenders. Any Britons still alive had been dispatched.

Anson stood behind and to the left of Osgar in the second attack, because Anson now had no spear and had drawn his axe from behind his back. He would fight two-handed with it and therefore not hold a shield to his front. He passed his back to the collected pile of retrieved weapons and those of the dead and wounded. Both of them fought with an even greater anger than before and each saw every attacker as the man who had killed their lifelong friend. Osgar now controlled his fury and channelled it, selecting each target in turn and striking hard at an exact point. Again, his spear was broken and he pulled his sword out. Anson was now fighting with his axe and they were covered from behind by the overhead spear thrusts of the Angles. When a shield appeared in front of Anson, he hooked the crescent shaped blade of his axe over it and pulled down. In that instant, Osgar thrust his tapered sword into the exposed Briton. Osgar saw a shield in front of him which was brightly painted blue and yellow. He could see the wood grain which was running diagonally. He swung his tapered sword over his right shoulder in an arc that brought the edge of his sword in perfect alignment to the grain. In an instant, the blade was through the sinew bound edge and had split one third off the shield. His arm came back and he thrust his sword through the gap that he had created, stabbing the Briton who was still shocked that one blow could cleave his shield in two. Osgar's sword point burst through the Waelisc leather body armour and into his chest and Osgar gave his sword a twist and pulled it back. The warrior dropped to his knees and Osgar looked for his next victim.

Whenever any horsemen neared their lines, aetgars rained down on them. Some of the riders were hit but it was mainly the horses that were struck by the throwing spears. Few horses would be killed by a single aetgar penetrating their flesh but they were sent wild with fear and pain. They reared and plunged, spun around and tried to flee while their rider fought to control them, causing more confusion and damage to their own ranks.

Cadrod recalled his foot soldiers and horsemen as he could see that they were not breaking through. The ridge was too steep and the army facing them too resolute. He could see, from the back of his horse, that the Sais were losing men to him, but not enough. Every time a gap appeared in the wall, it was quickly filled by another from behind. He looked along the line to the right. There, where the Sais army curved around to the river, the hillock flattened so that there was no ridge and in front of their lines, the Sais had planted pointed stakes. He had avoided attacking that flank for fear of the stakes and the nearby marshy ground but he now had an idea. He had watched when the Sais had charged forward from their lines when his men had fallen back. Waljan had been quick to see opportunity to counterattack. The Sais had been caught in open ground and every one of them cut down.

He called his men back to regroup and spoke to his commanders. He could hear the jeering Sais, shouting from their lines. He did not understand their words but he thought that they would jeer no more in a short while.

The retreating Britons were not followed by any of Cuthwulf's army. They waited until their enemy was a safe distance away and then their commanders allowed them out of the shield wall to collect arms and to finish off any Britons who were still alive. Some of them took the chance to strip arm rings from them while any of their own who were wounded were carried to the back of the lines. There they had to fend for themselves. They tore strips of cloth off bodies to wrap their own wounds while others just lay dying. Any who could stand were expected to rejoin the lines, which no one objected to as they knew that their journey to Valhalla was assured. They had grown up being told of Valhalla and the joys that it held and the scops had filled them with epic tales of heroes. To die in battle was not just the greatest honour, for them it was to fulfil their very reason for being.

Cadrod ordered his army to the right and they marched along the line of the Anglo-Saxon army. They stayed two hundred paces from their enemy who jeered and gesticulated at them. Cuthwulf could see that they meant to attack his left flank which had been left alone so far, during the battle. He sent a message down the line that he wanted one in three men from the right flank of Angles to reinforce the left. Henryk obeyed Cuthwulf's orders straight away. He walked down behind his men and tapped every third one in turn and told them to go left. He patted Osgar's shoulder and told him to go.

Anson said, "I'll go too." He was not going to let his nephew out of his sight. He still feared that he would get himself killed by being rash. Henryk was about to say no but stopped himself.

"Go on then," he said, "and show our cousins how to fight."

They jogged down the line, shields in their left hands, recovered spears in their right. When they reached the left flank, Ceol was angrily saying that he needed no Angles and that his men alone would win the day.

"I don't give a shit what you think," said Anson. "We are ordered here by your King. You need to face forward and then when you have time, thank the gods that we have come."

Cadrod threw his army at the centre and right. They were met by a hail of aetgars but although many fell, they passed through the stakes and pushed up against the shield wall. Behind them, men ripped and pulled at the sharpened poles making room for the horsemen. They were exposed as they had dropped their shields to use two hands on the stakes. Aetgars were thrown at them from behind the front line. As a man was hit another filled his place and slowly most of the stakes were pulled down. The battle raged most fiercely in front of the Aetheling, Ceol and though this was his first action, he fought like a wolf. He led from the front, his spear stabbing at the Britons until they pressed against his shield and then he drew his broad sword and swung it over his shoulder at the enemy. He wore a full helmet with face, cheek and neck protection. It gave him a ghostly look to the Britons and it saved his life on more than one occasion when a spear slammed into his face knocking his head back but not cutting into him. No one who saw him fight could doubt his skill or bravery.

The left flank had taken the full might of Cadrod's army and had held. This was in no small part due to the reinforcements that Cuthwulf had seen the need to send. The front row was tiring and those who had stepped into the gaps wondered how much longer they could hold on and resist the pressure from the Britons. Then suddenly, they felt their enemy give and its line fracture, Britons were caught alone and cut down. Some began to turn and scramble over the bodies of their dead and wounded and then they were in flight. Ceol only had one thought, which was to win the battle. He was drunk on the feeling of war and he had stood in the thick of the fighting. He ordered his men forward and they broke from the wall, hacking at the enemy in front of them as they ran.

Cadrod watched and knew that his timing was critical. When he turned his cavalry, he wanted them to run straight through the mob, which now pushed towards them. His cavalry had been told not to stop. The foot soldiers were to slaughter the Sais who had left their line and the cavalry was to pass through the now empty flank and attack behind the enemy. Their way would be clear as the stakes had been removed and the shield wall gone. With horsemen at the back of the Sais, victory would be inevitable.

Cuthwulf watched his left flank and saw the enemy flee. He saw his son order the flank forward. The fifty or so Angles held back and looked to him. He held his hand up for them to stay and commanded his thegns to follow the orders that he had warned them of earlier. He sent one hundred and fifty men from behind him towards the left flank. They ran along the brow of the ridge as it dipped towards the river and joined the Angles as the first horses approached.

Cadrod led his horsemen, who had not been able to break into a gallop as he intended. Although it took only a short time for them to get through the disorganised pack of Saxons, they found the ground littered with the dead, discarded weapons and felled poles. No horse can be made to step on a body or a thick stake rolling on the ground. Cadrod was surprised to be confronted by another shield wall already reformed. He wondered if the Sais had hidden reinforcements or had his spies been wrong in their estimation of numbers? Some of the Saxons, who had fallen for his feint, were now rejoining the shield wall and then, just when he thought that his victory was assured, the Sais did the thing that he was least expecting.

*****

Anson and Osgar stood in the centre of the left flank. When Ceol had ordered them all forward they instinctively saw that he was wrong. They had already seen many of their own lost by rushing from the defensive line and, though it was the son of Cuthwulf who had ordered them forward, they had looked at the King to confirm it and he had been clear in his signal for them to stand. The Saxons swore at them and called them cowards as they ran forward and the only Angle to go with them was Wilburh, shouting at the top of his voice, he surged forward with the rest. Osgar tried to grab him but he was gone. When the Waelisc turned, he was one of the first to die. Osgar watched him swinging his shield and broken spear in an ungainly circle knowing he was about to meet his end. He had been a pain in their side for two years but he did not deserve his dreadful death. The scops would always like tell of glorious battle and instant death but that was not how he fell. Wilburh took at least twenty cuts, stabs and blows before he lay still on the ground and maybe then he was still not dead.

Their Saxon cousins now realised how foolhardy had been their charge and they turned back. Many were chopped down from behind and then the horsemen came. They did not stop but wove through them towards the few Angles left standing. The Angles moved closer together awaiting the horsemen and now they realised that they were being reinforced and the shield wall lengthened again. It was thin though, as there was no second row with aescs to double their spear number. They were fending off the horsemen when the stragglers reached the shield wall and they were trapped because no one would open to let them through.

"Down," Anson shouted at them, "Crawl under our shields."

They started to drop to the ground and scrambled between the legs of those in the shield wall. Anson took the opportunity to knee Ceol in the face as he came by, 'Purely by accident' as he said later. They popped up behind the line of men and picked up anything that came to hand to hurl it at the horsemen. Anson kept an eye on the centre of the line on his right, from where he felt that Cuthwulf was now controlling the battle. He could only have reinforced them so quickly if he had been ready for his son to break the line and the Britons to execute a feint. Anson saw Cuthwulf look to his right flank and with his right arm waved it forward. He looked to his left and caught Anson's eye and made the same movement with his left arm but more slowly and then they did the one thing that their enemy least expected, they advanced.

A Saxon thegn commander, just by Anson shouted, "Advance, slowly," and they stepped forward over bodies, weapons and stakes towards their surprised enemy.

The line advanced and their spears met the horses which shied away. The horsemen who had spent years running down men in the open struggled to control their mounts and the Waelisc foot soldiers were pressed forward by those behind shoving at their comrades. Cadrod looked down the line of his enemy. Four hundred paces away on the ridge the Sais were advancing quickly as they were unopposed on that flank and even the centre was moving quicker than the flank that he had sent the main body of his army against. He now realised what was happening. By swinging the front of the army around, the Sais would trap him in the fork of the river. There in the marshy ground his horses would flounder.

Cadrod felt an aetgar hit him on his inner thigh as it ripped a gash a hands length and three fingers deep. It pieced the leather saddle below his leg and still had enough force to puncture the shallow flesh over his mount's ribs. Cadrod sheathed his sword and pulled at the aetgar while his horse span around. Finally, he pulled the javelin from his flesh and the horse's and brought it under control. It was the third time that the aetgar had been thrown that day. Each time a different Angle had hurled it at the horsemen. It had missed the first two times and the point was covered with dirt. As it passed through Cadrod's beautifully woven trousers it forced fibres deep into the wound.

Cadrod would not die here; he could not allow it as his destiny was to be a great victor like Arturius. He had to save his horsemen and as many of his army as he could. He turned his horse in a tight arch and his mount put its foot on one of the stakes that had been pulled out. It rolled and the horse lost its footing and went down and Cadrod was sent sprawling. Even in the melee of battle, a large part of an army is watching its King. They saw him vanish and believed then that the battle was lost.

Waljan rode his horse over to his King just as Cadrod was getting to his feet. Waljan ordered another warrior from his mount and had him help his King onto its back. The Sais advance was now close and it was all the more threatening for being slow and controlled. Waljan led his King and many of the horsemen towards the narrowing escape route between the advancing Sais army and the marshy bank of the Ivel. They made it through but the army did not. The Britons were in total disarray. Their formations were broken by them having to follow the cavalry to the right and now some had seen their King fall and others had seen him flee the field. They retreated away from the Sais towards the fork in the river. The ground became heavy and their feet began to sink into the ground near the river that few could swim.

Cuthwulf organised the advance and once he saw the enemy retreat, he was determined not to let them out of the trap. He would have liked to have caught the cavalry as well but he knew that it was unlikely. He had swung his army around and pushed the left and right flank forward, forming a crescent like a bull's horns. The battle was won by mid-afternoon but the killing continued to the evening. Cuthwulf's army were tired and few did not carry injuries but they did not stop until they had killed every Briton that they could find. They followed them into the boggy ground where they speared them and hacked them to death. They held them down in the shallow water and drowned them and when they had finished, they stripped them of anything of value and left them where they lay.

Osgar and Anson did not indulge in the butchery but went to find their friends' corpses. They were determined to protect them from the body strippers who had begun their gruesome acts.

Chapter 23
Reckoning

The day after the battle, Cuthwulf's army built great pyres for their own dead and stood while their souls were taken to Valhalla. Osgar, Anson and Henryk had carried the bodies of Wilf and Seward up the hill and laid them side by side. They helped Henryk to build a pyre for the seven Flems who had been lost. The Angles sat together on the grass by the smoking pyres and bandaged their wounds. Cuthwulf visited them and thanked all of them but hey noticed that his Aetheling stayed away. The King had a cut on the top of his shoulder that had been stitched. The sword blade had broken his chain mail and opened his leather jerkin. The King gave them each a copper ring and to Henryk and Anson he gave silver. He patted Osgar on the shoulder and asked to see his sword.

"So this is the shield splitter?" he said holding the tapered sword. They could see that he could not raise his arm above his shoulder because of his injury but refused to acknowledge that it hurt.

"It has no name, *sire*," said Osgar.

"Well it should have one, yes, it should have one," repeated Cuthwulf. "It is the Angle Sword," he said and passed it back to Osgar.

"Will we go to Bannaventa now, *sire*?" asked Osgar.

"Is this not enough death for one lifetime?" said the King, looking around to survey the burning pyres and strewn naked bodies of the Britons.

"The man who killed my father and stole my mother and brother fled the battle," said Osgar, "I will kill him and find them."

"Then you must go to Bannaventa," said the King. "But my army is weak and tired. I will take them home and return at the summer's end."

Cuthwulf looked at the young warrior. He saw him looking down and knew that he cared nothing for the famous victory that he had played such a part in. "I will take my army home but you may talk to my men and any who will follow you, go with my encouragement."

Henryk the Flem looked at Anson the Jute and they smiled for the first time since the battles end. "Come on," said Anson, "let's see who is daft enough to come with us?"

*****

It was a sombre ride home as Cadrod and Waljan made their way back to Bannaventa. They were no more than fifty men on horseback, many of the riders were injured including Cadrod and a number of horses were lame or had deep cuts to their necks, flanks and hindquarters. More had escaped but some had already left to return to their home villages. The horsemen from Glastening and Caer Glori had ridden off in disgust. They had told Cadrod that his incompetence had left their fellow men trapped. When they arrived the people of Bannaventa could not believe their own eyes. They had been used to a stream of victories when every week their raiding parties would return with treasure, slaves and tales of bravery. They rushed to the beaten warriors who were hunched over their horses and questioned them about what had happened. The riders could not bring themselves to tell them that no one else would be returning.

Not all in Bannaventa were unhappy, where the slaves knew that their people had won a victory. Only a few days before many of those leaving the town on foot and horseback had taken delight in predicting a great slaughter of the Sais army that had invaded their land. Aefre watched the horsemen return from a safe distance and knew that she would be called to clean and stitch wounds. She saw that Cadrod, helped by two guards to dismount, could hardly place his left leg to the ground but she knew he would not ask for her help. King Cadrod of Calchfynedd was assisted up the stone stairway in the tower that led to his rooms. He sat at his table and demanded wine. He refused to talk to Waljan and other senior warriors and leant over the table with his head in his hands. He occasionally banged the table with a fist or looked above at the beamed ceiling and cursed God.

Aefre was visited by Waljan who had a cut above his knee and needed her to treat it. He finally told her of the scale of their defeat and watched her carefully to see if she gloated. After eleven years as a slave, she could control her emotions completely. Inside, she was jumping in the air and shouting, outside she finished stitching his wound and then continued to dab her soothing paste on it. She always knew that her people would come and now they had. Soon the Angles would appear, she thought, and her husband Eafwald would be with them, maybe even Osgar. She imagined that he would be a fine freeman ceorl by now.

Once Waljan had left, Aefre ran to the pigsties to see Sigbert.

"We've beaten the Waelisc," she told him excitedly.

"What do you mean, Aefre? What are you talking about?" he said.

"All of Calchfynedd's army is gone, destroyed, finished. The Saxon fyrd came and Angles as I said it would. We will be free. Siggy, you must go and find them and lead them here. From what Waljan has told me they are east of here."

"All right, I'll go," said Sigbert.

*****

Osgar, Anson and Henryk assembled their army as they walked through the makeshift camp talking to all. Some said straight away that they had to be kidding if they thought that they were going to follow a boy further west. Others wanted payment first and were not so impressed with promises of treasure to come. Most of the fit Angles agreed to go, as they said, they needed someone to lead them home afterwards anyway. They picked up about fifty men from Cuthwulf's army. They were mainly adventurers who were ceorls with no land or money. No Saxon thegns opted to accompany them but they did go with the genuine good wishes of all. The only exception was Ceol the Aetheling, who told them that they were just looting on the back of the Saxon victory. Anson suggested that he might want to come and watch them fight as he had spent most of the last battle on his stomach.

On the second day after the battle, scouts brought a ragged figure in and held him in front of Cuthwulf.

"So you claim that you are an escaped Angle slave, do you?" said the King.

"Claim to be, Claim," said Sigbert with all the incredulity he could muster. "How bloody often do you have someone in front of you claiming to be a bloody slave swineherd held by the Waelisc? Would you believe me if I claimed to be the Thegn of Banna-bloody-venta or maybe the Ealdorman of Calch-bleeding-fynedd? But all I said was that I was a bloody slave and your bull here thumped me."

Sigbert pointed at the Saxon who held him and then at his swollen eye. By now, a crowd was gathering and Cuthwulf stood with his hands on his hips laughing. Anson, Osgar and Henryk had been talking to a group of Saxons and stopped to listen.

"He's no spy," Cuthwulf said. "Release him." Sigbert was freed and dusted himself down as if he was wearing the finest clothes while looking indignantly at the Saxon scout.

"So why did you come?" asked Cuthwulf.

"For a small fee I will show you the way to Bannaventa so that you may meet my Queen Aefre," said Sigbert in mock gravity.

Anson looked at Osgar as they both heard Aefre mentioned. They pushed through the crowd and caught Cuthwulf's eye.

"May I speak with him, *sire*," said Osgar.

"Please do," replied the King. "Please do, but I fear his mind is addled from years of captivity."

"Oi, I heard that!" said, Sigbert looking indignant.

"Tell me of this Aefre," said Osgar.

"What's it worth?" said Sigbert, eyeing the arm rings on the Angles biceps.

Osgar pulled a copper band from his arm and handed it to the scruffy man in front of him.

"Food?" said Sigbert pushing the ring up his skinny arm where it refused to lodge.

"Take him away and question him," said Cuthwulf, "Yes, take him away."

Anson and Osgar took Sigbert away to feed, clothe and quiz him. He confirmed to them that Aefre was indeed Osgar's mother and to his joy, told them about Leofric. Anson had never seen Osgar happier as he questioned the escaped slave continually. He even showed uncharacteristic patience with Sigbert's incessant attempts at humour.

Three days after the battle, they headed due west towards Bannaventa. They had ensured that their weapons were in good order and many were wearing new armour that they had stripped from the bodies of the Britons. They raided some villages on the way and took all that they wanted. The villages were mostly deserted and they gained the feeling that the whole country of the Chalk Hills was open to be taken. After a day's march, Sigbert and reported to Osgar that they neared Bannaventa. They stopped in a valley by the river for the night and Osgar was led by Sigbert to survey the fortress by moonlight.

*****

Aefre prepared her agrimony and melissa paste. She cared nothing for the Waelisc and hoped that they all suffered but she knew that, as a slave being a successful healer had kept her alive. She had found a dead bird that morning in the garden which had been deceased a few days and was rotten and covered in flies. She took a strip of cloth from her hovel and wiped it in the carcass. She rolled the cloth up and tucked it in one of the pouches that hung from the belt at her waist. She also tucked a small knife into the dress folds behind the belt. She had stolen the knife from the kitchen many years before and had kept it hidden in her hovel ever since.

She was taken to King Cadrod, by Waljan and found him lying on his bed in a fever. He wore only a tunic which was wet through, his head rolled from side to side, sweating profusely. He was unaware that she was in the room and Aefre approached him slowly and rolled up his tunic to expose his left leg. Between his knee and groin was the gash caused by the aetgar. It had been stitched but the inflammation had bulged the wound so that many of the stitches had torn through at the edges. Pus ran through the stitch holes and from the edges of gash. Aefre asked for a small sharp knife and Waljan passed her his. Two of the King's guards, seeing the knife in her hand, stepped closer to her but she indicated that she would cut the stitching. Once she had done this, she returned the knife to Waljan and the guards relaxed. She cleaned the wound with the cloth from her pouch and then covered it with her herbal paste. Then she carefully bandaged the leg, showing great concern for the wound. She left the King's rooms with Waljan and descended the stone tower.

At the bottom of the steps, Aefre turned to Waljan and said, "He is unlikely to live, you know. It has festered for too long."

Waljan took both Aefre's hands in his and looked her in the eyes. "You are doing all you can for him, aren't you?"

"I am," she said holding his stare.

"I'm going to the church now to pray that he will live and that the kingdom is safe," said Waljan walking towards the church.

"Do that," said Aefre and accompanied him to the church but left him to enter it as she continued to her hovel.

Bishop Cadrog Ddoeth said mass in his new church and prayed for the souls of those who had been lost in battle with the pagans. He told the congregation that they were already in heaven where they would live forever in peace. The Bishop had already discussed with his monks whether they should flee west. He wanted to stay saying that the Good Lord would protect them but the monks were not so sure. Leofric took no part in the discussion, he may have been a Christian but he was not a monk and he was not a Briton. The Bishop was impressed with Leofric as he had converted many of the Sais slaves to Christianity. Leofric did not want to flee west as this would take him further from East Anglia and freedom. As a Christian, he was not sure whether he should be joyous at the news of Cadrod's army's defeat.

The town of Bannaventa was almost deserted as most of the men had left with the army and had not returned. The scale of the defeat had taken two days for the people to understand. Without their men folk the women took their children, loaded their handcarts and left to join their families in safer lands. Even soldiers in the fortress deserted, leaving too few men to defend it.

Cadrod slept little that night. His fever raged and he was incoherent most of the time. He shouted that he was Arturius and that he had led the Cymry to recover Lloegr. In the morning, he was more calm and rational and his aides and commanders believed that the worst of the fever had passed. Cadrod issued orders that every Sais was to be put to death and there was to be no exceptions. He said that they were the cause of all their troubles and Cymru would never be safe while one lived. Waljan argued with him but finally Cadrod told him that he would also be put to death for treason if he did not obey. Waljan ran straight to Aefre's hovel to save her. He told her that they must leave straight away and go west. He had family in Caer Glori and there they could start a new life. He did not care that she would not convert to Christianity; he just wanted her to be with him.

"I would rather die here than go to the west," she told him, standing by the hovel that had been her home for eleven years.

He had tried everything to woo and convince her of his feelings. He had looked after her for years while he had heard the sneers from his fellow Britons. What had he ever had in return from her? His patience snapped that instant and he said, "Then here you will die," and he grabbed her arm and dragged her from her hovel towards the fortress courtyard.

The slaughter of the Sais slaves had begun. They were brought from the town and from the fields where they worked, tied with ropes and herded to the corner of the courtyard inside the fortress. Many of the Britons were disgusted with order to kill the slaves and refused to take part but many took to the opportunity with enthusiasm. Some men went gone to the church because they knew that the Bishop had a Sais slave.

"What are you doing in God's house bearing arms?" demanded Bishop Cadog, "Leave them outside."

The Britons were frightened of the Bishop and obeyed. They left their shields and spears by the door and returned. The commander pointed at Leofric and said, "We have orders from the King that all Sais are to be put to death, without exception."

"Is the King now above God?" asked the Bishop.

"I just have my orders," replied the Briton, without looking at the Bishop's eyes.

"Then I will see the King. Come with me," he said pointing to Leofric and the two monks.

They set off in a tight group towards the tower at the end of the second courtyard and passed the area holding the Sais slaves who were guarded closely by men with spears and staves. Once they had passed through the archway into the second courtyard, they walked alongside the deserted stalls and workshops. There was no longer the usual activity there, though many stalls still had goods displayed. Carpentry and leather workers tools were left and the smithy still had smoke rising from its fire and its doors hanging open.

*****

Osgar had led his men through the trees by the river until they were only two hundred paces from the partly rebuilt wall. The previous evening Sigbert had shown him the hidden river crossing and pointed to where the wall was still being rebuilt. Stones lay at its base and there was wooden scaffolding for the masons and slaves to climb but there was no activity and they could not even see guards on the walls. Osgar decided to act, though he knew that it could be a trap, it did not feel like one to him. He ran the men across the water meadow directly to the fortress and scaled the scaffolding. They were soon on the top and could see down into the large courtyard where Osgar saw a group of Britons stabbing at people with spears and one hacking with a sword. Then he saw a Waelisc warrior who he recognised, pulling a woman towards the slaughter. As he clambered down the wall and his men followed, he realised that the woman was his mother. She still wore her hair in the same manner that he remembered from childhood.

Waljan saw the Angles climbing down the wall into the courtyard and changed direction. He dragged Aefre through the archway and towards the tower and then pulled her up the stone steps. The guards let him enter the great oak door to the King's rooms. They had just allowed entry to the Bishop and three others. Behind them, they heard the bolts being drawn across the door. They looked at each other nervously, not knowing whether to stay at their posts or flee.

Osgar shouted to Henryk to attack the Britons who were killing the people. The Angles, who were pouring over the wall now, drove them from their victims. They trapped the hated Waelisc against a wall and slew them, while Osgar and Anson ran through the archway where they had seen the Waelisc warrior hauling Aefre. They ran into the smaller courtyard to see them enter a door up some steps and the two Waelisc guards saw them and held their spears at the ready.

Osgar and Anson ran across the courtyard and Anson delayed only to pull his war-axe from behind his back. He ran past the deserted workshops and stalls and up the stone steps two at a time to catch Osgar who was already facing the guards. Osgar had scaled the scaffolding at the wall without his shield which would have been passed over later. He suddenly felt unprotected as he looked at the two spears jabbing at him. Anson arrived alongside him but he was slow with his axe and could not strike the spear hafts which were prodded out and withdrawn quickly. Then a thrust came past him and Osgar struck downwards with his sword cutting clean through the haft which slowed the second guard and Anson used his axe like a hook, pulling his spear down. Osgar rammed his tapered sword hard into his upper chest and as he pulled it out Anson swung his axe onto the first guard's shoulder, splitting him down to his chest.

Osgar pulled on the door and barged his shoulder into it but he could feel that it was solid. Anson swung his axe at the door but the blade hit the rivets, causing flying sparks and after a few blows he gave up. They both looked around for anything that might help them.

Osgar said, "Wait here," and ran back down the steps.

He dashed across the courtyard towards the empty workshops and went straight to the smithy where inside he could see two sledgehammers. He carried one in each hand, holding them by the handle just below the hammerhead and ran up the steps again passing one of the sledges to Anson. Anson had been inspecting at the door, the better or stronger of which he had never seen. There were three iron hinges on the left-hand side which spanned two thirds of the door's breadth. The door was bonded crossways with iron strips and thick rivets appeared every hand's width. He could see that no axe could split this door and cursed it.

Anson took one of the hammers from Osgar and aimed a blow at the bottom hinge. He had made hinges all his life and he knew their weak points and where they would snap. No one used the best iron for hinges but these were strong. "Follow my blow boy," he said to Osgar and it was as if they were back in the forge.

Anson's first strike made the door reverberate and the sound carried across the courtyard. Osgar followed and landed his hammer face exactly where Anson's had struck. He struck left-handed with his left hand grasping the handle nearer to the head than his right. They found their rhythm and beat the hinge like a drum until it snapped and without pause Anson aimed at the hinge in the middle of the door. They were swinging their hammers sideways, Osgar on the right of the door, Anson on the left. The second hinge gave way and now they aimed their blows almost overhead. Their force and tempo never wavered and finally the third hinge broke and Osgar and Anson dropped their hammers. Osgar picked up his sword and Anson took up his battle-axe. Osgar barged at the door and with a splintering of wood from the inside, the door fell.

They both stepped through the doorway into the room. Inside their eyes adjusted to the light and Osgar could see his mother held by the Briton warrior. She was to his left, close to a doorway and on the right were four men wearing long gowns with hoods down behind their heads. They wore rope belts and wooden crosses around their necks. One was an elderly man, whose hair and beard were long and white, holding a staff with a gold cross at its top. Only the Waelisc warrior was armed and he held a sword in his right hand.

Aefre suddenly said, "It's you, Osgar."

"Yes," said Osgar, "it's me, Mother." He did not take his eyes off the Waelisc warrior.

"Anson," she said, recognising her Jute brother-in-law, "and where's Eafwald, is he here?"

"He died at the hand of the man who holds you," said her son, now pointing his sword directly at the face that he had not forgotten in eleven years.

He told his mother what he had seen from his hiding place in the pigsty. He had waited so long for this moment. In his dreams, he had imagined killing the

Briton before him and rushing to his mother and brother. He had learnt on the battlefield to control anger and hatred so he looked into the eyes of his father's killer and said, "You are dead."

Waljan could understand nothing that was being said. He gripped Aefre tightly with his left hand and knew that she may be his only means of escape. He recognised both the Sais opposite, having been close to both of them in more than one battle. The elder one held his axe across his chest and the younger one next to him, pointed his strange sword at his face. His eyes bore into Waljan's and he could see this was with more than just an enemy's hatred. He recognised him as the Sais who, two years previously, had fought like a devil by the great white bank, to try to get to him, breaking their line in the process.

"Who is he?" Waljan asked Aefre.

"He is my son, for whom I have waited these past eleven years."

"Tell him how I have cared for you and protected you," pleaded Waljan.

"He has just told me that you killed my husband Eafwald in the raid that took me here," she replied.

"That was war, Aefre. Men die. Our men die, your men die." He said desperately.

"He died in a burning hall, you bastard," she shouted. "Unarmed. Unarmed, damn you. You cut him down that's why he never came for me. You bastard."

Aefre reached into the folds of her dress behind her belt. Her hand gripped the handle of the small knife. She thought about the man who grasped her arm and who had almost won her over. All the time, she thought, that she had sat and talked with him, he had been the killer of her husband. She swung her arm around and hit Waljan hard in the centre of his chest. At first everyone thought that she had punched him and even Waljan just felt a thud. Then his chest felt cold and he looked down and blood was pouring out of his leather jerkin. He felt his strength leaving his body and as he dropped to his knees, he raised his sword. In an instant Osgar swung his sword, cutting Waljan's right hand off at the wrist and as it fell to the ground his sword fell from it.

Waljan remained conscious for a while as his life ebbed from him. Aefre's words echoed round his head as he remembered the only unarmed man that he had ever killed. He had never indulged in the child killing and rapes of their raids that the other warriors took such joy from. He had always concentrated on commanding the men in battle and once the fight was won, he had always found ways of avoiding the frenzy. His memory of that night was clear and in his dying moments, it went through his head because now he knew that he had killed the husband of the only woman that he had ever loved. They had approached the Sais village undetected and had cut off the exit from the hall and set fire to it. As each Sais ran out through the door, one of the men had speared them but suddenly one had charged out and despite a stab wound had downed one of his men with a punch. He had swung his sword and the man had put his arm up to defend himself. As he had pulled the sword from his victim, he had looked around and spotted a boy hiding in a pigsty. He remembered hoping that no one else saw the boy and that he remained safe. Waljan prayed to God for forgiveness as his life slipped away.

Osgar moved forward, with only one thought, to kill the other men in the room and so complete his revenge. For eleven years, he had sought vengeance on the man now kneeling and clutching his chest with his left hand, as his life ebbed from him. He had seen his mother stab him and was content that she had avenged his father Eafwald's death. He did not know if the Waelisc had their own Valhalla but he had ensured that if they had, then he would be denied entrance. Now he raised his sword and alongside him, he glimpsed Anson's war axe swing up above his shoulder. Both of them had seen the slaughter of the slaves in the courtyard and were in no mood to give quarter. They would slay the four Waelisc still in the room and suddenly one of them said, "No Osgar."

Osgar stopped and looked at the priest who spoke in the Angles language. He was a tall man with blue eyes and blonde hair, "Its Leo," shouted Aefre.

"Great Thunor, it is you," said Osgar looking at his brother and lowering his sword. He stared at his twin and the three men with him and calculated their threat. They seemed to have no weaponry and were not holding Leo who was grinning at him.

Leofric stepped forward and placed both hands on Osgar's shoulders, pulled him into a hug and said, "Put the sword away, my brother, the killing is done."

Their mother watched as Osgar's sword slipped from his hand and clattered to the floor. His shoulders began to shake as he sobbed and put his arms around his brother and embraced him. Aefre moved forward, joined her children, placed her hands on their shoulders and kissed each one in turn.

Chapter 24
Home

Aefre watched her two boys chatting to each other as they walked home. Osgar had his sword out of its sheath and was holding it out in front of him and pointing to the blade while explaining something to Leo. All three of them had survived the last eleven years in their own way and now that Anson had told her of Osgar's story, she thought that in a way he too had been enslaved. His life had had only one purpose, to rescue her and his brother and to avenge his father's death. Leofric, she thought, had found his own way of remaining alive. Aefre did not know whether the Christian God had saved him as he claimed but if he had, then she was grateful and would no longer despise his god.

Osgar had found it hard to understand why his brother followed the Waelisc God but when Aefre explained to him that Leo believed that the God of the wooden cross had been the reason for his survival, he accepted it. Leo had convinced Osgar and Anson not to kill the Bishop or the monks as they had rescued him and kept him safe for years. The Bishop had told him to return to East Anglia and spread the word of God. They had not taken the golden cross from the Bishop Cadrog or his ring but they had searched the fortress and town for anything of value. The townspeople had mostly fled and those who remained were butchered or taken as slaves. The Angles found plenty of treasure in the fortress where Cadrod had his gold and silver stored below the tower. This was later shared amongst the victorious Anglian army and their Saxon allies in the traditional ratio. They had entered the room where King Cadrod lay. He been delirious, his body convulsed and the wound in his thigh was exposed with flies crawling across it. The flesh around the lesion was black and the whole room stunk of the pus oozing from it. Aefre had said that killing him would be a mercy so they had left him.

Leofric and Osgar walked together along the chalk ridge heading northeast. Behind them followed their mother Aefre and Anson their uncle. The big Jute held her hand and told her all he could of the last eleven years. She told him nothing of her life in captivity and he did not ask. They walked through the waist high grasses and wildflowers scattering the butterflies and moths ahead of them. Swallows and swifts swooped, scooping from the air flies and midges which drifted across the heath. In the distance, she could see the white bank running along the horizon, to the left it disappeared towards the fens and to the right it rose towards the woodlands. On its ridge stood men holding spears, which rested on the ground pointing skyward and on their left sides they held round shields.

When they reached the dyke, they were greeted by crowds who had awaited the return of the army that had set out to join Cuthwulf. Many had run from the gap in the white bank as soon as they spotted them on the horizon. They joined the group of marching men looking for their fathers, husbands and loved ones. Many hugged their returning men and others sought news and explanations of why they were not with them. Less than half of those who had set out from Theod-Ford, so recently, returned. Most who did bore both the scars of war but also its rewards. Bannaventa had been rich and when its plunder was shared even the most humble ceorl received silver.

Osgar recognised Lynn on the ridge of the chalk bank and knew that he had to face the hardest conversation of his life. On the journey home first Anson had said he would talk to Lynn of the loss of her father and brother and then Leofric told him that he would explain death and console her. He thanked them but had decided that as he was betrothed to her, he had to tell her on his own. He looked at her excitedly waving to him and scanning the crowd for Seward and Wilf. Osgar strode up the side of the white bank and hugged Lynn who hung around his neck and kissed him.

"Let's walk along the bank," he said, taking her right hand in his and leading her away from the others on the crest, "There's a lot to tell."

They walked a hundred paces towards the fen ditch end and sat with their backs to the low evening sun. They looked towards home and their shadows were cast down on the heath below them. Lynn sat quietly and then said, "They aren't coming back, are they?"

"No," said Osgar quietly, "they are not. Seward and your father died in battle."

"Did they die quickly?" she asked as he put his arm around her shaking shoulders.

"They died swiftly and bravely, fighting alongside each other," Osgar said, thinking back to the battle and wiping a tear from beneath his eye.

"What will my mother and younger brothers do now?" Lynn said thinking of the woodwork shop that her father had built into a family business.

"We'll look after them and see that they finish their apprenticeships with the right people. Your mother can stay in Beo or come to our farmland," He looked at her profile and thought that she was the most precious person in the world and said, "Come on, let's go and meet my mother and brother."

They walked down to the heath where Aefre stood with Anson and Leofric. Aefre beamed at her future daughter-in-law and offered both her hands to her. Leofric welcomed her formally and Osgar waited for their reaction. After a pause, he looked at his mother and said, "Well?"

"She is as pretty as you described her," said Aefre, "and if she is as persistent as you say, then you two should breed the most stubborn children in all Anglia."

"What will you do now?" Lynn asked Aefre.

"I don't know," she replied, "I don't think I will return to my old ham, apart from to see my sister. Maybe I will live in Beo or if you will have me, I would move to your new land near Gippeswic. First, I have to meet with your mother to organise a wedding."

There was a commotion behind them and they all turned to see a tall well-dressed man striding across the heath, his cloak flapping behind him. Following him was a group of thegns and ceorls trying to keep up. Aefre could see that he was beautifully clothed and wealthy, from the rings on his left hand to the ornate gold pommel of his sword. Someone announced that it was King Wuffa and Aefre and Leofric followed many others in dropping to one knee and lowering her head. She looked sideways and could see Anson and Osgar standing. Wuffa went straight to them and greeted them as friends.

"Up, up," ordered their king, "No kneeling. Well, if it it's not Young Thunor and the old Jute, come home with more tales of glory and treasure. You have much to tell me but we can do that over ale."

"The sooner, the better," said Anson, "I'm as dry as a witch's tit."

"Not lost your poetic ability with words then Anson," said Wuffa. "And you two can only be Aefre and Leofric, brought home by Osgar as he pledged on more occasions than I care to remember."

Wuffa stared at the wooden cross around Leofric's neck and asked, "Did you wear that to keep yourself safe or do you follow the Waelisc god?"

"I follow him, *sire*," replied Leofric, "but he is not the Waelisc god. He is everyone's God and I would be happy to talk to you about him." He thought about how poorly his brother and uncle had received his attempts to talk to about his religion. Osgar had been polite and listened but he could tell was not interested in his creed and Anson just said that the battle had proved that their gods were superior.

"I would like you to tell me about this god but not today," and then he said enthusiastically, "Have you seen from the bank of the Great Dyke? Let's have a look while it is still light," and headed up to the top.

They stood in line at the top of the bank looking back into the Kingdom of the East Angles, casting long shadows a hundred paces across the grassland. The white dyke turned pink where the dying sun's rays hit it and the grass either side orange. The defended gap was being closed for the night. Carts and travellers had stopped passing through a while earlier.

"Our land is safe, thanks to the gods and you two," said Wuffa. Osgar and Anson bowed their heads.

Wuffa turned and looked west into the setting sun and the others turned with him. "Will they ever return, my King?" asked Osgar.

"No, I think not," said Wuffa, "these are our lands now. The Kingdom of Chalk Hills is finished and soon we will move west to take more land. Our people will once more farm new land and build new hams. We will be connected to our Saxon cousins and that will make it safer for all. The land of the East Angles is here for all time."

"So," said the king, "now that you have seen the great white dyke tell me what you think."

"It marks home," said Osgar looking into Lynn's eyes.

"It is truly awesome," said Aefre.

"The work of God," announced Leofric.

"And ten thousand Angles," said Wuffa.

"And a Jute," added Anson smiling.

The End

268

Author's Note

Living and working in Newmarket for most of my life exposed me to a town with three unusual features. It has the highest concentration of horses in the world, the largest managed grasslands in Europe and the greatest Anglo-Saxon earthwork in Britain. The Devil's Dyke, as it is now known, stretches from the villages of Stetchworth to Reach. It runs arrow straight across Newmarket Heath for eight miles. In places, the ditch is as deep and the bank as high as when dug nearly one thousand five hundred years ago. You can stand on the top of the ridge today and see how easy it would be to defend it.

My novel was set in the darkest period of the Dark Ages. This should prove a boon to any author not wanting to be tied by dates. However, although there is some variance amongst historians, I set my novel to begin in 560 AD. King Wehha was known to rule all Anglia by then. He was the first King of both the Suth and North Folk. East Anglia can claim to be the first English kingdom. It remained an independent kingdom for over three hundred years. Wehha ruled until 571 AD when he died and was replaced by King Wuffa. I had Wuffa as his nephew but he may have been his son. The Wuffing dynasty ruled Anglia for two hundred years. Wuffingas means 'the kin of the wolves' in old English and Wuffa's name means 'little wolf'.

It was not just the Angles who saw themselves as wolves. King Cuthwulf of the Saxons' name means 'famous wolf'. He lived up to his name, when in that auspicious year of 571 AD, he defeated King Cadrod of Calchfynedd at the battle of Bedcanford, thought to be modern day Bedford. The battle of Bedcanford was one of the most important battles in these islands in the first millennium. Nobody knows how the battle was fought, only the result, so I took the opportunity to correct King Harold's mistake at Hastings, five hundred years later.

King Cadrod died and his kingdom, which had existed for only fifty years, disappeared. Calchfynedd may well have come about after the battle of Badon Hill (Mynydd Baddon). It was here that the Saxons suffered an overwhelming defeat by the Romano-Britons possibly led by a general called Arturius. The site of this battle is still speculated and it may be that Arturius was the fabled Arthur of the Britons. Something stalled the advancing settlement of Britain by the Anglo-Saxons, so it could well have been their defeat at Badon Hill.

The Kingdom of Calchfynedd or Chalk Hills, occupied a large area in the centre of Britain cutting off the Angles from the Saxons to the south. It was almost certainly the reason for the building of, as I called it, the Great Dyke. We do not know what the Angles called it but after Edmund, the last King of the Anglia, died in 869, it was called Saint Edmund's Dyke. We have only called it the Devil's Dyke since the seventeenth century. It has been calculated that the Devil's Dyke would have taken a thousand men a year to build one mile so I had it finished in two. It was built towards the end of Wehha's reign and was only occupied for about three years. The Anglians built more dykes, possibly as they advanced south and west, but this one is their greatest. Others, in Anglia, include Fleam Dyke, Brent Ditch, Bran Ditch and Black Ditches. Black Ditches is on private land only a mile from where I live. It is given only a cursory mention in the story and I share my good friend, the landowner's view that it was abandoned before being completed.

There was only one route into Anglia, fifteen hundred years ago. If you travel by car today from where the A11 leaves the M11, then you are following the old Roman road from London to Norwich and the far older Icknield Way. The farmlands seem to stretch forever on either side and it is hard to imagine that this was once such a constricted route. Look more carefully as you approach Newmarket, where to the right, the rolling hills climb and become more wooded. To the left, they fall and flatten off to become the fens. They are drained now but only four hundred years ago, they were still marshes and open water. Neither travellers nor an army would walk far through a forest or fen.

Rivers are an obvious impediment to movement and create natural defensive lines. In East Anglia, they mainly run east-west. The Lark, running from Bury St. Edmunds (Beodricesworth was its early name) towards Mildenhall, forms the shallow Lark Valley with a line of ancient villages behind it. Nowadays, it has at least one crossing point at each village. I set the 'battle of the three bridges' at Icklingham and you can travel over them today, although the Lark is closer to the village now than it was fifteen hundred years ago. Icklingham is today a modest village of four hundred but had been an important crossing point of the Icknield Way for thousands of years. The Lark drains west to the Ouse in the fens and the Gipping drains east. They almost join in the centre of East Anglia. Fifteen miles north, the Little Ouse and the Waveney still form the border between Suffolk and Norfolk as they did in the time of my story.

There is an important Roman villa that is no longer visible, on the way from Icklingham to West Stow. I had to mention it in my story. West Stow is now the site of an excellent museum of Anglo-Saxon life. If you have read this far then you should visit it where you can see the two burned houses mentioned in this tale. The Museum tells the story of the early Angles and recreates the ham using traditional methods. In some ways, you do not need to visit a museum to understand the settlement of Anglia. It is in the names of every town and village. Travelling on from West Stow towards Bury St Edmunds, you pass through Flempton, proving that it was not just Angles in Anglia. The Germanic tribes, now called Anglo-Saxons, included Flemish people and here the village name records it. The town of Swaffham in Norfolk means settlement of Swabians, who were a tribe from central Germany. Between Newmarket and Bury St Edmunds are Saxon Street, Little Saxham and Great Saxham, showing that the Saxons were not confined to the south. At times, I used the term Anglecynn as a collective noun for these people, probably erroneously. It was a term and concept that was used by King Alfred the Great but that was 300 years later. I am sure though, that they had some feeling of connection and shared heritage, especially when there was a common enemy.

Bannaventa was possibly the capital of Calchfynedd and had been a Roman fortress on the road called Watling Street by the Anglo-Saxons. It is now the village of Weedon, just west of Northampton. Bishop Cadog Ddoeth built a church in Bannaventa. He travelled far and wide, during his life, including Ireland. He was known as Cadog the Wise and became a saint. My story had Taliesan the bard visiting Bannaventa. It is not known if this happened but he lived at this time and he was often referred to as Taliesin Ben Beirdd (Chief of Bards).

My main protagonists Osgar and Anson were a blacksmith and his apprentice. The word blacksmith is old English for one who smites (hits) black (iron) The Germanic peoples made the best swords in the world during, what is known as, the migration period. It has been said that the quality was not bettered until the industrial revolution. It was quite a process of driving out impurities and hardening the metal. Pattern welding is the best method of giving a sword a hard edge while leaving the blade flexible so that it does not snap in battle and a

271

thegn's sword made by this method, was worth a year's wages, the equivalent today is £24,000. The tapered blade began to appear at the time of my story. I had Osgar make it out of necessity but it was a superior design and lent itself to greater swordsmanship.

The Angles were not good horsemen, although they did use horses later but they proved time and again that a disciplined army that stands, will always defeat cavalry. It is ironic that centuries after the Angles built their great dyke across Newmarket Heath to stop horses, it had a gap cut in it to allow the running of horse races. To this day, the first two counties of England, Suffolk and Norfolk, have their borders where they were then.

There are five kings and a saint in this novel, who all lived during this period. Two of the kings probably died in 571AD. The dyke was built in Anglia by Wehha, the first king of Anglia at this time. The rest is just a story.